Praise for B

"Moving, powerful, and compulsively readable, *Better You Go Home* is the unforgettable story of a man's journey to save his own life, and how he discovers himself along the way."

—Garth Stein, *New York Times* bestselling author of *The Art of Racing in the Rain*

"Scott Driscoll delivers. His debut novel has the pace of a thriller and the grace of a literary novel. Although international in scope, the story has an intimate quality and it captivates our hearts."

—Bharti Kirchner, author of *Darjeeling* and *Tulip Season*

"Like the big Russian novels that gave us moral philosophy, this book raises the deepest questions about freedom and captivity, identity and place. Chico, a middle-aged Seattle lawyer in need of a kidney, vows to use his medical leave to find his half-sister, who was left behind in the old country when his father fled the Nazis with another man's wife. Chico's doctors in the US want more tests before they will grant him a transplant, but he's in Prague where tracing one's family tree isn't a popular preoccupation if it raises questions about what people did to survive the Soviet Bloc. *Better You Go Home* is at once an immigrant story, a medical thriller, and a tale of love. Driscoll keeps all the skeins taut in his hand."

—Kathryn Trueblood, author of *The Baby Lottery* and winner of the Goldenberg Prize for Fiction

"Scott Driscoll's account of one man's struggle to overcome death by leaving the Pacific Northwest to find his half-sister in the Czech Republic is full of intrigue and illicit love against the backdrop of Eastern Europe's tragic history. A fine tale with a most satisfying finish."

—Caleb Powell, author of *I Think You're Totally Wrong: A Quarrel* (forthcoming from Knopf, 2014)

"Compelling, unnerving, full of insight ... In this odyssey of an American trying to find his past and save his life, we're taken back behind the fallen Iron Curtain and the ghosts that still live and breathe there. Terse with poetry, broad in history (and heart), and with all the suspense of an Eastern Block espionage thriller. Driscoll delivers."

—Layne Maheu, author of *Song of the Crow*

"*Better You Go Home* is a haunting tale of how a diabetic's quest for a new kidney uncovers dark secrets about his family as well as himself."

—Nicholas O'Connell, author of *The Storms of Denali*

"With dramatic well-drawn characters, a climax scene with the tension of *High Noon*, and a peek behind the Iron Curtain, *Better You Go Home* is a page turner."

—Mindy Halleck, author of *Romance & Money - 12 Conversations Every Couple Should Have*

"A tale of a Quester in a Wasteland, led by a beauteous guide, his ominous path blocked by twin Dragons. One dragon is exterior, the Omnipresent State wielding the ugly gray weight of the Iron Curtain; the other is interior, the Quester's deadly disease, a genetic curse that can only be lifted by grafting on a sacred body part—one that matches, one that won't kill you—plucked from the body of a family member. *Better You Go Home* is a taut tale of irony, sadness, bleak romance, and man's fate."

—Robert J. Ray, author of the Matt Murdock Mysteries

"The story is complex, the characters rich and thick and vibrant. There's love and sex, there's hope and redemption, there's sin and forgiveness, there's death and torture. But, as Driscoll tells us,in the right circumstances '...even torture can be a sign of love.'"

—Jack Remick, author of *Blood*, *Gabriela and the Widow*, and the California Quartet series

BETTER YOU
GO
HOME

BETTER YOU

GO

HOME

A NOVEL

—◂ᴵ▸—

SCOTT DRISCOLL

cp

coffeetownpress

Seattle, WA

coffeetownpress

Coffeetown Press
PO Box 70515
Seattle, WA 98127

For more information go to: www.coffeetownpress.com
www.scott-driscoll.com

Cover design by Sabrina Sun

ISBN: 978-1-60381-170-5 (Trade Paper)
ISBN: 978-1-60381-171-2 (eBook)

Library of Congress Control Number: 2013938460

Printed in the United States of America

Acknowledgments

THE FOLLOWING WERE instrumental in helping this novel come to be and I extend to them my deepest thanks: Jennifer McCord, for her tireless editing in the developmental drafts; Catherine Treadgold for her time and wisdom with the final edits; Josef Kolar and Dana Wilkie, Czech transplants to Seattle who authenticated the details and language of my family's former homeland; Kate Trueblood, my writer friend who read late drafts; David Downing, Jasen Emmons, Nicholas O'Connell, Layne Maheu, Garth Stein, and Cindy Willis, current and former writing group task masters; my sister, Sandra Driscoll, who fed me medical information; my father, Glenn Driscoll, who introduced me to Czech family connections; my patient wife, Daiga Galins, who kept the roof over our heads while encouraging me to get this done; my daughter, Megan Driscoll, who provided technical support; and my son, Dainis Driscoll, who (at age six) coined the term "baguette ponytail" and allowed me to use it.

Additional thanks to Jack Remick and Mindy Halleck for helping with social media connections, to Roberta Trahan for aid with file management, and thanks to the friends who asked about the book and cheered me along.

Contents

Chapter One

Monday Afternoon at the Church:
September 12, 1994

THE DESULTORY FLAP flapping of the monk's sandals in the cathedral's cold, vaulted vastness reminds me of my father's attitude when I told him I was coming to the Czech Republic to find my sister. It was not indifference, exactly. He chewed right through his toothpick and left his thick-cut bacon untouched on his plate. It wasn't even so much him saying, "Those people are dead, it's not your concern." It was more the way he tossed my plan off as though it was of no consequence. The way the farmer who called the raptor center where I volunteer weekends said a random owl had flown into his glass porch and then, that out of the way, went right back out to his tractor to continue his row.

"Tell me again why you wanted to meet me here?"

"Sick people," whispers Milada, "come here from every place in world to pray to Bambino for cure. He is famous."

"A cure?" Milada is a doctor, she knows better.

Today was the day Milada was to drive me to my father's village in eastern Bohemia to begin our search. Instead, I'm watching the monk in his brown robe drape an ermine shawl over the shoulders of a wax Christ child mounted above the altar. He ignores us, the newest supplicants, with divine disinterest. The stone walls are unadorned. Kostel Panny Marie vitězně is a spare German Lutheran-built structure in Prague's Mala Strana district near the river. Not much here for tourists except this chapel.

"Bambino was brought here from Rome by Carmelites." She reads the Bambino's provenance off a placard as though that will nail the lid on my incredulity. Something about touching his cheek and Countess Kolovrat's sight and hearing came back and it was a miracle, and ever since then the lame and the sick have flocked like lemmings to our humble church in Prague to touch the Bambino.

"FYI, he's behind bullet-proof glass."

"*Ano*, but still you can pray. I have prayed to Bambino before I take medical school exams. I believe you have say? 'Do not put all bets in one basket'?"

"Eggs. Eggs ..." I've never met my sister. I only actually learned of her existence this year. My father grew up in Písečná, a farm village near the mountains bordering Poland. He would have inherited a large estate had he not been unlucky enough to come of age in time to be conscripted into the Nazi army. Or, would have, had he stayed. He was sixteen when he fled to Iowa with his father and two younger sisters, along with a woman from the farm next door and three of her children. He left his mother behind on the farm with three of his sisters. But he also left someone else behind, and this is the rub. He left Rosalye, the young "maid," pregnant. His daughter, my half-sister, was born four months after his arrival in Iowa and was sent away by her mother to live in an orphanage.

"I am so exciting to see you." Milada invites me to bend down. I'm a ridiculously tall man. She gives me a kiss on the cheek, then holds me at arm's length for a better look. "You look good but I see swelling."

"I know," I say, ruefully patting my belly. "Fifteen pounds of fluid."

Last winter, I was warned that renal failure is in my near future. Until then I'd led a pretty cosseted life—high marks in law school, a rapid rise to the position of city attorney in Kent Terrace, a suburban municipality south of Seattle. But, okay. That is what was. This is what is. Hating the thought of being idle, and hating even more the thought that there was a little girl who was my sister and whose existence my father had denied, I vowed to use my medical leave to find her. To find her, and, if a visa could be arranged, bring her back to Seattle. My sister, I've learned, worked most of her adult life as the director of the orphanage where she grew up. While my weekend warrior trips to the raptor center have nothing to do with abandoned children per se, rehabilitating wounded raptors ought to appeal to her rescuing nature.

"You bring the letter with you?" I can't avoid this indefinitely.

"*Vsechno je v pořádku*. Everything is fine. I am certain."

"Did you read it?"

"So many questions. Finally you are here."

"My internist is not happy about it and my father pretends not to care. But you look great." I'd forgotten how dark complected she is, how Slavic looking. Her eyes have an extra fold at the corners that I teasingly call her Genghis Khan fold. Despite having raised three boys, she's kept the compact figure of the Olympic skater she once was. Today, in Prague, she's wearing the same black Italian leather jacket and thigh-cleaving slacks she wore when we first met in February. A reporter took a photo of her that day that was later printed in the *Everett Herald* along with her essay on why she loves the Pacific Northwest. At the time she was attending an English language school for professionals, paid for by her employer, the Czech Ministry of Health. I tucked a copy of that photo into my passport pouch. In the six months that have gone by since, I've studied it as though she were the Holy Grail.

"What your father say about you come to Prague?"

"When he realized I was serious? Let me see if I can get this right. He said… it would be best if I don't get involved … quote unquote."

"I am *wary* sorry, Chico. But we will speak with his family. He had to know we look for your sister."

In these past few months so much has happened I hardly know if I'm coming or going. My amicable divorce was finalized in December. In January, my nephrologist dropped the warning that without transplant surgery I had at most a year before my kidneys gave out. Needing time to absorb everything, I flew back to Cedar Rapids to visit my father, only to find letters handwritten in Czech in his attic revealing the existence of a sister. With little more to go on than the name of a village, I sent a letter requesting information regarding a woman named Anezka who would be in her early fifties. Before the month was out, I had a call from Milada. She had grown up on the very farm that once belonged to my father's family. What did she expect from me? Was she looking for a sponsor? That thought did cross my mind. Age is a subject she avoids. The chemical black dye she uses on her hair seems to confirm my surmise—based on her having let slip that she was eighteen in August 1968 when she escaped, briefly, over the border into Germany—that she is forty-four or forty-five, two or three years older than me. Her family, one boy still at home, lives in a concrete high-rise flat—I've seen photos, it looks cheerless—a flat that she loathes but is stuck with. Her husband took a usurious loan from the Russian mafia so he could restore the mountain *chata* where his ill father spent his final years. Living under the hammer of the Russian mafia was not how she had planned to enjoy her freedom. Fair enough, I'll sponsor her if that's really what she wants. I did make her promise that first, as soon as my medical leave started, she'd take me to my father's village.

Here I am.

She couldn't get out of her shift today.

A letter arrived that probably means bad news.

⁓⁕⁓

"GUESS I BETTER have a look."

"*Ted' je dobrý čas.*" Milada pulls out of her handbag a manila envelope marked "Urgent!" The return address puzzles me, until I realize it's my ex-wife's new condo.

Inside is a business-sized envelope that has been cut open and resealed with tape. On the back, a hand-drawn smiley face is wearing a frown. *Frown? A frown?* Her note is written on a pad from Metro Bank—my ex manages loan officers—in large looping letters gauged to help me read without my magnifier.

Before you read this letter, she says, *don't worry*. Should I scream or laugh? *I called the UW Medical Center and talked to Julie.* Julie is the social worker who makes the arrangements once you've been accepted for transplant surgery. *Please look at the date on the letter. I'm very, very sorry I didn't get this to you sooner. You know how sometimes I get your mail and you get mine even though I put in for a change of address? Well. I didn't know if I should open this. But I thought it could be important. I forwarded it to your 'guide' (smiley face) I don't know the Czech word. Big hug, whether you want it or not. Your ex, ha ha. (I'm still Kasia.)*

"Could you read it for me?" I ask Milada. I'm a coward when it comes to facing bad news. *Feed it to me gently?*

A class of twittering uniformed school children chooses this moment to wing into the famous Bambino's chapel. They shush each other to avoid a swat on the ear from their chaperoning nun. They recite a prayer. The radiance of their voices cheers me up, until I notice Milada frowning and my heart stops again.

"I cannot understand your English insurance speak."

"Maybe read it out loud?"

The nun gives us a baleful look before guiding her twittering sparrows elsewhere. Milada waves the nun away with a rude hand gesture that reminds me of her impetuous side, not what you'd expect necessarily of an anesthesiologist who designed a portable machine for testing blood gasses and who has devoted much of her career—and suffered a lack of promotions from the Ministry of Health because of it—to coercing the government to pay for the installation of these machines in emergency vehicles.

We are alone in the Bambino's chapel. She reads. My blood tests, according to Dr. Stan Pomerantz, the signatory on the letter from Blue Cross, show a creatinine level averaging seven to seven point five. For someone my size, it would take a consistent reading over eight to trigger concern of imminent renal failure. Pomerantz concedes that the rapidity of my kidneys' deterioration warrants further testing. Before they can complete their *consideration for approval* of dual kidney/pancreas transplant surgery, I need to come back in for another round of blood and urine tests and chest X-rays.

Consideration for approval? The drop-dead date by which they want the test results is September 23rd. "That's a week from Friday. Ten days."

"Tomorrow you must speak with my colleague. Dr. Saudek will say you what is possible at IKEM. On Wednesday he will go with me to conference in Brno so we must see him tomorrow."

"Delay delay delay, that's their job, you know. They delay until you die and then you are no longer their liability."

"Kneel with me. Please, Chico." She tucks the letter back into her handbag, but of course I notice her doing it. "We will say prayer to Bambino."

"What's the point?"

"You are being crazy like me." She touches a finger to my lips. "Your family was Catholic. They would not say this is wrong. Now you must recite prayer exactly."

Typed copies of a standard prayer, translated into a dozen languages, are taped with yellowing sticky-tape along the marble banister's handrail. The lame and sick who feel inspired to ask for miracles are instructed to kneel at the rail and recite the prayer. Milada locates the English language version.

She won't accept a no, so I kneel beside her. After breaking the sticky-tape seal, she slips the crinkled paper with the prayer out of its plastic sheathing. She reads it, intact with grammatical errors, and I repeat it verbatim:

"Humbly understand, dear God, that I am aware that I asking for special consideration. Please know that I am willing to bear burden of my suffering if that is your will."

"Willingly suffer?" I repeat.

"It's a matter of faith," she reminds me.

"But if it pleasing to you, God, take away this suffering. Will you please humbly consider ..." Here the prayer instructs the supplicant to fill in the blank with a personal request.

"Now you must say request in your words." Age and smoke have darkened the Bambino's face and raised hand to ebony. He gazes down at me impassively. Obviously, he's seen this a thousand times before.

"First, thanks for not sending me a rejection. I *am* grateful for that." *Sorry, Bambino, I sound like the mumblers at city hall with too much time on their hands.* "I gotta do this silently."

I do have a request. Remind Blue Cross that if they drop me they'll lose the contract for a hundred and twenty thousand municipal employees in the State of Washington, not just my office. Just remind them of the facts. No threats. And make sure you leave no paper trail, but get me on the list. Okay, one more request? Help me find Anezka while I can still get around. I've got that room waiting for her in my townhouse. That map I hung on the wall is so detailed it shows every last village in the Czech Republic. We'll spend our days at the raptor center. Evenings she'll walk me around the map. I don't know if a reconciliation with my father, our father, will be possible, but at least he should be called to the witness stand to answer a few questions.

Milada strokes my arm. "*Ty budeš potřebovat protekci.*"

"That sounded lovely. Say it again."

"Is not joke. Here if you have pull, things can be done."

I shake my head. "No. I really can't do that." Despite knowing I feel that it would be a grievous betrayal, Milada persists in believing I should ask Anezka to donate a kidney.

"Tomorrow night you will eat dinner with my family. We will phone to your insurance. Maybe they will give extension and we will find Anezka."

"I get to spend tomorrow with you? You're not on shift?"

"*Já na tom trvám.* I cannot permit you stay alone. Perhaps you meet some hot young Eastern European tramp." She slides her thumb over two fingers, the international sign for money. "For one day you are my prisoner, Chico!"

She promises to call me at my rented room first thing in the morning. I watch her walk away from the Bambino's chapel. Here, in Prague, she has that Eastern bloc way of hunching her shoulders and shoving her hands into pockets to make herself less noticeable. When I took her out for a cold walk by the Skagit River this past winter I saw none of that hunching. While I waited on the bridge, braced for the cold, she disappeared into the tall, coniferous woods.

The children's sing-songy chanting of their Catechism reaches me from deep in the cathedral's recesses. My father, František Lenoch, *we call him Frank*, was pretty devout in his younger years. He once admitted to me—he'd never have admitted this to Mom—that church helped him remember his mother, my grandmother, whom he never saw again once he'd fled to Iowa. She had a chapel built in their farmhouse so she could worship nightly. The Dostals, her family, built the first and only church in the valley. He carries a lot of unspoken guilt surrounding his mother's death, guilt that no amount of going to confession, evidently, could expiate. But, these are his issues, not mine. I don't miss going to church. I do love the way the children's voices reverberate within these stone walls. It's nothing less than the clarion call of angels. Joy itself. I love it. I'm convinced that sound of unadulterated joy can only be cooked up in a pressure cooker like here. How would Anezka feel about that? Her entire life was spent in this pressure cooker. Would she have an ear fine-tuned for the subtle shades of suffering in her orphans' expressions of joy? Or would she have grown tone-deaf to all that, as though it were nothing more than desultory noise?

Chapter Two

Tuesday Night in Prague: September 13, 1994

MILADA'S FLAT IS on the eighth floor of a twelve-story high rise in a gray *sidlisté* of concrete block buildings. The street curb is dammed by defunct Skodas, the no-frills tin-can cars manufactured locally. The security mesh screening the outer door is rusted and dented. This is the depressing Khrushchev-era flat Milada is forced to continue calling home so that her husband could afford that Russian mafia loan. Okay, it's not lost on me that I'm taking risks, possibly for no better reason than to salvage my own father's dignity. Or my own. Still, Jiři goes too far. How is his pride any different than that of his father's?

She pushes the buzzer on the intercom panel to alert Jiři to our arrival. Jiři's family name is listed on the panel. Her name is Kotyza. Her grandfather was related to my grandmother. Most lights behind the buttons on the panel are burnt out. I avoid looking at hers. I don't want to see if they've troubled themselves to replace the bulb behind their buttons anymore than I want to think of Milada stuck here for the forseeable future.

We bounce in the elevator up to the eighth floor and walk down a corridor with cracked and missing tiles. A decorative strip of plaster above the tile, painted the color of mustard, has browned with grime. And the smells. Sour cabbage, urine, acrid tobacco. Nose wrinkling neglect has turned this passageway into a tableau of the torture I imagine it must have been to raise her family here. No wonder she obsessed over the Skagit, the baldies, the turbulent water. The stinking salmon carcasses on the flood banks must have been ambrosia to her eastern bloc nose.

Prague is earning a reputation as the world's black market capital for illegal organs. I know this, but I did not anticipate Dr. Saudek's insinuation—as he shoved me away from the shores of Prague this afternoon—that this was the reason I've come paddling into his little harbor.

Milada insisted that we phone Blue Cross tonight and request an extension. Jiří's black-light troupe—he's their business manager—is performing at a local theater after dinner. She wants us to attend his show. She admits she is proud of her husband's participation in the revolution. She will always love him for this.

In the entryway to her flat we exchange shoes for slippers. Blinds cover the windows, an old precaution to prevent paranoid neighbors from spying, a habit she admits she finds hard to break. Curious—*can't help it*—I lift a blind. In a littered lot between buildings is a rusty, partly collapsed play gym. All the reason I'd need to keep the blinds closed. Her dark furniture includes a massive armoire for coats and shoes and a credenza filled with the obligatory leaded crystal. Nothing in the details says *Milada*. Where does she keep her details? Following her to the kitchen, I ponder the degree to which the details we surround ourselves with ought to reflect our desires. To what extent does a paucity of details reflect self denial? My father kept his details in the basement. That amber bowl he flicked his cigar ashes into. The starched white undershirts, the ironed Union work pants. The bar of Ivory soap at the sink he brushed his teeth with, in the early days, when he still thought and acted like an emigrant. That stack of quarters, weekly replenished, that I was forbidden to touch. I liked to think they were savings kept from Mom in order to send money overseas to Anezka. What do those details say about him? That he was caught between worlds, a man whose heart desired a world that was in his past, that he longed for pointlessly? But he was kind. Those quarters, I'm convinced, were more than just beer and cigar money.

In the kitchen, her husband winces at my broad-voweled American accent when I politely return his "*dobrý den.*" Jiří is a short man with an athletic build through the chest and thighs. With his pale eyes, sandy brows, sandy hair cropped conservatively short, he looks more handsomely like the Olympic skater he once was than a revolutionary. You'd expect to see his face on a Wheaties box, not on a prison mugshot. Their fifteen year old son, Martin, takes my jacket. His hair is jelled into neon pink and green Mohawk spikes. Milada tells me he is crazy about Seattle grunge. I gave him a Nirvana disc and a Walkman to play it in—he's on his own for the batteries. Do I want coffee? he asks. I explain that I'd love it but it's a problem of fluid retention; I have to measure intake. Then I decide why not, I'm going right back home anyway. Why not enjoy the little time I do have here?

"Tonight," Jiři announces with a dramatic sweep of his arms, "we serve Czech specialty, *svíčková!*" Pronounced "*sveetch-ko-vah,*" the word rolls off his tongue with a sumptuous *ahhh*! The sauce for the marinated beef dish takes two or three days to prepare. It will be too rich and too salty for me, Milada warned yesterday when she invited me to dinner, but I said no problem, I'll take a spoonful and appreciate what I am missing. Throwing Jiří a stern watch-your-manners look, she disappears into a back room to change. While their son fixes coffee, I escape to the deck.

Wash is hung to dry on plastic lines. The deck side of the building faces the freeway, which is so close it roars like a thousand sewers draining all at once. The unfiltered exhaust makes my eyes water. I ponder the shove I took this afternoon from the esteemed Dr. Saudek. No doubt he was only being sensible when he said, "Better you go home." Still, how could I not resent the insinuation that I'm here to steal a Czech kidney and that I'd take advantage of my father's country in its desperation? Nothing I could possibly say would change the fact that in his eyes I'm an American and that's that.

⁓

AT FIRST DR. Saudek actually seemed willing to help. Short, wiry, with buzz-cut gray hair, the head of the Department of Diabetes wore a lab coat and had a clipped manner and was more at ease spouting statistics than in offering encouragement, but he did seem to take a special interest in my case. He proudly showed me a study he'd published in English entitled, "The Effect of Kidney/Pancreas Transplantation on Diabetic Retinopathy."

His secretary printed a copy. I read it using my magnifier while he watched. Eleven years in, more than ninety percent of the patients who received only a partial pancreas from a living donor had gone blind. Patients who received a complete pancreas from a cadaver are exhibiting a sixty percent rate of eye stabilization.

"You still have functional eyesight," he observed. "If you take only portion of your sister's pancreas, you will certainly become blind."

"What I need most urgently is a kidney," I said.

That's where the interview began to sour. To qualify for a legal kidney here, you have to be Czech, and I don't have a Czech passport. When I was a dependent my father could have made this possible but he never expected to return and so chose not to do it.

"Cost for surgery," he went on, I'm sure to scare me, "including mandatory first year of care, would be about thirty thousand. In cash dollars. If you have this money," he shrugged elaborately, "maybe we could put you on list."

I couldn't help but notice the contradictory messages and was reminded that Czech doctors work for the State and are not well paid. Many take private patients who show up bearing envelopes stuffed with cash.

He handed me a brochure that proudly announced the introduction of the immunosuppressant drug program ten years ago, in 1984. This program made it possible to transplant organs that wouldn't be rejected by the recipient's immune system. The annual number of kidney and pancreas transplants has risen steadily since then. Twenty-five are scheduled at his clinic for this year alone.

"Better you go home," he said tersely. "Among Czech people, six hundred thousand have diabetes. Patients on dialysis is up thirty-one percent from when we began our study." He opened his hands, palms up, as if to say sorry, what can we do?

Ushering us out of his office, he reminded Milada that the two of them are due to leave tomorrow for their conference in Brno. I'd forgotten about that conference. This might explain why she was so cavalier about my leaving immediately to return to Seattle. "Good luck to you," he said, clapping me on the shoulder. That was two hours ago. I still feel the steely pinch of his grip on my arm as he steered me to the door. During the metro ride out to Chodov, Milada assured me that he was only talking this way to avoid having to admit they take bribes. I assured her that I prefer to have the procedure at home with doctors I know and not to worry.

⚬⚬⚬

THE SMELL OF fresh coffee lures me back to the kitchen. My landlord, Tomaś— I'd forgotten that he's a family friend—has arrived. Wiry, bearded, Tomaś is a ball of entrepreneurial energy. He and his father are both engineers. They buy old buildings for next to nothing, pay the families in them to move, then refurbish the buildings for resale to investors who have profited from the switch to the private economy. A notable example, I'm told, is a guy from my father's village, Jungmann. The ex state security apparatchik was set to profit from the inn that burned the night of the government handover.

Milada rented a room for me in Tomaś' parents' flat in Mala Strana in the heart of Prague, near the cathedral where we met yesterday. Last night his father serenaded me to sleep from behind closed double doors with his chronic cough. Was Milada worried that I would feel too isolated out here near the end of the subway line? Or … what? That her husband would cause trouble? We've certainly given him no reason.

I sit on the *Eckbank* beside Tomaś. He points out the new knotty-pine paneling, the self-replenishing eight liter electric hot water tank mounted above the sink that offers—*get this!*—instant hot water. His remodel of Milada's kitchen ended abruptly. Martin uses a spatula to tug open drawers that have broken half-shell plastic handles with wickedly jagged edges that would lacerate unwary fingers. According to Milada, Tomaś tried in vain to talk Jiři out of diverting every *koruna* of that Russian loan into his father's *chata*. Bad business move, pure sentiment.

Milada re-enters wrapped in a kimono exposing a lot of bare thigh. Her husband catches me looking. She removes a place setting. A friend from the neighborhood, Yveta, was invited—she wanted to meet the visiting American—but she's recovering from radiation treatment for breast cancer and doesn't feel up to an outing.

"Too bad," Martin says to me. "Tomaś fixed up flat in home of Yveta. It has three private rooms. She will rent cheaper than this thief." A nod to Tomaś. "Okay, here is beautiful Turk coffee." He serves it to me grounds and all in a glass. An oily sheen swims on the froth.

"Ach, not that coffee for our guest," says Milada.

"What?" says Martin, offended. "We always serve to our guests this coffee."

Tomaś opens a few bottles of Staropramen Desitka, a local beer. "*Na zdraví.*"

"Drink coffee," says Jiři. "Tonight you must stay awake to see my black light play. Is another Czech specialty." He laughs and then says, "Your father is Czech, *ano?* He tell you about our black light? Why you do not speak Czech?"

"My father," I say into the awkward silence, "refused to teach us. It's something I regret, for sure. What did your father do after the war?"

Jiři sets down his glass of beer. His handsome features flinch and tighten. "*Dělal vše proto aby zůstal naživu.*"

Milada translates: "He do what he is told if he wants to stay alive." It's a sore subject. I do know a few details. Jiři's father, a registered Communist and the supervisor at Jáchymov, a uranium mine, got into trouble when he refused to cede control to the Soviets. They needed the uranium and turned the mine into a forced labor camp for dissidents. "They very nicely invited Jiři's father to become inmate."

"What about your father, Milada?" I've never been able to get more out of her than the fact that he still lives on the farm in Písečná that used to belong to my father's family, and that when she escaped in 1968, he was arrested, interrogated and tortured by Jungmann's state security.

"*Moje rodina je blaznivá!*" She throws her arms dramatically into the air. "My family is crazy!"

"She will never say more," Jiři says.

Tomaś says to me, "I think you are judging Czech people."

"Czech people," says Milada's son, "have inferiority complex." Leave it to youth to point to the white elephant in the room. "You wish to call us cowards? Okay. We need your money. Everything you say is okay."

Milada scolds Martin, reminding him that my father is Czech. She apologizes to me. "We love to complain. We do not learn how to live free like you Americans." She tosses back her beer and refills her glass.

"My father gave his life to protest Soviet occupation," Jiři shouts. *Lower the volume*, Milada chides. *We're not deaf.* "He defend what belonged to Czech people. For why? So we tell to every coward who fled, come back and take what you want? *Ne! Musíme to zastavit.*"

"My father really wanted to join the partisans." It's a lie. Actually, there might be some truth to it. "Imagine the torture, never knowing what happened to my sister."

"We don't need to imagine torture."

"Stop this!" shouts Milada. "It make me sick, always fighting!" Following another warning to her husband, Milada disappears again, this time to slip into her theater clothes. When she's gone, Martin confides that he has something I'll be interested in seeing. He unfolds on the table the opinion page from a last March issue of the *Everett Herald.* There is the photo the reporter took of his mother in February, when she came to Seattle to attend the language school at Skagit Valley College. The photo accompanies the essay Milada wrote. Milada doesn't know I keep a copy of the photo in my passport pouch. Martin, of course, would also have no way of knowing this. Or that many times I've pulled it out to study those eyes, squinty even though the light could not have been bright in Skagit Valley in February. Was emigrating on her mind as she pondered the Skagit flooding into the fields?

Wanting to practice his English, Martin reads the essay out loud. " 'One day, I saw an otter in the Skagit River. This is an animal that hasn't lived in the rivers of my country for many years because of pollution. I felt something nice in my restless heart.' "

"*Dost,*" says Jiři. "She feel something it is certain."

They stopped having conjugal relations two years ago—at least, that's what Milada claims—when Jiři borrowed that money from the Russians and Milada understood, finally, just how deeply the hook of shame had set in him, the shame of the occupied, so deeply that he would take out a high interest loan on their future.

Martin reads on. " 'I've seen in your country many miles of virgin woods. This is something that doesn't exist in my home. But not only nature excited me so much. The people I met returned something to my soul.' "

"She look like she is begging."

" 'Please take loving care of this nice country where the raptors that have died in Europe are still flying. Please regard the Native Americans who revere the sun and the moon. Your country must never stop being clean, good-smelling, and wild.' "

"*To je, hloupost.* It is stupid, yes?" Jiři rises from the table. "We have beauty here. You have some castles? *Ne,* you have Disneyland."

"Why don't you come visit? See for yourself. I'll take you to see the raptors."

"Him?" Martin says with disgust. "We live in this shithole so he can pay one hundred thousand dollars to rebuild his mountain house."

"We have wounded birds right here."

"He is *patriot*." Martin raises his hand in a mock Nazi salute. "Patriots believe only we are good and they are evil. They do harm for superficial reasons."

"Never do that again in my house," Jiři says, defeated. Judging by Martin's smirk, they've been round this bend before.

"Your father is nationalist," says Tomaś. "Is different. They believe in country."

"You call them nationalists, so now ethnic cleansing is okay?" Then he looks at me, knowing of course that his father is watching. "I think she will love Seattle. She hate how brown and sick everything is here."

Milada strides back into the kitchen to put an end to the bickering. "Yes, it is beautiful, but this is our home." In her evening outfit, a black gown with a high neckline and a flouncy skirt, an enormous rock of Baltic amber dangling at her breast from a silver necklace, she looks slim and beautiful, but in that way I've noticed Eastern European women seem wont to put it on: lipstick too thick, skirt too short, outfit too clingy.

Would she really consider such a thing? Has she spoken about this with her son? I read her essay when it came out in the opinions column. It seemed at the time like nothing more than what anyone would say who'd spent four decades growing up behind the Iron Curtain.

She pats her son's arm. "No provoking your father while we eat."

Their son fills soup bowls. Jiři dishes up *svíčková* with buttery dumplings and a red cabbage salad with sour cream. The sauce I can only sample. Way too much sodium. He hardly touches the sliced beef on his own plate before grabbing his jacket. Leaving for the theater, on his way out, he repeats his invitation. "You do not have something like this, yes?" When he is gone, Tomaś apologizes to me for his rudeness. "His own wife is not Czech enough for him. You must not take personal insult." Announcing that he must get to work at the train station, Tomaś says goodnight, then he, too, is gone.

Now it's Milada's turn to apologize. His black-light troupe is struggling financially and he has that murderous loan to pay off. "We will phone to Blue Cross. If they give okay you will stay here and we will begin immediately to look for Anezka."

"What about your conference? Aren't you going to Brno?"

She looks at me gravely. *What now? What haven't I understood this time? My God these people can be touchy. I see where my father gets it.* "I have agreed to conference so I will find some opportunity to speak with Saudek about your case. If you wish I will meet you there in three days. Or you will wait for me here."

It would be pointless to attempt this on my own and of course she knows that. "That was quite some essay you wrote. Sounds like your son wants to move to Seattle. You guys talk about this?"

"Later. We will have time for this later."

While Martin cleans up, Milada dials a long string of numbers on the old Bakelite rotary-dial phone hung on the kitchen wall, then hands me the phone. It's shortly before ten o'clock in Seattle's morning. A female voice answers.

My file has been assigned to a case worker, but she's home today with a sick child. For confidentiality reasons, the office manager cannot tell me over the phone what's in my file. Despite that, she says, "This claim was denied, but I see there's been a review ..." Realizing she's already said too much, she stops and asks for my patience while she reads the review. *Denied? Denied? But the board of surgeons, when they gave me their acceptance, they assured me...* A close friend of mine from law school chairs the board that negotiates the health insurance contract for the union representing those hundred and twenty thousand municipal employees. I asked him to put in a good word for me with Blue Cross. That must explain the review of the denial. *You don't need to be from an eastern bloc country ...*

"So, you're where?" she says, back on the line. "Did you say Poland?"

"Prague. Searching for my Czech sister. I'm hoping she can donate a kidney. That's why I'm here." *A lie, of course, but there's no reason these people need to know that.* "The letter I just received is signed by Dr. Pomerantz. The letter asks me to come back in for more tests. It sounds like approval of my transplant surgery is pending those results. But here's the thing. I need a little more time to find my sister. An extension of one week on the deadline would probably do it."

"I can't speak for Dr. Pomerantz. You should call the UW Medical Center."

"It's not a medical question. I'm concerned about making your deadline."

"We process a lot of claims here. Those deadlines are firm."

"So, I can't ask for even a week's extension?"

"I'll put a note in your file that you called," she says peremptorily. "Don't miss the deadline. That would delay processing your case."

Milada commiserates. It is best for me to go home immediately and straighten this out. She will proceed with her conference in Brno then phone me regarding any progress with Saudek. Then we will decide if now is the right time to look for my sister.

The very thought of waiting... Waiting is the privilege of the healthy. Waiting owns the luxury of a future. Now we are going to the theater. The theater is a public place. There is something we need to discuss without fear of being overheard. Not one scintilla of what she has to say can get back to her husband, nor can her son be trusted to keep quiet. What could be so sensitive? But the prospect of spending an evening with her overcomes the slavering exhaustion that dogs me on bad days like this.

◦〜◦

Vaclav Havel's wealthy family owns the theater tucked into a backstreet off Wenceslas Square. The theater resembles the *fin de siècle* high-school lunchroom of my Cedar Rapids memories: oak floors polished to a basketball-worthy sheen; elevated stage—I half expect to see a scoreboard when the curtains open. Certainly fewer than a hundred tourists fan out among metal folding chairs, lured by the promise of seeing a simulacrum of the black light shows that fostered the revolution. Scraping shoes and shifting coats, they arrange themselves with as much dignity as possible. Is this the best venue Jiři's troupe can afford? This sad little converted auditorium?

Jiři comes out before the show begins, ostensibly to welcome us but really to fret over the rows of empty chairs. His actors do have to be paid. "So, Charles. I am sorry. What does she call you? Chico?" He pronounces my nickname *cheeek-oh*. "Tomorrow you are finally off to Pisečná!"

"Blue Cross wouldn't give me the extension. I have to go back."

"But you've only arrived." Do I hear relief in his tone? "Tonight we give you beautiful memory. A gift you will take home for your father."

"*Na zdraví!*" I thank him and wish him luck. The house lights dim. He hurries backstage before the curtains open.

We move up to the balcony. We are alone. It will be easy to talk. Most of those in the audience below are overdressed European tourists in leather jackets and evening gowns. She points out a heavyset man at the rear of the theater wearing a cheap brown suit and standing with his hands braced on the back of a folding chair and gazing dully at the parting curtain on the stage. "He is not here for show," she whispers. "He is here to watch someone. Everyone watching everyone to see who will cheat. Maybe he is sent by Jungmann."

Just in case, I lean back until I'm no longer in the brown-suited man's line of sight. "Why would this guy Jungmann be interested in us?" Milada obviously still suffers her country's chronic paranoia. I like to think of it as the pinching effect. Pinched shoulders, pinched brows, pinched expectations.

"Hey, they're actually very good," I add. In the opening act, lithe actors in harlequin costumes perform incredible feats that combine balletic elegance with impressive gymnastic acrobatics. "As far as that goes, how would this guy even know we'd be here?"

Images of village scenes flash from a projector onto shifting screens—a fountain, a square, farm people in homely garb crowded into market stalls. The Eternal Wanderer—the story's hero, a bearded dancer swathed in black robes and suspended above the stage from invisible wires—floats through the night above towns where doors and shutters slam closed as he passes. No one admits to knowing him. No one will invite him into their home. Behind him is a deep void of inky night.

"Milada. How could that guy possibly know we'd be here?"

"You see this?" whispers Milada, still avoiding my question. "It could be your father. It could be my father. They float above two worlds. No one invite them." The Eternal Wanderer is unable to go back to where he came from, and is unable to end his tragic life by dying. He jokes and sings, but his jokes are sad and his singing melancholy. Only one thing can save him from his fate— the love of a woman from his home village who pines for his return.

"You see? He is your father. And she is Rosalye." She waves an arm dramatically. "I have seen this show many times but never before have I seen this connection for you. You must bring your father to here. He cannot say no. No more. You must convince to him. He will make known he look for Rosalye and they will come to us and you will find your sister."

"Milada. Why is this man here?"

"Okay, is what we must talk about, yes? I have friend, he is mayor of Piséčná."

"He found Anezka?"

"*Ne, ne.*" She leans toward me, looking around to make double sure no one is listening, which is of course absurd, right? We're the only ones in the balcony. "He search in archives." She launches into a description of the meticulously kept records that are only now beginning to be unearthed like buried corpses, records of orders to arrest and deport the well-to-do farmers who had no interest in signing over their land to the collective, who were accused of fomenting dissension among the *kulak*. My father, she reminds me, would have found himself among the deportees. Yet, I remind her, her father was not. She presses my hands and searches my eyes, for what? Forgiveness? Understanding?

"It is difficult to explain. My father collaborate with Jungmann so he can keep farm. He deal with Devil for favors and still he nearly starve. When I escape, he is arrested and tortured. Jungmann had to make look good, yes?" There's something more. Her hands press mine. They are sweaty and she keeps sneaking looks down at the brown-suited man. "Also he find two memos signed by Jungmann from September 1968. This was when my father was in prison."

"The memos implicate this guy Jungmann using torture?"

"I do not know details. I haven't seen. It is not your concern. I only say you this because my mayor friend, his name Zamečnik, he wants to bring human rights accusations in court against certain individuals."

"And Jungmann is one of them."

"*Ano.* I worry, if Jungmann finds out I am connected—"

"How *are* you connected?"

"I am not, not really. But I admit I will like to see Jungmann pay for how he betray my father. My father don't know about this. I only tell you because maybe Jungmann will make trouble for us. I think is better we find your sister and take her away before troubles begin."

"Jungmann has a good reason to look for her, right? The inn? The fire? She had plenty of motive to burn that place to the ground, from what you said."

"*Ano*, it is true. He took away her orphanage. Is better I think if she is gone before my mayor friend make trouble."

"This is why we came up here? This is what you wanted to tell me?"

"I see this brown man. Then I am sure. You must know about this."

The Eternal Wanderer calls out the name of the woman who loved him. Has anyone seen her? Anyone? The tumblers on stage, if they hear, refuse to respond. "The sexiest thing that ever happened in our city office is the TV news show, *America's Most Wanted*. They interviewed my police chief. People wanted to hear about the Green River killer." Only a month into my six-month medical leave, I haven't been forced yet to address the question of medical retirement. That world seems as far away to me as the world that awaits me post-transplant. I have to be optimistic about this. I am, but I don't want to face this alone. I don't want to get up and take my meds only to face my couch alone. I would have saved myself for what? No, this post-apocalypse of mine should be shared. I have a room for my sister. I want her with me.

"*Neboj se.* Are you afraid? I think you are."

It's a rhetorical question. We watch the final act in silence. The Wanderer does find his home village, but everything has changed. No one recognizes him when he calls out greetings. Then we see the former lover, alone on the stage, sitting hunched, her head shrouded in a shawl. He calls out to her. Her head never lifts.

Lift your head. Say his name. Say his name!

"Chico, go home, take care to Blue Cross, but you must immediately return. It is better if you take kidney here. I will help with recovery. I will speak again with Saudek at conference. Also I think it will be easier for your sister. She has probably never been away from our district. It would not surprise to know she has never seen Prague. Here she will be more comfortable."

"I made copies of her mother's letters." So she could see her mother pleading for a word from my father, for anything to indicate when he would come back to help raise his daughter. There was a promise veiled in that pleading.

The house lights come up. The man in the brown suit is gone. On our way out, I poke my head backstage to thank Jiři and tell him how much I loved his play. All he can do is lament. "Where is my Czech audience? Where are my people? You tourists understand nothing. Where are my people?" Looking pinched, he turns away.

Despite her saying it's not necessary—she's angry and I can't tell why, maybe because I couldn't promise when I will be back—I accompany Milada on the metro out to Chodov. We ride in clickety-clacking silence on an increasingly emptier train. We walk from the station past the Soviet worker statue sissified by vandals who painted his boots pink, then continue through a freeway underpass reeking of piss and approach her gray *sidlisté*. Hearing the dented security grate clang shut behind her, I finally understand that this is not about my sister, not *only* about my sister. Milada wants something from me. Of course, I'm her best escape option. No, no, I don't see the cynic in her. That love for the otters and the river? She would never be ironic about a thing like that.

Catching a cab back to Tomaš' flat, I decide I'll invite Milada to visit me as soon as we find my sister. Maybe we could find a getaway property on the Skagit not too far from the raptor center. We'll hang out, the three of us together. Our hearts will sing like the children in the cathedral. Can there be anything more joyous than having a future again?

Chapter Three

Raptor Rehab: Late September, 1994

THE FIRST THING that greets me in Seattle is the box of mail, kindly dropped off by my townhouse neighbor who has my keys. Flipping through the condolence cards from my staff, bless them, then the depressing stack of billing statements from labs and clinics—the law journals and bar reviews tumble directly into recycle—I come across a letter from the board of transplant surgeons. How the medical bureaucracy grinds. Nearly a month after granting approval, they send a letter reminding me that family should schedule blood tests? These tests were of course done long ago. My father was ruled out as a viable donor. Anne, my older sister in Iowa, not only had incompatible antigens and the wrong Rh factor, but the blood tests uncovered a condition that might jeopardize her own kidneys. That leaves my Czech half-sister who, as far as my medical team is concerned, does not yet officially exist.

The extra labs required by Blue Cross take me to the University Medical Center, where I'm told my creatinine levels are high, but we knew that. My blood pressure is unacceptably high, as is, obviously, my fluid retention. I'm checked in for a day and hooked up to catheters and subjected to a stern lecture about lowering sodium and fluid intake. It seems that my internist might have been overly optimistic when he informed me that I needn't worry about preparing for dialysis for another six months. Three, he's guessing now. In three months he wants me to have my left arm fitted with a fistula. For diabetics it can take weeks to heal and he wants the fistula in my arm and ready when dialysis can no longer be avoided.

Back home, taking in the view of the ship canal and the lofty Aurora Bridge, locally famous for its suicide jumpers, I decide I deserve pampering.

I walk up to the video store, then spend the afternoon and evening on my soft leather couch with a giant bowl of air-popped popcorn—no salt, no butter. But after my second time through *The Emigrants*, a riveting Swedish film dramatizing the quest undertaken by a young Liv Ullmann and Max von Sydow for freedom in the hinterlands of Minnesota—escaping a debt-burdened farm, a fate shared by an earlier generation of my Czech family—I can't stand it any longer. The walls are closing in on me. That evening, in the room I've prepped for Anezka—the room is small, with a full-sized bed, a desk, a treadmill that folds up; there's hardly room to stand without tripping over cords—I lance stickpins into the map, into every village in eastern Bohemia ever named in the letters I stole from the family Bible, villages with names like Ceské Libchavy, Oucmanice, Sudislav nad Orliči, Hnátnice. Somewhere in that district, maybe in one of those very villages, my sister is hiding—very likely with relatives, if Milada is right. The day the approval comes through from Blue Cross, I book my return flight.

The following day, faced with the gloomy prospect of more couch time, I find to my great relief a card in the mail from Rainy Waters. Okay, roll your eyes. It's a name the raptor rehab center director assumed after reading Rachel Carson's *Silent Spring* and falling off her ranch horse and into the cause. The card is a pre-printed thank you, but in the margins, in her hectic scrawl, Rainy lets me know that she has a possible solution to Isis' situation. This particularly uncooperative Peregrine falcon, she is well aware, is my favorite bird at the center. Also, she's taking sign-ups for the late September rafting trip on the Skagit to do the pre-winter baldy count. If I can't make it I need to let her know. This outing is hugely popular with newbie volunteers.

An attorney is neither a vet nor a wildlife biologist, obviously, and with my experience limited to municipal law, I can't even offer legal counsel to the raptor center, beyond reviewing county zoning regulations. I can't draft settlement proposals with Cock-a-Doddle-Moo, the ad hoc organization of local farmers that wants the center gone. Federal protections offered Peregrines and baldies restrict the farmers' use of pesticides, not to mention any shrub clearing that would reduce habitat. But I don't go there to use my law degree, and Waters understands that and hasn't asked me, yet, to sit in on negotiations. A month away from the office, I've begun to wonder if I would have gone into municipal law at all, had I not needed a career offering high-grade disability insurance without the stress of billable hours. This past summer, with the Wyroc hearing looming and committee meetings eating up my every morning and evening, and especially when it was no longer possible to go out for my long, soothing runs, I found my only calm around the birds. My first day as a volunteer, last March, fired up with a Milada–inspired passion for saving one of the last "clean, good smelling and wild" places on earth, I hungrily swallowed the sermon: "We are Giving Back to the Sacred Circle." Birds are more than just birds at Sardis. "By mending their bones and wings and returning them to their habitat," Carrie, the vet student chief of volunteers, explained, "we volunteers are healing our wounded world." *Healing*? I signed up, met Isis, witnessed his jitterbugging retreat from humans he ungratefully doesn't trust, and realized I needed a way to be useful. If I can't actually help, I bravely told Waters, send me away.

Thanks to progressive retinopathy, I have the option of having myself declared legally blind. I should not have the option of getting behind the wheel of my Saab. Concerned friends want me to give them my keys. By palming my eyes, I can actually clear the blur. What I don't tell them is that it's like defrosting a car window on a cold day; they have to be cleared regularly. So it's with foggy vision that I steer onto Interstate 5 during the late-morning traffic lull. Despite knowing that I could be arrested for such reckless behavior, I drive the two hours north to Sardis, my sanctuary.

⁓ˋ⸰⸝⸜

THE CHIPPED-BARK PATH to the raptor center meanders through a cathedral of Douglas-fir and hemlock and western red cedar mintily redolent of sap and needles. Listening to the shrill cry of the Harrier hawk that seems to have adopted the center, far from the roar of the freeway and doctor visits, my death sentence feels like it's been lifted. This is what I come for—this and my sentimental desire to free Isis.

The sprawling compound, an array of feeding barns and flight cages, also has a medical clinic with an ambulance parked outside. Waters and her husband and dogs live in a rough log cabin above the clinic so that Waters can be on call for emergencies. En route to see Waters and let her know I'm back, I pass Carrie among the holding cages.

"Wanagi says hello." Carrie slips on an elbow-length leather glove. Wearing no makeup, a sweatshirt draped over baggy jeans tucked into rubber boots, Carrie reminds me that I need to change if I'm staying to work, and that reminds me of the motto hanging above the changing room—"We are mending our relationship with the world one bird at a time!" Sappy, okay, but that motto inspired me to reach deep into my heart for the courage to save the sister I am coming to think of as a wounded bird, though I have no concrete evidence of this, nor any specific notion of what she needs to be saved from.

Carrie's forearm emerges from the cage holding a nervous, adolescent six-pound female bald eagle with one wing unnaturally canted. "You're becoming one of our prize show birds, aren't you?" Like ninety percent of the injured birds here, Wanagi flew into man-made trouble, in her case a fence. With her permanently injured wing she has a short flight range, maybe ten yards.

"How many birds on site these days?" The entire complex, including two net-covered flight cages that together comprise the area of a football field, occupies thirty acres. In this row of two dozen cages on stilts, the air is pretty acrid.

"We're up this week. Just shy of a hundred. The birds are on the move. We need to get busy with a baldy count. Hey, weren't you supposed to be in Europe looking for somebody?" She attaches leather jesses to the eagle's ankles while I explain what Blue Cross demanded. "You going back?"

"Absolutely. I just don't know when."

That last night in Prague, after the black light theater, Milada lit into me, shouting, "*Nemožné*! Impossible! You are impossible." She was so incensed I had to ask her to calm down. I'd been telling her that I planned to spend time with the raptors, assuming she'd find this prospect exciting after what she'd written about the Skagit, but her reaction took me by surprise. "You speak always about dignity," she said. "Even if you are sick you must keep dignity. Okay, but dignity is what my husband want. It is like living in cage. If you want freedom, dignity is burden."

She refused to explain what she meant and during that long silent metro ride out to Chodov I considered that maybe she was worried I would never come back, and that could only possibly matter if she wanted me to sponsor her.

Over the next hour, waiting for Waters to finish a surgery, I walk around the complex and say hello to Mote Man, a Barn Owl who thinks he's human, and to Bob, a blind American Kestrel hit by a car, and I manage to wake up Heyokee, a Harris hawk who makes a grinding noise in his throat to complain. I'm stalling. Isis is my bird, but I want Waters to be with me when I visit him.

It was Waters who introduced me to Isis last spring. My first day as a volunteer, waiting on the lawn outside her cabin, recalling an argument I'd had with Milada over whether freedom is actually liberating or a burden, I speculated that Milada might have reacted adversely to this place. That impression was only reinforced when Waters made her grand appearance lighting up a cigarette and wearing the outfit she's worn every day I've seen her since—a lab coat over a pearl-button shirt tucked into tight western-cut jeans and tooled cowboy boots—and you can't miss the ice-blue eye makeup.

Catching me staring, Waters laughed. "Hey, what can I say, I was a rancher's kid before I had my Paul-on-the-road-to-Damascus moment." Assuming from my reaction that I was a skeptical volunteer, Waters forewent the speeches and led me to Isis' cage.

With a ruffled blue tawny and gray chest and hooded, hyper-alert eyes, Isis looked scruffy and paranoid. He jiggered from foot to foot when we drew near, refusing to give us the satisfaction of a look that would say *I know why you're here*.

"Cooperate," I told him. "It's for your own good."

That wariness was making it impossible for Waters to help him. I made a joking reference to Isis being a male with the name of an Egyptian Goddess. That prompted Waters to explain how he'd become her special project.

Isis had been one of four young in an experimental nest seeded by wildlife biologists on the Washington Mutual Towers in Seattle, operating on the theory that downtown there are cliffs, and plump pigeons and tasty starlings, and we have to find a way to live together. The four nestlings were sickened by a protozoa from a pigeon fed to them by their mother. In the wild, they'd have died and that would have ended the affair. This could not be allowed to happen in front of nervous bank execs with noses pressed to the glass. The nestlings were whisked away to Woodland Park Zoo. Three of the four died soon after. Embarrassed by the bad press, the zoo biologist called Waters to say that one female nestling had survived and she promptly named her Isis.

Waters identified the protozoa and the falcon's true gender. The infection had very slightly widened the choanal slit in the roof of Isis' mouth on one side. These birds, the fastest on earth, fly at an incredible 200 mph swept-wing diving speed when hunting, and that itty bitty widening would make controlled flight impossible. Her only hope was to keep him, and watch. Eventually the opening seemed to heal, but no trainer has yet successfully coaxed Isis into the flight cage for a test.

Common wisdom in this business has it that the longer in captivity, the less likely they are to survive in the wild. We argued about what to do. Dragging on her cigarette, Waters admitted that Isis was too suspicious of humans to become one of her show birds. But she had a theory. If one volunteer could just spend enough time with Isis, the reprobate might actually calm down enough to be moved.

The challenge interested me, but with the Wyroc hearing coming up—an appeal that had been pending for two years and that in August would come to a vote before the city council—I couldn't give more than the occasional weekend at Sardis. The rock crushing plant sought rezoning permits that would allow them to move their operation into town where their trucks would have better road access and would not have to pay the county's higher excise fees. Nothing in all my decade and a half in city government had caused such partisan acrimony. The pro faction licked their lips at the idea of collecting tipping fees on twelve trucks per hour. The anti faction complained about overloaded stack lanes blocking traffic, not to mention flyaway dust and the usual noise pollution. As the city attorney enjoined to interpret compliance with the law, I was caught in the middle with both sides lining up expert testimony for the August showdown. There was no way to know at the time that this would be my last hurrah.

Wouldn't it be something if I could have my sister here for his grand release?

–⁓–

THE SPACIOUS ICU clinic occupies the downstairs of Waters' cabin. In front is an exam room with a gurney donated by a hospital. In the back, an operating room with Plexiglas incubators, one operating table, overhead drop lights, trays of sterilized instruments. That's where I find Waters.

"Welcome back, stranger." She's moving an anesthetized Barred Owl into a meshed cage. Waters has on her usual ice blue eye makeup. After checking to see that the gas is turned off, she lights up. "Hey, you find your sister?"

"Wasn't time. I'm still having trouble with insurance."

"You heard there's a rafting trip coming up?" I thank her for her card. "Last Saturday in September. We'll do the count now, then count 'em again in February to find out what percentage are over-wintering."

"Sign me up." A rafting trip on the Skagit to count baldies? What could be more perfect for Milada? "My friend in Prague, the doctor who's helping me find my sister ... I told you about her? She wrote that piece about the Skagit for the *Herald*."

"You say she's a doc? Could be useful. I'll sign her up. But don't talk about this. We can only take fourteen."

"What if we find my sister? This could be really inspirational."

"There's gonna be a lot of pissed off people as it is. Don't push it."

"What about Isis? You said you had a plan?"

"Same old plan. We take him downtown and hope he decides it's time to hunt again. But first we gotta get him into the flight cage. And that requires…"

"I might have some time. I'll know soon."

Waters' walkie-talkie squawks. "Sorry, another emergency coming in. Go get reacquainted with Isis. Make sure you get your name back on the sign-up board."

"Put two of us down for the raft," I remind her as she hurries away. In comes Carrie bearing Torkey on her arm. The twenty-seven-year-old red-tailed hawk, the oldest bird on site, has to be brought inside every afternoon to prepare for spending the night in a covered cage, like a canary. Torkey has arthritis in her limbs and hops around in her cage mad with fear whenever a new volunteer forgets to bring her in. I like Torkey. It's not a bad life, this captivity, and she's making the best of it.

"You driving again?" Carrie says. "That a good idea? Hey, I'll check the schedule, see who's commuting up from Seattle these days."

I stop by Isis' cage, but soon realize I'm torturing him. Establishing a rapport will not be easy. I leave before they can convince me I'm not fit to drive.

～ゝˈ⁄ˌ～

DOWN BEST ROAD through the Skagit flats, there's not much traffic. Instead of white-knuckling it all the way, I glance over at Mt. Baker and the glacier-notched Cascade foothills and wave to itinerant workers out in the fields and wish it were tulip season. I count the red-tailed hawks perched on the power lines, stopping at a dozen. Last February, when I drove Milada up here to have a picnic by the river, we came across thousands of migrating long-necked, graceful snow geese nosing into a pelt of new grass. She shouted, "Fantastic! Fantastic! Thank you so much for bring me here."

She wanted to see another river otter and insisted we drive up as far as Rockport. A heavy mist clung to the Skagit. The February air was a few degrees colder than 40, close to the temp of the water. When the mist parted, we glimpsed a swollen river plunging over its banks into the underbrush. Despite the whiteout in the sky, the water ran gunmetal gray and boiled against the bridge, stacking up log jams. Excited by the wildness of the current, I impulsively asked Milada if she'd ever consider coming here to stay. There were no otters to be seen in the turbulent waters. "I will come back," she said, "you can be sure." Then she left me at the bridge and ran past a stand of alders and scrambled over nurse logs and disappeared into the woods.

The river began to frighten me with its currents, its barely contained will. "It's going to snow," I remember telling her as an excuse to leave as soon as she returned. We hurried back to the car.

～ゝˈ⁄ˌ～

IT WAS A fluke that I learned of her existence at all. This past January, my townhouse had become a lonely place with Kasia gone. My ex has Polish parents. Our shared fate as the progeny of exiles attracted us to each other in the first place, but over time the combination proved too volatile. I figured my father could use some company, too. Mom had died from diabetes complications two years earlier. From what I could gather from our phone conversations, Dad had reduced his life to work—he still owns Lenoch Home Design and Build—and the Sunday drive to mass at St. Wenceslas and after to Bohemie town for the thick-cut, nearly fatless bacon he gets from his Czech butcher. I flew to visit him in Cedar Rapids. While he had me home—he still lives in the bungalow he built on Fruitland Boulevard, the same house where he raised my older sister and me—he asked me to poke through Mom's things in the attic, see if there was anything I wanted to keep before he purged.

A steel washer hangs on the end of a string in the landing where the stairs come up from the carport. When the washer and string are pulled, a drop down ladder gives access to the attic. My father has arthritis in his knees and hasn't climbed up there in years. Anne, who lives in Williamsburg, had sent her goth teen daughter—I get a real kick out of Megan—to pack Mom's things and haul them up.

In the freezing attic I found Mom's old trunk. Buried under the fine linens that came out only for Christmas and Thanksgiving dinner, I found the brown leather-bound family Bible with gilt lettering, the one I loved to thumb through as a kid. That swirling vine motif of the capital letters spoke of hidden castles and monstrous forests. It had been my favorite book in the house and I'd wondered why from one day to the next it was no longer on the coffee table by the rocker in the living room.

Pressed between pages of that Bible I found what might have been the explanation: fourteen letters, all addressed to my father, all posted during the year and a half after he escaped Czechoslovakia, all handwritten in neat cursive and signed by a young woman named Rosalye. I hid the letters in my suitcase without telling my father I'd done so. Later, feeling guilty, I asked if he knew the letters had been saved.

"*Tito lidé nežijí*," he said without any inflection in his voice, essaying what would become his standard response whenever I made inquiries into his Czech past. "Those people are dead."

Unbeknownst to my father, or even to Anne, who would have objected, I decided to have the letters translated. I drove to Solon, a town just outside of Cedar Rapids with a convent where, I'd learned, there lived a nun related to our family on the side of the Kacalek woman my grandfather had married bigamously in Iowa.

I dropped off the letters. A few days later we met again in the priest's rectory. "Here is your packet," she said dryly, handing me the same manila folder I'd dropped off with her. She averted her gaze. She paced the room.

"What did you learn? Who was Rosalye?"

Her penny loafers squeaked on the tiled linoleum floor. The light through the arched, leaded-glass rectory window was dim. Outside was overcast. A dreary winter day. Finally she stopped, brushed down her garments, looked at me, her brow furrowed in deepest concentration, and said, "There has been a mortal sin. A suicide. It was the first husband of Barbora Kacalka, Rosalye's mother, the woman from Pisečná who went to Iowa with your grandfather and then married him even though he had not divorced your grandmother." She continued to pace, her gaze averted. "But, it's not certain that the man who killed himself was Rosalye's father. I can say nothing more about this. If you wish to know more, you must go to Pisečná.

"There is one thing more," she added, before I could ask questions. "It seems that you have a sister, a half-sister, Anezka, daughter of Rosalye and your father. I give to you these letters and their translations. They are yours. I wish to speak of them no further." Hands folded across her rosary, she made it plain that our conference was over. "Please, never trouble me with this matter again." She waited for me to leave.

Mom, I realized as I drove back to Cedar Rapids, had to have known about Anezka. That would explain the mysterious letter she sent me not long before she died, "You should go to Piséčná one day, even if it means displeasing your father."

While I remained in Cedar Rapids, I called Anne to ask her to have her blood tested as a potential organ donor. She countered with a question, "How long are you home?" She's a generous person. She gives of her time enormously and I consider myself fortunate to have her nearby to take care of my father now that he's older. It's not that. My request, rather, threw her off her routines—she is as rigid as our father.

Upon returning to Seattle, I read and reread those translated letters. Written blandly to pass the scrutiny of censors, the letters revealed little about Rosalye beyond her demand that my father return to take his rightful place on the farm and raise their daughter. Not much use. Nothing for it but to go there.

—⁄⁄—

THANKS TO BLUE Cross being willing to do anything to win that union contract, a few days after my drive to Sardis I receive an expedited phone call from Dr. Pomerantz. The new battery of tests convinced him that my condition has grown acute. I'm accepted for transplant surgery.

"It's official! I'm accepted!" I shout this out loud.

There is, though, one more hurdle to leap. A home visit from an insurance rep must be scheduled to determine that they won't spend money on a bad risk. Meanwhile, I'm to get my affairs in order. Once given my beeper, I have to stay on call within twenty-four hours from the medical center.

I call Milada. She is guardedly ecstatic. This is great news, of course, but when does that mean I'll be coming back to Prague?

"First you're coming back to Seattle," I tell her. "I've got us both signed up for a rafting trip on the Skagit. The Skagit, can you believe it? We're going to count bald eagles. You can't say no. I'm buying your ticket. I'll put it on my credit card, so don't worry about it."

Soon as we hang up, I call SAS and make the reservation before she can change her mind.

Chapter Four

A Few Days Later in Seattle:
Late September, 1994

THE DAY AFTER Milada arrives from Prague, we drive north so I can introduce her to Waters and Isis before the rafting trip. We take the scenic detour over to Pioneer Road and then up Best Road through the Skagit flats. While we drive, Milada tells me about a famous radio series she and her friends listened to as kids in the sixties. To slip past censors, the series told what was claimed to be a fictional story of the Cimmermans, but Milada and her friends decided that the betrayal the Cimmermans suffered, the jail time, confessions forced by torture, seemed a little too authentic.

"Our families suffered like Cimmerman family. Suffering changes people. People are not heroes when they suffer."

My father could have stayed, he could have slipped over the border into Poland—it wouldn't have been far to go—and joined the partisans and slept in underground shelters in the forests and sniped at the occupiers. But, he left. If this illness has taught me anything, it's to assume you know nothing. "Czech hero," she adds, sensing my reticence to demote my father's status, "is man who stay by workbench and wait when his day will come." *And how is that not being complicit?* Of course I don't say this.

–∿–

WHEN WE ARRIVE at Sardis, Carrie has just returned with the ambulance. Another farmer reported that a stunned owl had flown smack into the glass-walled porch of his farmhouse. "This is your lucky day," Waters tells us. It's a rare Boreal Owl, a denizen of the Canadian boreal forests that strayed south. "In seventeen years doing this I've never seen one of these guys." Waters puts the bird on the scale. "A hundred and fifty-five grams. Weight fits the profile."

While Carrie holds our tiny patient on its back on a diaper stretched across the exam table, Waters starts a chart.

"I hear you're a doc," Waters says to Milada after apologizing for not having time for a proper welcome. "Want to do the exam?"

Carrie looks skeptically at Milada, who's wearing her waist-cut Italian leather jacket and ruby lipstick and ankle boots with spiky heels, hardly Northwest barn dishabille. Also, no doubt, Carrie wants this one. But Milada is accustomed to taking charge. She separates one wing from the thrumming little torso and stretches the wing over the diaper as though she were trained to this purpose. "Try closing your eyes," Waters advises. "I don't know about you, but my fingers see better than my eyes." Excited volunteers crowd near the exam table. "Run your fingers along the humerus up to the shoulder. You'll feel when something's wrong."

The lights suddenly dim. A generator starts up with a loud rattle. The tiny owl shivers. "That goddamn machine!" Waters turns to a volunteer. "Get somebody to oil it." Then to us, "We're getting more and more of these damn power outages."

When Milada probes the shoulder joint, the supine bird suddenly cocks its boxy head. The black pupils in their pumpkin orange orbs snap to attention.

"Nothing broken," Milada says. "A bruised shoulder." Then, emboldened by Waters affirming smile, "Some rest should cure. I think this one will soon be again free." She swaddles the northern owl in the diaper to keep it calm.

Waters promises to follow us after she finishes the new patient's chart. We head out to Isis' cage. En route we watch crows pester the Barred Owl from the week before, a graduate passing his final test in the flight cage. Waters soon joins us. She grinds out her cigarette beneath the pointy toe of her boot. To her credit, she picks the butt out of the bark and tucks it into an empty cigarette box in the pocket of her lab coat.

"*Vypadáš nějak smutně*," Milada says, stooping, peering in, observing Isis close up. She tucks her fingers into her jacket pockets and does that pinched thing with her shoulders. "Isis tolerate his cage because he has grown used to it."

"You think? You don't think he desperately wants out of there?"

"He is afraid. Anyone will see."

"Good. Fear is good. When they lose that they're done."

She says nothing at first, just stares at Isis, then suddenly, petulantly, "I want to go. I do not like staying here."

Wondering what could have caused her to react this way, I peer at him over her shoulder. With no one in his view but Milada, Isis has quit jiggering. For the first time with a human near, he is calm. His hooded eyes are alert, but he is as still as though he'd fallen into a deep meditation.

"Look at that," I whisper to Waters. She nods, she sees it, too.

"We need to talk," she says to Milada. "He's never been calm like this around anyone but you." Waters excitedly repeats her plan to give Isis a week in the flight cage, then take him downtown for a grand release on the Washington Mutual Towers. "That would be a cause for a celebration. I can see you now. There you are, shouting, 'Back to the free life!' "

"There will not be time for Isis I am afraid. I only can stay some few days. I must return to Prague after weekend. But you …" She looks at me, challenging.

"Let me have a private chat with her," I tell Waters, and then add, after Milada walks away, "The rafting trip is Saturday. Let's talk after that."

It's a warm Indian summer afternoon. Even late September in the Northwest offers plenty of evening light. We say goodbye to Waters and leave Sardis and on the way home we detour east on Highway 20 into the Cascade foothills to have a walk along the Skagit.

Brambles and Oregon grape and salal and huckleberries and ferns and devil's club and skunk cabbage fill the undergrowth. The yellow in the taller poplars indicates that the fall nights have already turned cold up here. The air is crisp. I'm excited to tender my idea of looking for property, but Milada only wants to talk about me hurrying back to Prague as soon as my business is finished with Blue Cross. I let it drop and enjoy watching her scramble barefoot—she ditches the heels—over nurse logs down to the rotten salmon smelling riverbank where she waves at me to join her. "Fantastic," she cries out. "Fantastic." I'm already shivering. These days I have a hard time warming up once I get cold, but this is a good sign. A very good sign indeed.

_~\\'/~_

SATURDAY MORNING, A converted school bus, painted with a mural of an Orca leaping from frothy waves, shuttles fourteen volunteers, including the two of us, along with two river guides and two fourteen-foot inflated self-bailing rafts, upriver to the Goodell Creek State Park campground put-in. We don wet weather gear and life jackets. It's heavily overcast. A morning mist hangs in the valley, but the river is running clear and only four feet deep in the shallows.

Leaning on a riprap boulder and waiting for the rafts to launch, I can't help but notice how shapely Milada looks in her form-hugging gear. During a walk along the ship canal by my townhouse the other day, she slipped a hand onto my shoulder, asked me to lean down, gave me a moist kiss on the lips and said, "Please, say nothing, I am just so enjoying to be here with you." She's been staying in the map room.

Last night, when I came out of the bathroom after brushing my teeth, she was in the hall wearing only a tee-shirt that didn't cover her hips. "Lovely," I said, unable to restrain the impulse.

Unsentimentally she said, "I considered to come to your bed, but I decide I do not want to complicate …"

I told her I understood. I did, but I didn't. What did she want? What did I want? We had never declared having feelings for each other. This morning early, packing for our river outing, there was a palpable awkwardness, as if each of us had admitted to a desire that had no plausible future.

The river bottom stones, ground smooth by sediment, sing a hollow tune as they rub together in the racing current. The salmon have attracted a few dozen bald eagles, most of them likely to overwinter, but Waters can be heard fuming from the other raft that we got such a late start we won't get an accurate count. Leaning over the front of our raft, Milada spots a Chinook the size of a small log nosing upstream. Closing in behind it is a dark shadow she mistakes for a river otter. She screams excitedly. In fact, it's a hungry harbor seal that has swum this far upriver.

The seal gains inexorably on the exhausted Chinook. I ask Milada if she'd consider doing a residency in Seattle so she could get a license to practice medicine here. Sponsorship for a green card wouldn't be an issue of course. "Where you will put your sister?" She's cheering for the probably doomed salmon. Cheering for the ambitious seal, I reply that my sister will take the map room, and she could share my room. Realizing that I've been too forward, I apologize and assure her that there are no expectations, it's a gratis offer.

"I think you are hungry like this seal," she says, laughing. The seal chews off his lunch, the bloody culmination of the hunt. The rest of the salmon drifts into an eddy to become eagle fodder.

That afternoon, we leave Waters and her disappointed crew warming up over beers and a late lunch at the Rockport tavern. We shed our dry suits and walk across the bridge, hoping to find privacy so we can finish our talk. Midspan, we stop and look down. The water is running crystal clear. The rocks rubbing together on the bottom whistle in minor-key notes that remind me of the children chanting prayers in the cathedral.

"I would be concerned for my sons," Milada muses. Her oldest is out of the university and working as a music critic in Prague. Her second is at the university. Only Martin remains at home, but next year he will be off to a music college where he will learn to make orchestral instruments, a practical skill that her wild son will need. "He is crazy for Seattle grunge. It would be for him fantastic to come here."

A baldy we'd failed to count, its white head and corn-yellow beak unmistakable in the dusky cedar towering over the south end of the bridge, is disturbed by our chatting and flies complainingly across the river. In its calm season, the river is narrower by a good margin than the Vltava in its Prague bend.

If Milada is a species indicator, Eastern European women don't share our puritan sense of modesty. Milada hurries across the bridge, slips down the bank and clambers through salal and ferns and skunk cabbage and over a nurse log to a stranded pool. She sheds her clothes as though it were the most natural thing in the world, though, I notice, she leaves her bra on. The current only looks calm, I call out to her. Her lean bottom flushes pink in the raw fall air. Despite having born and raised three boys, she still has the small-hipped, sinewy figure of the athlete she used to be. She laughs and beckons excitedly for me to follow. "Way too cold for me," I yell back. Moments later, she is hoisting herself out. The water truly is cold. Wisps of steam spirit from her dripping shoulders. Leaving her clothes strewn over the nurse log, she runs, laughing, into that same stand of alder she'd run into once before.

Only later, when my ankles itch miserably, will I realize that I'd been standing in Devil's Club. A rousing copulation is said to consume up to five-hundred calories, like a good run, if you stay at it and climax. I'm not convinced this is even remotely what she has in mind, but just in case, I prepare a carb load. I swallow half of the Snickers bar I keep with my insulin kit then follow her into the alder.

When I catch up to her, she is leaning against one of the sturdier mottled alders. She eyes me questioningly. You must be cold, I tell her. She says no. "Here, touch. My skin burns." My hand on her hip confirms that this is the case. She asks permission to unzip my jeans. "Do not worry," she says. "It will be to give to you pleasure. You will enjoy." She stoops and rubs until I'm erect and then continues with her mouth. There's no denying anymore what we both want. She braces against the mossy side of the alder. Her lean bottom inclines toward me. With one hand, she makes herself wet. We're not teens; it takes more work at this age. "I am so open for you," she says. I place my hand over hers. She brushes my hand away, I'm distracting her. I enter her and soon I hear her breathing grow rapid.

"Don't stop," she says just before collapsing against the mossy alder.

"Thank you," I whisper, breathing in the earthy scent of the damp woods.

Her face is pressed to the moss. "I feel so wild and free."

The chill does set in. We retrieve her clothes from the nurse log and clamber back through the undergrowth up to the bridge. Early evening shadows have knit across the river. Waters and the Sardis crew must be wondering what happened to us. It wouldn't even surprise me if the bus had already left to return the equipment—didn't they say something about reconvening at five?

In this pre-crepuscular light there isn't enough contrast for me to see the rounded rocks on the bottom, but that haunting whistle I hear well enough.

It was on this same bridge, when we were taking a walk in February, that she said, "One day maybe you will find your freedom here in cabin, why not?" It seemed like a wild fantasy at the time. Now anything seems possible.

Mistaking my exuberant mood for something else, Milada soberly pats my cheek. "You must not put on show of love. This was only pleasure."

Who would want to imagine a future with a man in my position? Besides, no small thing, she has a husband, a family.

The tingle of our lovemaking faded, the usual worries flood back in. Looking upriver, not at me, Milada says, "Your sister has been seen."

"Where? Why didn't you say so sooner?"

"A woman was one night coming from abandoned orphanage. This woman, maybe she is your sister. This woman was calling for stupid barn cat. Who would do this? Maybe some vagabond? I do not think is so. Your sister was known to be very fond of her cats."

Her mayor friend says it's urgent that we find Anezka and get her out of there. More memos have surfaced. These newest memos proscribed a particularly nasty torture known as "nose to wall." More than ever her mayor friend is certain he will have enough of a case to at least embarrass Jungmann et al sufficiently that they will go into hiding rather than face prosecution. There could be some collateral damage along the way.

We cross the bridge in the gathered shadows. She takes my hand. "You will need year for recovery. I have changed my mind about kidney in Prague. You have good medical team here. Your sister is trained nurse. If she will live in map room, she will help with recovery. I will visit of course."

I shiver. With the sun gone, chill and loneliness descend over the river.

Monday morning, before Milada catches her flight back to Prague, my friend, the one who negotiated the contract for the municipal employees union, patches us through on a conference call to his contact at Blue Cross. Milada does the talking on my behalf. They mistakenly believe she's part of my medical team. She doesn't disabuse them of that notion. She informs them that my sister's blood type is known to be compatible so she's a good donor prospect. After much impassioned explaining, she convinces Blue Cross to agree to a ten-day extension. I have until a week from Friday to be back for the risk assessment, at which time my name will go on the active list and I will claim my beeper. It can take a couple of months to process the tests for a live donor, should I be so lucky. Meanwhile it's in my best interest to proceed as if I have no live donor.

If for some reason I'm not back in time? My case will be denied. It takes, I am sternly warned, a year, minimum, to process an appeal.

I book an early Thursday flight, the soonest I can leave and still get everything in order. Milada will conscript my cousin, Josef, the one family member my sister might trust, into joining the search. Friday morning, we will drive east to my father's village. The search will fan out from there.

Chapter Five

Off to Pisečná: Friday Morning, First Week of October, 1994

IN THE GRAY Friday morning light, Milada's concrete, rust-stained *panelak* looks as charmless as a low-security prison. We haven't had a chance to talk yet about what we did a few days ago in that grove of alder. I push the intercom button. Their light, by the way, is burnt out.

My risk assessment is scheduled in Seattle exactly one week from today. I booked my return flight for this coming Tuesday. When I ran my itinerary by Milada, she pointed out that if we do find my sister I'll need a day in Prague to run tests at IKEM. Sometime today we have to call the airlines to change my reservation to Wednesday.

"*Ahoj!*" Eight stories up, her husband pops his head out of the window. I wave. "*Pravda vítězi!*"

He salutes with his fist. "*Pravda vítězi* to you, my American friend!"

Truth prevails. What did Milada say to him? Too late to worry about that now. We have five days, including today, to find Anezka and get her out of the country on a medical visa. That's assuming Milada somehow convinces her that this strange American she's never met could really be her brother.

Last night, Milada was on shift at the hospital. I took a taxi in from the airport. This time around we arranged for me to rent the remodeled upstairs flat in Yveta's lovely three-story brick house just a short walk away in an upscale Chodov neighborhood. With knotty-pine paneling and the latest in German plumbing, including an actual shower with running hot water, the three-room flat is impressive enough, but the garden... enormous. Rows and rows of late fall blooms, a sizeable fruit orchard, pears cherries plums, albeit fruit withered on the ground and leaves falling. The fountain, a bronze boy holding his penis and peeing into a pond, is rank with putrefying algae.

The chemo has Yveta too clobbered to work her garden, poor thing. Her two boys charged out with backpacks early this morning to pick flowers for her before catching the bus to school. Their frail grandfather sat on a concrete bench under a knotty old plum tree velveteen with moss. The hominess of the garden appealed to me greatly. It was with much regret I had to tell Yveta that I'm heading back to Seattle in a few days. Her exhausted look gave me pause. I paid her a month's rent to make sure I'd have a base, just in case.

⁓⋆⁓

THE WHEEZE AND rattle of the elevator is followed by a brisk tap of heels in the corridor. Bang! The security mesh explodes open from within.

"*Ahoj!*" Milada slams down her leather travel duffel and wraps me in a hug, but only after looking up to determine that Jiři is not watching. She's wearing a simple black cardigan over tight jeans. Compact, a piston of iron will. *Look out, Anezka! You don't stand a chance against this irresistible force.*

We carry our travel bags across the street to her shiny black brand-new Skoda, which is parked strategically under a streetlight, though the car has the latest in anti-theft electronics. Noticing my raised brows, she admits the new-car purchase is retribution for him taking on that Russian loan. I remind Milada we have to call the airlines.

"*Jiři a já jsme bojovali protože já jsem zabalila mojí cestovní tašku.* Jiři and I fight this morning yes? He don't like I pack my *cestovní tašku*. My travel bag. He say I must drive back to Prague tonight, leave you in village."

"What did you say to him? Does he know …?"

"I say him it's not reasonable, so much driving."

"But does he know, I mean, what happened with us?"

"When you are married twenty-three years, some things you don't have to say."

We'll have to make the call from her father's house in Pisečná. We stow our bags in the trunk along with a food basket and a case of Czechvar beer for her father and I show her my gift stash, token bribes for anyone who might be able to help: a pound and a half bag of Seattle's Best Coffee that I've subdivided into baggies, two hip-size bottles of Jack Daniels bourbon whiskey, a half-dozen yellow tee-shirts sent to me by my sister in Iowa with a logo commemorating the annual "beach" party in Williamsburg. Seeing the tee-shirts, Milada laughs heartily. Sand is trucked from God knows where into a farmer's field. In the logo, a pink sunbathing pig is sipping a tropical drink. My goth niece, feeling sorry for teens in this "iron cage," sent along pirated Die Form CDs.

The start of our trip takes us past block after block of concrete enclaves, most limited to five stories since dwellings taller than five stories were required to install costly elevators. The Skoda's caramel leather interior still smells of factory chemicals. I buzz down a window to let in fresh air, regret it, and close the window again.

"*Bud' bez obav*. It is ugly now, but you will see. Hey, good news." Her expression remains rather deadpan when she says this. "I phone to your cousin, Josef Kolar, yes? He will meet us tonight at pub. He say this morning we must stop in Hradec Kralove so you will meet his mother. She is your aunt. She must have information about your sister." A warning follows the good news, "She will be nervous to meet you."

Once we've left Chodov behind, Milada plants her foot on the gas and we jet eastbound on the E67 motorway past a phalanx of Communist-era rust buckets and she reviews our itinerary. Two appointments this afternoon in Písečná. The first with the mayor. We'll find out what his surveillance has turned up on Anezka. Later in the afternoon we meet with Pavel Halbrstat, the town historian who has agreed to show us the family records.

"I am not happy, but I do this for you." Halbrstat is the former Party apparatchik who carried out Jungmann's security orders. Ordinarily, Milada's family does not speak to Halbrstat's family, not even in the pub where the men play cards.

"Do we need his help?" *How protective I've been feeling, ever since our tryst in the alders.*

"In this book we might learn interesting things about your family. And mine. I am curious, too. My grandfather and your grandmother, you know, they were related."

More and more, I'm coming around to seeing that my father needs to be here. If there's trouble, he should face it.

Clipping along at a breezy 160 km per hour, we whiz past the Skoda factory, a palace of steel and glass. Further east we sail through agricultural flats where the air smells of damp earth and fertilizer and it occurs to me that I should be taking notes.

To make best use of my five days here, I've decided to interview anyone in my family willing to talk about crimes committed against our fathers. Really, it was Milada who put me up to it—her sneaky way of making sure I wouldn't object to her helping the mayor with his case—but I thought why not, and then got excited about it. What is my generation, the progeny of exiles, angry about? Should we be angry? Or should we just forget what happened to our fathers and make the best of our lives?

Milada throttles down suddenly and steers the Skoda onto the shoulder. I see it too, rotating blue lights in the rearview. Between curses, she touches up her lipstick and gives me a hard look that says, *This is how it is.* The cop taps at her window with his clipboard. Along with her license, she tucks four hundred-koruna notes into his palm. He writes a warning. The next cop, he lectures, will not be so sympathetic.

Milada swears bitterly when he's gone. "*Ještě jednu pokutu a nebudu moct jezdit.* One more ticket and I would not be permitted to drive more."

"We were speeding for my sake. I'm sorry ..."

She waves away my offer of money. "I speed because I love thrill. But now I must drive more slowly. Perhaps we don't have time for stop in Hradec Kralove."

"But we have to talk to my aunt, right?"

"It is Friday. If we are late Zamečnik will go away to his weekend *chata*."

Zamečnik is the mayor who's supposed to help us. "My father spent his entire adult life feeling he was living in exile. The only family I ever heard him say he really missed was his little sister, Magda." Magda is the aunt we're slated to visit.

"Exile? Your father was not exile. He escape by choose. Is not same."

"Escape? Exile? How is it not the same?"

Ignoring my question, she turns off the motorway onto Highway 11. The narrow two-lane road will be less patrolled by police. Immediately we run into a backup of long-haul trucks chugging eastbound to Slovakia and Ukraine. The muddy valley is flat and vast, the soil in the fields chocolate brown, the sky mauve, the air heavy with moisture. *If you didn't look at road signs you'd swear you were in Iowa.*

"What's the difference between escape and exile?" I persist.

When after a time she still says nothing, I nudge again, "You tried to escape in 1968. You called that an escape, right?" I open my Steno and ready my ballpoint for my first interview. "By the way, I never heard you say why you came back."

"I was thinking for my father." She heaves a deep sigh. "I was foolish enough to believe my family would be okay if I say absolutely nothing to no one." Family members of escapees were forbidden to travel outside the country, and that, she assumed, was the worst that would happen to them. The rare escapee who dared to return could expect four years of harsh treatment in prison, but she wasn't expecting to go back.

"The worst thing for my father was never seeing his homeland again."

"Is easy to miss cage when you can't go back in, yes?"

"You only see it as a cage because you couldn't leave. For him—"

"*Ne*, I could leave. I left. But my father suffer because I do this."

"So. Tell me what happened?"

"*Ne*, I do not wish to speak about this."

"Maybe it would do you good to speak about it."

"*Ne*. You will judge me. You will not understand."

We drive on in awkward silence. The genealogy passed on to me by the nun in Solon indicated that my father's family owned the farm when he left, the same farm her father eventually took over and where she was raised. It's a subject I've avoided before, but I bring it up now. "Would my father still have a legal claim to the land?"

"My father sacrificed everything to save this farm," she says icily.

"Look, I'm sorry. I'm just trying to understand what happened. So your father was tortured? That why you came back? You knew?"

"I came back. Is enough for your notes." She studies the passing fields as if corn were the last living thing on earth.

"My father abandoned his daughter here and never came back. Believe me, it's not a joke for me either."

Milada gestures wildly. "My father risk everything for his pride. So what do I do? I marry zealot just like him."

"Your father have any scars from his time in prison?" A lot of international human rights groups formed in the 1960s to monitor Soviet doings. This scrutiny had the unintended side effect of encouraging torturers to do their work "cleanly," the word used in the case studies I reviewed at her request. If possible, they left no marks.

"His feet walk funny. You will see."

"Would he make a statement?"

It's a tender subject. She doesn't want to talk about it, but my pestering helps her decide we should stop after all to see my aunt. Maybe my aunt will be willing to talk about these matters.

─✳─

AFTER CROSSING A stone bridge into Hradec Kralov, we pull into a car park beside the narrow Labe River. A row of blond, nineteenth century stone buildings casts its reflection in the channeled, glassine water.

"This place is beautiful. In a way I envy you."

"You might as well envy prisoner in cell."

Nearby is a public phone box. Her plan is to call her mayor friend to warn him we'll be a little late and ask him to wait for us. When he knows that we're talking to my aunt he'll understand, though the Friday afternoon pilgrimage to the country *chatas* is a powerful ritual, a ritual not easily resisted.

Trimmed birch and linden trees line the riverside promenade. The clouds have begun to break up. The sun warms benches where old men wearing jackets with elbow patches sit and smoke and talk. One of them, much taller than the others, sits off by himself smoking a pipe and intently reading a book. He's wearing a beret and an embroidered peasant shirt and looks rather professorial in his contemplations, not lumpy like the others. He would be my father, had my father stayed and studied history as he wanted.

"We have time for short visit," Milada announces, returning to the Skoda. "Zamečnik will wait for us at school in Letohrad. He is headmaster."

I point across the river. "That man smoking the pipe?" I repeat my hypothesis that he is the image of what my father would have become.

"*Poslouche.*" She clips her hair back so tautly it raises her eyebrows. "This man you find so elegant is Jungmann."

"Jungmann? Here? What would he be doing here?"

"Somehow he has heard that you will be here. Is best I think if you will speak with him. Don't worry. He speak excellent English. Don't give away anything about your sister. We must learn what he can tell us."

Milada seems worried for some reason that if Jungmann knows that I have Rosalye's letters he will find a way to get his hands on them. I assure her I'm no neophyte in these matters. Back when I took cases to court, I advised clients if they had to travel to leave original documents home. The originals of Rosalye's letters to my father are locked in Yveta's flat in Prague. I did bring copies with me, in case they are needed for official purposes, and of course I have my translated copies. She gives me a backward skeptic's glance then heads in to let my aunt know we're here and to find out if Jungmann has bothered her and what she might have said to him.

Chapter Six

Jungmann in Hradec Králové

WEDNESDAY, THE DAY before returning to Prague, I spent the afternoon buried in the university law library. Milada had asked me to research case law that might help her mayor friend in return for his help. One case in particular stood out. The defendant was Ukrainian, a security officer. His rank made him the equal of Jungmann's officer, Halbrstat. He stood accused of torturing a political prisoner in 1962 using an electrical device placed on the victim's head. The device was alleged to have traumatized the victim psychologically. The judge threw the case out. In his summation, the judge opined, "Electroshock therapy has been known to have beneficial effects on the insane." The rule of law in these human rights cases relies heavily on the judge's discretion. Somebody was obviously being protected. What I told Milada was that the threat of a trial might be more effective than the trial itself. Most judges now would have been young prosecuting assistants then, and could be personally implicated in having turned a blind eye to torture when it was useful for extracting bogus confessions.

But I had an image of these torturing security people as lantern-jawed, bulldoggish thugs. Jungmann does not fit the stereotype. His glasses have slipped down his slender, aquiline nose, and he doesn't notice me standing near, so engrossed is he in his book. The shock of white hair under his beret lends a dark tone to his skin as though he were a retired snowbird accustomed to wintering in Florida. Like my father, Jungmann must be in his seventies. The smoke curling up from his pipe scents the damp river air with vanilla.

"I've been told to introduce myself."

"*Jak se daří?*" He peers up at me over his bifocals. No hint of greeting softens his expression until I explain that I'm the son of František Lenoch, visiting from America. At the sound of my family name, followed by "America," he pulls the pipe out of his mouth and inspects me closely. His goatee and mustache are fastidiously trimmed. He'd be capable of cruelty, I decide, no doubt, but he's got an intelligent and curious look that appeals all the more to my desire to see something of my father in him. He'd be a good subject for an interview.

"*Jak je tvůj otec.*"

"I don't speak Czech, sorry."

"You come to see village of your father?" Jungmann draws ponderously on his pipe. His command of English makes me feel ashamed of my lack of Czech and I find myself suddenly fascinated by the idea of soliciting his views.

"Yes, and to ..." I almost slip. "To meet family. It's my first time here."

"Second, actually," he says.

So Milada was right. That brown-suited man at the black light theatre a couple weeks ago was working for Jungmann.

Jungmann snaps his book closed. He gives his pipe a hard suck. The pipe went out while he was looking me over. His long slender fingers probe the pocket of his peasant shirt, withdraw a plug of tobacco from a pouch and tamp the plug expertly into his pipe, albeit, oddly, without him first cleaning the dead plug out of the bowl. "But I am puzzled. Your father is not with you?" He doesn't bother to hide that he's had me watched. I appreciate his candor. "Why has your father not come with you?"

Return candor for candor? "I don't know. I certainly asked him to come, but every time I'd bring up the subject he'd say, 'Never mind, all those people are dead, there's no point.' Why would he say that?"

He tries again, without success, to stoke his pipe. The old plug is preventing it from lighting, but he doesn't seem aware that he left the old plug in. "Dead. This is word he spoke?"

"I've had a really hard time getting him to talk about ... any of this ... why he left, all that."

"You must bring him here. Today is Friday. Friday night I play *Mariáš* at pub in Žamberk. Your escort will know this pub. I will see you there. You will hear some story."

"I have a meeting tonight with my cousin," I tell him, "but I will try."

He laughs, but his laugh has an edge. "You do not ask why am I here? You think I have nothing to do except to follow you? You Americans are so arrogant." He waves his pipe at me dismissively. "Of course you are arrogant. It is your privilege. Only we are jealous. But I really hoped to see your father." I nod and keep my mouth shut. We are being watched by the lumpy men on the benches. "Your father is Czech. He will understand this."

"Understand what?"

"Let's start to chase, as I believe you Americans like to say. I know why you are here. Don't look surprised. Even your poor Aunt Magda know this. Everyone know you are coming to find her."

"Okay."

"I make you proposal. Bring your father. You will hear stories then you decide. You decide what is right."

"What is right? I'm sorry, I don't follow—"

"This woman, Anezka, whom you believe is your sister. If you bring your father and he agree to talk, Anezka will have no trouble from me."

"But if not?"

"My inn. You have learned about fire?"

"What does this have to do with Anezka?"

"She will be arrested for arson if you do not agree."

"What's her connection to the fire?"

"This is not your concern."

"Say my father cooperates. You get charges dropped and she's free to go?"

"It is gamble, yes? But is your best gamble I believe."

Seeking a diversion, anything to stop me from calling attention to the obvious hole in his reasoning, my eye settles on the book, folded now in his lap.

"You are curious? It is novel by Josef Škvorecký. Surely you have heard of him?" My inventory of Czech authors is exhausted after Kundera, Klima, Havel, Hrabel, Hašek, oh yes, Kafka of course. "You father will be disappointed. Škvorecký was on short list for Nobel prize." That air of bemusement drains suddenly and his expression turns cold. "In English, it is called 'Miracle Game.' It is about lies and deception. We excel at this game."

Waiting for that to sink in, he points to the reflection in the mirror-smooth water. "Beautiful, yes? In Žamberk there is also beautiful building. Alas, born too soon for Jugendstil, but still beautiful. This building is district prison. I will happily arrange inside tour of this beautiful building for Anezka. But it is messy. If we can avoid, is better."

"Let's talk tonight."

He returns his attention to his uncooperative pipe. "Good. Tonight."

Sensing I have been dismissed, I hurry back to the Skoda. Milada is waiting. The fact that he was talking to my aunt she finds more disturbing than his threat of prison for Anezka. "*To jsou pitomý lidi.* There are stupid people in village. They are still very afraid to Mister Big Shot. They talk."

I mention the meeting we agreed to at the pub tonight. "What do you think?"

"*Starý dluh.* I wish only to pay old debt to Jungmann. *Ty by si asi použil slovo odplata.* But I do not wish that your sister will be hurt. First she must be away. I think you must bring your father to speak with Jungmann."

That doesn't settle what we should do tonight, but I let the matter drop for now. Leaving the Skoda in the car park by the river, we enter a neighborhood of trim concrete apartment buildings separated by manicured patches of lawn. My aunt has emphysema and breathes on a respirator and Milada warns that her blood pressure is low and she becomes dizzy if up for too long so we will have to keep our visit brief.

Before going in, there's an issue I still want to clear up. "Most people have a day that tethers their lives to world events, yes? Even though I was just a kid, for me it was the day President Kennedy was assassinated. I'd never seen so many grownups crying before. For you? Let me guess. The night of August 21, 1968?"

"You think you can so easily trick me to talk?"

"Something happened to you. It's like it's still happening."

"I will tell to you some background. Is all you need to know."

～✺～

THE WRITERS' UNION had pushed Dubček to relax censorship that spring. He was sympathetic to the cause, but Brezhnev was not. Upwards of 200,000 Warsaw Pact troops marched into Prague that hot August night. Milada joined the mobs of student protesters changing street signs in an attempt to confuse the invaders.

Wenceslas Square was a dangerous place to be. Molotov cocktails flew out of windows and the tanks drove into the crowd. That night the reformers were packed onto a plane bound for a Moscow-style brainwashing. The next morning Praguers awoke to a Soviet tank parked under the tail of King Wenceslas' horse. Prague Spring, that window with a peek-a-boo view of freedom, had just been shuttered.

"You escaped, but you underestimated the consequences for your family?"

"My father," she says, choosing her words deliberately, "refuse to give farm to cooperative. His 'non-cooperation' had consequence for me."

It was impossible to get recommendations from her college teachers, so she was refused entrance to the medical school at Charles University, and studying medicine was the thing she cared about most. Only by escaping to the west could she pursue her avocation. In Austria, Milada slipped away from her skating team and asked for asylum at the police station. They sent her to Johannesbrunn, a refugee village in Bavaria.

"I stay one week at U.S. military base in Munich for interrogations." They slapped her file on the desk, warning her not to lie. "They ask if I am member of communist party. I say absolutely no." Next they asked about her father. "They say they know more about my family than I know myself. I am afraid they will send me back." So she told the truth about her father, Bedřich Kotyza. He was not a party member, but he paid Jungmann in pork for *protekcé* so he could keep the farm and he was accused by villagers of collaborating with the Soviets.

"How much you need to know? Your aunt is waiting."

"You still haven't said why you came back."

She was granted refugee status. She had distant relatives in Iowa. They were contacted and agreed to sponsor her, but a plane had just flown with refugees bound for America. She couldn't leave Germany until all seats were filled on the next plane. "I am warned I may wait as much as one year in Johannesbrunn."

She was housed in a monastery and shared a communal barracks-style room with refugees from Poland and Albania, a few from Lebanon, but despite the crowding, Milada found to her surprise that she liked life in the camp. This had to do with Fritz.

"Fritz? You fell in love?"

"You don't want to know about Fritz." I've pulled my Steno pad from my daypack and I wait, pen poised. "Okay, if you must." Fritz was one of the military policemen who did the head count each evening. A year older than Milada, he was waiting for a place in the university. They were forbidden to work outside camp, but Fritz pretended he didn't see.

"Why was Fritz so eager to be helpful?"

"*Ne*, I see I have said too much already."

My aunt is waiting, but I warn her. Soon as we're underway again, she's going to tell me about Fritz.

Chapter Seven

Visiting Aunt Magdalena: Late Friday Morning, First Week of October, 1994

CONFINED TO DRAGGING around an air tank, Aunt Magdalena is fortunate to have a ground floor apartment and a spacious one at that. On a table in the entry hall, a black leather-bound Catholic missal is displayed so it can't be missed.

"Your aunt pulled some brown strawberries from her freezer. She wanted to offer something for you but she said, *ne*, this I cannot serve." Milada had to convince her we would only say hello and ask a few questions about my sister.

We enter a glass-enclosed terrace, a kind of hothouse filled with plants and steamy with a tropical heat, the glass foggy with condensation. Once we're in and the door closed, my aunt appears through another door.

An air tube, connected to a portable tank on wheels, hangs from her nose. She pushes the tank ahead of her and leans on it like a walker, shuffling along in slippers. A plastic bag dangles from one wrist. She breathes in measured gulps. She's small, lost under a billowing robe. She has my father's round head and protruding ears, but that's the extent of the family resemblance. We smile awkwardly at each other.

"Do you enjoy your visit?"

"Everyone has been very welcoming, thank you."

My aunt beckons for me to approach. She clutches my arm with the strength of the desperate. "Jungmann ask some questions, yes?" She pauses to gulp air. "If I like my flat? He say he will purchase this buildings."

"I'm afraid I'm the cause of this trouble."

Her strong fingers dig into my arm as though to cut through any false modesty. "He ask if my brother is coming." By brother she of course is referring to my father. "I say him I don't know, is very long time since last I have seen

František. When he will come to see me?"

"He wanted to come." But I see in her earnestness and frailty that we're beyond pleasantries. "Actually, I don't know. I was hoping you would know."

"He was like father to me. He read to me stories."

"What kind of stories?" Not on task, but I need her to trust me enough to open up and talk.

"*On mi vyprávěl povídky, které byly zajímavé, ale také strašidelné.* He tell me stories which are interesting but also scary." Milada confers with Aunt Magda.

"Your father liked to tell story that is called Little Otik."

It's a gruesome folktale about a couple who can't conceive children. The woman, obsessed, pretends that a rough doll carved out of a gnarled tree root is her child. To her surprise, the root comes to life, but he is a monster who eats every bit of food they have and then eats them as well.

Who could blame me for thinking of Anezka as that root child who eats up her parents' lives. I ask permission to take notes. She is certain that I do not want to waste my time with her "foolish granny stories." It's her brother she wants to talk about. Anything I can tell her, anything at all. I should leave out nothing.

"Your father married that Kacalek woman in Iowa, you know." She does know, and she isn't surprised to hear that Frank—growing up we called him Frank, not Dad—never spoke again to their father after that. "He also refused to allow me to ever visit my grandfather." I mention that when I was sixteen, I snuck a visit anyway. "Unfortunately, he found out." She insists that I tell her what happened. She won't let me go until I do.

－◢ﾚ◣－

REACHING SULPHUR SPRINGS required roughly an hour and a half drive on mostly unpaved county roads. The town amounted to a post office, a brick, three-story school house, perhaps a dozen clapboard bungalows clustered around a crossing of two roads. My grandfather's whitewashed bungalow set at the rise of a grassy knoll overlooking a community garden. Below the garden, railroad tracks ran alongside a stream, Dead Man's Creek, screened from view by fronds of pussy willows and cat o' nine tails. Josef Lenoch worked in his old age at the school across the road. He was the custodian. He was easy to locate. I simply asked a nosy woman out hanging her wash, a Mrs. Lookingbill, who had dark hairs growing out of a mole on her chin.

I found my grandfather sitting alone on his back porch. He wore overalls, a blanket draped over his lap. He was thin-built, like my father, but smaller.

Mrs. Lookingbill hollered over at him from her back porch to put his hunting cap on. He ignored her and she marched over and shouted at his left

ear and retreated, shaking her head. His wife, Barbora Kacalka Lenoch from
Piséčná, had died earlier that same year.

"Kacalka, she steal my father. We don't speak about her."

My grandfather's eyes were watery and pale and his slender fingers would
have better suited a pianist than a farmer. Like my own father, he seemed
to have been meant for a different life. Sometimes he understood who I
was, sometimes he mistook me for his son. He'd gone mostly deaf. When
he did speak it came out in an idiolect of Czech and German and English;
a conversation was out of the question. On the several occasions when
I returned to Sulphur Springs, usually without letting him know I'd come,
I'd walk along the railroad tracks, and when the season was right, I'd climb
the pile of feed corn spilling out of the trap door at the bottom of the grain
silo. The words "Superior Seed" were painted on the cylindrical metal silo
in large black letters. One cold wintry afternoon, I realized that no matter
how many times I walk these tracks and look at the seed spilling out of the
silo, I will never know what it felt like for him to be torn from his family in
Czechoslovakia and forced to live out his life in the end of nowhere. That
afternoon I pestered my grandfather with a seventeen-year-old's overheated
questions. *Do you miss your home in Czechoslovakia? Would you ever go back?
Why won't my father speak to you?*

"He only patted my head and smiled. I will say he had a kindly smile."

It was after dark and the roads were icy when I drove home. "I'd missed
dinner, and missing dinner was not an option in our house. I knew there'd be
trouble, but I had no idea." At the back door, the entrance from the carport,
my father was waiting for me on the landing. He must have heard me drive up.
The moment I pulled open the door, he cocked his fist and said, "I don't know
why I stop to hit you." His eyes were red and dilated. For a moment I thought
he was upset because I'd driven my unreliable Ford Fairlane after dark in such
weather. I assured him I'd checked the oil and put in a quart.

"He said if I ever went to see my grandfather again, and he found out, I
would no longer be welcome to live in his house."

His anger that night surprised me, but what followed was worse. He
seemed to withdraw from his own family. Every Sunday morning we went to
mass as usual at St. Wenceslas, then stopped for his usual bacon and samizdat
at the butcher in Bohemie town, and we'd take the usual bag of kolatches, as
we called them, home from the Czech bakery, but it was as though we were
only doing it for the sake of appearances.

"I worried about him. But your two sisters"—my two aunts never married
and live together in an apartment near St. Wenceslas where they shave
candles—"they don't like to talk about the past. I do remember them once

claiming they knew Rosalye had poisoned your mother, but, well, you know, I just assumed—"

"That whore wanted your grandfather."

"You mean the Kacalka woman?"

"*Ne, ne.* Rosalye."

Anezka's mother wanted my grandfather? Seeing that I'm scribbling this down, Aunt Magda backs away from an outright accusation. Between gulps of air, she says, "It is so long ago. I had only four years when they left. When our mother died I was sent to live with family in Oucmanice. I waited for František to rescue me. I waited and waited." She pauses to breathe. Milada suggests we curtail the visit and come back another time but I wave her away.

"Rosalye was maid. She lived in our house. Terrible business, what she do."

"My father had to have known she was pregnant when he left, yes?" After I told him I'd found Rosalye's letters, he took me for a drive in his Oldsmobile Delta 98 through the Amana colonies. The boat of a car with chrome fenders looked as new as the day he'd bought it. We stopped in Ox Yoke to have lunch in the stone communal dining hall built by German homesteaders. Mom had especially like Ox Yoke, she liked to visit the millhouse to shop for the Americana that decorated our home—washboards, kettles, butter churns, irons—so I knew our coming here was for my father a sentimental journey. On the ride home, his gaze roamed the passing hills. The north sides of the hills were hard from the winter freeze. Where the earth was turned the fields were covered with white foam, the frost that hadn't thawed. He pointed to the frost on the hills and said, "Those people are dead. Forget about them. My life is with my family here."

Aunt Magda has turned away and gone silent. Her breathing comes in hard rasps. My visit seems to have upset her. Milada helps Aunt Magda settle into an overstuffed chair and insists that our interview is over.

Before we leave, my aunt asks Milada to give me the plastic bag that has been dangling from her walker. "Open now," she says between gasps.

Inside the bag is a black and white photo in a fold-out cardboard frame of four children. At first I wonder if one of the girls in the picture is Anezka, then I realize that the boy must be my father and the three girls are his sisters. The little cutie is Magda herself. The other two are the sisters who stayed behind. The eldest, Katerina, named after their mother, has plain looks, with small eyes and a plump face. Her most striking feature is her furry eyebrows, two black caterpillars that nearly join in a v-shaped frown. My father looks to be maybe sixteen; the photo must have been taken right before he left Pisečná. His hair is slicked behind protuberant ears. He was a handsome kid with a broad bashful smile.

"Take it," she says. Gulp for air. "Tell František he is very bad for not come to fetch me. Tell him I want to see him. Oh, which way you will drive?"

Milada explains that we're detouring south to Letohrad to track down the mayor.

"Letohrad. Oh, then you will pass Brandýs nad Orliči." Aunt Magda raises an admonishing finger. "Look for sign to Oucmanice." She glances around as though afraid Jungmann had bugged her flat. "Katerina live there. She is nosy one in our family. Maybe she will know where is Anezka. But I must warn to you, she is very suspicious. Very suspicious. If she do not trust, she will say you nothing."

"Who would she trust? What about your son? What about Josef?"

"I don't know. He is friends with Rosalye. I never understand why he betray family to help Rosalye. My own son. I just don't know." She pats my arm. "My sister hate Rosalye because what she has done to our mother. Don't speak this name."

That's it. Visit over. On our way out, I promise I'll pass her invitation to my father. In the hallway, the two baggies I leave beside the missal, filled with Seattle's Best Coffee beans, look sadly inadequate as a token from home, but I can't imagine she'd want a tee-shirt with a pig sipping tropical drinks. Outside, the late morning sun is bearing down on the river. The old men are still on their benches. Jungmann is gone.

─╼╳╾─

THE ORLICKÉ MOUNTAINS, a sub-range of the Carpathians, swing down from Poland and run like a spine through Eastern Europe. We drive into foothills where the woods are thick and the road follows the terrain and squeezes into stomach-churning turns. There's no traffic to speak of. To recover lost time we speed past meadows resplendent with wildflowers and flush geese out of tall grass. A domestic white goose crosses the road honking at our rudeness. At last we have found the fabled Bohemian loveliness I've heard so much about. I glance at my Steno notes. I'd jotted in the margin to be sure not to mention the "maid" to Aunt Katerina. That will be difficult of course, considering that the "maid" is Anezka's mother.

I ask Milada what she knows about Rosalye. Why does everyone in my family have this strong reaction when she enters the conversation? "Remember the inn," she asks? The inn burned to the ground just before Anezka disappeared. The inn's upstairs rooms had become Jungmann's private "club." Anezka's mother was the mistress of the inn. She was beautiful and wore jewelry and lipstick and grew her luxuriant hair down past her hips and ate lean meat whenever she wanted at a time when other women in the village worked until their hands looked like turnips and their bodies like potatoes and they consumed goulash with fatty gravy. They hated Rosalye. No one knows how the fire started. Anezka has not been charged, but she is wanted for questioning.

Chapter Eight

An Unplanned Detour

THE WOODS WE pass through are thick with spruce and lodge pole pine. The occasional mushroom hunter's bicycle with baskets leans against a trunk. "It is beautiful here, you know. You're way too hard on your country."

"No one can destroy beauty of soul, yes? Is like flower that so want to be free it will grow through crack in stone wall."

"That would also be true in a refugee camp, right?"

"You still want I should tell you about Fritz? Don't deny, I see your questioning mind turning, turning." The road drops off the hill and follows the river and we cross a stone bridge into the charming baroque town Aunt Magda mentioned, Brandýs nad Orlicí. Milada pulls over and parks near the fountain in the town square. "I must explain something. I only say you about Fritz so you will not wish to become involved with me. We must not allow this."

"It's understood."

"Is not about you. Anyway, you will see." Desperate to find out what was happening to her father, she devised a crude plan to return by obtaining a fake passport from Turk *Gastarbeiter*. Together with Fritz, who would pretend to be her German brother, they would cross the border to check on her family. If there was trouble, she would not go on to America.

A complication delayed her plan. Fritz was ordered by his superiors to stop the shop owners from illegally employing refugees and to strictly enforce the curfew. Having tasted freedom, the women resented being again confined to the monastery. It was decided that in exchange for the Albanians using their black market contacts with the Turks to buy her a passport with Fritz's last name, Milada would keep Fritz distracted.

I jot in my notebook: *Here comes the part I'm not going to like.* "Were you, how would you say this, experienced?"

"This is question you should not ask."

"Go on."

Fritz found an open cattle-car on a sidetrack, a train car that had been used by the Nazis—and later by the Soviets—to deport dissidents to forced labor camps. She found holes bored into the boards. People trapped inside the cattle cars, often for days at a time, bored so many peep-holes they allowed in "bands of chilly air." I jot this in my notes. *Bands of chilly air.*

Fritz presented her with a gift he'd smuggled under his coat, a machine-gun belt from WWII. He draped it across her chest and said she looked beautiful. Returning to that moment, her eyes gleam and I see a glimpse of that willful dark young beauty who wanted to be ravished by Fritz. I find myself feeling absurdly jealous of him. If only that could have been my coat she spread across the straw on the floorboards near the door—she had a fear of being locked inside.

Three months later, a Czech family arrived. They had obtained a travel visa and had driven their Trabant into Yugoslavia and continued back through Austria and into Germany, where they asked for asylum. At dinner one evening, she overheard the family talking about the castle in their home town. From their description of the castle's portraits, she knew they must be from Letohrad, less than five kilometers from Písečná, where they had relatives. Yes, they had news of her family. The news was not good. Milada's father, the only local farmer foolish enough to refuse to give his farm to the cooperative, had been arrested. Many of the locals were saying he deserved it.

"There were two kinds of farm collectives," Milada explains. "The *Jednotné Zemědělské Družstvo*, known as JZD, were owned by State but run by local farmers. There were also *Státní Statky*, SS collectives run by State. We had this one." Jungmann had her father locked up and interrogated. Every animal on his farm was expropriated.

Her father would starve, she knew, rather than give the farm to the SS, but under torture his resistance broke. Milada's mother had coughed so hard through the previous winter, fighting off viral pneumonia, she'd separated ribs from her sternum.

"So I went back. I gave myself to authorities."

"That must have been hard."

"Now I am disgusting to you."

"You really think I think you're a coward for going back? Milada."

"*Ne ne!* You think I am whore for what I do with Fritz." My predictable denial is met with a reminder that she only told me this story so I will not suffer any illusions about getting involved. This cold Milada could not be more different from the Milada who waved wildly for me to join her in the alders, the Milada who said she'd found paradise on earth when floating down the Skagit in a raft and coming upon the harbor seal chasing the Chinook.

"This place changes you."

"*Ne*, I'm sorry, Chico. This is me, too. This is more real me."

"I sometimes wonder," I muse. "If my father had stayed, would he have voted for the communists? He used to vote Republican because there was only one issue he cared about. Whoever he thought would be toughest on the Reds."

"Here we knew to expect usual tricks."

Her father avoided starving by running the co-op dairy the SS built on his farm. Her mother died that winter. Her older siblings were married and gone. She only avoided prison by signing a bogus confession denouncing the decadent west. She got pregnant, used Jiři's *protekcé* to obtain a letter of recommendation, studied medicine at Charles University, had three sons, and the rest I already know.

"Were you watched? You have to constantly worry about going to prison?"

"*Nikdo se nebál, protože oni byli snadno k poznání.* No one worry so much because they are easy to recognize."

"They?"

"*Tajná policie.* Secret police. Okay, they could be anyone. But you know."

"How did you know?"

"They are like you. They ask so many questions."

At the center of the fountain, the statue of the Madonna mounted atop a lofty granite column wears a shawl of pigeon poop on her shoulders. Reminded of the ermine shawl the monk draped over the Bambino, I laugh, loudly.

"Chico, I think you must eat soon."

Ordinarily I resent being told that my blood sugar is off, as though diabetics had no emotions not sugar strained, but, I do the poke. My blood-sugar reads 78, just under the low range of normal. I pop a couple of Life-Savers just to be sure.

We drive on. Exiting town, we come upon an arrow-shaped road sign with black lettering on white pointing south: "Oucmanice 7 kilometers." Milada corrects my pronunciation. "*OOTS-ma-NEE-Tsa.*" The town Aunt Magda mentioned, where my Aunt Katerina lives. Something about that town sounded oddly familiar the first time I heard it. Using my magnifier, I skim my packet of genealogy papers and make the surprising discovery that my grandfather was from that village.

"That would explain why Aunt Katerina lives there."

"*Ne*, Chico, *ne ne ne. Ne.* My mayor friend is waiting in Letohrad. He is making for us favor."

"It's only seven kilometers. There's no traffic. Look at it this way. If Aunt Katerina can tell us where to find Anezka, we don't need to meet with the mayor, right?"

"If it could be so simple, Jungmann would have been here."

"You have other reasons for wanting to meet with the mayor?"

Milada gives me a pitying look. "Chico, Chico." She puts the car in park and pats my hand. "You cannot be jealous with everyone I speak."

"Who said anything about jealous?"

She turns skeptically south, following the arrow's direction. "Okay, you must leave on Wednesday flight. Okay. We ask for your sister. But if we frighten your aunt today, we will not have second chance. Is why I think we should speak with Josef first."

"We'll just be careful not to mention Anezka's mother."

Crossing a stone bridge that arches over a rocky gorge, we pass three fishermen in black rubber boots standing with their legs thrust apart in the pellucid waters of the Orliči. They look so much like the stolid figure of the Worker statue in Chodov I find myself staring. Can they be real? They turn as one and watch us pass, their expressions absolutely scrubbed of curiosity. Maybe it's a mistake after all to talk to Aunt Katerina right away. I mention my worry to Milada.

"Everyone is paranoid, yes?" Jungmann, she explains, is the great great great grandson of the venerated scholar credited with saving the Czech language by translating the Bible into written Czech. "Jungmann senior was for us like George Washington for you. No one will cooperate with American if it means go against Jungmann family."

"What about Anezka? If we do find her?"

"You really should bring your father here."

"Not much I can do about that now."

Cresting a steep incline, we pass fields bordered with a windrow of birch. Their fall yellow leaves quake in the breeze. We come upon Oucmanice on the down side of the hill. The village has prospered in the three years since the Velvet Revolution. Most of the slope-framed homes have been freshly stuccoed and white-washed. Flower boxes adorn windows. Roaming chickens poke into blooming gardens. A woman wearing a beaded vest and white blouse, her hair twisted into ram-horn braids, leans out of an open window and gives a rug a few smart whacks with a broom. Seeing the new model Skoda slow down, her expression hardens into a mask.

Milada lowers her window. "Which house is Lenoch house?"

The woman offers terse directions, pulls in the rug, closes the window, and releases a metal shutter that rolls down with a snap.

"*Lidé stále bojí. A nemají rádi cizincům.* These people are suspicious, yes?"

"She sure got quiet when you mentioned my name."

"You think she is afraid by your name?" Milada gives one of her hearty laughs. "Maybe Lenochs were *tajná policie!*"

It could obviously mean that Jungmann has been here. At the low end of town, we approach a decaying farmhouse. The slate roof is sloughing tiles. Sections of stucco have peeled from the walls, exposing mud and straw chinking. Gaps in the chinking remind me of the "chilly bands of air" from Milada's train story. I imagine trapped people looking furtively out at us. Milada parks out of view of the Lenoch house just in case. We walk back. You can't help but catch the eye-watering smell from the outhouse. "This place could use some work."

"In village, it is man job to move outhouse each month."

"Guess there aren't any men at the Lenoch house."

Though it's midday, the windows are tightly shuttered. Milada declares that no one is here. We can drive on to Letohrad to meet the mayor. At least we can knock, I insist. A tunnel of rosebushes has overgrown the arbor leading to the porch. Forced to stoop to walk through, I manage to tear an inch-long gap in the shoulder seam of my fleece vest and swear out loud. Milada admonishes me to be quiet, just in case.

The porch stones are wet. Recently mopped? "Someone *was* home."

"If your aunt is home, we say only hello and make time to visit tomorrow."

I lift and drop the brass lion's-head knocker. Hearing shuffling footsteps, I give Milada a thumbs-up. The front door creaks open. A tiny white-haired woman peers up at me. Her face is deeply furrowed, like a helium balloon with the gas leaking out. Thick, furry, snow-white eyebrows knit together in a frown.

"Katerina Lenoch?"

"*Co chcete*? What do you want from me?" She blinks in the bright light, peers myopically past me to see who is translating her words into English.

"Is this the house of Josef Lenoch?"

"Not here." She attempts to slam the door shut, but I grab the handle. Milada gives a disapproving click of the tongue. If we want her trust we have to be more diplomatic.

"*Co chcete?*" she says again. "What you want from me?" Her furrowed face pokes like a turtle's head out from the wedge of opening. "*Sie sind Polizisten, nicht wahr?*" she says, reverting to German.

"We're not police." Now I do regret my hasty move. "I'm your nephew. From America? Frank ... František's son?"

"*Sie Sind Polizisten! Já nevím nic a nikdo tady není.* I know nothing."

A female voice from inside chastises the older woman for being unwelcoming to visitors. She steps aside, though not before casting a baleful look my way.

"I'd like to ask a few questions about my family," I shout to the woman inside. "The Lenochs?" The vinegary smell of fermenting cabbage is familiar from my aunts' apartment in Cedar Rapids. My eyes adjust by degrees to the interior gloom. She's a head taller than the older woman and is wearing a plaid wool skirt over white knee-stockings and loafers, what appears to be the outfit of a school girl. But she is no girl. She has a porcelain smooth, round face traced with wrinkles like fine cracks. Her steel gray hair is pulled efficiently back and clipped. She's leaning against an object that could be a cane, but in this light it's hard to be sure.

"Come back another time." Her eyes never leave their study of me.

"How about tomorrow? What would be a good time?"

"*Ano*, tomorrow. That will be best."

"What time?" I decide to take a chance. "Josef Kolar will come with us."

"Josef Kolar can stay with whore." It's the older woman who spoke. Catching me in a distracted moment, she yanks the door out of my grasp. Shouting, so I won't miss her meaning, Aunt Katerina says, "Our roof fall down and no one fix. Maybe Josef Kolar will fix."

No mistaking her sarcasm. "Maybe I can help."

"*Já mám ráda osvobozené země!*" She slams the door. Two deadbolts shoot into place. Pop! Pop!

"What'd she say?" I say to the brass lion's head knocker.

"She said, 'I love liberated countries.'" Milada guesses that she's frightened of being fingered as a Communist sympathizer. "She believe you say her nephew name to trick her so she will make confession."

A "chilly band of air" leaks through the hole the rose thorn tore in the seam of my vest. "What do we do now? Dammit, I should have kept my mouth shut."

We retreat to the Skoda. Milada fastens my seatbelt for me when I forget and reminds me we need to stop and eat lunch. As we speed back into the hills, she makes an observation that catches me off-guard. "The younger woman, yes? How well you could see her?"

"I did see what looked like a school uniform."

"I thought she look some like you. Her forehead slope back like you. She is tall and she have same long straight nose like you."

"What are you suggesting?"

"Maybe she is your sister."

"Anezka? No, really? If it's so easy for us to find her, Jungmann would have been here first."

"Not necessarily. Maybe he know, but he keep her like bait."

"Bait for who?" But then I catch what she's saying. "We have to go back!"

"*Ty si vymýšlíš*," she says. "You have strong imagination. It would be useless to go back and knock on door. We will speak with Josef, hear what he think."

To make up time, we eat our lunch from the picnic basket en route. Between gulps of a dry sausage sandwich—one slice of bread—and plums chased with bottled water, I grill her. If this woman is my sister, why didn't you recognize her? Why didn't she recognize you? I roll down my window. Steam eddies rise off a pond warmed in the sun. Frogs are bellowing.

"She was in Hnátnice. I was in Prague."

"But she moved back to your village, right?"

"State close orphanage only few months before Velvet Revolution. There were not so many kids left, I think. Anezka lived with her mother at inn from Jungmann only for short time." Even in that short time, Anezka certainly had eyes. "Inn burn down on night our government was given to freedom fighters. Probably it was accident, too much celebrating. My father will know some story."

Despite that it will delay our arrival in Letohrad, Milada wants to show me a castle ruin. It's along the way, and seeing it and hearing the story of its fate she believes will help me understand my family. After ascending a steep, winding road, Milada pulls over and parks under a choked stand of pines. Tramping uphill through monoculture woods, we pass a wooden sign with a poster photo of a fox that says: "*Prosim, Pozor.*" *Please beware of danger.* A rabid fox is loose. Milada snorts. "Even our animals are polluted."

On the crown of Zampach Hill, a triangular limestone peak looming over the valley where my father spent his youth, we come upon a crumbled stone wall with the remnant of a tower, all that remains of the castle. The breeze up here is bracing. "Sit with me?" Milada pats a smooth spot on the stone beside her. She's a little heater. I snuggle close.

The castle's owner, Baron Jan Pinčer, was a friend of the beloved emperor, Charles IV. Why this matters will be clear in a minute. In those days, the 1300s, the main road through the valley passed an immense land-holding that belonged to my grandmother's family, the Dostals. Baron Pinčer's posse was known to swoop down the hill and extort "protection" fees. Everyone in America, I tell Milada, claims their family was once connected to royalty. We don't need this, do we? Really? She takes offense at my attitude. The Dostals were not royalty, but they owned enough land they were able to bend Charles' ear with their complaint. It could also be that he wanted to send a message to other rogue barons. In any case, in return for his help, Charles asked only one thing of my family. He was a devout Catholic known to sneak out of the castle in Prague to pray privately and meditate. He asked that they remove the stones from the castle and use them to build Pisečná's first church. My family of course agreed. Good to his word, Charles put the sword to greedy Baron Pinčer. Good to their word, in 1350 my family, the Dostals, built a modest church using the castle's limestone. That church stands today in Pisečná and is still the only church in the valley.

"*Ja jsem ti řekla tuhle povídka aby jsi věděl jak hluboko jsou tvé kořeny v téhle zemi.* I tell you this so you will know that your roots grow deep in powerful family. It would not have been allowed for your father to marry maid from poor farmhouse."

"If my father had inherited the farm. There's something I'm still not clear on. How exactly does your father end up with the farm?"

"My grandfather, Antonin Kotyza, was half-brother to your grandmother. When she is dying, he and my father take over farm." She laughs. This means we're related, all the more reason I must stay away from her.

I write in my notebook: "In exile my father and his father could not speak the language of their dreams. I wonder if their dreams over time grew rancid with anger and longing and shame."

Milada takes my pen away. "There is something I must say you. *Tahle vesnice je můj domov.* Village of your father is also my home. *A já mám ráda mojí vesnici.* I love my village. Your father also love his village, don't believe if he say different."

"That's ironic considering you both couldn't wait to escape."

"There was no future for me here. I had to leave. Your father had trouble with Rosalye. It could not be allowed."

"You get excited every time you say *trouble.*"

She looks up at me with eyes the color of wet scorched earth. "I think you want to kiss me?"

"*Ne, ne,* I am afraid." But I laugh and bury my nose into the warm lotion-scented nape of her neck, under the collar of the cardigan, and pull a long deep huff.

"Come." She stands and takes my hand and leads me to the lip of a precipice on the northeast side of the ruin. Our footsteps crunch on windfall twigs. It's very windy up here and cold. The season is changing, winter drawing near. "Engels said of Czech *narod* we don't exist because Czech people don't have history that belong only to us. But he is wrong. Czech people exist in village like Pisečná. You will see."

She parts blackberry vines. "*To je ono.* There it is. Pee-SETCH-nya."

The slopes of the curving valley are quilted with grassy fields so vibrantly green the view has me silently supplying ridiculous clichés like "lush" and "pulsing with life." A pumpkin-colored river rolls southwest and loops around

Zampach Hill. The village farmhouses string out along the river like bows on a kite tail.

"*Malý, ale náš*. Is Czech say. It's mean, 'It is little' "—I love the way she says *lee-tell*—" 'but it is ours.' "

"The river?"

"Is name Potočnice. Is not usually muddy. They are digging chemicals from pond beside Jungmann inn." Milada directs my gaze along a tractor path leading to a dry pond where a giant yellow crane is taking muddy bites with its bucket. "There was inn. Fields of your father started by river and came to end of valley."

"What's left of it now?"

"Eighteen-hectare." She points to a long section, narrow like a runway. I make that to be a not so glorious forty-five acres.

"You said your father doesn't want the rest of the land back?"

"He is old. Not so easy he start over. But please, write in your Steno. For us, place is identity. Is not something you sell like car."

We're running late for the mayor. She leads me back past the castle ruins and down through the woods past the rabid fox warning and races the Skoda down the hill and we drop into the valley onto a tiny paved road and turn south toward Letohrad where the mayor, anxious to depart for his precious weekend *chata*, impatiently waits for us.

Chapter Nine

The Orphanage: Friday Afternoon, First Week of October, 1994

WHEN IT COMES to sorting out identity, it's the memories we don't have in common that define us. One of my father's persistent memories, one he told me about in any case, was of waking in the loft above the stalls at night filled with dread. When the heavy duvet would slip off and he'd wake up to freezing cold, the first thing he'd do would be to listen for the "angel breathing" of his little Magda. If he heard that, he'd then listen for the familiar snorting of the mare in the stalls. If he heard that he knew the world was in order and he could go back to sleep. While we take a circuitous loop and squander precious time to throw off hypothetical pursuers, Milada tells me that her father still wakes up with that acid burn of fear in his gut if he so much as hears a stray cat in the stalls. The dark void of early morning is when trouble came. To this day he'll still get up and go to the stalls to check. I of course grew up never feeling anything remotely like mortal fear for our safety.

Rounding a fishhook bend in the road, Milada suddenly shouts "*H-NAHT-NEET-tsa*," and jerks the Skoda to a stop. "Orphanage. It is your sister's home." It's a tiny village. A half dozen log-walled farm homes fold around the bend under a canopy of chestnuts. We've stopped near a manse with gargoyles leering out from beneath massive eaves. The old orphanage with its swayback roof and flaking plaster is pretty dilapidated. A muddy hayfield separates the manse from a newer brick flat that Milada believes might have been my sister's domicile when she was the director.

"I do not usually go on this road. I forgot is here."

"How old was Anezka when she was sent here?"

"Small child. Her mother was not welcome to stay at farm. She give Anezka to orphanage, then she have arrangement with Jungmann for his club."

Creeping ivy is colonizing the orphanage walls. What plaster still covers the square-logs is painted cerulean blue, the color of a naked summer sky. In my notebook, I add, "sky blue covering shame." And then wonder, why did I write "shame"?

"We are late. We must not make Zamečnik wait more."

"This is where my sister was seen, right?" Against her protests I open the car door and step out. "You said the woman might have been my sister? That was here, right? Just give me a minute." My jeans are soon damp from scrambling through knee-high alfalfa or timothy grass or whatever it is, but no matter, I'm anxious for a peek inside. The threshold has broken away from the stone foundation. The front door is thick and solid but hangs askew on gate-sized hinges. An official notice has been posted on the door. The word "*Pozor*" catches my eye. Beware. Must be condemned. Milada gives a nervous cough with the horn. I shove in before she can stop me.

The interior is dark but for a shaft of daylight sluicing down through a hole in the roof and loft. When my eyes adjust I see a row of stout posts framing a long hallway. A tiled wood burning stove is missing its flue and doors. Scavengers must have removed any usable metal. Rotted studs and broken furniture are piled by the stove for kindling. Near the pile is a bedroll. Cold ashes fill the stove's belly.

A plump feral cat I've managed to startle skitters up ladder stairs into the loft. The musky odor of rodent is strong. More prey than one cat can eat. There's another odor. Piss maybe? Stale sweat from the bedroll? I jot in my notes "smells like a homeless person's camp." Near the pungent bedroll is a folded clean white child's blanket. A closer look using my magnifier shows the little figures on the blanket to be saguaro cacti and bucking broncos and flying lariats. A touch of the Wild West in Bohemia?

Somebody is staying here, at least occasionally. Why a child's blanket?

My sister grew up here. Worked here. I flash on an image of Sulphur Springs, the community garden, the train tracks and cat o' nine tails, the Superior Seed silo, the pile of corn spilling out. Her grandfather in exile, living out his days, staring off at something only he could see from his back porch. What concept would she have of him? And her father. Did she wonder who he was? What would she have thought if she knew he attended the annual kolatch festivals in Cedar Rapids' Bohemie Town? Could she have imagined him dancing the polka to the accordion strains of Cervenka and his orchestra Friday nights at Danceland while she was stuck here? Would she have conceived of him teaching Czech history to children at the Czech Saturday School but refusing to come back for her? Poor Anezka never got to feel the tender grip of his hand at the back of her neck. Would she have minded him leaving smears of the Vaseline he used to clean his hands on the doorknobs? Would she have chided him, like Mom did, for his habit of chewing toothpicks after dinner? All that life lived there. And she never got to be a part of it. How sad. How utterly utterly sad.

The sound of the door scraping shatters my reverie. "We must go. Police are coming." I hear it, too, da-doo-da-doo, distant, but drawing nearer.

Back in the Skoda, we head south, away from Letohrad in case we're followed. This will cause another delay, but Milada knows the farm roads; it will only be a small detour. Safely away from Hnátnice, she curses me lustily, "Someone has seen you go in. They call police. Are you satisfied? Now we will be watched."

"It was my sister's home. I had to go in."

"Ne. You don't had to go in. You had to listen and do what you are told." These things, she insists, must be arranged with permission from authorities.

"What authorities? It's an abandoned building for god's sake."

"*Moc se ptáš.* You ask too many stupid questions. Now you must do what I tell you, understand? People are helping us. I have someone watching orphanage, your family, a cousin. We must not make trouble for her."

Careening around a blind curve on the down slope into Letohrad, we nearly plow into the back of a Mercedes tour bus and avoid a collision only when Milada whips into the on-coming lane and passes. Take it easy, I tell her. We're late as it is. Not the most judicious thing to say. She keeps her temper on simmer, but warns me, no more screwing up. What she tells me, I must do.

Chapter Ten

Letohrad: Friday Afternoon

KNEELING WORKERS IN blue overalls are scrubbing at four decades of grime with hand brushes, one cobblestone at a time. Pressure-washers thread hoses through throngs of Friday afternoon shoppers. A tower of scaffolding covers Letohrad's Madonna statue, which, I notice, climbs above even the castle's tower. What I find fascinating is not the mother of God's loftiness so much as the scarved ladies armed with yellow plastic shopping bags. Bobbing stiffly side to side like penguins, they march through the arcade with a missionary zeal as though afraid that Monday the shops might not reopen.

Milada parks outside a *Konditorei* that fronts on the square. Wait in the car, I'm told. Do I want anything? I ask for a coffee. I should avoid using coffee as a fluid, but looks like I'll miss my afternoon nap so I need it to stay awake. She knows the people who run the bakery and plans to use their phone. The mayor asked her to call before we show up. He might need us to pick up some files at the records office.

‒⁣◦⁣‒

PREPARATIONS FOR A gala reception are under way at the castle. A row of Mercedes tour buses idles, motors rumbling. Flowers for the reception are rushed through a side door under a banner bearing a photo of a man with a broad face wearing square black glasses and a sardonic smile, a politician of some stature I take it. When Milada does not immediately return I grow restless. What if the shops close for the weekend?

If I'm going to buy a gift for my father, this might be my only chance. She did say wait in the car, but the shops are right here. If she's back before I am

I'll see her. I follow the penguins into the arcade. The window display at a dry goods store features a pyramid of sun-faded washing powder boxes and a rack of Marlboro knock-offs and plumbing accessories. Under the display, blanketed with dust, are several seemingly forgotten hand-blown crystal vases. A vase would appeal at least to my aunts.

Inside, I muster a few words of Czech aided by a grope with my magnifier in my traveler's dictionary. The sullen clerk ignores me. "*Vázu*," I say, again. "*Pro České lidi.*" A penguin looks me up and down, accusing me with her eyes of being German. She bumps my leg with her yellow bag. "*Pro moji Českou rodinu*," I add, still not sure I've gotten it right. Vases for my Czech family. Then I remember to add, "USA, *Českou rodinu* in USA."

"*Ano.*" She brightens at last. "American!" It's in my favor apparently that I am not after all one of the Germans from the tour buses.

Detouring around the belligerent penguin, I follow the clerk back to the display. Her stooped shoulders, shapeless gray smock, the seam up the back of flesh-colored nylons, all remind me how much locals must resent foreigners waltzing in with open wallets. Much as I don't want to be one of those obnoxious foreigners, their resentment might be the price I have to pay.

She's promoting a slender, sea green vase, fussy with gold filigree, but near it is an amber vase, stocky, solid but for a narrow hollow, that refracts the light streaming through the window in a layered coppery pool, like a pond recumbent with autumn leaves, and I know instantly, that's the one. I point. That one. I'd forgotten about this, but my father has that small amber bowl on the desk in the basement where he keeps the books for his remodel business. As far as I know, it's real Baltic amber, a gift given him by his mother before he fled Bohemia. He'd flick cigar ash into that bowl while he watched his Friday night fights on the portable black and white Magnavox he'd lug down there because Mom couldn't stand that "racket," as she called it.

"*Ne, ne.*" The clerk wags a finger. Not for sale. It has a slight wobble in the base and an interior fracture that causes the light to refract in that layered manner, which as far as I'm concerned makes it the perfect gift. That vase will remind him of his amber bowl. That vase will be my Trojan Horse.

"*To je místní výroba.*" She keeps promoting the other vase. No, I tell her, I have to have that one, that one, I keep pointing, but she's turning away. All right, I say, all right. I'll take that granny vase and I point as well to a cobalt blue bowl on a wine-stem pedestal, I'll take that one, too. My Czech aunts in Cedar Rapids will love them even if my father won't. They had an identical bowl they used as a candy dish—likely nothing but carnival glass won at a county fair ring-toss—that I broke as a child. My total comes to just under 1,500 kc, less than thirty dollars. She's beaming. Must be a good sale for her.

"*Děkuji*," I mutter, exiting the shop frustrated but excited. One way or the

other I have to convince Milada to persuade the clerk to sell me that amber
vase.

⁓\⁄⁓

BACK AT THE Skoda, Milada's tongue is molding a chocolate ice-cream cone
into the shape of a volcano. She hands me a lukewarm coffee in a plastic cup.

I show her my purchases. "I also found the perfect gift for my father, but
she wouldn't sell it—"

"Charles." She never uses my real name unless she's truly angry. "You
think we have time for shopping?" She fills me in on what's transpired. The
mayor called the *Radniční úřad*, the district records office. No answer. The
woman who runs the office might be at the castle for the reception, which,
as it turns out, is for the famous author whose book Jungmann was reading,
Josef Škvorecký. He fled Czechoslovakia following Prague Spring and ran a
publishing house for *samizdats* in Toronto. Now he's back and on the lecture
circuit.

"Zamečnik want us to bring files. Maybe she is there and she don't pick up
phone." He'd requested that she set aside files from September and October
1968. If we have her call him, she should let us take them. Knowing we're
here snooping around, Jungmann's suspicions will be raised. The mayor wants
those files in his hands before Jungmann gets to them.

"Why those files in particular?"

Zamečnik found a report from the Truth and Reconciliation Commission
claiming that in the late sixties, during the time of Prague Spring when Milada
escaped and her father was arrested, police in some Soviet bloc countries
electrically charged water thrown on the floors of prisoners' cells. It was a
more efficient means of forcing confessions than the stress positions that took
so much time. The mayor expects to find evidence of this torture having been
used by Jungmann at the prison in Žamberk where Milada's father was held.
Zamečnik has been detained by an incident at the school and couldn't get
over here to collect the files himself.

The *Radniční úřad*, in a two-story steel and glass building more devoid
of personality than even my city hall office, is tucked into a back street off
the main square. The downstairs door is unlocked. We let ourselves into an
enormous room filled with desks stacked high with loose files. The place looks
deserted. A browse through a few stacks—Milada cursing and muttering the
while—reveals nothing more recent than the 1880s, *useless shit*. The director's
office is up a steep flight of metal stairs. I wait below. Milada runs up. Locked.
A sign announces that the office will reopen on Monday.

"Chico, if we had been on time—"

"Look, I'm sorry. But if your friend can't get the files, neither can Jungmann, right?" We retreat to the car. "Since he's stuck at his office anyway, can we please just take a minute to buy that amber vase?" It's unpleasant to have to plead, but this vase has become my golden ring, so certain am I that my father will understand the significance.

"*Ne*, Chico, *ne*. No shopping. You will find crystal vase in every village. Tomorrow morning in Žamberk I am certain shops will open."

It has to be this vase. I describe the flaw in his amber bowl. She scoffs. Memory is unreliable. When was the last time I saw his amber bowl? No, we'll find a vase tomorrow. Back at the square, a worker in blue overalls has made a point of planting his bucket behind the Skoda. Milada shouts at him. A grin cuts like an incision across his grizzled face. Cursing, Milada slips him a twenty-koruna note to speed things along.

But speed is not to be had. The great weekend escape to the mountains is in full flood. Stuck in traffic, we creep past row after row of concrete *panelak*. By the time we reach the bottom of a long curved drive leading up to a colonnaded school, Milada is seething. She parks. We climb out.

Before we manage much distance from the car, the mayor's teenage son, a student at the high school, slouches down the drive, greeting Milada with the barest of nods. He's playing a Walkman so loudly I hear the Techno scourge assaulting his ears through the headphones. She asks if his father has waited for us. He shrugs.

"*Kde je tvůj otec. Nechal pro mě nějakou zprávu.* Did your father leave some message for me?" She yanks off the boy's earphones. She's a mother of teen boys. She understands guerilla tactics.

He looks wide-eyed, offended. But now that she has his attention he admits that his father is in his office and the door is closed.

"Why should this time be different, yes?"

Translating that, Milada's sour look suggests he's hit a sore spot. He eyes me up and down as though I were some exotic brand of fool. Fritz, I want to tell him. Just another Fritz.

She dismisses the smirking sullen boy. He continues slouching down the drive.

"You meet with your mayor friend. I'm going to nap in the car."

Perhaps not surprising, she doesn't even attempt to argue with me. Her pride is wounded. Something is wounded. I'm inconvenient. "Go. Do what you have to do."

─⎬⎨─

FOR THE NEXT twenty minutes, unable to nap because of that coffee I should have dumped, I scribble in my Steno, as she calls it, now and then glancing at the housing enclave. Trimmed linden trees are planted like potted lollipops along the road bordering the housing development at exact intervals. A woman wearing an old-fashioned print dress, hair under a scarf, hangs wash out to dry on lines strung across her deck. Her persistence with the clothes, hanging them just so, knowing that if they are out for too long they'll turn gray, reminds me of my father in the basement he built for himself in the house in Cedar Rapids. He persisted in maintaining a few of the old habits from home, the Czech butcher, the Saturday language school, despite that over time they only managed to hold him in a gray world that never belonged entirely to one place or the other, and never, at least in his own mind, would he be able to do the one thing that would enable him to escape this gray netherworld: never would he be able to go back for the daughter he left behind.

I write, *Torturers and their collaborators live together with their victims in these projects.* Jiří's father died of lung disease five years after his release from the uranium mine. One of his former jailers lives one floor below in Jiří's mother's building. Milada's father lost some of his teeth during his interrogation and his hair went white—perhaps from the electroshocks?— but they left no mark except the injury to his feet. *He walk like his tender feet are on ground glass,* she had said. He continued to live in the village with Jungmann and Halbrstat for neighbors. It would be no different if my father and Anezka lived in adjacent *panelak.*

⁓⁕⁓

ABOUT THE TIME I'm longing for a hotel room and a bed, Milada rushes down the drive and climbs into the Skoda. Her dyed black hair has been loosened from its ponytail and flung back of her shoulders like loose straw. She apologizes for taking so long. "You have napped? All is okay?"

"Shouldn't have drunk that coffee."

"You look like you need hotel." When I don't immediately reply, she adds, "Okay, I will meet with Halbrstat. You rest." She proceeds to tell me that Zamečnik found Anezka's birth certificate, a document we need to go with her visa. "But, Chico, something is crazy." He did confirm that the woman with Aunt Katerina, the woman wearing the school-girl outfit, could very well be Anezka.

Even though my legs feel like concrete blocks, I tell Milada I'll nap later. Halbrstat keeps the village record book. I'm not going to miss the chance to see Anezka's name officially listed with my family.

We drive over the ridge to the valley on the far side. The one-steeple church that my family built nearly six-hundred and fifty years ago stands alone on a slope above the farmhouses. The only thing taller in view is the yellow crane scooping chemical mud out of the empty pond. The skeleton of Jungmann's inn beside the pond is a black scar on the face of an otherwise tranquil village.

Before we see Halbrstat, she warns, there's something we need to discuss.

Chapter Eleven

Strategizing: Piséčná, Friday, Mid-Afternoon

BAROQUE ARCHITECTURAL BEAUTIES are common in Bohemia, but Piséčná's square missed the pageant. Shops surround what amounts to a cobbled junction of two roads with a dry fountain in the middle. All but one dry goods store have been abandoned. Ground floor windows shuttered, second story windows shattered by vandals, stucco exfoliating as though it were necrotic flesh … The concrete statue in the fountain commemorates Charles IV's routing of the robber baron. Charles is missing his nose. What could such a repair possibly cost?

Milada parks and points to an archway with two flower boxes filled with geraniums. A courtyard beyond the archway leads into a modernized dairy barn.

"Flat from Halbrstat."

"I don't like that look you're giving me."

She opens the console between our seats and pulls out a Sani-Wipe to remove invisible bacteria from her hands. "I will just say it. Please don't interrupt with your questions. Be patient and I will explain." She gives me a piteous look. The square is quiet but for a passing diesel tractor.

"Birth certificate of Anezka list her family name as Kacalka, same as her mother. Rosalye Kacalka. But father is František Kacalek, not František Lenoch."

"František Kacalek? That can't be. It should have listed my father."

Why does that name sound so familiar? I pull the genealogy papers out of my daypack. There it is, the name the nun in Solon brought to my attention. František Kacalek was the one who committed suicide. The geneology lists him as Rosalye's father, not as Anezka's father. "I speak about this with Zamečnik.

He say you should not worry. This name, František Kacalek, is very common. In time of war, young women with children which are illegitimate will forge birth certificate with name of fallen soldier. They collect pension from dead man."

"Any way of knowing who this guy might have been?"

"He search files. He found František Kacalek in Czech air corps. He is shot down in 1940, close after time when Anezka is born."

"What about Halbrstat's record book? Why wouldn't the authorities have tested her claim against those records?"

"This you must ask to Halbrstat. Village will hide record books in times of war. It will pass secretly around village so authorities cannot … how do you say—"

"Confiscate." This just can't be. The record book will surely set this matter straight.

⁓⋇⁓

BEFORE WE GO in to see Halbrstat, she warns there could be more trouble. According to Zamečnik, Anezka had a motive for the fire that looks pretty incriminating. The fire happened on the night of December 28, 1989, the same night Havel was elected president. A crowd gathered at the inn that night, but the talk was mostly about who was brave enough to go to Prague a month earlier, when the growing protest first spilled out into the streets. Heavy snows had been falling in November for days and the temperature was reported to have plummeted to as low as minus 15 degrees Celsius but that didn't deter a busload of Piséčná villagers from joining the million or so protesters gathering in Prague in Letna Park.

"What about you? You were in Prague that day?"

"I stand home with my sons. Too much risk. If I am in trouble with police I would go immediately into prison. Jiři don't care. He is zealot. He join riot on Narodni. They arrest him for five days. Fine, I say, you can have him."

"You gotta admit, he acts on his convictions."

"I refuse to admire him for being crazy." But there's pride in her voice, too. Admit it, I tell her, come on, but she turns angrily on me and says, "This stupid pride, *ne*, it make me sick, sick."

The night the handover was announced, Rosalye invited all villagers, whether or not they'd gone to Letna Park, to the inn's pub. They kept it open late and served, compliments of Jungmann, an unending river of free *pivo* and *becherovka* and *Slivovice*. Card games were interrupted to make room for toasts and speeches.

Maybe Jungmann correctly assessed the sea change in the air and wanted to come down on the side of the victors? "Was Anezka there that night?"

"*Dost*, Anezka was there. One witness claim she leave because she protest having children around so much drinking. Other witness say she fight with Jungmann."

"What's her motive?"

"Orphanage was closed only few months before. Anezka was forced to live with mother. It is said those two fought like Czechs and Russians."

"Still, that doesn't mean she burned down the inn."

"Jungmann make some claim she did not like."

"The witnesses are credible?"

"Halbrstat is witness. That night Jungmann announce that Rosalye Kacalka has agreed to marry with him. Halbrstat confirm this to police. Why now she say yes? What have he told to her? Whatever he say, it made Anezka very angry."

"They got married that night?"

"*Ne, ne.* There is fire, so, no wedding."

What does Jungmann gain by pursuing an arson case against Anezka now? Must be something personal. Maybe he wasn't kidding when he hinted he'd make trouble for her if that's what it took to lure my father over here.

While she talks, I jot notes in my Steno:

> Trials inevitably pit villager against villager. In a transitional government, courts run the danger of (intentionally or not) sanctioning revenge. For a stable transition to liberal democracy and a capitalist economy, there has to be the assurance of recourse to law that rises above partisan interests.

What exactly is Jungmann's interest? What does it have to do with Anezka?

Chapter Twelve

Our Meeting with Halbrstat: Friday Afternoon First Week of October, 1994

THE HOMELY REEK of cow piss fills our noses while we wait for Pavel Halbrstat to respond to our ringing on his bell. A satellite dish is mounted above the archway. A sign of affluence in this village no doubt. When the town historian does hobble down the stairs and open the door, lurching on a prosthesis—the stocky gnome lost a leg during the war—he bows deeply. "Allow me." He sounds obsequious even without the translation. We slip off shoes, pull on the slipper sandals he proffers, and follow his creaking progress up the stairs.

After sitting us at a wooden table covered with an oilcloth, he sets out a cut crystal bowl filled with Italian plums from his trees. "Please, please enjoy." Rather than disappear immediately to fetch the record book, which is mainly why we've come, he lingers to watch until we've eaten several over-ripe plums, obviously picked a couple of weeks earlier, and yummed our appreciation. When finally he's gone, I cast a curious eye about the cluttered space. A dozen or so carousel horses, mounted on brass poles, lean wherever they have been left. Our guest, I take it, is not above accepting gifts for whatever his *protekcé* is still worth. Tall double doors close off an adjoining room. Through those doors canned laughter explodes from a popular American TV game show, *Wheel of Fortune*. Milada and I exchange a look. Who could be in there? Rosalye? The mayor did tell Milada that Rosalye stays here occasionally.

Several dozen framed wood-block prints line the walls. In one that catches my eye, villagers cower in what is recognizably Piséčná's square while a man with a bullhorn harangues them. Halbrstat is the artist. Her own father, Milada tells me, hangs a few of his prints. Halbrstat was born and raised in this village and earned acclaim as a young artist in Prague before he went underground—his art's un-ironic social realism should have appealed to the Soviets but he fell out of favor for depicting Party bosses in what was deemed an unfavorable light. Zamečnik believes he allowed himself to be recruited as Jungmann's enforcer to divert scrutiny from his *ideological failings*. This will make him vulnerable should the mayor need him to turn on Jungmann.

"I'm feeling fuzzy. Where's the bathroom? I need to do a poke." Milada directs me to a back room. *Thank God, an indoor toilet.*

—✲—

A CRAPPER, SANS TOILET seat, has been retro-fitted in a storeroom against the outside wall under a window. No nod to privacy. Wash hangs on lines strung across the room. Curing sides of pork dangle from brutal looking hooks. Jarred garden vegetables are stacked wherever there's space. I perch on the crapper, prick my finger, squeeze. Sixty-eight on the digital readout. Too low. I pop three Lifesavers.

A dirty plate has been left on the washer. Cheese rind, bread crust, a few plum seeds. Someone's lunch? Beside the toilet is the usual stack of rough gray wipes. *So, even former appartchiks don't rate soft toilet paper.* A door at the far end of the storeroom has been left slightly ajar. For a moment I entertain the creepy notion I'm being watched, but when I tap on the door there is only silence.

Rejoining Milada at the table, I tell her about the plate. We agree that it couldn't have been Halbrstat or I'd have heard his prosthesis squeaking. But if Rosalye is here, why wouldn't she come out and join us?

—✲—

HALBRSTAT REAPPEARS, CRADLING a book the size of a photo album. "My beautiful child." A tracery of wrinkles creases the book's leather binding. I write in my Steno: *This looks like an authentic original.*

Halbrstat is wearing square black glasses similar to those worn by Skvorecky and I wonder if he's deliberately cultivating the intellectual look. Despite that he's in his seventies, Halbrstat's mane of gelled hair is still dark and hangs theatrically to his shoulders. Halbrstat kisses Milada on top of her head. She allows this intimacy without flinching, though she does avoid my look of surprise.

"Your father will be happy for your visit," he says. And then to me, "How long you will stay?"

"Only a few days …" We should have rehearsed how much to reveal.

"I am sorry. If you could stay one month we have ski run. Have you seen? You must be our guest for Sunday dinner. My daughter will make *svíčková*."

Daughter? Must be who's watching TV. "By the way I have something for you." This we did rehearse. Despite his worldly education, Milada assured me he would not be above accepting gifts from America. I offer him from my daypack the hip flask of Jack Daniels. He solemnly sets the bottle in a place of honor on the mantel above the wood-burning stove. It's chilly in here. Though we're well into October, the villagers, Milada warned me, save their wood. It's not winter yet.

When he's returned to the table, I give him one of the Iowa beach party tee-shirts. He grins like a kid, showing four chocolate brown teeth amid empty gums. He gleefully tugs the yellow tee-shirt on over his starched white shirt and suspenders. Even he must realize he looks ridiculous with that pink pig sipping a tropical drink stretched over his sagging belly, yet his enjoyment seems genuine. "Look, I am American! Like your Kennedy. *Ich bin ein Berliner.*"

"My father wanted me to hand those out." A lie, of course, it was Anne. My father didn't want me coming here, but I don't want Halbrstat to know that yet.

"Your father loved history." Drawing himself up like a senator, he proceeds to lecture. "In your school lessons, is it said that there was great celebrating in Europe in 1848 when Emperor Franz Josef free *robotnik*? *Ano*?" I nod. I don't have the heart to tell him that the demise of the Austro-Hungarian Empire rated hardly more than a few paragraphs. "But who explain to *sedlak* how they will pay wage to workers and pay taxes, too?" He beams, pleased with himself for his brilliant analysis. "This was plan to allow greedy estate owners to steal land."

Calm only a moment before, Milada is suddenly livid. "*Dost*! Open record book. We will see who own this land before 1848."

Without asking anyone's permission, I'm taking notes.

Small land owners, Halbrstat explains for my benefit, were forced to offer sections in trust to pay debts after their serfs were freed and began to demand wages for their work. In 1867 Prussia defeated Vienna. Sensing a revolution brewing in Bohemia and hoping to appease the malcontents, Franz Josef passed a civil rights law that legalized private property.

"Your family," he accuses Milada, "purchased parcels for next to nothing when other farmers default." Known as "handkerchief" plots—most no more than ten to twelve acres—the parcels were too small to afford a living and most of the tenant farmers were ruined by debt. It didn't help that cheap grain from the American Midwest was killing profits in Europe. "Our family has photo from this time." He locates an album in one of the stacks and extracts a sepia-toned print. A family is huddled together on their bundles at the railway station in Prague. "You see? Kacalek family is waiting for train to Hamburg so they will catch boat." Their heads are bent. They look clobbered.

"Dostals paid for that land." Milada is shouting.

The person in the other room jacks the TV volume to drown us out, then switches the channel to what must be an NBA rerun, judging by the squawking klaxon. Halbrstat apologizes. "My lazy daughter. She love to watch Chicagos Bull."

Seeing that the feud between these two is only likely to escalate, I ask if he minds if I have a look in the record book. This business with the name on the birth certificate has me more anxious than I'm letting on and I don't want any trouble to come between me and seeing Anezka's name listed with my father's family.

"*Samozrejmé!* You are my guest." Oh so delicately, as though it were the only extant edition of the Bible itself, he lays open the record book. Entries date back only to 1753. He apologizes for that. "If you want to see earlier records, they are in Letohrad." The pages, crosshatched like graph paper, have certainly yellowed with age, but the feel of the paper is less brittle than I expected.

"Turn like this," he chides. Because I am a coarse American, proper handling methods must be demonstrated. "Start with Farmhouse Number Seven. It is house from your father."

The farmhouse my father grew up in is also the house Milada grew up in. Even her curiosity is piqued. She leans over the book with me.

By 1753, the immense Dostal estate, which would briefly become the Lenoch estate before it became the Kotyza estate, had shrunk to just over two hundred hectares, but by the 1860s the estate had swelled again to over three hundred hectares, a size it would retain through the time my father was born in 1922.

Milada pushes up from the table. "You stole land from my father. You dare deny you tortured my father so he will sign papers?"

Far from daunted, Halbrstat pats her hand as though she were a confused child. "Once you were big star. People in village worshipped you. State paid for you training. You will win Olympic gold we are sure!" She says nothing. He pats her hand again like a dear uncle. "We all have disappointments. We. You. Everyone."

Lest we never get to the records, I beg her to please calm down and sit.

"*Ano,*" says Halbrstat. "You like some food? My daughter will bring."

Slowly, achingly, protesting in every inch of her, Milada lowers herself back into her chair and then turns to our host and in a monotone says, "No thank you, we're fine."

"You remind me of my Aunt Rosalye." He appraises her as though seeing her for the first time. "Beautiful, *ano,* but also very … stubborn."

"You speak of aunt?" says Milada. "Rosalye Kacalka is your cousin, *ano*?"

"Ach, I show to you something." He hobbles to one of his stacks and searches for a photo he doesn't seem able to find. *My God, no, another delay? No, it's not possible.* I eye the book, already turned to the pages devoted to Farmhouse Number Seven. "Your grandfather. He cause this trouble."

He returns to the table with a photo he sets on the oilcloth in front of me. "Here. Your grandfather, Josef Lenoch." The young man who married into the Dostal family and took over the estate wears a bushy, Stalinesque mustache and looks keenly, his eyes predatorily alert, out of a gaunt but handsomely proportioned face. Nothing in this assertive young man bears any resemblance to the deaf defeated silent old man I visited in Sulphur Springs.

"Your grandfather go to Iowa with my other aunt, Barbora Kacalka." He and Milada argue about who is related to whom. Convinced the bickering will never stop, I interrupt and ask one of them to please translate for me what's been written on my family's pages.

Milada pores over a column. Lighting on an entry with her finger, she says urgently, "Chico, look!" I scoot my chair closer. "First husband from his aunt, Barbora Kacalka, commit suicide in 1922. You see?"

I bend near the page with my magnifier. "František Kacalek. Must be the suicide the nun in Solon told us about. Rosalye's father, or so we think, right?"

"Maybe not. Look at these dates." Barbora—Halbrstat's aunt—married František Kacalek in 1917. They lived at Farm Number Eight, which at that time was listed at only forty-eight hectares, too small to support their large family. The Kacaleks ran the inn, which they sold to Jungmann in 1939, a few months after my father and my grandfather and Barbora Kacalka and several children left for Iowa.

"Hanging by rope." She taps her finger at the entry. Then she points to an adjacent column. The dates show up under the lens of my magnifier, but I can only see one column at a time.

"Look here, this column. First three childrens from Barbora list František Kacalek for father." She jabs that column until I see what she's talking about and nod. "But he hang himself by rope in 1922. After 1922, three more childrens are born to Barbora. You see?" Jab, Jab, Jab. "But, who is father from them? Look down this column. No father is written. All three are blank."

This I can see even without the magnifier. "She must have remarried?"

"Ne, ne. See here? She remarry but not until 1939 when she is in Iowa." She runs her finger down an adjacent column. "Now look. For every six childrens from Barbora, one man is godfather. You see?" Jab, jab, jab, jab, jab, jab. "All six same. Who is this man? It is Joseph Lenoch, your grandfather." Halbrstat threatens to take the book away if she doesn't stop jabbing it. "Now look here. Which are name of childrens born after 1922? Can you see?"

I bend close to the book again. It has that musty smell of old paper mixed with pine, probably from the box it's kept in. Shifting the magnifier, I see the entry she has in mind. "There's Rosalye, my sister's mother. Born in 1923."

"Exactly. She is born one year after Kacalek hang himself."

"So, we have a mystery. Who was Rosalye's father? You think it could be my grandfather?" *What an ugly possibility.* Milada shrugs but clearly this same thought has occurred to her. If my grandfather fathered Rosalye, that makes my father and Rosalye siblings and means my father had sex with his half-sister. I sit up straight and take a long breath. The nun in Solon must have figured this out. Did my father know? He must have known. That could explain why he left and why he wants nothing to do with his daughter.

Halbrstat asks what the problem is. After listening to the explanation, he laughs avuncularly. "Someone I know will object to such crazy story."

I search further down the columns for any sign of Anezka's name, but in my agitated state it's impossible to focus.

"My father," I say, "you remember him?"

"Of course." Halbrstat raises an eyebrow. "Your father was …" Halbrstat and Milada search in vain for the precise word. We settle on "gullible."

"Gullible?" *This doesn't sound like him.*

Halbrstat shakes back that greasy mane of hair. He's still wearing that yellow tee-shirt with the sunbathing pig. "Someone have three childrens after suicide, but who? Not Barbora. It was my other aunt, Aunt Rosalye whom I spoke about." A Marlene Dietrich look-alike with stabbing eyes, this ambitious Aunt Rosalye planned to go to Prague to find work as a photographer's model, but after Kacalek's suicide, she was forced to stay on at the farm to help Barbora. Desperately unhappy, she began to sleep indiscriminately with men who stayed at the inn. Her profligacy resulted in three children born out of wedlock.

"Because she never marry, her three childrens are listed for Barbora."

"Your Aunt Rosalye named her first born after herself?"

"*Ano.* My cousin Rosalye, she was beauty, like her mother."

"Okay. We don't know who Rosalye's father is, but there's no doubt that Anezka is the daughter of Rosalye and my father, right?"

Halbrstat says only, "Look what it will be written." My magnifier follows my nervous finger down the column. There she is. Anezka. I feel as excited as if I'd found *her* and not her listing in a book. Born April 2, 1939. Mother: Rosalye Kacalka. Father: but here the entry is in pencil and is faint. It looks to have been hastily erased. "Milada? Can you please take a look?"

"You will see imprint of name from your father, František Lenoch. Someone erased, but you will see it there."

"Why pencil? Some of these others are in pencil, too."

In the Soviet decades, he claims, the record book was passed from house to house. Entries were written in pencil by whoever had the book and only rewritten in pen when they could be officially verified. "Verifications take time."

"Who erased my father's name? Why?"

He looks at me, considering his answer before speaking. Milada frees her hair from its ponytail, scrunches it back in. "My cousin belly is big when he leave. Why he is in big hurry? He is afraid from Nazis? He know Chamberlain will allow Hitler to annex Czech lands? I do not think so. Nobody know this."

"But who changed the entry in the book?"

After careful consideration, he says, "You must ask Jungmann."

"He had access to the book?"

"It pass around."

"What about Rosalye?" I'm thinking of that name on the birth certificate.

"Ah, Rosalye. *Ano*, if you wish to speak, I can arrange."

"We were told she sometimes stays here."

"*Ano, ano.*" He leans close over the table and speaks in a conspiratorial hush. "But you will trust what she will say?"

"I'll see Jungmann tonight. Shall I tell him you said to ask?"

He shakes his head. Locks of jelled hair rake his shoulders like chain mail. "We were comrades. We were like this!" He's entirely forgotten that I'm taking notes. "Some people," he looks knowingly at Milada, "say we were brutes. We wished only to cause harm for some pleasure." I'm scribbling furiously, trying to jot down every translated word Milada spits at me. "Maybe few are like this. If we knew of it, they were punished. But we, *ne. Ne.* We have cause that is beautiful. We want all of mankind to be happy and to live in harmony." I'm convinced he's merely spouting Party propaganda, but when I look up from my Steno I see none of that stentorian attitude I saw before when he was rewriting history for my benefit. "What price could be too high to pay for happiness and harmony for all mankind?"

"Price?" Milada no longer holds back the venom. "What price you have paid? Is easy for you to say happiness and not feel nausea in your fat belly."

He folds the record book closed with a shaking hand.

"What you want from me? Why you are here?"

"Apology. I want apology for what you did."

"Apology? They were running dogs for bourgeoisie. Traitors."

"It is my father you speak about." Impatient suddenly to remove herself from the company of this greasy man, as though moral pustulence were a disease one could catch on contact, Milada rises from the table.

"He was worst of them. He is not worth to lick bottom of my boots."

Milada slaps Halbrstat hard across the face. "You deserve to be held in fountain with pole until your filthy mouth fill with water."

"Milada." I take her hand. Rage vibrates through her like an electric shock. "Come on, he's not worth it."

From the other room, his daughter shouts, "Beaten dog! Go to your bitch!"

"Women!" Halbrstat looks pointedly at me, his obsequious grin restored. "Always complaining. What can you do?" As though to be conciliatory, he makes a sign to indicate that his daughter is demented and needs his attention. He extends a hand and pumps mine. "Sunday dinner then?" Lowering his voice to a whisper, he adds, "If you like, I will invite Rosalye. Is no problem, I will arrange."

Milada's expression remains stony. "Don't expect apology from me. It will never happen. I will be with harmony only when I see you in prison."

~\!/~

ON OUR WAY out to the car, I notice a shadowy figure with a wild nimbus of silver hair peering down at us from a window above the archway. Halbrstat's daughter? Rosalye. She clutches at the sheer curtain as though intending to throw open the window, but then apparently thinks better of it. I tug at Milada's arm, but by the time she looks the apparition is gone.

We pile silently into the Skoda. Scattered dry fall leaves skitter across the deserted square, propelled by a breeze with a nip in it. I ask Milada if she would mind driving by the farm before we head to the hotel, but my request is met with moldering silence. "You know, it's to avoid scenes like this that people hire lawyers," I say, trying for a lighter tone. She only digs deeper into her silence. We round the fountain. Whatever caused that damage to Charles IV also sheared off part of his horse's tail. A Soviet tank took the turn short? But why assume it was the Soviets? There seem to be plenty of local zealots. By leaving the damage unrepaired they are at least complicit, are they not?

Chapter Thirteen

The Old Farmstead: Late Friday Afternoon, Early October, 1994

THE CRUSHED GRAVEL road follows the river north through the heart of the village past log-walled farmhouses, most centuries-old, solid, sagging, original but for the shed roofs added to keep out the weather until renovations can be afforded. A chicken lurches like a sudden surprise into the lane in front of the Skoda. Rather than slow to miss it, Milada speeds up as though daring it, too, to end up under her wheels.

She has yet to say a word since leaving Halbrstat's. She won't look at me. With each farmhouse that we pass, each barn nesting on its stone foundation, each leaning wooden scythe, each Hunter green shutter, I imagine my father walking here, gazing out of one of these low windows longing for his family's maid to walk by, inspired by her coltish beauty to what? Risk everything for a night or two of forbidden love? Not that I'm in a position to take the moral high ground, here, but look what he stood to lose. What did Jungmann have to do with it?

At a bend in the road we cross a low bridge and Milada pulls over at the site of Jungmann's inn. The silent crane looms over the mud hole that was once a pond. Apparently the crew is taking Friday afternoon off to make their great escape. She opens the console and pulls out another sanitary wipe and scrubs her hands and then she pinches the wipe gingerly between fingers and drops it behind her as though it carried dangerous germs. What she deserves, I decide, is a good scolding.

"What did you expect from him? Did you really think he'd apologize?" She takes that as a rhetorical question and doesn't deign to respond. "If he's unhappy with the way Jungmann is treating him he could have helped us." When still she doesn't respond, I add, "At the very least he could bring us to

Rosalye. Maybe he still would." The mere suggestion that we could cooperate with Halbrstat breaks through the silence she's erected between us like a Berlin wall.

"Chico, I have realized something today. I have been telling to my friend Anton, no, I cannot help you, I must not be involved." She's referring to Zamečnik, the village mayor. When did he become Anton? "I have said this for you, so you will not have trouble. I am sorry, but I cannot anymore pretend that this trouble is not belonging to me. You see how they are."

Not sure what to say, whether to console or reprimand or plead, I climb out with my Nikomat and set about snapping off shots of what's left of the inn. The stone foundation still supports a fretwork of charred posts that look like cauterized amputees. Rosalye lived and worked in this inn for something approaching five decades. Five decades of wanting to tell my father something she couldn't say in a letter? In the letters it's all about coming home and taking over the farm, very little personal detail about Anezka, nothing sweet, nothing that would particularly appeal to the heart of a bereft young father. About the time Anezka was sent to the orphanage, the letters stopped.

When I'm back in the Skoda, Milada turns to me, her eyes red-rimmed. She was shedding tears while I was out snapping photos. She clutches my arm. "You must know that I will help Anton now. It will not be safe for your sister if they choose to retaliate."

The crane's bucket has dredged to the surface an oily bluish sludge that smells like a toxic sewer.

"What can happen between now and Sunday? I know how you feel, but another day or two?"

Suddenly the softness is gone and the bottled rage erupts again. "*Jste plný sraček!* You are so full of shit!"

I wait for her to calm down, but she swipes at me again.

"Some things are more important than your sister. Why she need to be saved anyway? Maybe life here is best for her."

I let down my window. The solvent in the mud leaves an astringent taste at the back of my throat. "Jesus, Milada, you're starting to sound like him. Harmony at any price. Sacrifice a few people, oh well."

"Who sacrifice? You want to blame, maybe you should blame to your father."

"All right, yes, I should blame to my father, but he's not here is he?" Obviously neither of us is in a mood to be reasonable. "Can we drive by the farm?"

"Okay, but we don't stop." She's already explained that if we stop, her father won't let us get away without staying for dinner and drinks and talk and we have to get to Žamberk and book a room in the hotel and give me time to nap before our meetings tonight with my cousin and Jungmann.

"Maybe I shouldn't meet with Jungmann tonight. If you and Mr. Zamečnik"—I can't bring myself to call him Anton—"are going to let him have it with everything you've got, you don't want me getting in the way."

"Do what you want. I will do what I want."

⸺ ⁓ ⸺

A SHORT WAY PAST the pond, near a bus stop, a side road bends under a tenting row of chestnut trees in the season of dropping their pods. We turn down that lane. The pods littering the road batter the Skoda's undercarriage and the vibration I find surprisingly soothing to my swollen ankles. A bank of indigo storm clouds is piling up behind Zampach Hill.

About two hundred meters along, a U-shaped enclave of buildings stands alone in a run of fields. The farm where my father grew up. A mammoth slate roof overhangs the farmhouse and its adjoining house and stalls. Low windows deeply set into logged walls peer out from under that overhang as though shy of revealing what's inside. Though I don't doubt I will see the shabby details Milada has so often apologized for, from a distance the farm looks pretty grand. The notion that my father would walk away from all this simply because his lover was pregnant is obviously absurd.

Nearing a plum orchard, Milada brakes to a crunching stop. A small man in the garden is stabbing a pitchfork into a compost pile. He lifts his head, hearing us pull up. He pointedly does not look our way.

"*Ty něco slyším a hned si myslis, ze to musi být pravda.*"

"Excuse me?"

"You hear one thing and you assume you know truth."

"You mean about Rosalye and my father?"

The little man stabs the pile as if there were something in it he wanted to destroy. Pausing to blow his nose, he straightens his upper torso with military correctness and pushes back the cap squashed onto his head and takes a moment to ponder the clouds banking behind Zampach Hill.

She leans over the console. Suddenly full of mercy, she presses my cheeks between her cool hands, not tenderly, but as though I were a sandwich she wanted to squeeze sense into. "My father know nothing about what Anton is doing. You must understand; he refuse to join Party but he is fanatic nationalist, more even than my husband. Yes?" I attempt a nod. She lets go of my cheeks. "I am not certain I understand this myself, but it don't matter what they do to him in prison. He will not betray Jungmann. He don't like Jungmann. He will not say kind things. But betray? *Ne*, he believe Jungmann protect our village from Soviets."

In the end, maybe nothing will be salvaged, maybe not even her father's dignity, but for three years she has been paying the taxes on this estate. "I want to see is possible to save this farm, even if my father say he is tired and he don't care no more. Kacalek family have taken most of it because my father sign paper in prison. Jungmann will not be happy until he take all."

"I see. Between this and the human rights trial—"

"You should be thanking me, Chico. It was once your father land, too."

The man with the pitchfork sees the black Skoda, looks confused, recognizes it, and suddenly he's waving a friendly salute and coming our way along a twin rutted path. His steps mince. Each foot lifts flatly and sets down the same way.

"My father. Now we will have to speak with him. Give to me promise. You will say nothing of what I have decided to do."

"Does he speak English?"

"*Ne, ne.* You will remember some Czech."

When he's near, Milada waves out her open window and hurls a cheery "*Ahoj!*" He's beaming. Happy to see his daughter. Eager to meet the American.

"*Dobry den, dobry den.*" Limber for eighty-two, Bedřich Kotyza stoops and peers in. His fine, silvery hair is smoothed under a flat cap but even with the cap it's easy to see that he has the round head and back sloping forehead of the Czech side of my family. He's dressed in baggy chinos, plaid shirt open at the collar, brown corduroy jacket with elbow patches. His grin displays a mouth empty of teeth but for a lone brown stalactite.

"*Nazdar!*" I say. He continues to grin. Is my pronunciation that awful?

We step out. Milada hugs him, but then he pushes away. Jungmann stopped by here less than an hour ago. Must have been while we were with Halbrstat. He parked his black diesel Mercedes right here in the lane where we're parked.

"Warn your daughter to stay out of this, he say. I am confused. I tell to him I don't know what he is saying."

His common-law wife, Marie, picks this moment to lean out of a window to sprinkle water over her flower box. "*Ahoj!*" She waves and her heavy bosom rolls under the print dress she obviously pulled on anticipating an occasion.

"Oh, no." Milada sounds genuinely worried. "Marie has seen us. I will have to explain why we cannot stay for dinner." She walks the path with her shoulders hunched and her hands tucked into the pockets of her cardigan, worn down by the weight of everything she's trying to carry on her own.

Bright red geraniums planted in window boxes add a touch of zest to my father's old house. That enormous slate roof wears a sweater of moss. Where the plaster sags, gaps expose the logs underneath—What was it? I wrote in my Steno, "Bands of air, something like that"—and now I'm thinking of Milada and Fritz in that railroad car that might have transported my father's neighbors to those terrible camps, and I see me alone on my couch with my beeper waiting for the phone to ring, and it seems too sad and lonely and pointless. If there were a way to get a kidney here ... No, no, I can't start thinking that way, no, I need to get my sister out of here, take her home and wait for a kidney. She can drive up to Sardis and help me with Isis.

Her father wants to show me what's left of the land. We stop at a metal Quonset hut the size of a small airplane hangar. What I catch from his impassioned speech is that this milking barn was forced upon him by the SS. He agreed to run their dairy. It was that or enjoy more time in brainwash hotel, I gather. What seems to bother him most—judging from what I'm able to catch between his gestures and the smattering of German thrown in for my benefit—is that he'd become a Soviet lackey and would be judged for that. For that betrayal he blames Jungmann. At least Jungmann's name comes up.

Our path follows a creek toward Zampach Hill. Bedřich points to the fields to the south and spits the name, "Kacalek," as though it were vomit in his mouth.

"*Toto je můj kus země! Toto je moje půda!*" He makes a wistful sweeping gesture with his arm. All that was once the Dostal farm. *All that land!*

The packed soil cleaves to the ribs in the soles of my Teva shoes. This would have been my father's, most of what we see in this valley. When I was in first grade, I got into a fight with a kid on the playground who called my father German. I wanted him to know that my father was Czech so I told him my father lived in the forest in underground shelters with *Party Sons*—I had no idea there was such a word as partisans. I remember his admiring stories about the men who'd been disbanded from the army, but who refused to give up their guns. Whether he meant it or not, I assumed from his stories that he longed to have been one of them. *Maybe that's just what I wanted to believe?*

A chilly breeze swoops down off the hill, pushing back the ammoniac smell of manure. Bedřich hasn't had livestock in four years. Outhouse leavings? He looks up at the purple clouds over Zampach Hill. There's a crackle in the air.

"*Pojd'te, pojd'te!*" He motions for me to follow him back to the house before the clouds burst.

~⋆~

WE PASS THOUGH a brick archway and enter a courtyard. He disappears through a low door after gesturing that I should wait while he checks on the status of things inside. Waiting outside is fine with me. I'm exhausted and the thought of a bed dampens even my desire to see the inside of my father's old home.

Rusting harrows and plowshares lay abandoned in the waist-high grass that fills the courtyard. The windfall timber Bedřich and Marie drag out of the woods to use for stove fuel is stacked a good twenty feet high in an open shed. Across the courtyard is the house the older generation moves into when the younger family takes over the main house. *My father would be living there. Anezka and her husband and children, if they existed, would be in the main house.*

Two massive wooden posts support a beam that runs the entire length of the house and stalls and supports the loft above the stalls. My father and his sisters slept up there. The warmth rising from the animals kept them from freezing in the winter. *That should have been where young Anezka slept.*

The creek runs past the open end of the courtyard. Beyond the creek, a grove of birch screens the Lenoch house from the Kacalek house. The leaves have begun to dry out and yellow and are chattering in the breeze. A wooden footbridge that once crossed the creek has caved-in. I'd be willing to bet this little bridge was kept in good repair in my grandfather's time. He had only to walk over that footbridge and through that stand of birch to see Barbora Kacalka.

"My father want show to you his rabbits." Milada bursts out of the door, her father high-stepping close behind. "Tomorrow, I told him. We will not have time for this but I told him tomorrow so he will stop pestering." A shed attached to the wing house used to be the pigsty. Her father is using it to keep the angora rabbits for which he is locally famous and of which he seems especially proud.

I ask Milada for the *suchy zachod*. Between that coffee and the diuretics I take to reduce fluid retention, there may not be a lot of time between impulse and urgency.

"If you can wait for hotel is better I think."

"I can wait." Bedřich is waiting, his shoulders ramrod straight, palms open in supplication. Are we going? We can't be going already …

Walking along the path to the Skoda, I look back. Bedřich is preparing to spread composted rabbit and outhouse slops under his plum trees. Fruit rotting under the trees purples the ground. Bedřich used to take his plums to the Saturday market in Letohrad, but gathering more from the harvest than he and Marie care to can is too much effort these days, if it's only to rescue the old trees' dignity.

Chapter Fourteen

To the Hotel in Žamberk

A SHORTCUT ON A farm road hardly wider than a tractor winds north through fields and woods and we pass an industrial dump with black, acid-scarred oil drums stacked three high behind chain-link fencing. The industrial waste that's been leaching toxins into the groundwater? Too tired to take notes, I don't bother to ask the question.

A few kilometers later, jolting through a cow pasture, Žamberk dead ahead, Milada comes to a decision. "I have tried to phone Anton from my father house, but phone is not working." For the first time since our spat she looks at me with some tenderness. "I will miss you, Chico. But I think is best if you go home as soon as possible."

Of course she would say this. An urgent loneliness takes over me. I say, no doubt sounding desperate, "I've had time to think about what you were saying before. I could rent Yveta's flat. It's plenty big enough. If they were a way to get a kidney here, without a long wait …" I don't have to add how afraid I am of dialysis, that I only have a few months. She knows that very well.

"Perhaps you do not understand." She strokes my cheek. I nudge her hand away. It feels patronizing. "Marie has just told me about Jungmann visit." He knew we were seeing Halbrstat and he guessed better than we what the result would be. Before our meeting tonight, Jungmann will know everything. It will require only a small leap of logic to assume she has enlisted in the mayor's human rights campaign.

"Where does that leave us?"

"My guess? He will send police to arrest Anezka."

"He has to find her first."

Despite everything, she laughs. "He only must follow you."

"Give me until tonight. Let me talk to him. Call off your ..." *Dog*, I wanted to say, but think better of it. "Let Mr. Zamečnik wait."

⊸⊷⊷

WE COME INTO Žamberk from the south on a wide boulevard clear of junkers and with streetlight posts festively painted primary yellows and reds. It's Friday, after school hours. Passing a playground with kids, I hear the joyous sound of their laughter and remember that sound in the cathedral. A heaviness like a fog settles over me as I see myself alone on my leather couch, no one staying in the map room, not one detail out of place. Even the image of Isis jitterbugging in his cage fails to rescue me from this funk.

We pass an abandoned concrete factory. The windows have been shattered, interiors gutted, the chutes and conveyor belts and machinery of the massive labyrinth left to rust behind a brick enclosure topped by concertina wire. Looming beyond the factory is a five-story structure crowned by a wooden cupola fashioned as a watchtower. It's the district prison where her father was held for interrogation. If Anezka is arrested, Milada speculates, this is where she'll be held.

But Žamberk is a lucky town. It lies on the main route to the Orlické Mountains, a popular destination for the new generation of recreation seekers. That's why my cousin Josef lives here. He hires himself out as a climbing guide.

The town square surrounds a park with mature lindens and chestnuts and old men relaxing on benches. Shops are open. People out strolling the paths that crisscross the park are dressed in pleated slacks and fashionable V-neck sweaters as though Friday afternoon were a fancy gala.

A mausoleum in the park supports a tall column atop of which is a gilded Madonna statue with a moon face and knee bent in a renaissance S-curve. The Mother of God, holding in her right hand a slender olive branch, gazes down—*I swear she's looking at me*—with a furrowed expression of pity. I sorely want to point out the olive branch to Milada when it dawns on me that this Madonna looks familiar. Maybe they all look alike, I don't know. I do remember that the Madonna in my father's stories was a beacon of the faith that couldn't be stolen by the occupiers, but it was also a reminder that faith could not prevent them from conscripting him into their army.

Milada parks before a pink stuccoed building shrouded by scaffolding. Our hotel. "Before we go in I want you to see beautiful Žamberk church."

Looming down a side street, the cathedral with its gothic vault and Renaissance domed towers looks like something straight out of Salzburg and *The Sound of Music*. It's a beautiful thing to behold, but my family preferred worshipping in the humble church they'd built in the village, and besides, I tell Milada, if I'm going to make it through tonight what I need immediately is a nap.

In the hotel lobby, a plastering machine whirs and clatters, raising a mist of throat-clotting dust. Plastic has been draped over everything but the reception counter. A minute at least, arguably a rude amount of time, grinds away with no response to Milada's tapping on the bell. Wait here, I'm instructed. I clear a space in the dust and set down my daypack and my soft-sided travel bag that converts into a backpack. The two crystal vases I purchased in Letohrad are wrapped with newspaper several layers thick in my daypack. The room we're booking is strictly for me. Milada decided she would spend tonight at the farm to keep up appearances with her father. I didn't argue. The sensible thing for me to do is to leave now and forget that things are about to get ugly and let Milada do what she has to do, and take care of myself. God knows, that's a big enough job.

Instead of the familiar *Čau*—locally pronounced "chow"—a lovely young woman, rubbing food from her mouth, appears through a side door and says, "*Guten Tag.*" I'm not German, I explain in English, to which she replies, "*Nerozumim, prosim,*" a polite way of saying she doesn't understand. "*Nemluvim* English."

"*Nemluvim* Deutsch," I say. She giggles as if this were the funniest thing. In fact, I do speak a smattering of German, but I don't want to be mistaken for German and sure enough, when not bent on practicing her German, she speaks halting English.

"You are American? We have been told you will come." I lift my brows. Did Milada call ahead to book a room? How? If the phone at the farm isn't working … I'd place the clerk's age at about eighteen. She has a moon face that bears an uncanny resemblance to the Madonna in the square. Her bobbed hair is dyed lamp black and she has multiple piercings in her ears, even in the cartilage, and a nose stud, and a tongue stud. All she lacks is black lipstick and she'd be as goth as my niece in Iowa.

"Please make you comfortable." Her eyes open wide like fountains, drinking in everything about her rare American guest. Her form-fitting pullover, a brash mustard color, showcases generous breasts that wobble like jellyfish with her every excited hop.

"Thank you. But, actually, I have a question. I'm looking for somebody. Do you … live around here?"

Milada chooses this propitious moment to return. She gives me a warning look before engaging the clerk in a heated exchange. "She demand 880 koruna for double room with shower. I explain we are not double. You will stay alone." A quick calculation works this out to be about $32 for a night, roughly what a cheap motel would cost at home.

Milada tells her to wait. Out of her hearing range, Milada says, "She won't give Czech price to foreigner. She believe I wish to cheat her. She demand full price for two." Milada taps her head in frustration with the inability of her compatriot to understand basic capitalism.

"Let's not squabble over a few dollars."

"There is another hotel, not far." She looks at me dubiously. "Maybe you prefer here because you like this cat at reception?"

"Please." But this is good. She can be jealous, too.

"What have you said to her?"

"Nothing. I said I was looking for someone."

"Chico, *ne*. After what I have spoken to Halbrstat, we must be careful. How do you know Jungmann has not paid this boopsy girl to spy? You think she is eager to pleasing to you because you are too sexy?"

The deal is consummated. The clerk, surly now, hands over a key that looks like it could have opened a chest in Charles IV's day. The newly installed elevator is not yet operating. Milada and I climb two flights of stairs to a modern room with two queen beds invitingly covered with white, thickly-piled down comforters. Hung between them is an original oil painting signed by Eduard Landa. Milada whistles appreciatively. He's an artist of considerable local renown. Executed with thick, rough brush strokes, the painting depicts Žamberk's square with the Madonna prominently silhouetted against a chalky winter sky, the cathedral in the background, balconies and roofs all wearing snowy eyebrows. The painting's somber tone seems wrong for hotel decor. A closer look—my eyes are adjusting to the dim light—suggests that this assessment might have been hasty. In fact, there is warm ochre in the square where sun has penetrated the overcast. I find that heartening. I am so grateful for that touch of warmth I feel like weeping. *Obviously you need to nap.*

"Look at bathroom," Milada says excitedly. "German plumbing. Fluffy towels. Look at this. Tonight you will have nice soft tissue for your bottom."

Milada jokes that she might stay after all. "Unless you wait for your boopsy clerk?"

I follow her out the French doors and onto a balcony fronting the square. Forgetting my exhaustion for a moment, I take in the view, feeling like royalty in a box seat at the theater. At the low end of the square is the local "mayoral" house, their version of city hall, a prim, two-story nineteenth century palace painted an arrogant sunflower yellow and with flowerboxes under tall French windows and a bell tower rising out of its steeply canted roof. Most of the buildings crowding the square shoulder to shoulder are similarly restored mini-palaces. In the days of the empire, Žamberk was a popular resort town for visiting Viennese. By the prosperous look of the square, Žamberk is prepping for the empire's triumphal return, at least the capitalist version.

Together we watch the "boopsy" goth clerk exit the hotel and hurry across the cobbled road to the mausoleum where she steals a few puffs from a friend's cigarette.

"My number two son is same age like this girl. We fight for freedom. Now they enjoy, but we are afraid to be wild and free."

Surprised by this rare admission of fear, I look at her more closely. The wrinkles in the folds of her eyes are not entirely from squinting. She has lived through hell and it shows and I can't possibly blame her for wanting to join forces with Mr. Zamečnik. It's just that her timing couldn't have been worse for me.

"Let's say tonight I convince Jungmann that I can bring my father here."

"*Ne*, I know what you want to say, but, *ne*. You find Jungmann so interesting. I tell you, he is not to be trusted."

"What are you going to do?"

"Tonight while you meet with your cousin I will speak with Anton."

"You have to keep calling him Anton? What happened to *my mayor friend*? Look, I'm sorry. I'm tired. Can't it wait, just a couple more days? Give me the weekend. Then I'm out of here, with or without Anezka."

Refusing to bite, she announces peremptorily that she will be back for me at half past seven. "Get some sleep. You have busy night ahead. Oh, also, be sure to keep Rosalye letters safe. Another thing I learned from Anton. Jungmann very much wants those letters. Maybe we can use to bargain."

"Those letters belong to my father." I don't bother to mention that I only have one original presently with me. "You would need to ask him." But I am curious to know why they believe Jungmann would place so much value in those old letters.

"Like any tyrant, he is desperate for proof that someone love him."

Before leaving, Milada gives me a kiss to make up, but she's distracted, with the mayor no doubt, and I'm too tired to ask for more. When she's gone, I transfer the manila envelope with the translations of Rosalye's letters, including the original, into my travel bag, just in case. I've forgotten where I put the padlock key. Exhaustion turns my brain to mush. Everything will be so much easier after a nap. I unwrap both vases and set them out on the window sill by the French doors. The late afternoon light passes softly through the green vase as though illuminating a mossy patch on a forest floor and I take out my Steno and scribble:

> Paradoxically, history in this place is both alive and a graveyard full of buried family secrets. What price are we, the progeny of exiles, willing to pay to unearth those secrets? What price am I willing to pay? What

if I don't hear what I want to hear?

–⁕–

"*Wachen Sie bitte auf!*"

The tapping repeats. I check the time: 7:05. Preparing to lecture Milada for being early, I laugh at the sight before me when I do open the door. The boopsy jangling goth clerk is hopping with worry that I might have overslept.

Without waiting to be invited, she breezes into the room and crosses to the French doors. I step into the bathroom and give myself a poke and consider the readout on my test strip and then decide to give myself a couple extra units of fast-acting, just in case. When I return, she has picked up the candy dish and is grimacing at it. "*Sehr hässlich.*" The thick stem supports a plump-bottomed bowl garlanded with tiny porcelain forget-me-nots. Okay, it is old-fashioned, but to call it ugly is going too far.

"I have two Czech aunts in Cedar Rapids who'll think it's beautiful."

She hides the candy dish coquettishly behind her. "Show to me something you have brought from America. May I look in armoire?" The light from the square accentuates her tight waist and round hips. By modern measure she'd be described as voluptuous, though compared to the Renaissance Madonna she's positively svelte.

"There's nothing to see. Some clothes stuffed in a bag."

She approaches swinging those hips.

"There something I can help you with?"

"I have message from your girlfriend."

Picking through a three-language gorp, I gather that Milada will not be coming back to the hotel at half past seven as planned. She's made dinner reservations at the Snack Bar around the corner. The clerk will show me the way.

Noticing that she still seems eager to chat, I ask when she will finish her shift and I show her my Steno and suggest that I'd like to interview her for my notes. She looks at me with a smile that says easy prey. *She's wrong. I have my methods. She'll give away more than she realizes.*

"I work desk until *Mitternacht*. Shall I come to your room after?"

"That's late for me. Knock three times. If I don't answer, I'm asleep."

After assembling the necessaries in my daypack, and remembering that I still need to find that tiny key to my padlock, I follow her down to the reception desk in the lobby, only then realizing that she's taken my Aunt's candy-dish vase with her. A bland friend with a thick blond baguette ponytail, non-descript in the way friends of beautiful girls often are, has been watching the desk while she was away. Seeing the phone on the desk, remembering that the phone at the farmhouse is out of order, I ask how one would go about calling the airlines. It requires a cash deposit. She offers to make the call for me, right now if I prefer.

I hadn't expected to have to make a decision so suddenly. Dinner is waiting at the Snack Bar. In a short while I'm to meet my cousin at the hotel pub. After that, Jungmann. Common sense would dictate that I do nothing until I've spoken with Jungmann, and yet I don't want the pressure of Milada telling me what to do. Would it be foolish to stay? Am I deserting Anezka to an awful fate if I sneak away tomorrow? I watch the clerk light a cigarette, metal jangling, chest wobbling, brash with teen certainty. I'd love to just hand her my credit card and have the decision made, but I really have to take care of this business with Jungmann.

"What are your plans for my vase?"

"This granny thing?" She gives my granny vase to her baguette ponytail friend behind the desk. "People will say Czech people are behind times. *Ne*, tomorrow I will trade for better in shop."

It's 7:15. By the way I've calculated my shot, I need to eat in the next fifteen minutes or so. Whatever this silly game is, there's no time to argue. Outside, she pauses to light up another cigarette, a knock-off brand of Marlboros. Around the corner, at the entrance to Snack Bar, we stop under a mirrored globe. She grabs my shoulder and pulls herself onto her tiptoes and gives me a peck on the cheek. She smells like her cigarette.

"What's your name?"

"Dana," she shouts as she spins away. Sounds like *Dunna*.

"See you tonight at midnight, Dana. If I'm not asleep. *Děkuji!*"

⚬⚬⚬

NOWHERE IN SNACK Bar's vast interior is there any sign of Milada. A throbbing disco beat bounces out of an impressive set of speakers and a revolving mirrored ball throws opals of light connected by filaments—the pattern reminds me of the veils my aunts wear over their hats when they go to church. The DJ apparently doesn't start until the Friday night dance crowd shows up. Currently, I am the only customer. Waiting for a waiter, suffering through a taped loop of oldie goldies—the Bee Gees, Abba, a wrenching twist into Santana's *Abraxas*—anxiety begins to gnaw at my stomach. She's got better things to do with Mr. Zamečnik, obviously. Where treachery is concerned I'm out of my league. I should take her advice and leave tomorrow.

A lugubrious waiter wearing a starched white jacket shows up bearing on a platter a dinner Milada must have pre-ordered. The first course is a "Vitamin" salad, a frothy concoction resembling an ice-cream sundae. A prod with my fork digs up sliced beet and celery root buried in a mound of whipped sour cream. The main course, delivered soon thereafter—obviously he's been told to hurry this along—is a platter with wafer-thin slices of cold pork arranged like a row of little corpses next to slabbed vegetables, in the middle a heap of greasy *pommes frites*.

The cream gives the "vitamin" dish too many carbs, and *pommes frites*? Milada wouldn't have ordered those. Must be the house special, disco fuel. The bill, I am told by the waiter, who stares disinterestedly at me while I eat, has been prepaid. This can only mean Milada knew very well she wouldn't be here.

En route to the pub, I stop by the hotel reception to look for Dana and ask whether Milada might have mentioned anything about Mr. Zamečnik, but once again Dana has abandoned her post. I cross to the square.

The paths are unlit and meanwhile it has grown dark so I confine my search to the perimeter where there are streetlights. The *petite palaise* that earlier looked so charming now look only smug. The melancholic strains of a busker's violin drift my way from the side street that flanks the cathedral. None of the evening strollers in the park venture down there to hear the violin. No one throws *heller* in his open violin case. He doesn't appear the least concerned. It's a perfect sound chamber. What is that? Dvořák, must be. Who wouldn't recognize those languorous strains from his *New World Symphony*, but then the violin's mood shifts, this time to frenzied Slavonic dances and I'm reminded of the folk dances my father took me to see at Danceland in Bohemie Town, when he would still admit to having some pride in being Czech. The lilting sound fills my heart with an ache for something hard to define, something that must be nostalgia for the child who watched those dancers in their peasant shirts and billowing embroidered skirts and imagined an exotic world that belonged to his father. The music lifts me above the palaces to that world—a world with no illness no occupation no torture, a world in which my father inherits the family estate and raises Anezka and plums—but then I notice that I can see from the park the actual cupola atop the actual prison, actual spotlights aimed down at the actual prison yard. The fantasy vanishes.

The bell in the mayoral house tower chimes the three-quarter hour. I'm now officially late for my meeting with my cousin Josef. Maybe I should just go back to the hotel and have Dana call the airlines and get on with it. But maybe Josef could help. At the very least, before I go, I have to ask Jungmann what the deal is with that erased entry in the book and see what can still be negotiated.

Chapter Fifteen

At the Pub Friday Night

THE AIR IN the hotel pub is blue with smoke. Somewhere in that blue ocean, somewhere among the *Mariáš* players shouting and slapping down cards and bawling to the squeeze of an accordion, is my cousin. The walls are greasy from the smoke, but the lead mullioned windows give the pub a medieval charm that's complimented by the coffered ceiling and the tooled backrests of booths that look to be hundreds of years old. Despite the nearly unbreathable air, I feel an odd affection for the place. "Affection" isn't the right word. It *feels* familiar, though that's absurd, too. I've never been here before.

Long tables are crowded with thick-backed farmers and workmen in blue overalls and denim shirts. While I search through the smoke for my cousin, a drunk grabs my arm. His eyes plead for something urgent he can't seem to remember. He asks for a cigarette. I signal that I don't smoke. He pulls out a pack of Spartas and offers me one of his as though we were best chums.

A passing waiter, wearing a white shirt and black bow tie, whispers into the guy's ear. The guy mutters an apology. He isn't a bother, I indicate to the waiter. God knows, this is his pub, not mine. The moment the waiter darts off, the guy lifts his hands as though conducting a symphony. "*Co jste hasiči, co jste dělali,*" he sings, which I will be told by my cousin translates, "You, firemen, what did you do when the brewery burned?" To which they reply, "There's not enough beer, but we won't drink water 'cuz that's what frogs drink, and we won't drink rum 'cuz that's what old women drink." He presses his head to my chest as though we'd agreed this were the saddest song in the world.

A strong hand claps my shoulder. A kind voice sends the drunk sailing off into the haze. "*Ahoj* my American cousin." He's my age give or take and wearing a snug pullover that shows off a muscle-bulked chest. He wears his hair cropped athletically close. I don't see much family resemblance. A broad, back-sloping forehead like my father's, he has that, but otherwise Josef's is an uncomplicated stranger's face with a welcoming smile.

"Jungmann here?"

"Jungmann is playing *Mariáš* in back room."

"I should head back. You and I could catch up later?"

"They are taking his money. He will be here for some time."

Steering me to a booth, Josef totters, I can't help but notice, and I am not usually prissy about these things, but I wonder if he's already had a few beers too many. This is worrisome. If I decide to stay, he could be my liaison with my sister and my paranoid aunt, but will he even remember what we talk about tonight?

There are no empty booths. We share with a young couple. The man, wearing a Tiroler hat with a Gemsbock, repeatedly says to me while pounding me on the shoulder, "Where are you come from?" Meanwhile he is downing, one by one, the half-dozen shots of corn rum lined up in front of him. His giggling girlfriend, wearing a polka-dot bow in her hair and sipping *zelena*, a syrupy peppermint schnapps, admonishes him to stop pestering. He continues punching my shoulder, saying, "Hey big guy, you are American." Before there can be trouble, she hauls him to his feet and I watch them jig a wobbly polka around the accordion, glad for a moment's calm.

Josef orders a Turkish coffee for himself, a *desitka*, a light, ten degree lager for me. The *pivo* has more carbs than I can afford on top of dinner, but those extra two units of fast acting should take care of it. Brushing aside my protest that I've just eaten—*and, I suspect, to suggest that he's doing well*—Josef orders food. "No goulash and dumplings." He winks. "Not for us anything so ordinary."

"So," I say when the waiter leaves. "My half-sister, Anezka. You know her? I was told you know her mother pretty well."

"No one really knows Anezka except her children." He confirms that Anezka and her mother did not get along in that brief time Anezka shared her mother's upstairs rooms at the inn. "But children. She loved children. Children loved her."

"She ever marry? Any children of her own?" Nothing of this nature was written in the record book; of course it would change everything if she had a family here.

"*Ne, ne.* She had orphans and cats. They were family."

"I understand she's hiding from the police because of the fire?"

"After fire she disappear."

"Would Rosalye know how to get in touch with her?"

He gives my shoulder a bruising squeeze. "Don't expect help from Rosalye

Kacalka." That hand is gnarled, part of two fingers missing. Climbing injury? "She say me she refuse ever to speak again with her daughter."

"I met your mom, by the way." His brows lift inquiringly. "This morning. We stopped on our way through Hradec Kralove." We commiserate. The oxygen. A shut-in for years, and she never a smoker. "She seemed pretty disappointed that my father never came back for her."

"She don't really put blame to him. It was so, she know this."

"What do you know about the night of the fire? Were you there?"

"Police already asking to me these questions. I tell them Jungmann say something that make Anezka very angry. She accuse her mother of being big liar. Next thing I know, smoke is everywhere."

"Why is it alleged that Anezka started the fire?"

"Halbrstat tell to police he has seen her in kitchen arguing with Jungmann. Burning oil in kitchen start fire."

"So Halbrstat was also in the kitchen. It could be him."

"She tell everyone Jungmann should be hanged."

"Any sympathy for that view in the village?"

"Of course, but everyone have business with Jungmann, yes? You want favor, he has *protekcé*. He is Big Shot."

I look at my watch. Blurry. "What time is it?"

"*Kdy se naučíš mluvit Česky?*"

"Actually. This is one thing I can say in Czech. But now I'm too embarrassed."

"It is nearly a quarter past eight."

While I stew over what Milada could be up to with the mayor, Josef pulls from his shoulder bag a book-length manuscript typed and hand-bound on cheap paper. The title translates into English as *The Death of Mr. Balthisberger*, a collection of stories by Bohumil Hrabel. This censored manuscript was circulated illegally before it was officially published sometime around 1963— he can't remember when exactly—and still bears in bold letters across the bottom of the title page the stock disclaimer: "*Výslovný zákaz dalšího opisování rukopisu.*" Translated: "It is strongly prohibited to reprint this manuscript." Obviously a wink to censors.

"In Czech Republic, we don't forgive success." He's referring to writers like Kundera, whom he accuses of defecting. "I love this manuscript. It speaks to Czech soul."

I pull out my Steno. "You're familiar with Klima, yes? Klima claims the very word *revolution* so tempted leftist intellectuals they turned a blind eye to what was actually being done. Like, torture, for example."

"Okay, Young Pioneers were brainwashed."

"What about the stuff Jungmann was doing in his club?"

"Young sexy girls, they want to eat meat, they work for Jungmann."

"Is that what Anezka was upset about?"

"It could be. Clients are strictly Party higher-ups. Very exclusive. Rosalye, she protect girls."

"Maybe Anezka wanted him shut down?"

"He warned her, never judge your own family."

"What did he mean by that?"

"You must ask to him."

"What about you? You enjoy his Party *protekcé*?"

"*Ne, ne!* I was thrown out of university and they put me in jail." He tosses this out with a wry smile, as though it were a badge of honor.

Our drinks arrive. I shove the noisome ashtray to the far end of the booth, take a cool sip of my lager. "What happened?"

His story takes us back to the twenty-fourth of January, 1983. Biting cold, driving snow. Brezhnev in Prague visiting. Josef was a forestry grad student at Charles University. Climbing was his passion, but that could never become a career in cold war Central Europe where product endorsements went to glam models such as Eva Herzigová, the super model from Litvinov whose bra billboards caused accidents on freeways. *No one crashed from admiring my billboards. Ha, ha, Josef. Very funny.* That Sunday in January, the day Brezhnev arrived, caving in to an impulse to join a few hundred other foolish—depending on how you choose to see it—student protesters, he ripped down Soviet flags. He was caught and held in jail for the usual five days. He was married at the time. Jitka, his wife, also a student, was pregnant and not feeling well and had decided to stay home. Until his release the following Friday, she had no idea what had become of him. A trial resulted in a three-year prison sentence. Jitka's mother contacted a former lover, a highly regarded swimming coach, who petitioned the court on Josef's behalf. Upon appeal, his sentence was reduced to two years' probation.

"Mind if I ask what they did to you in jail?"

Picture, he says, a freezing cell with no window. You're only allowed to wear underwear. They gave you nothing to sleep with except a torn piece of blanket. "Food, *my God!* Thin soup, it taste like dirty water. Something is wrong with bread so I am sick with diarrhea and shivering." He refused to rat on his friends. For this he was beaten repeatedly. It was then he thinks that he became sterile.

"I'm worried this could be Anezka's fate."

"Security police were trained in Soviet times. They know how to force confession. It could be rough." His arrest was only the start of his trouble. Josef was kicked out of the university. Couldn't find a job. Jitka was allowed to continue her studies, but was harassed, her study group disbanded. He was watched by the secret police. There were knocks in the middle of the night.

Jitka couldn't take the stress of living with a target of police surveillance and she lost the baby and then she left him.

I nod at the gnarled hand. "That happen in prison?"

He examines the claw. "Climbing in High Tatras. Three years ago. My legs … how do you say … gave up on me? But my hand catch in crack, like piton."

He's forty, it turns out, two years younger than I am, and from what I can see, exceptionally fit. If I were to stay. If his blood type and antigens are favorable. If he wouldn't mind being laid up for a couple of months. If I paid him for the clients he lost.

The waiter drops off a platter with a round of breaded and fried cheese served with *pommes frites* and tartar sauce. Josef smacks his lips. "Czech specialty!" *Another specialty. I'm really getting the treatment.* He carves a wedge of fried cheese for me, assuming that I'm only being polite when I say no thank you.

"Actually, I'm diabetic," I explain. His expression devolves from surprise to furrowed concern. "Type I? Yes? Shots?" I feign a poke in the rear.

"I had client, he was diabetic." He nibbles a wedge of fried cheese, looks away. "Is how I lost fingers."

But Josef wants me to understand that behind the Iron Curtain not everything was grim. He cut his climbing teeth on the Adržbach Mountains bordering East Germany. "We liked to say, you could climb from hell to hell," he adds, laughing. There he made the acquaintance of Orolin. The name means nothing to me. Josef looks perplexed. My ignorance of my father's homeland apparently exceeds even his modest expectations.

A Slovakian climber who earned his fame in the Himalayas, Orolin introduced Josef to day climbs in the High Tatra Mountains at the north of Slovakia, a short way south and east of here. One of the more popular areas, Prachov, a series of limestone pillars, had earned the reputation: "*Český ráj,*" Czech paradise. Josef perfected his technique on a brutal spire nicknamed "Jehla," the Needle. Rising vertically 50 meters, the tallest, thinnest spire in Prachov is a mere meter square on top.

"View up there is amazing." Unspoiled pine and birch woods, rolling slopes that seemed to go on forever. "When you are on top you fall in love with paradise. You forget that it is only oasis in hell."

At the top of Jehla was a metal box. "Inside is book to sign your name. My client, he is diabetic like you, he meet me at top." He frowns. "This part of story is too sad." I encourage him to go on. In a morbid sort of way, I welcome bad news these days. It makes my own situation look brighter. "My client's arms are shaking. I say him, you sign first. I will wait."

"I bet he was having an insulin reaction."

"He said he was clipped. He was experienced climber. Still, I should have checked." Josef takes a deep breath. "I try to catch, then I fall and my hand is wedged in crack. For I don't know, few seconds, he is dangling." He abruptly changes the subject. "What's about you? You are lawyer, yes?"

"City attorney. Let's just say I'm taking a forced early retirement." How in the world do you say to your Czech cousin, hey, but if I could have a kidney, and you have one to spare. "*Kde je záchod?*" I ask. "Where is the bathroom?"

"*Kam i císař pán musel chodit pěšky.*" He laughs. "Where even emperor has to go on foot." He directs me past the bar into a corridor.

Leaning over a stinky hole framed by feet stands—at least it's not an outhouse—I worry that my asking him to consider donating a kidney will make him feel uncomfortable, and that's a risk if I want his help with Anezka. On the other hand, if I'm just going home to wait for dialysis, what do I have to lose? Heading back, still uncertain how to solve this dilemma, I find Josef bent over the table, his beloved Hrabel manuscript open before him. He has slipped thick-lensed glasses onto his nose, but gives up reading with a look of disgust and removes the glasses.

"You still climbing?" I sense that something is wrong.

He picks at the cheese and potatoes.

"The accident?" I prompt.

"I still have reputation."

"Can I get you more coffee?"

"Oh, no." His claw covers his glass. The sludge at the bottom is thick like a mudslide.

"Someone told me Czechs believe you can read your future in the grounds."

"I don't need coffee to read future."

I look at him questioningly. "Because of what happened?"

"*Ne, ne.* I have multiple sclerosis. My mother did not say you this?"

After a rough silence, after watching this thin hope piss away down the same hole every other hope has gone, I finally manage to come out with, "I'm sorry, Josef." He accepts my condolences without comment. "How long have you had it?"

"Doctors say maybe three, maybe four years already."

"How did you ... what symptoms ...?"

"Reading bother my eyes." Josef describes going to an ophthalmologist, who could find nothing wrong, but who had seen enough to do a series of X-rays. " 'Secondary progressive' they call it. It march forward and leave me behind." I force a polite laugh. "Is worse on left side. On bad days I know I have leg but I cannot move. My brain command, but my leftist leg is like student. It rebel."

Lesions attack the myelin, the protective sheathing around the nerve cords. The nerves degenerate. It weakens the heart. "There are injections. But very expensive and bad for heart. Drugs kill you faster than disease."

"What about surgery?"

"There is no surgery that can fix." He shakes his head. "My doctor push drugs. I say no. What do you think? You think is wrong that I say no?"

"No, I get it, I totally understand." Sensing the probably not so well hidden edge of despair in my tone, he looks at me quizzically. "I'm looking at renal failure. My doctor gives me a few months, tops. If my internist had his way I wouldn't be here now. I'd be home on my couch preparing for dialysis. There's a long wait for transplant organs. Even Milada wants me to go home. Halbrstat said some unkind things to her today. She's going to do everything she can to help the mayor set up his human rights case. She wants me out of the way."

"Is better. You really don't want to see inside Hotel Jungmann."

I study the logo from the brewery on my beer glass. A cloven-hooved creature standing on hind legs holds out a stein with a smug little smile. I avoid looking at Josef. "Know why I never had kids? I used to tell my wife, my *ex*-wife, all kinds of bullshit. But, the real reason? I didn't want to pass this fucking disease on to my kids. I don't know." But now I do look at him and he rubs his eyes and I detect a slight tremor in that gnarled hand and remember his tottering when he walked. God knows, he's got enough worry of his own. "Who knows?" I attempt a wan smile. "My father refused to talk to his father once they were in Iowa. Imagine you're his father. For most of your adult life your son refuses to have anything to do with you?"

"He had his reasons, I am certain."

I shake my head. "That's partly why I'm here. To find out."

"Rosalye refuse to speak anymore with her daughter."

"Yeah, you were saying."

"That generation. Maybe we just need to forgive."

"Yeah. And I should just go home."

"Rosalye Kacalka, people say bad things to her, but she was kind to me. Without her *protekcé* no client would hire me because of my time in prison. She made Jungmann put out word I am okay."

I explain that I have letters she wrote to my father a long time ago and ask if he knows why Jungmann is so keen on seeing them. His reaction is curiously like Halbrstat's when I asked about the erased entry in the book.

"Jungmann is telling some story. Even Rosalye would not say, even to me. Some story about Anezka. You must ask to him."

An uproar at a card table in the room behind us is followed by a trill of hysterical laughter that bobs like a cork on an undertow of grumbling.

Before taking me back to see Jungmann, Josef has some advice to offer. "Be like *Mariáš* player. Do not expose what you are holding. Bluff."

—✧—

HE'S WEARING THAT same beret and bloused peasant shirt he had on when I met him this morning by the Labe River. Still smoking that pipe. Only after taking a long draw does he reach across the table and shake my hand. A farmer just won a sizeable pot. He pushes up from the table to take a break outside.

"Sit down," Jungmann says to me, indicating the vacated seat. "You like to play? Sure. We will take your money." The others laugh uncomfortably.

"I'm not familiar with the game. I'll watch."

"It is simple. Anyone can learn. Well ..." He makes a disgusted face, taps out a hot plug of ash from his pipe. "Anezka did not learn so well."

His gray piercing eyes fasten on mine. Remembering Josef's advice, I wait to see what he has in mind. He has an aquiline nose and a sensitive mouth, lips etched like a doll's, a feminine mouth. That coiffed goatee seems to be an attempt to distract from the mouth's vulnerability. The cards are dealt. A hand is set out for me. "You visited with Pavel Halbrstat today," he observes. "I know everything so don't bother to deny." He leans over the table toward me. "Not everything written in record book is accurate, you understand?"

Standing behind me and looking over my shoulder, Josef gives me a crash course on how the game works. The *Mariáš* deck holds thirty-two cards, counting up from seven through ace. The goal is to make marriages, the more highly valued the better. If someone has high cards, he starts the betting by saying "*Flek.*" The next one, if he thinks his hand is better, says "*Re,*" then "*Tuty,*" and up through "*Boty*" to the final challenge, "*Kalhoty.*" With each bet, money is added to the pot. The play goes in rounds. In each round one of four colors is named trump. To play you have to follow suit. Friends shout advice, good-naturedly threaten to unmask an opponent's hand.

Josef reaches around me to play my hand. "My father's name was penciled in as Anezka's father, but someone erased it. You know anything about that?"

"Villagers pass book from house to house. It could be anyone."

"Who would have an interest in erasing his name?"

A drinking song erupts. Something about a general, and what kind of a general is he, and then it's a woman, and what kind of a woman is she. Meaty arms embrace me. I play along. No way to know who's working with Jungmann.

He takes some time to restoke his pipe. "Your father is coward. If he want to know what is true he must come here."

Despite knowing better, I nibble at the bait. "Why did Rosalye keep writing those letters to my father?"

"You stay in room 201, yes?" He busies himself dumping out the plug that won't stay lit and scraping the crust in the bowl with a metal tool. When he looks up, he regards me with a faint smile. I cast a look to Josef. He nods. Play along.

"Yes, why?"

Noticing a hairline crack in the stem of his pipe—the crack gives him more distress than anything I've said—he gathers his pipe and pouch and tool and stuffs them in a pocket under the peasant shirt. "You have read these letters, of course?"

"In translation."

"In translation, do Rosalye say precisely that Anezka is child from your father?"

"She asks him to come home and take responsibility for his family."

"Just answer question."

"Not precisely, that I recall. But it's certainly suggested."

"I should very much like to see these letters." He stands. "I am bored with this game." He folds his hand. "Tell your father Rosalye never loved him. She was using him." He collects what's left of his stake from the table. "I was her love, first and always. If he dare, he will come to hear what Rosalye will say."

"What about Anezka?"

"She is not your concern." He smiles that sardonic half-smile. "You think you know who she is, but you don't know. What has your lovely escort told you? Of course, if maybe you are wondering, I know she will help Anton Zamečnik. *Ano?*" The smile spreads. "I see I have guessed correctly. It doesn't matter. Send your father here. I will make deal. If he comes here and Rosalye say to my face that Anezka is his daughter, I wash my hands. She will go free."

"Free? What do you mean?"

"Never mind. Tell to him." He leaves the table and soon is lost in the haze.

Waiting for Milada, waiting for Josef to finish out my hand, joining in the singing when it hits the chorus, I decide that there is only one sensible thing to do and that's to leave tomorrow. Who am I supposed to believe? My father won't talk about it, I can't talk to Anezka. And I'm tired. God, I'm tired. Tired of it all.

It's just before ten. I'm about to head upstairs and take a booster shot—with all this stress my blood sugar is taking a loopy swing—when Milada rushes in, parting the ocean like Moses at the Red Sea.

She looks exquisite, as usual, shapely in tight jeans, hair swooped into a French bun, leather jacket catching neatly at her hips, stiletto heels beating a fast rhythm on the linoleum. But, pancake makeup? Once we've settled into a vacant booth, away from listening ears, she admits that she's just come from meeting with Mr. Anton Zamečnik.

She scans the room. "I have persuaded Anton."

"Persuaded?"

"I am Czech, remember? We find refuge in lies." *Don't ask.* "*Poslouche.* He agree to do nothing until you have gone. But then he want me to find witnesses." Her steely look convinces me she's not going to back off on this.

"Tell Mr. Zamečnik he won't have long to wait. I'm leaving soon as I can book a flight." She gives me that patronizing look I can't stand.

"Would you like to meet Anezka before you go?"

"What are you talking about?"

"Anton have someone watching *syrotčinec* in Hnátnice. Anezka is there tonight."

"The orphanage? She know we're trying to find her?"

"She has spoken with contact. Anezka say she know she will be arrested soon so she wish to talk. She will trust if Josef will come. She trust Josef."

"Jungmann is suggesting Anezka could be his daughter."

"He will say anything to get what he want. Don't be stupid."

"Why not go tonight?"

"She want night with her cat before she is taken to prison."

"Cat? That's crazy."

"That is her wish. Tonight you will have good night sleep. Tomorrow will be long day. You will meet Anezka. By tomorrow evening you will be in Prague, maybe even Anezka will go. Josef will help to make arrangements with airlines?" Josef nods. He's willing.

It's decided that later tonight Josef will bring his bicycle up to my room along with a stocking cap and an old coat. Tomorrow morning I'm to ride the bicycle to the orphanage and I'm to make certain to not be wearing or carrying anything recognizable.

"Stay with me tonight? You'll have soft tissue for your bottom."

"I must not be seen in hotel or tomorrow you will be followed."

"Who's going to see you?"

"Your boopsy, of course." She gives me a waxy lipstick kiss. "Tomorrow morning, Chico. Take care. It might be your only chance."

Disappearing into the haze, she pinches her shoulders and jams her hands into her jacket pockets, reminding me of clients who realize that winning damages will never repay them for what they've lost. Back up in my room, nervous about tomorrow, I do my booster shot, gobble a snack, slip between the sheets, and manage to forget entirely that I've scheduled an interview.

Chapter Sixteen

Interviewing Dana after Midnight

AFTER HAVING THOSE letters translated this past January and learning that I have a sister in Czechoslovakia, I came up from the basement to find my father sitting at the kitchen table a good hour after he should have driven off to a job site in his pickup with "Lenoch Custom Home-Building" stenciled on the side-panels. I was staying at the house on Fruitland Boulevard, in the basement, the only place where I could hack my way through a forest of emotions without him chewing toothpicks just down the hall. On his plate was his usual two crisp, dry slices of bacon, one fried egg sunny side up, smothered in pepper, a small glass of orange juice. Not a bite had been touched. *He looks frail*, I remember thinking. *Through the chest. When did he turn frail?* He sat with his shoulders ramrod straight, his arms folded in his lap. He'd never liked coffee, but kept a percolator on the counter. Mom had liked coffee and that's where she kept it. After waiting for me to dump in the pre-ground Folgers that had to be at least two years old, Frank asked if I still intended to find Anezka. We had begun to talk about this the night before. I confirmed that I had not changed my mind. He greeted my answer with a simple question. What would I do if I found her? It occurred to me that until that moment I'd never quite understood his Czech pride as having been built on a foundation of humiliation, and of course what I was planning would only stretch his threadbare dignity further. What would I gain? I told him, I don't know, it just seems to me the right thing to do. The honorable thing, I added. With that he looked away and I saw in his pained wince that he understood, but still could not help me for reasons he would not disclose.

Hearing a knock, I remember suddenly that I'd asked Dana to come up. I slip on jeans and not a moment too soon. She lets herself in with a pass key, apologizing in case she has disturbed me. Not at all, I assure her, albeit nonplussed at the sight of that key. She's changed into a black tee-shirt with a scooped neckline that displays a generous view of her plump breasts. An innocent flower she is not.

She rushes past me to the French doors and throws them open. Hip-hop throbbing from a boom box down in the square invades the room along with the chill midnight air. Lifting onto her toes, she gives a tiny wave. She looks positively seraphic with that moon face, those baroquely curved hips. I look across to the park, see no one paying us any attention, and decide that she might be harmless after all.

Her black hair shimmers when she turns and smiles. A crooked finger beckons for me to follow her to the bed where we might comfortably conduct our interview. I close the French doors and follow.

With Dana coiled like a panther beside me on the bed, I suffer self-consciousness over the edema in my belly and ankles and though I doubt very much it matters at all to her I feel compelled to tout the man I used to be, the man who jogged thirty miles a week, jumped rope, did daily push-ups, sit-ups, a doable regimen when you have no children and your wife consumes her weekends dabbling in real estate. It wasn't about vanity, either—*maybe a little, I wasn't above admiring my cut abs in the mirror*—so much as relentless blood sugar control.

"I was sure I could beat the odds." She gives me a distracted purr. My pride counts for nothing. Yet, she is here, she wants something. "Let's get started. What was it like for you to be suddenly free?" She gives this some thought. I backtrack over standard profile questions. Turns out she is nineteen, needs one year to finish at a teachers college. Her dream is to study woodcarving at a Bavarian village famous for its religious icons. She'd settle for teasing uptight burghers by sunbathing nude in Munich's English Gardens. *Just kidding? Not at all.* Parents divorced. Lives with mother.

Suddenly remembering, she slips a folded envelope from a wafer-thin crevice in her back jeans pocket and flips it casually onto the bed. "Key for your bicycle."

The envelope contains a squarish metal spoke-lock key. I'd forgotten about that bicycle. Josef must have left it out in the corridor. Did he knock? Did I not wake up? Now we have trouble. What's to stop her from reporting this to Jungmann? I'm surprised Josef wouldn't have been more careful, but then, how would he know Dana was coming up to my room?

Dana demands to know what I intend to do with my notes. "Maybe you will say some insult to Czech people?" She uses the German, *Beleidigung*, which carries heavier shades of snobbery than the American translation. I assure her this is strictly for personal use and not to be reprinted. She laughs and I feel her relax beside me and again I wonder what she's after.

She wants to tell me a story. "This will explain how it is to be suddenly free."

She talks about hiking Europe's "Green Roof"—the Czech name I can't make out—in a forest in southern Bohemia. A *backpacking camping story? That's the best you've got?* I tune her out and instead worry that when I meet Anezka in the morning she will want to see her mother's letters, and not my translations.

But then Dana is telling me about an encounter she and her boyfriend had with some *Arschlöcher* from Munich in an overnight shelter and my interest perks up. The word means "assholes" but it is said without venom, as though just another word for Germans. Squinting at me, she says, "like you … I mean older, like you." There were four of them, *Anständige*, decent, wearing Bundhosen and carrying walking sticks. They commandeered the crude hut as if by right of noblesse oblige.

"It was neúnosné . Unbearable." Her boyfriend wanted to throw them out. "He was *sehr* …" she searches for the word, comes up with "*eifersüchtig*."

"Jealous? Of the Germans?"

She laughs naughtily. "My boyfriend knows I love German things."

She offered to dance for them, Salome-style. *That would contribute to my jealousy.* They offered to throw Deutsche Mark for each item of clothing she removed.

"Did you? Did they?"

Yes, she says matter-of-factly. Yes. They threw bills at her but she left the money on the shelter floor and walked naked into their circle. They hooted and applauded, but she silenced them. "This is our home," she claims to have told them. "Remember that you are guests and be polite." Her nakedness stopped everything.

"How did your boyfriend react when you took your clothes off?"

"My boyfriend say I am whore to Germans."

"How did that make you feel?"

"I am very angry. I say him dignity does not come free."

Hearing the mention of that word, "dignity," I realize I am looking at a young version of Milada. What Milada did with Fritz—and is obviously doing now with Mr. Zamečnik—and what Dana did with the Germans only confirms what my father has been trying to tell me. Dignity is the last refuge of the weak.

"Before Velvet Revolution, we were protected. If you don't say nothing, life is okay." I'm scribbling notes furiously. "Now? We are like wife who is rape by her husband. Sure, we are free. But where we can go? We have no money.

We have no pride. Big bully in house of Europe can rape us and we have to accept."

"Is rape the right word? I mean, if you strike a bargain with the bully?"

"I only have power if I am Czech *Hure. Alles klar?* Now I will dance for you."

"You want to expose my naked desire?"

She laughs. "You are funny. But you are also old."

"I hope to get to be a lot older."

"Haben Sie Angst?"

"More afraid than I've ever been in my life." Afraid because my belly is swollen tight like a gourd? Because my feet are wooden posts? Because rogue capillaries in my retinas are filling like the tide rising into the canals of Venice? Yes, I am afraid. I'm afraid of dialysis. I'm afraid of being that weak. That dependent. That isolated. That alone. I certainly don't give a shit about Jungmann, if that's what she's thinking.

"We are finished with interview?" She looks at me with round earnest eyes. "I want to give you small gift. I think you like my breasts, *ano?*"

"Did Jungmann send you to spy on me?"

"If it is so, you believe I will say it?"

"Why are you here? And don't tell me it's for the interview."

"You have some love letters." She points to the armoire. "Old love letters are best ever, man. I want to see."

"If Jungmann told you about the letters, that means he wants you to steal them. Well, sorry to disappoint you. Like I told him, they're in Prague."

"Schade." She pouts, then brightens. "Show me something from you."

After one of my visits to my grandfather—looking up at that silo beside the tracks, in the cover of that draw, the cornfields behind me and hills beyond, I felt as though I could walk for hours for miles and miles, just keep walking and never look back—I purchased an M. Hohner blues harmonica and attempted to teach myself to play railroad blues. If there's one thing I'm not it's a musician. Another thing I'm not is a wallower in blues. But I brought that harmonica with me. It's in my travel bag in the armoire. The one tune I did teach myself to play is my father's favorite, "Clementine."

"Want to see my harmonica?" I sing a verse: *"Light she was and like a feather, and her shoes were number nine ..."* She wants to see into the armoire. "Want me to dance for you?"

"Of course!" She laughs. *"Ne,* I make joke. That would be *neúnosné."*

"It's not that awful. When I have a new kidney and pancreas, you'll see."

"Schwarz!" she exclaims, visited by a sudden epiphany. "Now I understand why you are here. You want Czech kidney from black market." She stares at me as though I were the rapist.

"If you want to know the truth, I'm here looking for my half-sister." This I'm sure is a mistake, but I will not be thought a rapist, under no circumstances, I will not. This is my father's home. My sister's home.

"Your sister? She is Czech?"

"As Czech as you. Anezka Kacalka? That sound Czech enough?"

"But you are Lenoch!" she says. "Your sister will not marry Kacalek."

"Her mother is Rosalye Kacalka. I'm assuming she took her mother's name."

"I know Anezka Lenochova. She was big shot at orphanage."

"You know her? How? What do you know?"

Her eyes take on a childlike excitement and she says, "I will say you about your sister. But first you must show to me something you do not wish to show to me. I think you are ashamed for your water belly?"

She lifts the tail of my thermal shirt and peeks at my edema-poofed belly. There's nothing more than curiosity in her look, so I relax and let her look. "Okay I touch?"

I wince, but not from the brush of her fingertips—I feel only a scratchy sensation on my belly. "I'm a little sensitive about this."

"I have to make confession."

I grab my Steno. Now I'm going to hear that she does work for Jungmann.

"My parents. Is not true what I tell you." Her father, three months before her birth, refused conscription into the Soviet army and was sent to a gulag, where he starved to death the following year. To punish her family, the NKVD officers gang-raped her six-month pregnant mother. That resulted in a venereal infection that killed her mother the same year her father died. "I hate Soviets. Is why I prefer Germans."

"How do you know my sister?"

"Until I have seven years, I am in orphanage. Then I live with aunt in Žamberk. I still live with aunt."

"What was Anezka like?"

"I love her. She always say I am her dear child."

Heat steams off her hands. "You're too tense," she tells me. "*Sei locher. Locher.*" Be loose. "When she is *nervös* or upset," Dana adds, "she talk to her cat and call herself by name, like this, 'Anezka loves you, little golden bug. Anezka will always love you.'"

When you've been tossed from clinic to clinic like broken machinery, the thought of more hands on you is revolting. But Dana's kneading hands bring back the desire for touch. The light streaming in through the sheers casts a coppery reflection, like the tea-colored surface of a pond, with leaves rotting in fall, and that washes over my belly and produces a sensation of floating that's the most delicious imaginable. I feel it down in every blasted nerve and bursting capillary.

"Usually being touched makes me feel twitchy. But, your hands ..." I tell her about Torkey, the hawk who has to be taken in every night. Her tenebrous features suggest that she's not interested in wounded bird stories.

She's come to some decision. She slips her tee-shirt off and tosses it like a rag onto the carpet and thrusts her shoulders back and flattens her tummy. Her breasts are full in the way a ripe gourd is full. Dark areolas surround fat, erect nipples. After massaging her heavy breasts, she tugs on them as though they were puppies in need of discipline. She seems to be into pain. I'm surprised her nipples are not pierced, considering the studs in her ear cartilage.

"*Sehr hübsch.*" My rudimentary German makes me sound like a horny school boy. "Thank you. But you can put your shirt back on."

"You do not like?"

"You're beautiful, Dana. But I told you, I am not a rapist."

"I will make nice pillow. Rest your poor tired head."

When I hesitate, she lowers my face to her chest, pressing my nose into the under girth of those sumptuous lobes. "Rest my child. Sweet rest." Her heated scent is a delicious mélange of wood soap and smoke. Her pulse—*or is it mine?*—throbs against my ear. Reminds me of logs pounding against the bridge in the flooded Skagit.

"I really am afraid. Actually." It is not easy for me to admit that.

"Shhh." She sags back against the bedstead with an exasperated oof! "Maybe my boyfriend is right. But if I am *Hure*, it is because I want something better than this shithole!"

There is something to be said for the comfort of a modern bathroom, I decide, when I excuse myself to do my nightly ablutions. I consider the shower, but my bleary eyes remind me that tomorrow morning will come early.

Dana is gone when I return from the bathroom. My heart sinks a little, just a little, though of course it is better this way. Still, I worry she'll report the bicycle to Jungmann and he'll have us followed and I will be the cause of Anezka's arrest. I'll leave extra early and take a longer route. The plan is to meet up in Letohrad and catch a bus to the orphanage so that we won't risk Milada's Skoda being followed. Drifting at last into sleep, I wonder if any of it even matters. If she's going to be arrested anyway.

Chapter Seventeen

Saturday Morning: Six Days till the Drop Dead Date with Blue Cross

BLOOD PRICK. GLUCOMETER readout. Shot prep. Twelve units, two fast–acting. *Going to be a long hard day with more exercise than I've attempted in months.* Cornflakes, orange juice. My little padlock key falls out of my passport pouch as I'm packing. So that's where it was. Should I lock the letters in my bag and leave them in the armoire? Would she at least like to see the original? I could read the translations to her.

The manila envelope's red thread is looped loosely over the clasp. Odd. I would have bound it tightly. Was I having a reaction?

I heft the envelope. Too light. Really? I look in. Thirteen translations and one original gone? Every one of them?

"Un-fucking-believable!" I yell. That whole thing last night, *use my chest as a pillow, rest your poor tired head.* "Fucking bitch!"

By now Jungmann must have read the letters. I wish I'd read back through them last night. What did Rosalye really say about Anezka? Jungmann's name was never overtly mentioned per se, that I recall, but did Rosalye effuse, actually, over her love for my father, actually? What I recall is a demanding tone. She was young. She had an infant. Thanks to the Munich accord the Nazis had just walked into her country as though it were their backyard. She could not have understood what she was demanding from my father, the impossibility of it. But did she love him? What exactly was she threatening without expressly saying so?

~᛫~

I PULL ON THE stocking cap Josef left for me. The duck canvas hunting coat is scratchy; it'll chafe my neck. No helmet. I commandeer the steel-framed black one-speed with fat tires quietly down to the lobby. Plastic sheathing everywhere. No Dana at reception. So far so good. Being a chronic early riser is coming in handy for once.

Cold early morning ground fog shrouds the pastures and meadows south of Žamberk. I take the farm road, avoid the main road. Everything is drenched in dew. Fence posts, barn roofs, birch leaves. The hoo-hooing of a mourning dove serenades the crunch of my tires on the packed gravel. Reveling in the sensation of crisp air stinging my ears, I wonder why I've abandoned my Raleigh International to the storage closet. Fatigue is like a governor on an engine. It slows you down, sure, but it needn't stop you. And I've let it stop me for too long.

Cornfields, dense woods, back to the main road. An occasional Zastava or Volga chugs past, but no one slows or seems to take an interest. A beige seventies-era bus belches cindery black clouds of diesel exhaust into my face. I welcome the warmth. Soon enough I'll be alone on my couch waiting for the nightmare of dialysis to begin. This will all seem like a dream.

~·¹⁄~

A FEW SHOPPING PENGUINS have gathered for their Saturday morning march in Letohrad's square, and the team of street workers in blue overalls is already, at seven-fifteen, on knees prying out cobble stones one at a time like removable teeth. I lean Josef's bicycle against the Plexiglas bus shelter, lock it with that spoke lock, look around. Nothing suspicious. A beige bus shows up, more exhaust, more stench. The driver snaps his ledger closed, Milada and Josef materialize as if out of nowhere, the bus doors hiss shut. Before a word has been spoken, the shock-less bus is laboring over the ridge and then bouncing down at a breakneck pace into the valley and wrenching into a sharp turn south and throwing us around like a roller coaster.

The morning fog is burning off. Sun dapples the old hardwoods. The bouncing jars my ankles painfully. I tell them about my interview with Dana, declining to mention my head nestling into her *pillow*. Josef knits his brow. He's too polite to upbraid me for briefing the enemy. Milada, not so polite.

"This means we will certainly be followed."

"I was careful this morning. No one saw me leave."

"Don't be stupid. You make sex with your boopsy so now you think you can trust?" I've seen her angry before, but never so coldly angry. This is a Milada I don't know. "What do you think I am doing last night? Anton used his *protekcé* to help you. We have birth certificate. We have medical visa. All that is required is X-ray and check-up to know she will not have tuberculosis. He even arrange for passport with falsified stamp. He take risk so we will send Anezka to Prague with you today."

"Why didn't you tell me this last night?"

"You see why." Her tone is hard, beyond exasperation.

"Stop it. Dana lived in the orphanage, okay? Her parents are dead. She thinks of Anezka as her mother. Push come to shove, her loyalty will be on our side."

"If this is so, why she steal letters?"

"She said she wanted to read love letters. I believe her."

Milada deems this unworthy of even one of her cynical quips. She turns on the bench and keeps a keen eye on the road behind us.

"Look, I know it sounds silly, but I'll tell you why I believed her." If I really did. "After the funeral Mass we celebrated for Mom?" Josef listens patiently, still frowning. Milada won't even turn to look at me. "This grandfather was chatting with my Czech aunts when a boy runs up to him and this grandfather lifts the boy off his feet and dances around with him, and I see the expression on the grandfather's face and I hear the boy squeal and I realize, I'm seeing unadulterated joy for the first time in my life."

"What this has to say about stolen letters?"

"Patience. So my father comes around in his big Oldsmobile. He's chewing a toothpick. Mom would never have allowed that at church. He doesn't say a word. One of my aunts puts a hand on his shoulder. He just keeps chewing his toothpick. Then he says, I'll never forget this, he says, 'There's probably something in the fridge.' Suddenly it's like I'm seeing my father for the first time. Mom just died and that's the best you can do? 'There's probably something in the fridge?' "

Josef gives my shoulder a reassuring squeeze. Milada stonily keeps her vigil.

"I realized something that day. I realized I'd never seen my father show a strong emotion. Corny jokes, okay, he was great at that. That's how you knew he was having fun. But actual joy? Sorrow?"

"Chico. What this has to do with your stolen letters?"

"Think about it. An actual expression of genuine love? Real honest to god longing? That's really what she wanted. Of course, not to say she didn't pass the letters on to Jungmann."

"You can be certain of this."

Josef admits his mother was like this, too, every emotion guarded. Every day like she was anxiously waiting for something that never arrived. We commiserate. One of those somethings was my father. Their generation had it hard.

~✵~

WE GET OFF at Lansperk. From there we walk two kilometers through the woods and come the back way to the *syrotčinec* in Hnátnice, past a barn and through a muddy cornfield. No sign yet of police or Jungmann's Mercedes.

Josef approaches the brick caretaker's flat first. An African violet has been set in the window, the sign that we have the all clear. A woman roughly Milada's age, my cousin Frantiska it turns out, is at the door, waving us hurriedly in. A loose wool sweater tents a thickish shape. Her straw hair, shot with premature gray, is chopped soberly short. She peers at us over the top of heavy-framed glasses. "You are absolutely certain no one has followed?"

"*Děkuji, děkuji.*" I thank her for helping arrange this.

Milada warns her that I might have given us away last night. Her weary look suggests she's not surprised. Her engineer husband, who is working on a building contract for Jungmann, said nothing about trouble before he left this morning, so it's possible Jungmann is not onto us yet. By the way, Anezka is in the orphanage tending to her feline "child." Would we like a nibble of cheese and *koláče* while we wait? She sets out a tray, starts a kettle on her new two-burner electric stove for tea.

Frantiska's flat has been modernized: a bathroom with a shower, wall heat behind pine panels, a cast-iron spiral staircase winding up to loft bedrooms. Winter tourists have started coming for the skiing. For two weeks each Christmas, the height of the season, Frantiska and her husband are required to vacate the premises so that Jungmann can put up clients here. Yes, he has owned the property since 1990. He bought it shortly after evicting Anezka and the kids from the orphanage. She shrugs. It's a quiet life with little trouble, a price she and her husband decided they were willing to pay.

Waiting for Anezka, nibbling snacks, I ask her what she meant by trouble, exactly, and would she mind if I took notes? No notes. She does not want to chance that anything she says can be used by the police. Frantiska explains that she trained to be a school teacher. Her husband studied mechanical engineering. They currently take care of this property and farm the few hectares out back. She is Mr. Zamečnik's mole. Her husband doesn't know this. He called the police yesterday when I was snooping in the orphanage. He claims he's worried that the building is a fire trap. Does he know Anezka was here last night? No way to be certain. We should not stay long.

"Did you know Anezka growing up?"

"*Ne, ne.* I studied education at Charles University. Prague was my home. I only come back here in 1990." At my prompting, she admits that after landing her first teaching job in Prague she foolishly signed Charter 77.

"You were original signer?" Josef sounds impressed.

"*Ne*, I was not dissident. But I felt is wrong we must look over shoulder at each step for StB. Why we should live like this?"

" 'There are certain causes worth suffering for.' " Josef admits he's quoting Havel.

The cost outweighed her feeble protest's worth. Not only did she lose her job, so did her husband. Their friends in Prague had telephones disconnected, driver's licenses taken away. Neighbors no longer spoke to them. She and her family had no choice but to move home with her mother, my aunt Marie, in Žamberk. With no opportunity to teach, she earned what she could as a nanny. Her husband found pick-up work as a mason. In 1990, with the new government, she landed a teaching position at the high school in Letohrad. That's how she got to know Anton Zamečnik.

We are encouraged to finish our tea. Time is short. Anezka must be fussing over her precious *child*. We'll find her in the orphanage. Frantiska will keep an eye on the road. We should watch for her signal. She'll put the African violet in the side window if her network alerts her that the police are approaching. If we're quick, we can escape through the field past the barn into the woods. She'll stall the police, but, if questioned, she'll claim she had no idea we were here. If we're caught and say otherwise, she'll testify in court that we're lying. Her sacrificial days are over. Understood?

Chapter Eighteen

Saturday Morning's Meeting with Anezka

THE IVY DISMANTLING the stone foundation has sent legions of runners up the log walls. It's an inexorable process I understand well and I feel a great deal of sympathy for the besieged orphanage. Those shrinking aqua-blue islands of plaster and rotting eaves and chipped gargoyles once graced a handsome building. Is it nostalgia for better times that lures my sister back here? What does she want with this place?

"In a cavern, in a canyon ..." I finger the harmonica in my pocket. I brought it to show her. Dana gave me the idea. One thing from home.

A panel wagon with a yellow lightning-bolt logo is parked in the mud between buildings. The engineer husband's wagon, no doubt. "Want to disable it?" I say to Josef. "Pull a spark plug wire?"

He gets that I'm joking and smiles, but his smile is thin-lipped.

After crossing the muddy field we wade into the uncut tallgrass near the building and my toe stubs something immoveable. I stop and part the grass and discover a grave monument, a gray slab, canted almost horizontal. Scraping away a layer of algae, I uncover a decoupaged photo of a pilot in the Czech air corps. I ask Milada to read the inscription. Neither Josef without his glasses nor I without my magnifier can see it. There he is. František Kacalek, the name on Anezka's birth certificate. Cast into the concrete pad at the base of the fallen monument is a weathered bronze statuette of an American bison maybe six inches tall, the size of a child's toy. We can speculate about the grave, but a toy buffalo?

"Save questions for your sister. Come. We must hurry."

─⟍⊩⟋─

THE CAVERNOUS INTERIOR of the orphanage is damp and chilly. The stout beams bearing up the loft will support the sky long after the roof has collapsed. Somewhere behind that shaft of sunlight streaming down through that gaping hole, Anezka must be watching me, but I can't see her.

"Ciao," Milada says to my invisible sister.

The answering "Ciao" is hesitant. Gradually my sister—if she's actually my sister—coalesces out of the ether like a developing Polaroid. By degrees I notice a cane leaning against a chair. Sitting on the chair, back erect, knees primly locked as though waiting to be deposed, she's wearing the same fifties-era schoolgirl outfit—gray wool sweater over white blouse, plaid wool skirt, knee-high sheer white stockings, loafers—I saw on the woman I met yesterday at my aunt's house in Oucmanice. Lounging on her lap is the same plump cat that skittered away last time I was here, its gray fur blending so well with her outfit the cat would be invisible if not for the sweep of its tail.

"If you wish to ask questions, we must begin," she says matter-of-factly. "We may be interrupted soon."

"I understand you have some questions for me?"

"Would you mind to sit? You are very tall. When you stand like this …"

Milada shakes, sniffs, spreads out the crib blanket. We sit on cacti and bucking broncos. Having trouble today with his left leg, Josef excuses himself and stands to one side. He volunteers to be the one to check for Frantiska's signal.

"Blanket was gift from my father. I never know him. He was shot down over France when I have one year. You have seen his grave?"

"The monument with the buffalo? Yes, just now, coming in …" She's looking at me earnestly, but not, I suspect, for the reason I'd hoped. "It's true, Mr. Zamečnik did find a birth certificate listing the pilot as your father." Her round face with its porcelain pale skin varies its blank expression with just a hint of a curious smile.

"You have reason to doubt?"

"Yesterday we saw a record book at Halbrstat's that lists my father as your father. Your date of birth is April 2, 1939, right?" She nods agreeably enough, her hand the while stroking her cat's fur. "Someone tried to erase my father's name, we don't know who. It's faint, but you can still see his name written on the page for House Number Seven on the line beside your name."

"Your father?"

"František Lenoch."

"My mother has spoken of him. Where is he?"

"In Cedar Rapids, Iowa. He left Pisečná in December, 1938. He was sixteen. A few months later you were born."

"I have been told you have letters written to your father by my mother, yes? I should like to see them."

"As a matter of fact, I was the one who found those letters. I had them translated. That's how I learned about you. I was told you are my half-sister."

"I am sorry for this mistake you have been told. You see it is not true."

"But why would your mother write to my father in Iowa when she was pregnant with you?" The way she methodically strokes her cat, I see she's going to believe what she came here believing. "Anyway, tell me ..." I blurt this before better judgment can stop me, "why is there a buffalo on your ...?"

"I have not lived here for three years. It gave no money for repair. Someone cutting hay has knocked over stone. Buffalo, it was my toy. It came with me. I do not remember, of course. I had only two years then. Nuns say I asked to put to grave so I might feel close to my father."

The theft of the translations might work to my advantage. "Those letters are in Prague. I'd be happy to show them to you, but we should probably get going. Come to Prague with me. I have to return to Seattle. I'm sorry I can't stay longer, but at least we'd have a chance to talk and you could read your mother's letters." Hearing the distant grumble of a truck on the road, Josef ducks out to watch for Frantiska's signal. Anezka leans forward, tipping her chair. Her alarmed cat ceases sweeping her lap with its ragged tail. "I'm not trying to convince you of anything." The chill is getting into my bones, the odor of rodent is unpleasant, and I especially don't want to be here when the police arrive and risk any bureaucratic entanglement that could delay my departure. "If you are really not my sister, then you're not. I'm sorry I bothered you. I didn't mean to cause trouble."

"Don't worry, is trouble already." Did I really imagine she would simply fly away the moment I opened her cage? Images of jitterbugging Isis come to mind. "My mother said to me, if you will live at inn, you will work for Jungmann. Is good enough for Anezka."

"Work for Jungmann? In his club?" Some mother. I'm more curious than ever to meet this strange woman.

She strokes the cat until it lies quietly again. "Rosalye, my little gold lady bug. Anezka will not leave you alone. Never again. Anezka give promise to you."

"You named your cat after your mother? That's sweet."

"*Jsi příliš laskavý.*"

Milada translates this in a whisper. "She say you are too kind. She does not of course really mean *kind.*"

Lest we think she's merely being sentimental, she explains that for three years she's been hiding in Oucmanice. She has taken the train to Lansperk and then walked here, moving mostly at night, so she could bring food to her *child.* "When she was kitten, one hind leg almost chew off. She is left to die by her mother." Calling on her nursing skills, Anezka sewed and bound the ripped tendon. "In 1989 Jungmann close orphanage. I am forced to move to Piséčná inn. My little golden bug is terrified. She hide. This is only home she has ever known. I could not find her to bring with me. She is grown now, but she expect me to bring food."

"What if Frantiska fed her? Just while you were away, I mean."

"Husband from Frantiska will put poison."

"Frantiska will explain to her husband."

"*Ne!*" she says, losing her composure. "You must keep your tongue behind your teeth."

Milada asks me what I want to do. It seems unlikely that I can convince her to take the train to Prague today. If only to help her elude the police, Milada would be willing to put her up in the storm cellar at the farm, though Anezka would have to be kept hidden from her father as his loyalty in this matter might be questionable. It would be at best a temporary solution. What, I ask, if Anezka doesn't want to go?

"What do you remember of the orphanage, I mean when you were growing up?" I'm trying to understand her attachment to this forsaken place.

"Oh, in early days it was crowded." I nod, pen busy in my Steno. "More than fifty childrens are pushed together in one room for school. Room was just here." She points along the corridor of posts where interior walls have been removed. "We sat at desks that are like table. Two kids to one table. Boys with boys. Girls with girls. We sat always with shoulders very straight and say respectfully 'yes sir' to teacher. A nun watch at back of room. If you are not giving eyes to teacher's authority, *budete se cítit bič její hůl.* You will feel lash of her stick. On wall was old map of Europe left from war. It show our land belonging to Germany. I look at map and think my father die to save our country, but is like he die for nothing. Still, it gave to me comfort to know that my father was hero."

"Did you receive visits? What about your mother? She lived not very far away. You knew this, right? She come to visit?"

At this mention of her mother, Anezka's eyes take on a drifty look. Though she continues to sit with her knees primly locked, her hand ceases stroking the cat and its fur bristles.

"It was unlucky child who receive letter or visit. We hid ends of candles. If girl receive letter we force her to light candle and we put heads under blanket and she must read so we will pretend what is in house of them." She points upstairs. The dormitory for the girls was in the loft. "We were very jealous, so if she don't cooperate we report to nuns and enjoy when she is beaten with stick for stealing candles."

"But what about your mother? You hear from her?"

She pauses before answering. Her arms encircle the cat, which shows no sign of protesting. "Saturday afternoon was visitor time. Each Saturday afternoon when I am small I refuse to go outside and play with others. Each Saturday afternoon when I am small I stay inside. I am certain she will visit so I am waiting."

"She never visited?"

"She send money. Yes? On Sunday I eat fresh *kolač* and fat sausage." She sighs and releases the cat and the cat reclines again and its tail resumes its sweep of her lap. "Is better she never visit. There was such terrible crying after visit." She shakes her head at the sadness of this memory. "We pitied those children. Their hearts never stop breaking."

"Ever hear from the guy's family?" I resist the impulse to add *the pilot you claim is your father.*

"*Ano, samozřejmě.* Each week." I catch the sarcasm even before Milada translates. "If your father is my father, like you say, why he did not write letter?"

Milada is giving me the high sign. We shouldn't be here when the police arrive, which they're certain to do before long. "It's a fair question. I don't know. I was hoping you or your mother could enlighten me."

"He say I am his daughter, why he is not here? Jungmann say it, too. It is funny, don't you think? All my life I have no parent. Now everyone want to claim me."

"Come with me to Prague. I'd love to talk some more."

"You know what will happen to my little golden bug?"

"Happen? What do you mean?"

"My child. If I leave, what do you think will happen?"

"We'll bring her along." I look to Milada for confirmation. "Not a problem."

"This is her home." She leans toward me again. So far no sign from Josef, but how long can we chance it? The cat again arches its back, threatening to leap from her lap. "Jungmann took away my home but he don't care. Is nothing to him. Investment. Maybe he will build ski resort." Her porcelain visage, oddly smooth given her age—this may just be my eyes and the dim light—hardly shows a flicker of the emotion in her words. "You know why I am here? Why today I do not hide? I am here to make deal with him. I want my home back. You understand, yes?"

"Not entirely sure. What about the fire? What's to prevent him from simply having you arrested?"

"It make me sick how he make big business from young girls. It make me sick at heart. I raised some of those girls. They were my children."

"I have a room in my home in Seattle with a giant map of the Czech Republic. It takes up most of the wall. It has every village. It even has Hnátnice."

I see by the way she hesitates that she is surprised to hear that her tiny tiny village might be visible to the world I inhabit. "I was hoping I could convince you to come there and live with me. You and your ... child."

She wrinkles her brow. Isn't it true that beginnings often happen suddenly? The door opens to the flight cage, the bird hesitates, and suddenly the world is new again?

"We have a passport for you and a visa."

"If I try to leave I will be arrested. What I must do with my child?"

"Looks to me like if you stay here you'll be arrested. What will you do?"

"I did not start fire. Jungmann know this."

"Anyone else know this? Any witnesses?"

"One. Pavel Halbrstat."

"He was there? He saw?"

"He was in kitchen. He saw oil spill. Jungmann always smoking pipe. Jungmann drop match, oil leap to flame. Halbrstat is near sink. He could throw water, but it is oil, maybe only sand will stop fire. Soon is smoke like crazy. I leave. My worry is to warn to everyone take children immediately outside."

"If Halbrstat cooperates with him, you get blamed." I look at Milada, I can't help it. She doesn't need the reminder. "Could your ... could Mr. Zamečnik hire a good lawyer for her?"

"Of course. But Anezka can be held for months without hearing." She's looking meaningfully at me. Anezka, as far as we know, has not been apprised of my medical situation. "Is better if she will leave now before arrest."

But it's not to be. The plump cat, feeling her mother's agitation, leaps from Anezka's lap, throws itself along the hall with a hitch in its stride, swivels, slips, and skitters as though possessed up the ladder stairs into the loft. Anezka rises, steadying herself with the cane. Trouble with a hip slows her down.

"She run away when I was forced to leave. It is week before she trusted me again." Her sagging shoulders, her tone, her weary expression, everything about her is resigned to the inevitable. "Go now," she says. "It is best if you are not here when Jungmann come."

"You know for sure he's coming?"

"I have arranged. I will offer deal. I am prepared."

She never says what deal. It doesn't matter. Nothing I could do or say would convince her to leave with us. My last image, in her waning moment of freedom, is of her shaking and folding the crib blanket and pressing it to her cheek, her slate hair pulled back into a knot that is mirrored in her expression as she looks up, despairingly, toward the loft. Her mistrusting *child* has disappeared again.

An anxious Josef is outside watching the road. The main thing is to stay out of sight and avoid unnecessary trouble. We keep to the birch woods, ducking deeper into the trees the few times we hear a vehicle approaching.

At most a half hour after leaving the orphanage, ensconced on the bus to Piséčná that's making the milk run and stopping in every village, wondering how any of this can come to anything but an unpleasant end, I tell Josef and Milada I regret leaving her there like that. Milada shrugs. It was her choice to stay. Still. I tell them a story of something that happened to me when I was three.

It was winter. It had snowed the night before into the early morning but the snow had stopped falling and long icicles dangled from the gutters, just waiting for a snowball. My sister, Anne, two years older, had been allowed to walk on her own through the city park behind our house to the playground. Stuffed into a bulky snowsuit and mittens, I disobeyed mother's orders and trailed her at a safe distance so I wouldn't be sent back. Anne wanted to join the older boys' play, but they wanted to go faster on the merry-go-round and one of them—a boy named John, who wore a leather belt with a broad silver buckle that I deeply coveted—shoved her off. Anne still didn't know that I had followed. She pleaded with them to let her back on. They were enjoying her pleading, and I began to feel angry over the injustice. John said she could get on, but only if she pushed first. She tried to push but the ground under the snow was frozen and there were several of them and she was small. John jumped off. He shoved her down in the snow so she'd let go of the merry-go-round. My bulky snowsuit made running awkward. I remember the slick material chafing my thighs and making a scraping sound I was certain would give me away. Tackling John—that I also remember, the satisfying vertigo sensation of tumbling with the big boy. The element of surprise had given me the advantage. What I don't remember, but Anne proudly reported later to Frank, was shoving snow into a startled John's mouth. "Her praise struck me as unearned. I only did what a brother should do, right?"

Milada's eyes narrow with suspicion. "Why you are saying this? She has made choice. Is nothing more you can do. What?" What does she see in my expression? I'm not going back. I'm going home. That's all there is to it. "You wish to push snow on Jungmann? Believe me, we will push snow. But we are not children."

The bus comes into the village on the back road, past the church my family built. It's a simple gray limestone structure, utterly unadorned. One steeple. The clock added to the steeple tower not functioning. My grandmother must be buried in the small cemetery behind the wall at the back. There was satisfaction in that moment on the playground, the satisfaction of justice having been served. They let my sister play. Why? Because John repented? Because John was afraid of me? Of course not. Well, maybe a little afraid of my determination. No, because I pushed that merry-go-round. I thought I could make a deal for that fancy silver belt buckle so I pushed, and fell, and got up and pushed and fell and pushed. They were amused. I wish I could summon that determination now. But it's too late. I'm exhausted. Why wait three months for that fistula? If dialysis is inevitable, let's get started. Why wait until everything falls apart?

Chapter Nineteen

Returning to Seattle: Early October, 1994

M Y FLIGHT HOME includes a stopover and plane change in Detroit. From a pay-phone, I call my father in Cedar Rapids to let him know that he need no longer worry. He doesn't pick up. This is not especially a surprise, though it is Sunday and that means he's not working. His pickup—a round-hooded '49 Ford with running boards, his first ever pickup, which he continues to use—will be parked in the long driveway and covered with a tarp. After mass at St. Wenceslas, he will have driven his two sisters in his spotless Oldsmobile home for lunch at their apartment with the priest. Father Josef rewards his "girls" for their volunteer work with distracting meal-time conversation starters such as, what accounts for the Catholic church's failure to prevent genocide in Eastern Europe? The priest, like my father, was a young émigré.

I leave a message on his answering machine—a machine I bought for him when I was back visiting in January. In a few days, I should receive notice that I have Blue Cross's approval for the surgery. My kidneys, unfortunately, have been deteriorating rapidly. So if he wants to visit, I add, maybe see the raptors, which he's said he wants to do, he should come sooner rather than later. By the way, I met Anezka, I tell him, pretending the thought just crossed my mind. I'd be happy to tell you all about that if you're curious, but she doesn't believe you are her father and I've decided to drop the whole thing. Come out for a visit? I'd love to see you, if you can get away.

Home that night at my Seattle townhouse, the first thing I do is check phone messages. Nothing from my father. I have a pounding headache from the high blood pressure and jet lag, but I can't bear to look at my untouched bed.

Whatever deal Anezka offered Jungmann didn't work. I learned that waiting for my flight out this morning. She is being held at the prison in Žamberk where Milada's father was once tortured. Mr. Anton Zamečnik will hire an attorney to solicit the court, but we were warned not to expect anything to happen any time soon. The worst of it is that poor limping cat of hers now won't eat. My cousin, Frantiska, promised to search the orphanage until she was found.

In my message to my father, I said nothing of her arrest. I want him to visit and I don't want that trouble to stop him. He can stay in the map room. He'll enjoy that. The map room's high, narrow horizontal window faces north to the interior courtyard. When the blind is closed, the room is nearly cave dark like the room in his basement where he keeps the cot. I enter and close the door and push a towel against the aperture at the bottom to make the dark as dark as his basement. I close the blind. With my lousy vision it would be easy to trip over the feet supporting the folded treadmill, or the cords snaking to my PC desk, but I know this room well. Anezka will spend her first few nights in a cold, brightly lit cell. This is how Jungmann will break her down for questioning. This warm dark womb of sympathy is for you, Anezka.

What I told her was not a lie. Even Hnátnice, even her tiny village, population something under fifty, is on my wall map. Is it really? Suddenly I wonder if I made that up. I snap on the LED light from my key chain and focus the concentrated beam. Not only is Hnátnice on the map, it's designated as a bus stop and postal pickup, a veritable metropolis. It's just above the navel in the triangle that contains everything of consequence that my father left behind. If Žamberk is the north corner, Letohrad the southeast corner, Oucmanice the southwest corner, my father's village, Písečná, is the triangle's heart. It's a tiny world, and yet I'm more convinced than ever that his life in Iowa is nothing but a prolonged interruption of his life in this tiny world.

If fixing the world starts one bird at a time, is the corollary also true? Will failing to fix that bird diminish the world? My head is convulsing, my ankles throbbing. I'm desperately exhausted and I can't sleep. The bed in the map room, a black cast-iron frame with an arched headpiece stabilized on thinly spindled columns, salvage from a European hotel—my ex bought it for next to nothing at a rummage sale and left it when she moved out—is made up for my sister. It's covered with an amber bedspread, has a skirt that hides the frame, and has throw pillows decorated with views of Prague's spires braced against the head stead like greeting cards. The slender forest green vase with gold filigree from Letohrad is on the computer table. First chance I will add flowers. I pull a down comforter from the closet and spread it out on the bed. I crawl under the comforter. The womb is complete. No farther to go. I will ask my transplant team to sign me up for the fistula.

—\|⁄—

THINGS GO AS expected with Blue Cross, a minor miracle in itself. Wednesday their rep shows up at my townhouse wearing a stethoscope around his neck and carrying a valise full of forms. Looking out the south-facing plate-glass windows of my unit, he exclaims what an excellent view I have of the Aurora Bridge. "Famous for suicide jumpers," he says, grinning. Those high arching steel girders frame my view of water, hills, and the concrete gray sky. "It is lofty," I say, feeling called upon to say something. He sniffs around my cast-iron wood burning stove, asks about smoke leaks. He's concerned about my high blood pressure and asks for a full list of medications and asks me about the sodium in my diet and what I'm doing to control that. Of course the real reason he's here is to ascertain how I'll manage when I'm incapacitated. He looks at my burgundy leather couch, the neatly folded blanket, the TV with the VCR under it. And he looks at Kasia.

My Polish ex-wife with her movie-star cheekbones and limpid brown eyes has taken a few hours away from her mortgage broker's office today to act as my liaison. Kasia enchants him with tales from our two-hundred mile Seattle-to-Portland bicycle adventure, omitting mention that this happened several years ago. Her ability to sell low down-payment mortgages with arms that crush you later comes in handy. He's charmed. He's been thinking of jumping into the market himself. He finishes with a battery of questions concerning my consumption of alcohol and diet, tests my reflexes, looks at my swollen ankles, mutters, makes notes, accepts her card, and leaves.

Kasia stays.

Would I like to enjoy her *restorations*? For old times' sake? We speak often by phone, but it's been since before the Wyroc hearing that I saw her last. Between her personal trainer, a serious weight regimen, and her bike club, she's lost weight and toned up. Milada is out of my life, as far as she's concerned, and since we have an entire afternoon ahead of us … Your trainer won't care? She was sleeping with him even before we officially filed for divorce, though if asked she will vociferously deny this. I've met him a time or two. He likes to wear tights and spend his weekends in the saddle with boys and he's very nurturing and that's why she likes him. I'm sure he's gay but in denial but he's a distraction and apparently a good dancer and she loves being feted by her *boys*. Don't get the wrong impression. If she's a party girl now it's a reaction to the dry years with me.

Familiarity is a comfort at times like this, let me tell you. If you're in your forties, male, and diabetic, you worry about erectile dysfunction, but she's playful and the new definition looks good on her, though it can't hide the dimples on the backs of her thighs left over from the indulgent years. In those dimples I take solace. I am obviously no longer the whippet I used to be. How I miss her unapologetic way with pleasure. In fairness, though, it's a pleasure shaded with sadness. She looks at me so wistfully. Now that she is thirty-nine, her shot at children is looking like a long shot.

It's the second week of October. The days are growing shorter and chillier, but we haven't yet descended into our winter's perpetual gray. We enjoy a lovely walk along the ship canal. We stop to watch tall-masted pleasure craft cruise past the long row of poplars, the occasional commercial fishing boat with booms and pulleys and nets chugging out to the locks. The Fremont drawbridge goes up. We gloat over our good fortune at not sharing the misery of the backed up commuters. Kasia brags of her training climbs on Queen Anne Hill across the channel while I shiver at the sight of tourists crowding the deck of an aquatic-capable duckmobile honking its indignant goose-sounding klaxon at passersby, including us. That water just looks so cold. We walk on. I can't look at the boats anymore. We stop by the twin silos of the gravel plant, where the path shared between pedestrians and bicyclists turns away from the canal. The gray, chalky dust covering the lot reminds me of Wyroc, which reminds me of that rusty labyrinthine monument to abandoned industrialism in Žamberk, and that reminds me of the plaster dust in the hotel lobby where I met Dana, the goth-girl who stole my letters, the translations anyway, and suddenly I long to be back there. I mention this to Kasia. My ex makes the mistake of asking about Anezka.

My father did call me back, finally, yesterday. He apologized for taking so long to get to it. Winter pretty much puts a stop to outside work in his part of the world and he has a remodel project going that he can't abandon to his foreman until the frame is bolted into place. When I told him about the orphanage and the grave and Anezka's claim that the World War II flier was her father, he dismissed it outright as nonsense that Rosalye cooked up. I asked him point blank: are you her father, or aren't you? Silence followed my question. "Your name was penciled in beside hers in the record book." I did not mention that it had been sloppily erased. Instead of answering, he asked if I'd met Jungmann. "We need to talk about that," I said, "because he had Anezka arrested ..."

Well, while this was an awkward way to deliver the news, it wasn't clear to me that he would particularly care, so his reaction stunned me. I was unprepared to hear him say "That is unfortunate." He repeated it, "That is unfortunate." Not his usual anthem: *those people are dead, it's not our concern.* No, this time it was *unfortunate.* We agreed that he should come out to visit as soon as he could get away.

Since that conversation, I've concluded that no one will catch Anezka's child. That child is hiding and will wait for its mother to return. Suddenly I hear "on your left." I step out of the way of bicyclists on the path. Her child is starving, slowly. She will starve to death. There is nothing I can do about it. I burst into tears.

"What's wrong?" Kasia's eyes fill with the surety that she could fix this, whatever it is, if I'd only let her.

"Kasia," I say through the snot and tears. "Anezka's child is going to starve to death. I'm so sorry I couldn't give you children. You would have been so good with children. I'm so sorry."

"You mean I wouldn't have starved them?" She holds me until I stop shivering. Her thin riding jacket smells of the funk of hard earned sweat. There is a bracing marine saltiness in the breeze. I'm reluctant to part from her warmth; it's so hard to stop shivering these days. "Let's go back," she says, "I'll make you a nice low-sodium mushroom and celery soup. It'll have a little cream in it for flavor. You'll feel better."

On the walk home I can't talk for the sadness of it all.

After dinner, Kasia offers to head up Fremont Avenue to the video store but I tell her I'm not up to it. She offers to spend the night so I won't have to wake up alone—as much, I suppose, so *she* won't have to wake up alone. I thank her for a lovely day and assure her it's just exhaustion, it would make anyone weepy. When she's gone, I go into the map room, close the door, and curl up under the comforter on Anezka's bed. Except to go to the bathroom and take medication, that's where I stay.

─ᴖ─

WHAT DOES A child look like who's starving to death? What will poor little golden lady bug look like? Will her mouth wrench open? Will she curl up quietly and wait for her mother? The refrigerator hums now and then. Wind claps the stove flue. Buses growl out on Fremont Avenue. The whoop whoop of a helicopter? Another suicide jumper on the bridge? She's curled up in some recess in the loft. Rats will find her. I am the cause of it. I've failed. Failed at everything. Failed everyone. Kasia. Milada. Anezka. Failed my father. I am not a cause worth fighting for. Dialysis will be wasted on me.

A boat blasts its klaxon. The sound is muffled, far away. What if the bridge went up and wouldn't go back down? What if there were no alternate route? What if you just waited? At what point would it be acceptable to say, okay, it's time to curl up?

I'm curled up. I have no reason to exist. I am necessary to no one.

In the university law library I read about a landmark 1980s Chicago case, Wilson v. Cook County. Wilson was told to confess to the killing of a police officer. When he refused, under the direct supervision of the commanding officer, he was trundled in a sack and beaten severely. When still he wouldn't confess, the detectives applied alligator clips to his ears and nostrils and shocked him. He screamed from the pain. He fainted and had to be revived. The shocks were repeated until he said what they wanted him to say. If they said he killed the officer, he killed the officer.

What was he thinking when his nerves were being stimulated and his neurons and skin were frying? At what point did he curl up and say *enough*?

They hadn't counted on him squealing about his treatment and suing everyone. Plenty of witnesses corroborated Wilson's testimony and the allegations were proved to the satisfaction of the civil court. Still, all that ever came of it was the dismissal, more than ten years later, of the commanding officer involved. No criminal charges ensued. Why? More than a third of the judges in Cook County were assistant district attorneys at the time when torture was used routinely. They got their confessions. They looked the other way. Now these same people were the judges hearing human rights cases. I told Milada that if she decided to help Mr. Zamečnik she would obviously salvage nothing for her father, he might even say things she'd rather not hear, and it would only break her heart. She countered with the observation that to do nothing is to be complicit.

Even if Frantiska puts food out, the rats will eat it.

Around the time of Prague Spring, with so many human rights watch groups snooping around, the prisoners had to be kept looking unharmed for show trials, so guards switched to using so-called "clean" exhaustion tortures. These could tend to take a lot of time, requiring guards to keep going at the prisoner around the clock, but they didn't cause visible damage, like even the electroshocks did, often leaving a corpse or a lobotomized zombie. The prisoner would be kept awake in a near-freezing cell under bright lights for two days. On the third day—by then most prisoners would cry in terror at the least sound, the least stimulation—the prisoner was forced to do deep-knee bends or pushups until they fainted outright. The interrogators would then have the guards wake up the prisoner with ice water and start again. After one or at most two rounds of this, most prisoners signed whatever was put in front of them. For the more incorrigible cases—or for the more famous prisoners, such as Milada's father, who could not be allowed to get off so "easily"—an especially ingenious torture awaited, a stress torture that no one could withstand indefinitely, but that would make the prisoner foolish enough to complain in court sound like a whiner.

Zamečnik told Milada about the "nose-to-wall" technique. It's not a torture I've read about. He told her that this was certainly done to her father. After her insulting conversation with Halbrstat, hearing about this was enough to push her into his cause. According to Zamečnik, the guards forced Milada's father to stand with his toes and the tip of his nose against the cold wall in the interrogation room. His hands were wrenched up behind his back and bound in such a way that his shoulders were nearly pulled out of their sockets. After an hour or so of enduring this, according to Zamečnik, and especially after two days of being kept cold and awake, followed by maniacal exercising, you would scream for mercy. "Your eyes would feel like they were bulging out of their caves. You felt like heavy rocks were squeezing you from all sides." Your ankles and feet in that hour would swell to double their normal size. Most prisoners were crying or praying out loud well before the hour was up. But there was no visible damage, and that's what Jungmann and the courts counted on. Apparently a few hard cases sometimes did hold out. If they didn't give in and sign confessions and point the finger at others, the nose-to-wall procedure was repeated three times over a twenty-four hour period. During this time, the prisoner was given no water to drink. The pressure and the lack of fluid caused their kidneys to fail. These were the disposable prisoners. There was no dialysis in their future.

Is there a higher order of value here? If one holds out, not out of bravery necessarily, but because one believes it is wrong to be complicit, yet the result is that one dies, is that sacrifice more valuable than a bogus confession that keeps one alive to tell the story? Now and then the phone rings in the living room. My phone enjoys my view of the Aurora Bridge. At one point I hear my father's voice leaving a message but I can't hear what the message is. If I leave the map room, it's only to eat a few nibbles of low-sodium crackers and skim cheese so I won't fall into a glucose coma. I want to stay awake for this stress torture. I want to feel what Anezka is feeling.

The Red Cross had nothing but rumors to report to the United Nations. The United Nations did nothing. Prisoners died. They didn't even die for a cause, most of them, they were merely victims of chance. Wrong place, wrong time.

Kasia calls. "I called your father," she shouts into my answering machine. "I know you're listening. Get your ass out of bed and answer or I'm coming over."

How he gets himself here, lets himself in, and finds me curled up in the map room I'm not entirely sure, nor do I ask. He's here. Now I have to deal with him. Frank. František Lenoch. Silver hair, neatly combed, sparse on top. Frail in the chest now that he's into his seventies. Wrinkle-free Union work pants, royal blue. He's wearing a sleeveless undershirt and I know it will be as white as freshly fallen snow.

"I have to tell you I'm sorry," I hear him saying. This is confusing. Sorry that Anezka is in prison? Sorry I'm feeling this way?

"She is an admirable person," I hear myself saying. I sit up and lean into the pillow, braced against the iron head stead. These things weren't built for comfort.

He thinks I'm talking about Milada and effuses over her helpfulness. "No," I correct him. "Anezka. Your alleged daughter. She is admirable." I have some clarity on this situation, I tell him.

"We should act because it is the right thing to do," he says, quoting me back to myself. "Remember you said that?"

"We don't. We like to think we will, but we don't. She did, though. Now she is in prison and her child is starving to death."

"Child? What child?"

He can't help it, he slips a toothpick into his mouth and chews. It's semi-dark in the map room. Cocoon-like under the comforter. It has the vinegary odor of unwashed me. Must be late afternoon. He sits at military attention on the swivel chair at my computer desk. *Who does that remind me of?* Picks up the slender vase with the gold filigree. Pokes at the flowers with a work-blunted finger. "Nice," he says, being nice. He aspires to look at it more closely but I ask him not to turn on the light. I don't want him looking more closely at me.

"Milada asked me to pass on a message to you." He waits for that to sink in. I let him wait. He goes on. "She made me repeat this until I had it more or less memorized." He fiddles with the vase until I ask him, given its fragile nature, to please set it aside while we're talking. "It's a quote from Vaclav Havel. She said you needed to hear this. I was really impressed. My Uncle Alfons certainly would have been—"

"Frank."

"Okay. Sorry. Okay. Hope is not being convinced that what you're doing will turn out well. No." He fidgets with the vase again. I give him a look. "Hope is finding a way to believe that it makes sense to do what you're doing, that it is the right thing to do, whether it turns out well or not."

"You can sure see why Havel would say this." But I can't summon the will to argue. "Milada really told you to say this to me?"

"She's worried about you. She told me about Anezka's arrest."

Suddenly I'm up, the comforter sloughed. I'm dizzy and head-achy but I'm off the bed. I shine my LED light on the map. Show him the triangle. Show him Hnátnice, home of the orphanage where I met Anezka. So many questions I have. Why was she sent there when she had two perfectly live and healthy parents? Did he ever send money or try to contact her? I search for my Steno on the computer table. "I'm going to take notes." He advises me to calm down.

"I told Milada I'm coming over there to see what I can do. I might have some influence with Jungmann. She said she wants you to come with me. I told her I'd check to see if you're feeling well enough."

"Really? I'm surprised. She say why she changed her mind?"

"I'm concerned about your kidneys."

"Dad. Anezka says she's not your daughter."

He looks at me, fiddles with the vase, catches himself, stops. "She could be."

"Could be?"

Now he's worrying that toothpick.

"Jungmann? There something to that?"

"What did he tell you?"

"Me? Nothing. It's what he told Anezka." When my stubborn father merely chews that toothpick, I tell him about Jungmann's offer to cut a deal.

"After all these years."

"What are you talking about? Maybe you didn't notice, but I'm not doing so well here. I don't have time for any more nonsense."

"How is Rosalye doing? You spoke with her?"

"No, actually. And apparently she's not speaking to Anezka these days. But your old buddy, Halbrstat, he can put you in touch. If she'll talk to you."

"If I will talk to her."

"You know what. I think you just better go there yourself."

"Yes, you are probably right."

The image from Jiri's black light play comes back to me. The older woman, who once pined for the Eternal Wanderer's return, sits hunched, wrapped in a shawl, refusing to look up. *Look up, look up,* I tell her, but no, she can't hear it, or won't.

⎯⎞⎛⎯

A DAY AFTER MY father's arrival, the second Friday of October, I get the congratulatory call from the University Medical Center. Come in and collect your beeper. I am now on the official waiting list. My best chance to make the short list—*maybe only six months*—is to sign up for the dual kidney/pancreas transplant. My internist consults with me. With medication and a strict low-sodium diet we can reduce the swelling and lower my blood pressure and that should reduce or even eliminate the headaches. My creatinine is high, but not dangerously so. "Hold out for the transplant," he says. Regarding dialysis, he wants to wait and see. He thinks it's premature to fit me with the fistula. Wait and see how long? "Oh, three months," he says, blithely. "Let's revisit this in three months."

Milada calls me back late Friday night, early Saturday morning in Prague, with unexpected news. Dr. Saudek, her colleague and head of the transplant team at IKEM in Prague—she reminds me, in case that bit of information has slipped my wracked mind—informed her that they have an unexpected opening on their surgical calendar a week from Wednesday. Ordinarily it would take at least a month just to process the necessary tests for a live donor, but he would personally arrange to have the process expedited. I laugh. Is she serious? If I had a live donor I wouldn't be starring in this horror show. Your sister, she reminds me. Your half-sister. Anezka. If her blood antigens are compatible … Such tests can be run on a patient in prison; a blood draw can be ordered without the patient's consent if the clinic claims to be looking for tuberculosis. For a medical "emergency," she could be transported under guard to Prague. Anezka could obviously refuse to cooperate, but if all went well I could have a kidney as soon as the end of October. In Milada's view, I should feel grateful for this offer. She used up a lot of *protekcé* to arrange this. "If it does not happen, okay, better you go home and you will begin dialysis."

"What about her child? Any word?"

Sadly, Frantiska has not been able to find the cat. We can only hope the cat is feral enough to have returned to hunting. This is an absurd assumption. The selfish thought of escaping dialysis puts me over the edge. I tell my father I'll accompany him, if the invitation is still open. He admits there is another worry. Rosalye. "I thought I never wanted to see or talk to that woman again in my life," he says. He asks me a strange question, uncharacteristic for him. Have I ever wondered why I was forbidden to visit my grandfather? Have I ever wondered?

Have I ever wondered.

"Well," he says, "now I guess you're going to find out."

Chapter Twenty

Back to Prague: Third Week of October, 1994

A CHILLY LATE OCTOBER wind whips around the south bell tower of St. Vitus Cathedral. The vantage in Prague Castle up on the hill offers an excellent view of the Vltava in its Prague bend, where it curls shallowly past Old Town and under the Karluv Bridge. I talked my father into coming up with me to the cathedral's tower parapet—he was game for it, despite his knee trouble, though he took his time—as I wanted to see if my comparison was apt, if the Skagit, in flood, was as grand as Prague's river, but now that I'm back here I can't find any honest point of comparison. Between the rotten salmon and the baldies and harbor seals and a racing current that piles downed giant conifers against bridges as though they were matchsticks, what similarity is there to a restaurant barge featuring a string quartet playing Dvořák and Janáček while floating under a medieval bridge so crowded with tourists it might as well be nicknamed pickpocket row? A teen couple mounted the tower's two hundred and eighty-seven spiraling steps just ahead of me, boots clinking with metal. My heart pounded and my ankles screamed, but I kept up, step for step. I still have it in me.

Despite the sting of the wind, they grope each other with abandon. "What else do you do with that tongue piercing?" I say but they ignore the funny American, if they hear me at all. My creatinine at last check had climbed to just under eight, near to crossing into the red zone. My internist was dead set against my leaving Seattle. I told him to tell the surgery team I'm here to ask for my sister's kidney. I did not mention the possibility of surgery in Prague. Squeezing past the lovers, I inhale the perfume of their lust with a hunger that's pure nostalgia, no real appetite.

He's leaning over the parapet, my father, František Lenoch. Frank. The ear flaps on his lemon-yellow cap are tied under his chin to prevent the cap from flying in the wind. The brand new Rockports with cushiony soles he bought just for this trip give him an added inch in height. I suggested he ask for Bata at the shopping mall, a more European style. A sales clerk working on commission convinced him Rockports were more popular. For a man who went through what he did, he can sometimes be so, I don't know, naïve? Okay, he was young when he left. I can't suppress a sigh. He looks like a tourist in his own homeland.

"Any of this look familiar?"

"I only came once to Prague. I was with my Uncle Alfons."

"Has it changed much?"

"I don't remember everything being so gray and brown."

"What do you remember about your Uncle?"

"I've told you about him. He was the history professor at Prague University?"

Looking out over the sea of steeples and spires and chimney pots, I remember how my mysterious Great Uncle Alfons grew to hero status for me when, as a boy, I learned that he'd been executed by the Nazis. I pull out my Steno, thinking to take notes, realize it's too cold and windy for that. And besides, I get the feeling that if he knows the story is strictly off the record he'll talk more openly.

"He invited me to visit him in Prague to watch Masaryk's funeral procession. At that age I was very patriotic. I didn't understand what he wanted to warn me about."

"When was that?"

"September ... '37? I was fifteen, so, must have been."

"Did he encourage you to leave?"

"Yes and no. Let me tell you what happened. If you are still curious then you can ask your million questions." The night before the procession, my father begged his uncle to take him up to the castle, up to this very cathedral, St. Vitus, to view the casket and honor their hero. Masaryk had been president during most of their short-lived democracy and was enormously popular. The press was warning to expect a long line and they were not disappointed. By the time it was their turn to walk past, the casket had been closed. Pointing to the tricolor flag of the republic draped over the coffin, Alfons said, "Do not trust Beneš." That was the new president. Don't believe anything that traitor says tomorrow when he gives his speech.

"Did you think he was exaggerating the danger?"

"I thought he was being unpatriotic."

Alfons took my father the next day to join the procession. Frank can't remember if Beneš delivered his speech in Old Town Square or Wenceslas

Square, but he thinks it was Old Town Square, maybe even from the very balcony where the Communist takeover was announced eleven years later. The speech was quoted verbatim in the papers and my father committed it to memory and recalls bits of it to this day.

"Those were words you don't forget." My father looks off across Prague's vaunted spires as though he could still hear the joyful sound of the cheering multitudes. *I call you all without exception, from the left to the right, from the most remote hamlet to this capital city.* The crowd was quiet. Everyone expected this much. But he finished with a line that made everyone cheer like they had heard St. Peter's call to heaven.

"In English it translates, 'To the bequest which you placed in our hands, we shall remain faithful!' That's a famous quote from Hus. He was a patron saint for us. 'Faithful we shall remain!' '*Věrni zůstaneme!*' You should have been there. You should have heard it."

"What did your uncle think? Sounds like he might have been suspicious."

"That's when he finally admitted the real reason he invited me to Praha in the first place." Under a clear autumn sky, more than a million people—my father is obviously impressed by these astonishing numbers—lined the streets along the casket's route into Wenceslas Square. "It was so quiet you could hear the horses' hooves. A general on horseback rode ahead of foreign heads of state. That was exciting."

"What did he say? Why did he invite you?"

"He reminded me that I was his sister's only son. He advised me not to be here when the Nazis came. 'When you will come back,' he said, 'then you and young men of your generation will help us rebuild our freedom.' "

"How did you react?"

"I told him he was crazy. I told him there was no way I was ever going to leave." He laughs. "I had no idea how much influence he had with your grandmother."

But it's cold and I'm shivery so I ask if he'd mind if we leave the tower and head down into St. Vitus and talk out of the wind. He's fine with that.

It occurs to me, as we descend the narrow stairway, that what we more urgently need to talk about is Anezka. Saudek put me on the schedule for a kidney transplant at IKEM for Wednesday next week. Because I'm one of those rare lucky individuals with AB positive blood type, it's all but certain Anezka could be a donor provided she has at least four out of seven blood antigens favorable to mine. If indeed she is my half-sister, that's an added value. Live-donor organs from family have a significantly lower rejection rate post surgery. Anezka's blood has been drawn and is currently being put through the lab tests. Anezka is still in prison in Žamberk. Of course no one has found her cat at the orphanage. My father is probably right. It makes no sense to distract ourselves with a search for a cat that is surely already dead. Still, I have to know. I have to have something definite to tell Anezka. It would be too cruel to simply show up with a shrug, especially when I consider what I'm asking of her. Shame can be a powerful deterrent, I get that, and I sense that my father is making excuses to avoid having to see the place where his daughter was forced to grow up. If he wants to help me he'll have to understand that this is the right thing to do.

Before we finish our talk, my father wants me to see the wooden panels in the cathedral that depict Bílá Hora, the infamous battle of White Mountain. "This defeat began our shame," he says, showing me brown carved story panels. It's so dark in this vault I can't see the details, but I do remember reading about this bit of Czech infamy. Bílá Hora ended in 1620 with the foreign-born king and queen forgetting their own child, they were in such a hurry to flee. I remind him of this, goading him for a reaction. "Oh, I just think that makes a pretty good story," he says dismissively. Sensing I've touched a nerve, I decide to let it go, for now.

The cathedral's echoey stone interior is hardly warmer than outside. Now that I've started I can't seem to stop shivering so I ask if he'd mind continuing our talk back at the flat. We stroll down the hill and catch the trolley to Wenceslas Square and descend the escalator to the metro platform and catch the "C" line out to Chodov and I escape to my room for a nap.

―――――

OUR LAST TWO evenings have been devoted to revisiting our memories, which, I'm discovering, lurch and crash into one another like bumper cars that only rarely hum along peaceably in tandem.

This evening we put off talking until after dinner. Josef has joined us at Yveta's flat in Chodov and has turned out to be quite the cook. Tonight's menu includes celery root to clear the palate for garlic soup with floating sausages. The soup and sausages have too much sodium so I take nibbles and sips. After dinner, with Turkish coffee for Josef and my father, decaf tea with lemon for myself, we convene in the family room on the pine corner bench like three old bourgeoisie bachelors and nibble dumplings filled with plum compote—sweetened only with apples, no sugar—from the bounty of plums we harvested a few weeks ago out of that mossy old tree in Yveta's garden. To give us a chance to talk privately, Josef retreats to his room and watches reruns of *Dallas*.

An American calendar hung on the wall near our corner bench features a photo of a river cascading through a canyon somewhere in the American West. A diesel locomotive races alongside the river on tracks that would send it roaring right over the viewer. The photo looks familiar. I bet I saw it in *Life* or *Look Magazine* when I was a kid. The prospect of travel would have excited me even at that age.

After elevating my swollen ankles on pillows, I take a good look at my father. He looks wary. Not without reason. He has for a fact become frail through the chest. The wall heater has finally warmed the cozy knotty pine paneled room. He's down to his bleached undershirt. For the record, he does not think of himself as a contractor. He's a wannabe historian. He would prefer starched white collar shirts with a bowtie.

I ask him to finish telling me what happened to his uncle, my real concern being to understand why he left but others, like his uncle, stayed. We start with dates. On October 5, 1938, Beneš fled to London. A month and a half later, on November 21, 1938, my father set out for Prague with the contingent that included two younger sisters and his father and the Kacalek woman and part of her brood, and by December, 1938, they were on a ship for Ellis Island with Iowa as their destination. In March, 1939, Slovakia declared independence and placed itself under Nazi tutelage. Within twenty-four hours, the Wehrmacht strolled into Prague like they were on vacation. The Czech army had been disbanded back in October. There was no one to resist the invaders.

"Why was your Uncle Alfons shot?"

He chews through a toothpick and a splinter is caught between his teeth. I ask if I can bring him something, floss maybe? A glass of water, he says, but my ankles have stopped throbbing and he sees I'm pretty comfortable on the bench so he gets up himself and brings me a glass as well.

"My uncle believed the Allied powers would stop Hitler. But he also knew nothing would happen until a protest got reported in the international press."

Alfons and a cadre of dissidents gathered in Wenceslas Square, but only the local papers reported the incident. Accounts of protesters linking arms and singing *Kde domov muj*? "Where is My Home?" the Czech national anthem, did, however, attract the attention of the SS troops. Uncle Alfons and the others ran through the streets ripping route maps from the sides of the streetcars and throwing the hated signs—hated because they'd been translated into German—into the Vltava.

Two nights later, the Gestapo made an example of them. The press samizdats that found their way to Bohemie Town in Cedar Rapids reported that the Gestapo rounded up 1,200 students randomly from their dormitories that night and arrested them. Without trial, they were transferred by train in cattle cars to concentration camps, either to Terezín, near Prague, or farther to Buchenwald and Auschwitz. According to the papers, nine promoters of the protest, ratted out by students under torture, were shoved into the square and publicly shot. An additional twenty-two men, among them Uncle Alfons, and five women, fingered as organizers, were next paraded in front of an audience in Wenceslas Square that had been paid to hail the Führer. These additional "traitors" were similarly blindfolded and shot. The university was closed.

"I don't know if they knew they would die. But I do think they believed they would rather die than live like prisoners in their own country."

"You really admired your uncle, didn't you?"

"Very much. I wasn't cut out to be a farmer. I wanted to study history at the university like him."

"How did you hear about his death?"

"Your grandmother wrote care of my sisters in Cedar Rapids."

"Speaking of letters. You know I still have those letters Rosalye wrote? One was stolen by someone Jungmann paid to spy on me, but I still have the others. Any idea why Jungmann is so interested in having those letters?"

He gives me that silent toothpick regard, and I'm thinking that's all I'm going to get, but then he confides that he and Jungmann came from the two rival families in the valley. They were near in age, Jungmann a couple years older. Natural rivals, they fought for the attention of Rosalye. "She was the live-in maid in our house. At first I thought he was jealous."

"At first?"

"I have never talked to anyone about this."

I wait for him to go on.

"He turned up dead in the river. Drowned, they were saying. Pretty hard to believe that considering he was the best swimmer in the village, but that was Jungmann's story. Somehow he got away with it."

"What are you talking about? Who turned up dead?"

"Leoš Kacalek. He was Rosalye's younger half-brother …" He stops, rubs his temples, fiddles with a splintered toothpick.

"And? There's something you're not telling me …"

He shakes his head. "I should have said something. I should have told everyone what I saw. But Jungmann threatened me. I didn't say anything right away. Then it was too late. If I said anything later it would have made me look like I was trying to cover something up for myself."

"Whoa, whoa. Jungmann threatened you? With what?"

"He knew me pretty well. He knew I was ashamed of my father. We had our family name to protect. If I told anyone what I saw happen to Leoš, he said he'd tell everyone what my father was doing at the Kacalek household and that Leoš was my father's bastard. That threat probably didn't really stop me from talking. Everyone in the village already knew what my father was doing, I'm sure of that. What really got to me is I thought this trouble would make my father leave with Rosalye like he was always saying he would. I couldn't stand the thought of Rosalye going away with my father."

"Were you already … hanging out with Rosalye?"

He clicks his tongue. "*Kluci mají své sny*. Boys have silly dreams."

"Dreams?"

"I used to dream of marrying Rosalye and running away to Prague."

"She must have known you'd inherit the farm?"

"Sure. But my father already owned the farm. Why would she wait for me?"

"Never mind that he was married to your mother and had six kids."

He nods, refusing to look at me. "More. Two younger Kacelaks were probably his also. Including Leoš. Jungmann knew that. That's why he knew it would be easy to blame the poor kid's death on my father."

"Was your father involved in any way? I mean in the drowning?"

"No. No, he had some principles. He'd never stoop to that."

"When you guys left for Iowa, you knew Rosalye was pregnant, right?"

"We knew she was pregnant. Yes, we both knew that."

I wait for him to say more, but he doesn't.

We sip our water. The two boys downstairs are being noisy while Yveta gets them ready for bed. The common stairwell connects our upstairs flat to the downstairs. The top landing is closed off by a heavy drape. On the bottom landing a door sequesters their flat, but sound travels up so we share a muted version of their domestic hubbub. The sound of the boys' laughter reminds me of what a sad business this must have been for my father all those years ago.

"Your grandmother had other ideas about who was going to Iowa. So did Barbora Kacalka." His gaze roams over the photo of the train careening through a river canyon. When he talks again he chooses his words with care. "When we left, my mother was in good health. I thought my being gone was only temporary. I thought Rosalye would get kicked out of the house … my mother hated her … and she'd be sent back to live at the Kacalek farm. She would have her baby. Then I would come back."

"So you're saying you believed Anezka was—"

"I just don't know," he interrupts. "Only one person really knows. But then the Nazis marched in. Pretty soon it was impossible to get a ship back to Europe."

He chews his toothpick. The knotty-pine paneling is warm, the radiator gurgles. You can't miss the rat-a-tat-tat of the laugh-track from Josef's program down the hall, courtesy of satellite TV. The boys are quiet downstairs. Yveta is glum these days. Chemo is not fun. Dialysis won't be, either, I'm pretty sure.

"You ever write back to Rosalye?"

"*Ano*. Often. Maybe my letters were stolen by censors. Jungmann could have done that. All I know is her letters made it sound like she had not heard a single word from me. It was difficult."

"And you said what in your letters?"

"It was so long ago. I was so young. I probably bragged about my gymnastics tournaments. I probably told her I was angry. I probably blamed her for what she did with my father." He rubs his temples some more. "These are difficult memories."

We clear the table and leave everything in the sink for Josef to face in the morning, and I follow him in slippers, courtesy of Yveta—"no shoes allowed on inside"—down the corridor. There's much we still have to talk about, but he's tired.

The flat has three separate bedrooms, each adjacent and entered by a door off a long hall. The typical Soviet-era flat had no living room. Space was a premium, no tolerance for a room to show off nice crystal to guests. This flat once housed three families. Yveta had western renters in mind when she renovated but she still didn't catch the concept of comfy beds. Each of the three sleeping rooms has twin boxes like pedestals, each box covered by a thin mattress. Each room has a set of tall German windows that snap open with a view out back to the garden. Like he did last night, he throws on a jacket and strolls in Yveta's garden before bed. I watch from my darkened room, behind the curtain where he can't see me. Despite the night cold, he sits on that bench under the leaning, mossy old plum to let his thoughts settle. At moments like this, he seems a sad old man who was better off leaving the past in the past. Were it not for his old rival having arrested Anezka, and now me needing Anezka's kidney, I doubt very much he'd have come back here, if the pain I saw in his expression at the table is any indication. In the morning, you can be sure, he'll have a smile ready when he brings me my coffee. Yesterday morning, before we caught the metro line into Old Town, reflecting on a question I'd asked the night before, he told me he was very clear on one thing: *I did not want to leave. I left because I was told I had to.*

⁓✳⁓

THE NEXT MORNING, the call comes from Anezka's legal counsel. He has arranged clearance for us to visit her in the prison in Žamberk. She's being kept in a low security wing. Clearance was a formality. Anezka's legal counsel advises that we should nevertheless bring an envelope with plenty of cash. The plan is for Jungmann to join us at this meeting. A prison visiting room isn't exactly how I'd imagined this family reunion, but at least it's really happening.

The meeting at the prison is set for tomorrow. It's decided after a call to Milada—today is her day off in the rotation—that this afternoon we'll visit the farm in Písečná and my father can spend the night catching up with Bedřich and I'll stay in the comfort of the hotel in Žamberk and we'll plan our assault on Jungmann. That leaves one thread untucked. Rosalye. Milada calls Mr. Anton Zamečnik, her mighty mayor, to see if he can lure Rosalye to the farm to meet us.

Chapter Twenty-One

That Afternoon at the Farm

A T THE KACALEK farm someone is in the yard clucking and throwing grains to honking geese. A diesel tractor putt-putts off toward the fields; a gate clangs shut. Cows low plaintively to register their dissatisfaction at having been made to wait so long. On our side of the creek, the Lenoch farm is as quiet as a ghost town. No smoke curls up from the chimney.

It's a chilly fall afternoon with leaden skies. My father asked for time to collect himself before we enter the farmhouse where he grew up, the home he hasn't seen in more than half a century. Walking through the grove of birch by the creek, listening to the rustle of the dry yellow leaves, he recalls fond memories. Sleeping in the loft buried under mounds of downy comforters. The games they played with the chamber pot. In winter the contents would freeze. He, being oldest, owned the chore to thaw it by the stove and empty it each morning.

Milada went ahead to greet her father. They're waiting.

A limestone corridor connects the house to the stalls. The stone over the centuries has absorbed an aroma of animal funk and musty straw, an odor that remains sharp in the nose, though there have been no animals other than Bedřich's angora rabbits on this farm for nearly four years. My father looks around with a boyish grin. The funk from the stalls must be raising ghosts of forgotten pranks.

The room at the end of this corridor used to be the tack room. Rosalye stayed there when she worked here as the live-in maid. My father calls it the *blue* room. At the back of the house is a tiny chapel where his mother went nightly to pray. This part of the building has never been modernized so there's no light switch in the corridor. I fish my keychain out of my daypack and unclip the LED light and shine it on my father. That eager look has stiffened into his default toothpick chewing long-distance stare. Something about the blue room seems to be having this sobering effect.

Josef has been sent to help Mr. Zamečnik find Rosalye. She was here earlier but then she panicked at the prospect of facing my father after all these years and fled.

Saloon-style swinging wooden doors close off the blue room. "Your grandmother paid a carpenter to carve those doors. I always thought they were beautiful. She wanted Rosalye to have her privacy respected."

"By you?" I suggest playfully.

"Your grandfather."

He takes the light from me and examines the figurines carved on the doors. On the right side, he points out Libuše, the princess in Czech origin tales. She floats like a fairy on a breeze. Stars circle her crown. For lack of a male heir, Libuše took over the kingdom. To silence her critics, she married a plowman named Přemysl, an alliance that turned out to be her Trojan horse.

Instead of carving the unfaithful and treacherous Přemysl on the left door, my grandmother paid the carpenter to mate Libuše with Bořivoj, the ninth-century prince who was the first Czech ruler to convert to Christianity. Midget-sized Bořivoj wears a pointy crown, a robe, and a beard. The real Bořivoj died at the ripe old age of thirty-five.

"A perfect love story. Bořivoj the pious dies young. Libuše prevails."

"Knowing my mother, she had a lesson in mind."

I suggest we take a look in. His mouth hangs half open in anticipation, as though he were once again that sixteen-year-old boy. The first thing you notice is the chill and the stench of stale cigarettes and the medicinal odor of booze. A black heat pipe, roughly six inches in diameter, protrudes through the wall like a cannon barrel. It must draw heat off the stove in the main house. The pipe is cold. The plaster walls and ceiling have been washed in a cobalt blue. *Blue as twilight or blue as dawn? Guess it depends on your mood.*

"Someone sleep here last night?" I nod to the disheveled duvet slopping over a cot pushed against one wall.

A jar lid on the stone floor next to the cot is filled with butts from cigarettes that are brown and longer than ordinary cigarettes and look imported and expensive. The filters are smooched with maroon lipstick. Under the corner of the duvet I find a bottle, cap missing. Slivovice. Glistening plums on the label. Half-liter. Empty. Judging by the smell, whoever drank this drank it not that long ago.

"Someone in your old family a heavy drinker?"

"Your grandmother never would have tolerated this."

No toothpick this time. His narrow face is solemn. When my mother died, he was rather matter-of-fact about everything. Of course he'd had plenty of time to prepare. This is different. He doesn't know what to expect from Rosalye. "Think of today," I say, attempting to reassure him, "as a rehearsal for tomorrow. Enjoy this. It's your old home."

―ᴗ‍ᴗ―

MASSIVE SMOKE-CURED WOODEN beams give the great room the feeling of a lodge when you first walk in. The impression fades immediately when you look at the details, at the legacy of decades of communist degradation. Judging by my father's crestfallen look, the fall must have been precipitous. What was he expecting to find? Obviously not cheap pasteboard cabinets. Not cupboard doors strapped on with string. Not cracked floor linoleum patched with sheet metal. Still, this was his home. For one frozen moment, that long stare disappears, and if I'm not mistaken—admittedly it's hard for me to see details—he's got tears in his eyes.

Milada has posted herself by the far window. On the lookout for Anton Zamečnik, who is supposed to deliver Rosalye. The view through the double-window—the walls are as thick as an arm is long—is distorted. Everything vertical looks slanted and the distance is foreshortened. The fields looking west butt flush against a careening Zampach Hill, site of the robber baron's castle that was dismantled by my grandmother's family to build the church. The Quonset hut dairy built by the SS cooperative appears flattened between them. To the right is that unpaved farm road bordered by the chestnuts that were dropping their pods the last time I was here. At the start of that road is the blackened skeleton of Jungmann's inn. The pond, I noticed on our drive in, has been refilled in time for the winter freeze to provide skating for fledgling hockey stars.

A bare bulb, lacking any sort of lamp shade, dangles over a table planted on a square of sheet metal floor beside the kitchen area, which occupies the corner to the right as you enter. Bedřich is sitting at the table, waiting impatiently. Obviously he's been coached by Milada to give us a moment before the onslaught begins. Marie, his former housekeeper-cum-common-law wife, is on a sleigh bed the size of four full-sized beds pushed together over against the wall near Milada. Marie's gout-swollen leg is propped on a stack of pillows. She apologizes for not getting up.

The chill is working its way down into my bones. I ask my father if he remembers the house being cold like this. He looks admiringly at the mammoth stove. It's a beauty, with scenes of farm and forest on glistening tiles, albeit a cold beauty. The sweet aroma of something baked hangs tantalizingly in the air. One of the ovens must have been lit earlier.

"Welcome, welcome." Bedřich can't take the suspense any longer. He stands, thrusts shoulders back military style, extends a hand to my father, gives my father's hand two vigorous pumps, clasps his shoulder. Today Bedřich is wearing a clean brown corduroy jacket with elbow patches and freshly pressed chinos. His sparse snowy hair is slicked back. He grins at my father, unashamedly exposing that one brown tooth in a mouth full of empty gums. My father accepts the handshake as though he were a visiting dignitary who expects fawning.

"Someone sleep in the blue room last night?" I join them at the table.

Bedřich says defensively, "Where she is supposed to sleep?"

As we'd surmised, Anezka's mother had been staying off and on with Halbrstat, but with Anezka's arrest something flipped Jungmann's on-switch. He's been intimidating everyone, so Rosalye has been moving around, occasionally spending the night here at the farm. Those imported cigarettes are hers, the Slivovice hers. My father registers this with a knowing click of the tongue.

I feel like heaving one of Bedřich's vexed sighs. A shadow crosses the windows facing the fields. Storm on its way. Milada leans over the sleigh bed, whispers something to Marie.

"*Cítíte se příjemně?*" Marie is asking my father if he feels comfortable. In the kitchen area, a platter of poppy seed pastries, curved like a horseshoe, is giving off that sweet aroma. "Coffee will be soon." She'd earlier plugged a heating rod into a wall outlet and placed the coil into a pot of water to bring it to a boil. When the grounds settle we'll have Turkish coffee.

Bedřich delivers the platter to the table and shovels wedges onto plates.

"*Děkuji.*" I wipe crumbs from my lips. Marie's *rohlíky* are neither too buttery nor too sweet. A splurge, for sure, but anticipating something like this I compensated with my shot this morning. "Delicious. Tell Marie we appreciate the trouble she went to."

Under the harsh light of the naked bulb, my father looks his age and then some. His face is thinner, bonier than I remember. Maybe worry has kept him awake too many nights. In the soft light filtered through the muslin curtains, Marie's plump beaming face lends her the look of a child perpetually waiting for Christmas. This is how I'd always pictured my grandmother. It occurs to me I've never actually seen her in a photo.

"You have any pictures of my grandmother?" I ask Bedřich.

He waves away my concern. Sure, of course, by and by. Noticing that I'm eating sparingly, Marie swivels off the bed and straps on a metal cane. A ring clamps her left arm above the elbow. Her swollen left foot and ankle are wrapped in an ACE Bandage. Wincing with every step, she limps to the table.

"*Prosím.*" She cuts a second generous slice of the pastry, glowering at Bedřich for his bad manners. Marie curses her "new Russian stove," which was purchased in 1950 when goods from the east were subsidized. The stove has two large ovens and several smaller chambers. A box holds sticks the thickness of my wrist, the fuel they gather from the woods.

"What's wrong with the oven?"

"It heats unevenly," my father translates.

Bedřich dismisses it as nonsense. She has her "new" stove, what more does she want?

The Turkish coffee is ready. Milada abandons her post by the window and delivers the coffee on porcelain saucers and dumps four lumps of sugar into her *tata*'s coffee and gives him a peck to sue for peace. He ignores the peck. He watches my father to see how he's reacting. Life behind the Iron Curtain has left scars. I have no doubt he'll tell us all about it, and I'll take plenty of notes in my Steno, but lodged behind that overweening grin has to be the worry that this farm by rights belongs to my father. It was my father who snuggled into that sleigh bed to stay warm while the bedpan he'd brought down from the loft simmered on the stove to thaw and the smell of cow piss wafted in from the stalls, and he had to have wondered why the smell of his father was not here, why he was sharing his funk with the Kacalek woman across the creek, or was life simply awash in funk, was that it? Was funk life itself?

Talk requires lubrication. Bedřich sends Marie to a back storeroom to fetch liquor. Before Rosalye arrives and upsets everything and everyone, Bedřich wants us to hear his version of what happened.

~×~

OVER THE NEXT few minutes, we nibble and Bedřich complains about the fall weather turning cold early. If it gets much colder we could get our first snow tonight.

"Everyone wanted to escape to America. Be cowboy," Bedřich says with that toothless grin that's so hard to read. He reaches into his corduroy jacket and pulls out a black ledger book the size of a weekly pocket planner. "Someone had to stay home." He shows my father his little black book. "Here. Everything they took from me. It's written." Incredible. He recorded every last scintilla of milk and meat and eggs he was ever forced to hand over to the collective, everything, that is, produced on my father's farm over a ten-year period.

"*Tata, tata, tata.*" Milada smoothes down his staticky white hair. "We don't want to hear this old story. Where is Rosalye? We are still waiting for her."

"She is free. She will come when she want. Sit down."

Marie hobbles back in balancing a tray with two pint glasses of Czechvar *pivo* and three shot glasses and a bottle of Slivovice. The purple plums on the label are moist with dew. Milada gives me a stern look that says be moderate, don't keep pace with her father.

"*Na zdraví!*" Bedřich pours a round of brandy and raises his shot glass.

"*Pravda vítězí!*" I rejoin. My father corrects my broad-voweled pronunciation. He sips the pivo but declines the shot. "The truth will win out."

Bedřich and I down shots. Marie hobbles back to the pantry to fetch food.

"Ten years after you left," Bedřich says, eyes already shiny from the brandy, "KSČ start reforms." They got rid of, for example, any coins commemorating Masaryk. Thuggish men in cheap suits began to show up even in villages as small as Pisečná. Anyone obviously "bourgeois," and that included prosperous land owners, went to prison work camps for re-education if they didn't have good enough *protekcé*.

This is a delicate subject, but I have to ask. I open my Steno and ready my pen. "In 1968 you were sent to prison, but before that they left you alone?"

"My father, he buy farm from your grandmother. But they leave him alone because I have *protekcé* with Jungmann."

"Show us what they took," my father says, changing the topic, knowing I am certain to ask what Jungmann's interest was in helping this farm.

After glowering over his shoulder at his doubting daughter, Bedřich eagerly reads the ledger's entries. In the ten years between 1948 and 1957—in 1957, following the Hungarian uprising, there was a crackdown that changed everything—he handed over: twelve thousand liters of milk, six thousand kilos of potatoes, one thousand six hundred kilos of beef, one thousand three-hundred kilos of pork. The egg count was spotty and highly variable. He scrunches up his forehead, estimates two thousand a year. So, roughly twenty thousand eggs.

"They take, but they pay nothing! How I should feed my own family?"

"It was same for everyone, *tata*." Milada ruffles his silvery hair to calm him down. "I was too young. I don't remember much from that time."

"Winter of 1957-58 was worst ever. If farmer still believed in workers' revolution he put his tongue behind his teeth." They were forced to deliver to the co-op every liter of milk. Every kilo of pork and beef. Every egg. Most gave up the farm and went to work for the co-op rather than face starvation. He's looking at my father now. "Josef Lenoch was not so crazy after all."

"I remember that winter. Mother was very sick." Milada pulls her father's head to her chest and rocks him like a baby.

The rain's sudden pelting halts our conversation. Milada distributes pots under numerous leaks along the west wall where the building is apparently not covered by the loft. We have to talk loudly to hear over the symphony of plonking.

"To surrender!" He pours a second round of shots. The plum brandy burns less this time. Milada and my father both hurl a warning look my way. My kidneys can't take it, my blood sugar will soar, I know, but I have this fatalistic attitude that caution just doesn't matter today or tomorrow. I'm quickly getting drunk and I feel incredibly liberated and I'm going with it.

Marie thumps back in with a cutting board and a length of *klobása* cut into thin slices and offers it around. Chores done, she settles in for a nap over on the sleigh bed.

"So, Bedřich. How did you manage to hang onto the farm?" My father apologizes for my rudeness.

"Jungmann. Who else? You have no idea. People disappearing. Neighbors spying on neighbors. You want to keep *klobása* in cellar, you will be denounced as enemy of people and you go in prison."

"Jungmann must have wanted collateral?" When he says nothing, I add, "It wasn't out of the goodness of his heart."

Bedřich fixes my father with a pleading look. "We knew one day such madness would end. It had to end." He grins. "Look. Here we are."

My father refuses to comment. That happened a long time ago. He prefers a journey into his memories. "My mother said her rosary every night before bed in the chapel. She hung her rosary from the crucifix on the wall. The beads were lavender crystal. Every Palm Sunday she put dried palm fronds behind the crucifix. Those fronds stayed there till the next Palm Sunday."

Bedřich admits that he really only knew my grandmother during the two years he and his father lived here before she died, and she was sick for most of that time.

"I don't get it," says my father. "She was healthy as a bull when I left."

Bedřich watches my father as though expecting acid to drip cuttingly from his lips. "*Tvůj otec věřil v předmanželský celibát. Ano?*" He is claiming that he remembers my father, back when they were boys, being as Catholic as his mother. His mother believed in celibacy before marriage. "But then there was Rosalye." He pours himself a third shot of brandy. I cover my shot glass.

"Help me understand this. Her husband is sleeping with Kacalka at the farm next door. So what does my grandmother do? She takes in Kacalka's beautiful daughter and keeps her like a consolation prize?" In a clearer mind I'd never be so forward, but it needed to be said and I'm glad I said it.

"You don't know what it was like," Milada says.

"Of course I don't know what it was like," I say loudly over the rain's plonking. "But I do know what it was like to grow up with a father whose heart was always somewhere else."

My father refuses that bait. "What happened to my mother?"

"Children, children." Bedřich lifts his palms like a pontiff. "*Prosím.* Please."

I push up from the table. The vast room begins to swing. I clutch the table to catch my balance. "Please excuse me. I think I'll go lie down until Rosalye gets here."

My father gives me a worried look. Milada guides me out into the corridor and through the saloon doors. In the blue room she smoothes the duvet on the cot. The rain out here is a muffled thrumming, a lullaby. She pricks my thumb. Blood sugar over four hundred. *Can't get away with anything.* She gives me a shot of fast acting. For ten minutes I lie on the cot under a duvet that smells sourly of alcohol sweat. I keep my eyes closed. The room spins and spins. She takes her turn at ranting. No more alcohol. Let your father and my father settle their own business. We need everyone cooperating tomorrow. No word yet on the blood proteins. We might know as soon as tomorrow. Meanwhile, I need to be calm.

"I need to find Anezka's cat," I say convinced the reasoning behind this is self-evident. "We have to find her before we go to the prison tomorrow."

She looks at me like I'm seriously demented. I hear her telling me reassuring things. No, the cat, I repeat. Nothing matters until we find the cat. With her cool hand on my forehead, I pass out.

Chapter Twenty-Two

Later that Afternoon at the Farm:
Rosalye Shows Up

THE OIL CLOTH taped over the window nearest the table keeps out drafts, but plunges the room's midsection into a cellar gloom. In that middle is a simple wooden table covered by a utilitarian oil cloth and surrounded by rickety, glued-together ladder-back chairs. Around that is open space interrupted by stout posts and stacks of boxed sundries. The planked floor, radiating cold, is patched with sheet metal. A bench that looks like a church pew painted red abuts that mammoth sleigh bed. All of this is perfumed with essence of fermented cabbage and wood smoke. The breath of a lived-in home. My father looks up at my entrance, his eyes worrying. He is still sitting in the unflattering glare of that bulb dangling over the table. His elongated face looks gaunt.

"I have a request," I say. Our guest, a tall lean figure sipping coffee in the kitchen area, arrived while I was napping in the blue room. "We all drive over to the orphanage and once and for all find Anezka's cat." They look at me like they never heard of the cat.

A smoke-hoarsened voice replies, "Do not worry for this child. Child is ..." She searches for a word. My father translates. "Taken care to. Seen to."

"Seen to?"

Anezka's mother steps into the light. She is taller than her daughter, even a bit taller than my father, her waist-length white hair gathered behind her in a thick baguette ponytail. Rosalye's lank figure is draped in black silk, loose pants, a billowy top with embroidered seams bearing a pattern from the village. She's smoking one of those long brown imported cigarettes.

"You must be Charles." She squints through the smoke, scrutinizing me. "You are much taller than your father. More handsome, too. He's gotten too thin." Her angular face has an exquisite bone definition that I don't recall seeing in her daughter's saucer face. Her mouth especially fascinates me. If ever there were such a thing as an aristocratic mouth it's hers. Her thin lips tilt down in one corner, in the manner of one perpetually bored by the inevitability that she will get her way. Cherry red lipstick slops over the boundaries of those lips. Drinking brandy? Her sweat reeks of it, but her voice is steady.

"How long you are diabetic?" Rosalye looks at me with what I take to be an expression of sympathy. With her, sympathy could be merely pity.

"Seventeen years. Since law school."

"Milada and your father have told to me you wish for kidney from Anezka? This is true?" Her aristocratic lips press down with bemused disgust. "Maybe she will finally do one thing useful in her life."

"I intend to ask her. Tomorrow, when we visit."

"You think she had hard life?" She coughs. A chronic smoker.

"Growing up in an orphanage—"

"You are young. You are American. What would you know?" One unusually cold January morning, Rosalye tells us, one of the "girls" at the inn came running in from the yard, where she was collecting eggs, screaming that her fingers were turning blue. "She had diabetes. She had been sent to us by her mother. Her name was Martina. Her father was German. He had been killed in purge of German men. Her mother thought she'd be safe with us." To save her hands from frostbite, three fingers had to be amputated to the knuckle joint. Disfigured, she was no longer acceptable to the foreign clients. They wanted her eliminated when they found out her father was German. Rosalye refused. "I took care to my girls."

Bedřich is gazing open-mouthed at Rosalye as though she were minor royalty. Marie is napping over on the sleigh bed. The rain's plonking has slackened.

"When did my mother get sick?" my long-faced father asks.

"A year after you leave her stomach blow up like balloon." Bedřich looks at Rosalye, Rosalye looks at Bedřich. One of them has to tell this story. "Little Anezka called Lenochova *babi*. It was very sweet."

Rosalye snorts. "She didn't know Lenochova was so ..." They search for a word and come up with "cruel." My father scarcely flinches.

How can I say this diplomatically? "You were very very young. Were you even sixteen when Anezka was born?" Rosalye shakes her head all but imperceptibly. "My aunts in Cedar Rapids once told me they believe you poisoned Lenochova. Rat poison? I always assumed that was just a crazy story."

Milada interrupts her pacing. "It was probably stomach cancer."

"It was pillow." Peeling away that aristocratic dignity as though it were a mask, Rosalye seethes with righteous anger, the kind only a self-absorbed teen would display without irony. On the loose-skinned face of a seventy-one-year-old woman, this naked anger looks demented.

A few months after Anezka's first birthday, Bedřich continues undaunted, my grandmother's condition worsened. At her own request, she was given the cot in the blue room. "She demanded to keep child with her. She loved little Anezka."

"Where did *she* go, meanwhile?" I nod to Rosalye.

"There was too much work." He looks at my father. "After you have left, my father and I move into here. We give to Rosalye small house."

This proves too much for my father. "My mother should never have let you stay."

"Pride did not stop you from visiting my cot."

Bedřich waits for the two of them to stop bickering then he continues his story. Lenochova frequently woke at night with that terrible pain in her stomach. Bedřich indicates the sleigh bed behind him. "I slept there, but I hear cries through vent. She wake up little Anezka and then both of them wail like banshees. What could we do? Put in stalls? Cows will upset and milk will spoil." He laughs at his own joke.

One night in late summer, five months after Anezka's first birthday, he woke hearing Rosalye bang into the corridor from the wing house. This was not unusual. It was Rosalye's routine to come in after the inn where she worked the late shift for Jungmann closed, to check on Anezka and to deliver a dose of Lenochova's "medicine," corn rum from the inn. Rum numbed the pain long enough to allow Lenochova to sleep. Though he had to be up in a few hours to milk the cows, Bedřich magnanimously let the others sleep and went to the blue room to check on things.

"If this was the routine," I say, "what woke you?" Rosalye watches my father chew toothpicks.

"Little Anezka crying so hard wake me up. But then I hear voice say kind words. Okay, I thought. So I go back in bed." When Bedřich took breakfast to Lenochova later that morning, after finishing the milking chores, he was surprised to find her still asleep on the cot and the child gone. "I touched Lenochova hand. It was so cold."

"She was only forty-two." My father looks at me. "Your age."

"We ask you, give to us baby. Anezka will be raised Lenoch."

Rosalye stubs out her cigarette on a post but is too proper to drop the butt on the floor and instead places it in an empty pack in a pocket. "Lenochova was cold-hearted bitch. She only wished that I will be punished."

"What did you expect?" My father has chewed through toothpick after toothpick. He gathers the slivers in a pile that looks like a game of pick-up-sticks.

"You want to know what really happen?"

My father passes a hand over his face. He wants to hear what happened to his mother but he doesn't want to have to hear it from Rosalye.

"*Tata*, say what you have heard. They have right to know."

Bedřich looks from me to my father to Rosalye, taps the table with his shot glass, gulps down another shot—his fourth, at least the fourth that I've counted. Eyes shining, he says, "Is not like I have said. I did not go straight back to bed."

Rosalye says to my father, "I believed you went to Iowa because you are so angry with me. No, she told to me. He loves you. I could not allow it."

"Tell to them, *tata*," Milada says. "Tell to them what you saw that night."

Rosalye offers my father a look that is part sympathy, part warning. "She say to me pain is too much." Lenochova offered a deal. The Lenochs raise the child respectably and Rosalye goes away to live at Jungmann's inn. In return, they pay Rosalye a monthly stipend so that one day she could have a dowry and properly marry. "I laughed to her face. You will never take my baby. Never, you old witch."

Rosalye lights up another imported cigarette, leans over the table. My father turns his face away from her smoke. "She said, if you will not leave, then make yourself useful. I cannot have this pain. Put pillow to my face."

She touches my father's shoulder to make certain he is listening. "Your type, she said to me. Your type always wants what they do not deserve. She said she told you you must go away because I am sleeping with your father."

"She had her suspicions," my father says. "So did I."

Rosalye says to a chagrined Bedřich, "And you. Peeping on me. That is why Lenochova put herself in blue room and move me out."

"Was it true?" My stoic father in his old house with its patchings is begging from the woman who was once the maid. "Were you sleeping with my father?"

Mustering an indignation that sounds rehearsed, Rosalye says, "Isn't it late to asking this now?"

"I don't know that I would trust your answer anyway."

"Your only good reason was your mother. You were her little puppy. She could tell you anything and you believed."

"Jungmann wanted me to leave. I bet he never told you why."

"Ach, he know nothing."

"He ever say anything about Leoš?"

"Why do you speak about my brother?"

"That's what I thought. Jungmann never told you what really happened."

She eyes my father through her smoke and frowns and grows quiet.

"I saw. I saw them. Your brother and Jungmann."

"Why you didn't help Leoš? You know, he looked to you with high regard."

"I was angry. Even you, too. You and my father. But it wasn't Leoš's fault. That poor kid. Now I'm so ashamed."

Milada is streaming translations for me. My father is speaking Czech. He's forgotten I'm here.

I stand up, nauseous from the brandy and the endless uncertainty. "Tomorrow we're going to the prison to see Anezka. Is she my sister or isn't she?"

"*Já jsem jeho noční můra,*" Rosalye says quixotically.

Milada, before translating, looks at me a good while. "She is saying she could be your father's nightmare."

Rosalye announces that she will not be joining us tomorrow at the prison after all. She wants nothing further to do with that "ungrateful child."

Milada, the fixer, tenders a plan of action. I will catch the bus to Žamberk where she's booked a room for me at the hotel. My father will stay the night here. She'll join me later. Meanwhile, her mayor friend, Mr. Anton Zamečnik, is making progress on his human rights case. He has found a witness willing to speak to the court. They have documentary evidence. Enough to compel Jungmann to cooperate. Bedřich reacts to this news by leaving the table and going off to stare out the window looking west toward the fields. "Don't worry about him," Milada says.

"*Nepůjdu do toho vězení zítra, aniž by věděl o osudu kočka o Anežka.*" Milada is translating for Rosalye my rash declaration that I would refuse to go to the prison tomorrow without first knowing the fate of Anezka's cat. Rosalye haughtily says that I should go to the orphanage and see for myself since I don't wish to take her word. Milada jokingly adds, "Unless you will be too busy with your boopsy clerk at hotel?"

"That's not funny," I say, "considering my 'boopsy' was one of Anezka's children." Milada apologizes.

Nothing more is said. We leave.

Outside has that green freshness that follows a hard rain. Wanting to clear my head in the crisp air, I refuse Milada's offer of a ride and instead walk back under the dripping canopy of defoliated chestnuts to the bus stop near the skeleton of Jungmann's inn. The poisoned mud hole is now a pond. Its banks are covered with black plastic sheeting. After the spring thaw new plantings will sprout. The river is running clear under its many little footbridges. As I was leaving Milada gave me a funny look and said, "Chico, I know you are worried, but have faith. Tomorrow Jungmann will be forced to cooperate. Anezka will cooperate. Soon all will be well." This seemed optimistic for her, which led me of course to assume she believed the opposite, which of course led me to worry even more. But then, I thought—as I waited for the bus and smelled the rain-washed air and looked back at a bricolaged village, battened down for the approaching winter—maybe here is where my journey ends. I can languish on dialysis here as well as anywhere, yes?

Chapter Twenty-Three

Later that Night at the Hotel

MY "BOOPSY" DANA is not at reception. Her baguette ponytail friend offers me the key to 201, the same upstairs corner room I had a couple of weeks ago overlooking the square. In the Landa painting, the exalted Madonna thrusts her arms outward as though she were Christ hung on the cross. Against that backdrop of chalky snow clouds you have to look closely to notice the slender olive branch. Madonna wields it like a baton, like a conductor gentling an orchestra overstuffed on *Sturm und Drang*. I should be napping, but first, I decide, I've got some *Sturm und Drang* of my own to conduct.

I write Dana a note: *What happened to my letters? Does it even matter now? My father is here. But, she took advantage of my trust.*

Back down in the lobby, I surprise Dana behind the counter. *Ear piercings, nose stud, black hair shimmering like the coat of a foal. How young she is.* I have to summon the indignation I felt while writing the note, indignation that had been simmering like a sauce kept warm just for this moment but now feels stale.

She asks in her German English idiolect whether I read her note.

"Note?"

"I put in your packet."

"Look, Dana, how much did Jungmann pay you to steal my letters?"

"*Was! Sind Sie total verrückt?*"

"You're calling *me* crazy?"

"Okay, I take your stupid letters," she says, defiant as ever. "But you think I give love letters to sadistic old bugger?"

"Yes, I do. Why else would you have taken them?"

"*Liebe, du dumme Kerl.*" She reaches across the counter and punches me in the heart region of my chest.

"Love? What are you talking about?"

"He say these are his love letters." When I shake my head disgustedly, she admits that he promised to take her on holiday to Munich, all expenses paid.

"And to think I fucking trusted you."

"Fucking fucking fucking. Nice talk."

"Sorry, you're right. No need for that."

With tears welling in her eyes, she says, "Anezka is mother to me. Now she is in jail. It is terrible what I have done. Please can you forgive? How I can repay?"

"You should have thought of her before you got greedy."

"Please. Allow me to help. *Sie werden schon sehen.*"

Stealing the letters probably made no difference. Regardless of what he hoped to learn from Rosalye, he'd have arrested Anezka with or without the letters. Still, a contrite Dana could be useful. "There is something you could do."

"*Prosim.* I will do anything for her."

"Try to find out what deal Jungmann is going to offer us tomorrow. We don't have much to go on. Find out tonight if you can."

She promises to devote her evening to this "mission." I smile, thinking of how she shamed the Germans at the shelter with her naked dance. If anyone can help us it will be Dana. My lawyerly instincts tell me that this time her loyalty will be to our cause.

Back upstairs in my room, curious, I open the armoire and remove from my travel bag the manila folder I never bothered to get rid of. This time I thoroughly search inside. *To je ono.* There it is, a folded note just like she said, penciled crudely on the back of a receipt. Dana writes: "*Sie sind ein guter Mensch.*" You are a fine man. This is followed by lines in English that she must have labored over: "I hope you will have joy when you meet your sister. She is beautiful woman. Please say her love from me."

I cross to the French doors and peer out. The lights shimmer around the *petite palaise* enclosing the square. The remaining dry leaves of the lindens and chestnuts in the park glisten from the earlier downpour like stars from a faraway galaxy. Why has my father come back here, really? To face Rosalye's humiliation? To own up to whatever happened to Leoš, Rosalye's younger brother who drowned? To apologize to his daughter, if indeed she is his daughter? Wasn't she better off believing that her father had been shot down over France? Ah, Anezka. If I could do one thing for you. It might be too late for the cat, but the orphanage could still be yours.

⋅⋇⋅

A RAPID KNOCK AT the door wakes me from my nap. Assuming it's Dana with something urgent to report, I call out groggily, "Come in, come in."

But it's Milada. "Whom you are expecting?"

Inside—I left the door unlocked—she hesitates rather than approach the bed. She's changed. Short leather jacket. Skinny jeans. Platform heels. Pretty, in that hard, Eastern European way. It's the same outfit she wore in the photo from the *Herald* that I keep in my passport. *She now knows I carry that photo.*

"You must have a date with Mr. Anton. Don't forget, after we eat, you said you'd drive me to the orphanage."

"Cat from Anezka is not going anywhere."

Let her squirm a little. "It's the right thing to do." She remains by the door, looking at me sadly or wistfully, hard to be sure which. I mention confronting Dana. "Don't give me that look. Dana felt bad. She loves Anezka."

"Have you make sex with your boopsy?" Milada hoists imaginary breasts. "She is va-voomy. You are American. She will believe you have money. Why not."

"Isn't it a little disingenuous for you to be asking me that?"

"May we talk?" She motions toward the other bed. "We can talk there?"

She's indicating the undisturbed bed nearest the French doors and balcony. I had chosen the most interior bed in order to be away from the cold, but I switch over and tuck my bare legs under the downy comforter and pat the bed beside me.

"Is good to see your father here? What he think of his home now?"

"Tell your father he doesn't need to try so hard to impress him."

"He is only happy to have someone ear to stab."

"Bend. Ear to bend. What do you think will happen tomorrow?"

She kicks off her pumps and stretches out beside me. The radiator pings under the window beside the French doors. Heat coming on.

"You will ask Anezka to give to you kidney." She adds, "No pancreas. You must take pancreas from cadaver."

"The University Medical Center just started doing pancreas-only transplants three years ago. There's a shorter line for a pancreas only."

"Tomorrow I expect to hear blood results from lab. I tell to them they must phone to Anton. His phone is good."

"Do we have to involve him?"

"I am Czech. You are not. I know how things are done."

This might be the worst possible time to bring this up, but I've hardly seen Milada since returning with my father and I have to settle this. "I have to ask you something. Please don't be offended. Promise you won't be?"

"No I do not make promise."

"Okay, but be honest with me. Are you sleeping with Mr. Anton?"

"*Jakým právem mě soudíš? Kdo si myslíš, že jsi?* Who give you right to judge?"

Dark shells ring her eyes. She hasn't been sleeping well. She takes both of my hands in a firm grip. "I want you to know this. I have fallen in love with you that day by river. This has not changed. But we cannot be together."

She slips off the bed and switches off the light in the room. Standing beside the French doors, her back to me, facing the balcony and the galaxy of lights from the square, she unbuttons her tight jeans, wriggles, slides them down over her hips, kicks them off. Silhouetted, she looks small and vulnerable.

"If your dignity must know, *ne*, I am not sleeping with Anton." Still facing the balcony, she tugs off her underpants. Her parted thighs are long and shapely and sinewy with athletic cord-like muscles. Dropping her leather jacket unceremoniously but keeping her turtleneck blouse on, avoiding my look of surprise, she slides under the comforter and touches my cheek with her warm hand. I'd stripped to my thermal shirt and boxers. She smells of soap and baked eggplant. Her hair is coarse from the cheap dye she applies herself.

"I worry your father is disappointed. My father has no money for make repairs. Since my husband take Russian loan I cannot go to bank."

"I thought you said your father doesn't care."

"*Ano*, he say he don't care. But he have dignity, too."

"My father could help. It'd do him good. He's been in a rut every since my mother died. This is the first time he's gone anywhere. He doesn't take vacations."

Without explaining what she's up to, Milada leans over and pulls something crinkly from the pocket of her leather jacket. Not likely a condom. She knows I had a vasectomy, a unilateral decision I made when I learned I couldn't count on seeing many days past my next birthday. *That unilateral move accelerated the march to divorce.* She places a Snickers bar on the bed between pillows. Smiles, pats my cheek again, toying with me. "Let us nap. I just want to hold you. Is okay? You are not still angry with me because I send you away?" We stretch out and she folds like an "S" against my abdomen and bent thighs. Drifting into that calm before sleep, feeling her warm bottom against my edematous belly, it occurs to me that there is a lot that can go wrong tomorrow, and probably will. Better savor this.

⁓⋆⁓

A KNOCK ON THE door? Who could that be? I tug on jeans and check.

"*Ich habe für dich ein Geschenk.*" Dana is holding a gift behind her back. How long have we been sleeping? "You found Jungmann?"

She ignores my question. "I wish to say I am sorry for stealing letters."

The amber vase she shows me, if I'm not mistaken, is the very amber vase the clerk refused to sell me at that shop in Letohrad.

"I remember you say about this glass. I send my friend to shop."

"*Děkuji.* That's really sweet. How much do I owe you?"

"*Ne, ne.* You will please forgive. And tomorrow, when you visit prison, you will please say my love to Babi."

"Babi? You call her Babi?"

"She like us to call her Babi."

"*Babi* is what she called my grandmother."

"There you are."

"I'm sure she'd love to see you. Did you track down Jungmann?"

She gives that customary little hop and her breasts heave and she says, "I will keep him happy. He will talk. I will report tomorrow morning."

With that she turns and is gone. The amber vase, solid but for a narrow hollow, weighs more than you'd expect, as much as a sizeable cat. Quietly, trying not to wake Milada, I place the vase on the sill above the pinging radiator. The vibration sets off a slight wobble. The light from the square casts through the vase a reflection suffused with voluptuous colors ranging from carrot orange to tea to copper to verdigris to slate blue. It's a stunning thing to see and leads me to wonder what color really was that bowl on my father's desk in the basement? The color that comes to mind is butterscotch. In my child's eye that amber bowl was butterscotch. Butterscotch was the color of my childhood. Rich and sweet. I should forgive my father.

"Your boopsy bring this to you?"

I've managed to wake Milada. "She felt bad about what happened. Remember I asked you to go with me to that shop in Letohrad but you said there wasn't time?" I dive into the colors pooled on the sill, down into my father's basement, down to the butterscotch bowl, down to the stacks of quarters, to the cot where I rubbed his feet. How utterly utterly lonely he must have been when he learned his mother was ill and he couldn't go back and then Anezka was sent away to the orphanage, and he couldn't go back, and then he had us, his Iowa family, and he couldn't go back and he had this loneliness, his longing, his desire for something he couldn't share, that had nothing and yet everything to do with us.

Milada joins me at the window, small, thin, sleepy, naked from the waist down.

"I want to say I have been very wrong." She can never get the "v." *I am wary wrong.* "*Tak moc mě to mrzí, neměla jsem žádné právo to po tobě žádat.* If you do not wish, maybe you will say nothing to Anezka about kidney tomorrow. I understand you do not wish to obligate."

"Let's see what the blood tests say."

"I cannot believe she would say no. She is too generous."

"I'm more worried about Jungmann. You say she can be extradited to Prague for a medical emergency, but he'll find some way to interfere, you know that. I can't even … I can't imagine what they're doing to her in there."

"We'll nail that bastard to cross. You will see."

"You certainly have a lot of faith in Mr. Anton and the human rights court."

"I have faith in justice."

"Really? My little escape artist believes in justice now? What has Mr. Anton been telling you?"

"You think you are funny?"

"I'm glad my father is here."

"Now you see his Czech side, what must you think of him?"

"Honestly? I think he's still a little bit in love with Rosalye. I see it, what everyone's been saying. He's nervous around her."

"It was better when he was lonely in Iowa?"

"I didn't say that. It worries me a little, that's all."

The pub below fills the silence with accordion ditties. The radiator hums. I brush my fingers through her sweat-dampened hair, touch the tip of my tongue to that extra epicanthic fold at the corners of her eyes. A tide of desire floods in. Blood carrying willful little oxygenated protean hammers pounds its way to the axial point in my crotch. I touch her shoulder.

"Chico, we can be happy tonight. We can make love? Is okay? You okay?"

She hands me the Snickers bar. I chew it and swallow hurriedly and pull the sticky caramel out of my teeth. I run my tongue down her belly. Her skin smells even more down there of baked eggplant. My fingertip traces a figure eight along the inside of one taut thigh and over to the next. Seeking more stimulation, she nudges two of my fingers up inside of her. I put my tongue to work. She caresses my genitals, strokes my penis. For diabetics an erection is not a given. The Snickers bar is doing its job. Okay. Dissenting arguments make their case like so many judges. This makes no sense. It will only hurt worse. She pushed you away once and she'll push you away again. I tell the judges to recuse themselves. Is it hopeless? Am I tossing my dignity into the corner like a dirty shirt? Her hand guides me in. The room burns amber. The vase wobbles. She whimpers, "You are inside of me, you are inside of me." A home cast in amber. I am in it, tasting beaded sweat, inhaling baked eggplant. The amber preserves the moment, a container for all that longing that needed its object. I understand, I think, my father now. The hold Rosalye has on him.

Chapter Twenty-Four

Later that Night before our Visit to the Prison

SOFT LIGHT FROM the square caresses a drowsy post-coital Milada. Her chemical-dyed black hair fans out stiffly across the pillow. Curled under the comforter, she looks as small as a child. Much as I'd like to snuggle back into her eggplant warmth, I finally talked her into driving me to Hnátnice to search the orphanage for Anezka's cat. If she gets too comfortable I worry she'll change her mind.

"Did you by any chance unlock Isis' cage?" Before we go, there is one little thing I need to resolve. The night after our rafting trip, after hitchhiking back to Sardis, I knocked on the door of Waters' cabin to apologize for deserting the group while Milada slipped away to have a private moment with our indomitable Peregrine.

Her eyes struggle to open. "Please."

"I know." I caress her warm cheek. Her lipstick is still on, still too thick. *Those cheekbones, those squinty eyes. Memorize this moment, this bliss, this calm. Press it into your memory's passport pouch.* The form thank you card from Sardis included a scrawled note from Waters informing volunteers that Isis' cage had been left unlocked, and for that reason all lock combinations had been changed. "But, did you?"

She regards me as though I were fruit she wonders if she should have left unpeeled. "Remember Torkey?" I nod. How could I forget the red-tailed hawk that has to sleep inside the clinic lest she screech in terror at the least sound. "Torkey cry out. I thought certainly Waters will come."

"She and I were weighing the pros and cons of a cabin by the Skagit."

"I wanted to see if Isis would be calm with me."

"That means you had to open his cage?"

"Isis is bird. He have to have chance to do what instinct tell him to do. If cage is locked is not ..." We do a word search. "Authentic. Authentic freedom."

"Well, you know ... But, what did he do?"

"He is nervous but soon he is calm."

"He make any attempt to leave his cage?"

"He came to edge. Does he want freedom? I think okay, is not right for me to decide for you my frightened little man. So I close his cage."

"Apparently you forgot to reset the lock."

She laughs. "Maybe I thought he will try escape on his own power."

Reluctant to leave the womb of our lovemaking, she nevertheless hauls herself with some zeal to the modernized bathroom for a rare pounding sizzling hot shower. A to-go food order is waiting around the corner at Snack Bar. We'll eat en route. Tonight is my father's chance to talk privately with Rosalye. I picture them sitting side by side on the cot in the blue room. Rosalye in black silk, by turns funny and disdainful, sipping Slivovice, smoking those brown cigarettes, František in his blue Union pants and cushiony Rockports, yellow golf cap squashed over his thinning hair, chewing a toothpick, looking solemn, wondering what she did to his life. Our visiting hour isn't until mid-afternoon, after the prisoners have had their lunch and time in the prison yard. We can strategize over breakfast tomorrow. By then Dana should have something to report.

⁓ᴗ⁓

DANA IS NOT at reception. Must be on the job. Good. In the cool night, exiting town south along the boulevard with the street lamps painted optimistic primary colors and the curbs cleared of embarrassing pre-revolution Skodas, a route that first took us past the abandoned concrete factory, and behind that the guard tower cupola with its roving, menacing searchlight, we pass two headscarved older women. They're carrying yellow plastic shopping bags and have just departed a late bus. They recognize Milada, or seem to at least, turning their shoulders away, muttering, throwing caustic glances back as though her Skoda carried something contagious and shameful. Since she started working with the mayor to find witnesses to the torture she's been seeing this reaction. The human rights business is a trash pile many locals would not benefit by seeing turned over. Too many family rats might scurry out.

The spindly pines on the foothills are etched in the harsh silver glow of a rising gibbous moon. Farm lights cluster below, buoys in a turbulent dark sea. In the moonlight, from a distance, Anezka's orphanage with its gargoyles looks apocryphal.

Chapter Twenty-Five

That Night at the Orphanage:
A Surprise Talk with Rosalye

A SCANT SEVEN KILOMETERS separate Piséčná from the orphanage. Still, Rosalye confesses, tonight is only her second visit ever. Her first was the memorial service held more than fifty years ago for the flier incinerated over France. She admits she bogusly claimed to have married the flier. With Jungmann's *protekcé*, falsified papers were no problem. "Why I should not take his widow pension?"

Rosalye pokes a finger into worm tunnels riddling the logs. "So much money I send! See how my daughter take care to this place? You mustn't let her fool you. She is no saint. She refuse work for me but she will happy take my money. Little thief."

That Rosalye would be waiting for us at the orphanage came as a complete surprise. Well, not complete. Approaching through the wet yard, we saw a light through the boarded up windows and knew something was up, but we ignored the condemnation notice posted on the door, figuring that with Anezka in prison the worst had already happened. When we first entered, a rat skittered through one of the doors that lead into perimeter rooms, giving us a moment of false hope. Then we beheld what had become of Anezka's sanctuary. Furniture smashed. Bedroll ripped, tufts scattered like fur from a butchered animal. What happened to her crib blanket?

The odor of rodent dung climbs up my nose. "Cat must be on vacation." Rosalye laughs at her own joke, the morbidity of which is not yet known to us. She adds, "You like to see my tattoo, son of František Lenoch?"

"Tattoo?" I can't get over feeling incredulous, not that she would have a tattoo, given her trade, but that she would be here instead of with my father at the farm.

"Very few people have seen. But you I think will find interesting." Exasperated by Milada claiming that none of this is necessary, that we're here for one reason and that is to find the cat, Rosalye opens her stylish overcoat, a faux London Fog, and tugs down on her silk pants. On the exposed withered blue-veined buttock is a tattoo that looks like a bruise. Milada aims the flashlight. I bend over my magnifier. A butterfly with dangling legs? Actually—I don't tell her this—it resembles a mosquito.

How could I not see what is obvious? It is flying stork, thank you very much.

The stork is carrying something. I ask what it is. Look more closely, I am told. It's no use. Though I sense this is nearly the last thing in the world Milada wants to do, at my request she peers through the magnifier.

"I see two initials."

"F and L," Rosalye says, not one for prolonging suspense.

"František Lenoch?"

She grins. "I had a devil in me."

Rosalye hoists her pants and closes her coat and produces one of those brown imported cigarettes and lights up. "I wanted to please your father. That whore, she make impossible."

That the "whore" is my grandmother requires no translation.

"*Činíš hodně mužů šťastnými*? You keep all your men happy?" Milada says.

Rosalye drags hard on her cigarette. "What do you know about love? You love Fascist you have married?"

"At least we raised our own children."

"Don't step on my blisters!"

Before this spirals down a toilet of vituperative, I ask if she'd care to explain what she meant earlier when she said Anezka's cat had been "seen to."

"Do you know," she says, evading my question, "your father wanted to be cowboy?" I wait for her to go on. "True. He have big dream. Go out west and ride horse and round up cattle and shoot rattlesnake with six shooter."

"My father? The wannabe historian?"

Shivering in the draughty air, Rosalye tugs her overcoat tightly around her shoulders, pats her long silvery baguette braid to inspect for fly-aways. "My mother died when I am young. It was not choice for me to go on big adventure."

"Your mother? According to the record book your mother was very much alive in December, 1938, when she went to Iowa with the Lenochs."

"You speak of Barbora Kacalka. She is my aunt."

Now I remember the confusing details in the record book.

"*Posečkej, než nade mnou uděláš kříž.* You must wait before you judge." Her mother, she confirms, was the sister of Barbora whom Halbrstat had told us about, the Marlene Dietrich look-alike with the razor eyes.

"What about your younger brother, Leoš? Same mother?"

"Leoš I could not help. When I am fourteen, my aunt send me to your grandfather house. She say I am old enough, I must earn money."

"It was my grandmother who set you up in the blue room, correct?"

"*Ano*, but your grandfather gave to me for my fifteenth birthday satin bedsheets. They were red and so smooth. I was tall and beautiful like my mother. I have *krásná bujná ňadra*."

Milada laughs despite her agitation. "She say she had lively breasts, like colts."

"My mother has died crazy from syphilis. I never had something nice."

"Why would my grandfather give you satin sheets?"

She touches my cheek with a lotion-smoothed hand that reeks of her cigarettes. "Your grandmother was fat cow who gave hard kicks. He want me to feel welcome."

"And my father? What did he think about the sheets?"

Her brow furrows. A softness steals over her that I haven't seen before. "I must tell to you story. Is about your father."

It was a dry warm June afternoon on what she claims would become the best day of her life. There was time to fill before the evening milking and dinner chores. Rosalye and my father rode bicycles to Zampach Hill and climbed through the woods past the castle ruins to a meadow she'd discovered one day while hunting mushrooms.

"Red poppies spread over field like thousand beating hearts. It was so beautiful. Ah!" She pinches out her cigarette, adds the butt to the box in her pocket.

"He was shy, your father. Very … *čistá duše*." *An innocent soul.* Curiously, this sounds very like the words Milada's father used to describe my father. "I laid down blanket. I said to him we will only enjoy sun, nothing more." She lights another cigarette. "Your father admire me like … *hrdinku*." Milada considers for a moment then translates this as "heroine." Tears well in eyes already red from the earlier brandy. "He was sweet to me, your father. He pluck poppies from meadow and make bouquet and bring for me. He cover my breasts and belly with poppies. So sweet."

She sobs. It's an awkward moment. I want to throw a comforting arm around her shoulders, but Milada's impatient squinting persuades me to censor the impulse.

"You don't ask if I was virgin," she accuses, composure restored.

It's cold in this draughty hall. Our breath escapes in puffs. Feeling a shiver working through my resolve to stay warm, I ask if we can talk while we search for the cat.

"This stupid cat is all you care about?"

"It's just cold, is all."

"Even your father don't know this. I have never told to him." Rosalye proceeds to tell us about a visitor at the inn. The visitor when she was ten took her into one of the upstairs rooms made up for overnight guests and showed her his penis and made her touch it. She laughs, but it comes out as more of a *humph*. "I have seen penises. Who cares? Is nothing special. But, Leoš. He is sent to this room to clean. This man is regular customer. I don't know, but I think something happen with Leoš. I cannot protect him. I am sent to Lenoch house. There is nothing I can do."

"What did Leoš have to do with Jungmann?"

"It was so long time ago." She puts out her cigarette. Instead of lighting up again she gives me a strange look, a look that seems to draw back the curtain on a world she is not accustomed to exposing.

"For more than fifty years I have lived with Jungmann. Never, until your father say about Leoš, have I understood him."

We hear the soughing of the night breeze. If the cat were here, and alive, we'd hear skittering that was not rats.

"You wish to know why I come here tonight?" Those aristocratic lips press ruefully together. "Before he leave for America, your grandfather demand return of satin sheets. I say him no. They are mine. I still have satin sheets. I am still waiting."

"Waiting?"

Milada presses my hand, urging me not to encourage more of this confession that in Milada's view is at best disingenuous. I frown at Milada. I want to hear it.

"Charles, *poslouche*. You are listening now?"

"I'm listening."

"Good. I must tell to you something. Anezka is your sister. This is why I have come here tonight. You must know this."

"But, why couldn't you have simply said so? Have you told him? You have to."

"It has become complicated. He would believe? I don't know. I didn't want to see his look."

That look. I know the look she's talking about. That faraway look of betrayal, of distrust, of longing for something that can never be.

"You must believe."

"I do. I believe you." *Unless plum brandy has rotted your brain.*

She shoves her face close to mine. Pores bloom like rancid poppies in her drink-reddened nose. "Your father think I am greedy donkey. He think I make love with your grandfather so one day I will have farm."

"But you didn't."

"*Ne*. Your father loved me. True love is rare. I never would betray. Jungmann was horribly jealous."

Of course, there is Jungmann. "You have to come with us tomorrow to the prison. I need you to tell Jungmann what you just told me."

She reaches a hand to my shoulder. "But you must make promise to me."

I nod. She takes my silence as encouragement.

"Promise you will take Anezka away from here."

"Away? You mean to America?"

"This old building is worm food. She must go away."

"Then, you promise to talk to Jungmann and my father?"

"*Ano. Tvému otci bylo ublíženo.* Your father was very bad hurt."

"I have to ask you a difficult question." What could I possibly ask that would surprise her? I press on. "Why did you send Anezka away? Why did you send her to grow up here?"

"You ask why I send her to live in filthy place where no one care?" She touches her withered chest. "I know what girl will see at inn. I cannot have her around this. Is no place for child."

As she herself pointed out, I can't possibly know what it must have been like. "Everyone was just doing what they had to to survive, I suppose."

"Crap." I get the downturned lip curl. "I had my own orphanage for lost girls. I kept them safe. I hired teachers. After one year I make Jungmann use *protekcé* to find for them work in government. I like to think of it as finishing academy."

"But with your own daughter it was different?"

"Don't step on my blisters." She's livid, the rancid poppies in full bloom. "I make sure my daughter will never become whore like me." She turns. She peers into the orphanage's dark interior, into that vandalized hollow abandoned place.

"Do not worry." Rosalye acknowledges our impatience to continue our mission. "You will find cat in loft."

Chapter Twenty-Six

The Cat and the Loft

A COLD NIGHT BREEZE susurrates through the slabs of broken slate where the section of roof has fallen in. The cherry trees in the orchard have dropped their leaves. Corn stalks are bundled into sheaves. The last hay crop of the season is stacked in a hayrick right up to the loft. This handkerchief farm fed Anezka's children. Thanks to Jungmann, it was never expropriated by the SS cooperative. Behind the iron curtain of the official story, Jungmann spent valuable *protekcé*, a risk that could have placed him in a show trial that could have ended with a cold re-education in a Siberian gulag. Whatever else we might think of him, Rosalye claims, he did it for Anezka.

Looking through the window at fields and orchards etched out of the dark by cold moonlight, I ask Rosalye why. Why would Jungmann do that for Anezka?

"I made to him promise," Rosalye explains.

Behind the dank smell of mildew and dung, there's a faint but unmistakable odor that's hard to place. I'm beside Rosalye under the crowned center of the loft. Wielding the better flashlight, Milada pokes into cupboards in the covered recesses. Finding nothing, she demands that Rosalye stop playing games and show us where to find the cat. Rosalye refuses to be rushed.

The breeze blows smoke from Rosalye's lit cigarette in a swirl back into her eyes, causing her to lift a hand to clear them. That gesture, the lift of her hand, that and the odor call to mind an incident that happened when I was four and my father took me on my first hunting trip. It was fall, late October, like now. He flushed a male pheasant in the full glory of its plumage out of a cornfield, aimed, shot, and boom, down it tumbled with a thump like a bag of flour. Its breast feathers ruffled in the breeze. Was the bird still alive? I waved my hand in front of my face to make the awful smell go away. Until after he had showered, I would not allow Frank to touch me. That odor of violated flesh is here, but so masked by the smell of wet earth and hay and sour silage blowing over from the barn that I might have imagined it.

"What did you promise Jungmann?"

"Your grandmother. You should have heard her beg. Put pillow. Put pillow."

"Rosalye, you were telling me about the promise."

"Know what I said to her? I shouted 'He never loved you you stupid cow. He never loved you.' I wanted to be sure is last thing she will hear in her stupid life." While telling me this she's looking out the window at the bare orchard. "She sent your father away. You understand? How could I forgive? I could not."

Rosalye lights a cigarette, puffs. Her mood seems to lift, as though this admission had removed a terrible weight. "Thank you." She pats my hand.

"Your promise?"

Milada warns that her patience is running out.

She crushes the cigarette out against moistened fingers, drops the butt into the box in her pocket, immediately lights another cigarette. "He asked me to marry. To say no in my circumstance was not possible, really not possible. I say him I promise I will marry to you but you must wait. He said, if I agreed, he would adopt Anezka. She would inherit everything when I am gone."

"Why did you make him wait?"

"Why, is obvious don't you think?"

"But you were prepared to marry him the night of the fire."

"He got drunk. He never got drunk, I never see him so drunk. He had not asked again for many years. But that night he ask."

"The night the government was handed over?"

"*Ano.* He would have title to property. I was thinking for Anezka future. He could leave us with nothing. I knew his tender side. He wanted to be loved, just like everyone. I decided that night why not. For what I am waiting?"

"You had been waiting for my father?"

"Jungmann had softness in his heart for children. He know I send money for taking care to this place. He understood."

"Did he know Anezka was my father's daughter?"

"Ach, they were no rivals. Men, women, what difference to him? He like to dominate. But he was very especial to boys. Not like you think. He was not ..."

"A pedophile?" I suggest.

"*Ne, ne,* never something like this. He like them to call him John Wayne. He saw movie once, something like *Searching.* He want to be that guy."

"So, he asked you. And you said yes ..."

Milada shines her flashlight into the recess where the roof slopes down. The crib blanket is hanging like a curtain from a low beam. It looks inconsequentially small in that dark void, like a truce flag waved from too far away to matter.

I don't have a good feeling about this.

"Cat is playing peek-a-boo?" Milada says snarkily.

"Wait," I say. "Calm down, please. Who really started that fire? What happened?"

"*Ano*," says Rosalye, the only adult I've ever known to actually huff out loud. That December night, she tells us, everyone in Písečná had been invited to the inn to celebrate.

"Including Anezka?" I ask. "She was there?"

"Why we are wasting time?" Milada says. "We have deposition from Anezka."

"I want to hear her story. When we talk to Jungmann I want to be sure."

"*Dej mi konečně pokoj.* Stop it. Give me a room."

"What happened?" I say, this time more gently.

"Anezka has said lie. She was not in kitchen. I was in kitchen. It was accident. I spill some oil by stove. Jungmann is smoking pipe. Flame catch in oil. I think, good. Let whorehouse burn."

"But why would Anezka—"

"When she learned I agreed for adoption—"

"She was angry? She didn't want the adoption?"

"What difference. It burn. Is nothing else matter."

"She's in prison because of it. Why in the world would she confess ..."

"Maybe she want her hour in court to denounce Jungmann."

"It must have been the deal she was offering," I muse, recalling what she told me in this very place. "She confesses to the fire. He gives her title to the orphanage without the stigma of adoption. But once he had her confession, he had her arrested. No more problem for him."

"I would have married him."

Milada announces that she has heard enough. I follow her across the creaking, sagging floor. The night breeze rattles through the slate. I can't help shivering.

"*Chudák kočka!*" Rosalye gasps. "*Chudák kočka!*"

Milada stops before the hanging blanket. "She say we must feel sorry for cat." The cacti and broncos and lariats look to my blurry eyes like the tattoo on Rosalye's hip, like dark bruises. That odor of putrefying flesh is strong.

"Let me do this." I pull down the blanket.

Caressed by the breeze, Anezka's gray cat twists with excruciating slowness. Its head is canted at an acute angle, its mouth wrenched open, though not wide, not as though in protest but rather as though struggling to draw a last breath. A wire hung from the rafter loops under its chin. There's something odd about the body's posture. Rigor mortis would have had time to set in, then relax, and the body would have bloated, but none of this could have happened recently. This flesh is partly decayed. Were it not for the cold, the smell would be worse. Its legs are curled in toward the abdomen, suggesting either that it was tied up or that the cat died while curled in that position.

"You knew the cat was here," I say. Regretting my accusatory tone, I add, "We'll give her a proper burial, of course."

"Police do this when they make arrest?" Milada says.

"*Ano*, it must be police," Rosalye says in a timid voice so unlike her.

Height works to my advantage. I unloop the wire. The over-fed cat has shed much of its bulk but it still weighs several pounds. Breathing through my mouth, I lay the big gamey stiff cat on the crib blanket. There I see without a doubt what I only suspected when it was hanging. Allowing for the inflexibility of stiff limbs, the cat's posture suggests an animal that had curled up and died, which, if true, could only mean that someone found the deceased cat and subjected it to a post-mortem noose. But why? As a cautionary tale of some sort?

"Rosalye, how did you know the cat had been 'seen to'?" The rear legs tuck in, one under, the other stretched from the lower joint as though in the moment before expiring the cat had thought to attempt one last time to uncurl and search for its mother. "Why would the police bother to stage a mock execution? Would Jungmann do this?"

"Do not blame to him." Bathed in the moonlight, chin quivering, lips parted in supplication, eyes open, dilated, Rosalye looks grief-stricken.

"Rosalye? You all right?"

"I came to feed child. I find cat in cupboard." She points vaguely into the recesses. "I think she maybe eat some poison."

"Anezka warned us, remember? Did you tell anyone? Why not bury the poor thing?"

"One day Anezka will leave prison. I fear she will come back and never leave."

"But, you can understand. This was her home."

"Home? This is home?"

Rosalye pinches out her last cigarette. Pulling the back of her hand across her mouth, she smears cherry lipstick in a long gash. Sensing that she will accept comfort from me, I leave the cat on the blanket and go to her and wrap her thin shoulders in my arms and hold her and smell her sickly sweet brandy sweat but there is no fear in her smell. She sobs exhaustedly against my chest.

"He really loved you." It's all I can think of to say. And then stuff pours out I didn't know was in there. "My father loved you more than he loved my mother. I'm convinced of that now. There was always something missing, something he'd lost. I think I know now what it was."

She pushes me away. "Is very kind for you to say. Now go."

We offer a ride back to town. She says no, she wants time here alone. She'll catch a bus later. I remind her of her promise to meet us tomorrow at the prison and warn her not to be late. Without the authorization letter, which we have, I'm not convinced they'll allow her inside as far as the visiting room. It might be best, I suggest, to spend the night at the farmhouse and then accompany my father to the prison, just to make sure. Too readily she agrees. Okay. I'm not going to argue with her now.

I fold Anezka's child into the blanket and lead the way down the stairs and Milada and I plod through the muddy cornfield—she managing awkwardly, her pumps sinking—and in the barn we find an ax with a digging blade. The plan is to bury the cat in the birch woods behind the barn. Despite the cold, the ground has not frozen yet below the surface, but this just seems too unceremonious. What will we say to Anezka tomorrow? My suggestion, that we sneak into the graveyard behind the Písečná church, draws a horrified gasp. For one, Milada doesn't want this smelly corpse in the trunk of her Skoda. For another, that would be unthinkably sacrilegious. Instead, we dig a hole beside the grave monument to the flier killed over France. To bury cat and blanket requires a considerable hole. We bury the cat close to the bison that had been Anezka's toy. If she feels so inspired, Anezka can dig her up and move her, but for now we let the poor thing rest in peace near her mother's home.

Chapter Twenty-Seven

The Prison: A Visit with Jungmann and Anezka

THERE ARE TIMES when it's best to close your eyes and work on instinct. That line I owe to Waters. I jotted it in my Steno. I recall it at the prison.

Political detainees were routinely tortured while awaiting trial at Žamberk's infamous prison. Their sentence was either deportation to a gulag, or, if the vaccine of re-education was deemed to have taken, repatriation to a happy labor camp. The really lucky ones returned to the cooperative barracks or were sent to a cellar to shred documents. The rusty pulleys and belts and silos of the abandoned concrete factory buffer the prison from public view about as effectively as the official view that only what was necessary to protect the revolution went on here.

After walking through an arched iron gate, we approach a ten-foot high wall topped with concertina wire. The prison wall is taupe, a scraped, peeling stucco. We face two doors. A large brown set of double doors allows for vehicle egress. We enter through a small metal door off to one side, a door painted the blue of old enamel pots, and find ourselves in a room closed off by a barred gate.

A ceiling mounted camera watches our every move while we drop our personal items, including my daypack with my money envelope and insulin kit, into a blue box and remove a key. A voice on an intercom tells us to use the key and enter. When the bars close behind us we are instructed by a guard to approach the reception booth. A grinning toothless granny, flanked by five guards in the standard royal blue uniform, asks for our passports and the letter from the court authorizing our visit.

We are shown to a wooden bench. We sit and wait to be admitted.

-\|/-

FOR THE SAKE of appearances, Milada spent the night at Josef's flat. This morning, she picked me up in her Skoda and drove me to the farmhouse. Rosalye had left. I would never have taken her to be a coward, but sure enough she reneged on her promise. Josef was sent out to find her. Bedřich harangued my hangdog father for having driven Rosalye away. To make matters worse, Dana told me she was unable to find Jungmann last night and had nothing to offer to our negotiations.

Even Milada reneged. This morning, of all mornings, she decides her time will be better spent with the mayor? The lab results from Anezka's blood tests should come today, she reminded me by way of excuse, as though I needed reminding. The chance of a good protein match, meaning a match that produces minimal antibodies, we were told by Saudek, is about one in four if the living donor is not family. With a family donor—and if what Rosalye says is true, Anezka is family—the odds are better, though there is still some debate on this. Since we are not in Prague and not near a fax machine, Milada asked that the results be called in to the only absolutely reliable phone in the village. Besides, Anton deposed a witness whose reputation is unassailable. If Jungmann gives us trouble, there's our trump card. Tomorrow, regardless, she has to return to Prague to her medical practice and to her neglected husband and son. Today, at the prison, it is just my father and me. Anezka's counsel is due to join us.

We wait on the bench. The granny seems to forget about us entirely. My father asks me to have faith in him. I do, but, still.

"Feelings don't lie," I say. "I've seen you two together." The intimacy is still there, like a dormant reaction waiting for the right allergen to flare it up. "Rosalye and I had a deal. How could she screw this up now?"

A tight-lipped guard interrupts, insisting that we follow him. He leads us through a series of three clanking barred gates into a corridor. The plaster walls and floor tiles are peeling and cracked. On either side are wooden doors with round peepholes. The guard ushers us through one of those doors into a small room with a wooden table the size of a desk and flanked by four polished wooden chairs in much better shape than the corridor. A tall wooden coat rack, a pole with hooks and rings, is the only other piece of furniture. No windows but that peephole. My father respectfully reminds the guard that Anezka's legal counsel is supposed to meet us here. The guard says he will report our concern and then leaves and the door shuts automatically behind him with a resounding click that leaves us wondering if we've been locked in.

We feel around the furniture for hidden bugs but can't find any. We hear shreds of conversations through the walls. When convinced it's safe to talk, I repeat a factoid Milada shared with me this morning. Anton Zamečnik found a 1973 Amnesty International report claiming that in the preceding ten years in Czechoslovakia there were no incidents of torture. These dates precisely correspond with the use of "clean" stress techniques like the nose-to-wall torture that left no permanent scars. "Her mayor friend is preparing an eyewitness. We should use this to squeeze Jungmann. She wouldn't tell me the name of the witness. Has to be confidential until the trial."

"I think I can persuade him to cooperate."

"You keep saying that. You haven't persuaded Rosalye to help us."

My father's brown tweed jacket with elbow patches, the calico shirt, the pressed chinos, have been borrowed from Bedřich. He's still in those Rockports, but he did eschew the yellow golf cap, at least, thank god. Catching me appraising his transformation, he says, "I want Jungmann to see I am still Czech."

"I brought up that business with Rosalye's brother. She didn't say much."

"We'll see."

"What are we going to see? What do you think's going to happen?"

"I understand your worry—"

"Don't say 'don't worry.' Please. Please, don't say that. Okay? I don't mean to sound harsh. But this is it. If we blow it everything falls apart."

We've been waiting a good half hour when five guards rush us out of the waiting room and then escort us through a series of barred gates and down a long corridor to an unheated "processing" room. In the factory days, the room we're led into might have been a dining hall. Windows two stories above the ground floor have been painted the same institutional taupe that covers the walls. The tower cupola appears as a hazy silhouette through the glaze. Guards in the tower watch over the prison yard. Our guards look young. Post-revolution. A good sign. But not the lead guard. He's older and has a phlegmatic bureaucrat look that I don't trust.

The leader wags his nightstick and commands us to stand facing a plaster wall mapped by the smudges of countless sweating hands. My father whispers the translation. It's obvious from the guard's brusque tone that we would be advised not to argue. The younger guards kick our feet out until our legs are spread wider than our shoulders. Lean against the wall, we're told. Hands above heads. We're pat-down searched, a needless precaution, it's all about humiliation, of course. We're forced to stay in this uncomfortable position while we're questioned. They ask ridiculous questions, accuse us of hiding riches in Swiss bank accounts and thinking we can buy justice. We can't deny that charge. They went through my daypack and found the cash envelope.

After nearly an hour of this, my ankles and feet have swollen so much that my shoes tighten like clamps. I make the mistake of looking back at our interrogators to gauge their mood. The older guard with the nightstick commands me to turn back around. Using that stick, he whacks first one swollen ankle then the other. A little reminder, he says, as I obviously need one, of who is in charge.

An intense sensation of burning courses up my legs, which are quivering from the strain. The neuropathy that is causing me to lose sensation in my feet for once works in my favor. But the swelling will worsen. I will have to remove my shoes.

Translate, I tell my father. Quiet, he warns. From working outdoors he's used to being on his feet for hours on end. Despite his age, he will, I realize, endure this. "I can't do it," I whisper. "I have to get out of these shoes. Tell them the Universal Declaration of Human Rights prohibits the use of torture. They don't have to let me sit down, but they do have to let me to take off my shoes. If that doesn't work, mention the Geneva Conventions." They're laughing at me even as he hesitantly translates. "Tell them the Conventions require that they give me medical attention. I have to be allowed to protect my kidneys. Also, tell them I'm diabetic. I need to test my blood sugar."

"Not another word," my father says through clenched lips. The lead guard steps behind me. That nightstick slaps into his palm. My breathing is shallow. I get a good grip on the clammy wall. My father pleads with him in Czech. The searchlight from the guard tower strobes through the room. There's an unpleasant smell of rust and cold sweat.

The first blow hits my left kidney. My knees buckle. As if from a faraway chamber I hear an echo of a cry of pain. The second blow hits my right kidney. I crumple to the floor. Clumsy, heavy, boneless. I am the pheasant. Boom, down. Guards on either side drag me roughly back to my feet. My back clenches and spasms. I can't stand unsupported. They let go of me. I sink to my knees.

They laugh. Do I want more Geneva?

The lead guard gives an order. They exit, boots scuffing on the filthy tile. I'm still on my knees. Swaying. *Don't look at him, don't look at Frank, you don't want to see that naked worry. Worry won't do you any good now.*

When no one immediately comes back in, he straightens up from the wall. "You okay? I think they just want to scare us."

I'm only listening with half an ear. I ease myself over into a sitting position on the cold tile floor and remove my Teva shoes. The shiver and clang of barred gates in the corridor. The thud of approaching boots. Fevered praying. Sounds drive the fear in deeper than the pain. The only furniture in the room is a long wooden table, four wooden chairs, a coat rack. An enormous tin ashtray smelling of vanilla-scented tobacco is on the table, beside it a notepad with yellow graph paper. One of the chairs has been knocked over by a previous visitor. I pull myself to the chair. Right it. Take a ragged breath. Heave myself like a bag of concrete onto the chair.

If this is our warning, what have they put Anezka through? A similar thought must be going through my father's mind.

"Look at me?" He clicks his tongue. I can't, I tell him. "Look at me," he insists. I look. Instead of that useless worrying, his eyes glitter with resolve. "I do the talking. I mean it. No demanding rights. I mean it."

It's overcast. Late October. The windows have been painted. It is already dark outside. Visiting hours must have come and gone. It must be too late to see Anezka. Wouldn't surprise me if Jungmann didn't bother to show. The guard tower's revolving spotlight strobes. The crying and praying that is somewhere out there won't stop. When the lock on that door clicks and the door opens and Jungmann rushes in, it's a relief just to have the suspense over with.

He greets my father with a distracted air, as though he were late for a meeting. The light continues to strobe. The moans perseverate at unpredictable intervals. In stiff but fluent English, Jungmann apologizes for keeping us waiting. My father answers in Czech. Taking his advice, I keep my mouth shut.

Jungmann is wearing his usual blue peasant shirt. Rosalye claims he has a weakness for wanting to be liked by the villagers. In this place it seems more a kind of uniform worn to exonerate him from following protocol.

"My son is hurt," my father says in English for my benefit.

"I'm very sorry for this. What have you said to my guards?"

Giving me a look to remind me to stay quiet, my father says, "Your guards obviously had no ... no ... discretion in this issue."

To me, "I will have you escorted to see medical officer."

"I go with him," says my father.

"I am sorry, but this will not be possible."

"I'll be okay. But I need my insulin kit."

He agrees amiably enough to have my daypack returned. "Now you will please stand and allow your father to sit." When I object, he says, "This is not request. You have said you do not require medical attention. Then you will stand and allow your father to sit. If you need medical attention I will call guards."

My father sits. Jungmann takes the chair opposite. Despite that there are two unoccupied chairs, I stand. The room is cold. I'm sweating. My back is spasming. My ankles scream. I brace my weight on the table.

"Stand," says Jungmann. To straighten requires breathing until I can relax my back. He calls for the guards to escort me away. My father objects.

At least my shoes are off. I kick them under the table where he can't see. Jungmann produces a leather tobacco pouch. He lights a fresh vanilla scented plug in his briar pipe, the pipe with the hairline crack. "Sorry I have no smokes to offer."

"We wish to have Anezka's lawyer present," my father says.

Jungmann observes him over his pipe. The vanilla scent reminds me of the air freshener my ex-wife used to hang in my Saab to cover the odor of moldy half-eaten apples collecting in the cup holder. The familiarity of that sweet vanilla induces a Pavlovian urge to trust him, an irrational urge I have to fight off.

"So, at last my old friend, you have come home." A smear of tar oozes from the crack in the pipe. "You have not changed so much."

"Nor have you."

"Oh, I have. But you. You always had this look ... how can I say ... like you were too good for us."

"Where is Anezka?" says my father.

"I have sent for her. Guards will bring soon."

"Let's not waste each others' time. We need to get her to Prague for an emergency medical procedure. Her legal counsel has the court's authorization."

"Excellent. But she has agreed?"

"We haven't been given access to talk to her. As you know."

"She signed confession. She must go before judge before she can release."

"A judge can be persuaded. Tell us what you want."

"What I want." He puffs at his pipe, fiddles with it, dumps the hot ash plug, refills, relights. A wave of nausea breaks over the room. I'm swaying, sweating, shivering. My back clenches like a fist. "What I want is to fix some misunderstanding."

"Go on," my father says cautiously.

With my kidneys on the precipice of failure, I suddenly realize why I'm here, really why I'm here. "I want the orphanage." Speaking helps me steady myself. "I want to purchase it for Anezka. How much—"

Jungmann laughs. "I love how you Americans make business."

"I am Czech," says my father.

"Are you?" He sucks at his pipe.

"I haven't forgotten Leoš."

"Then you are not so Czech as you think." Jungmann regards him with that feminine mouth, ill camouflaged by the goatee, looking drolly amused. "What do you remember?" Watching them is like watching two chess players, each wary of the other's move, both aware that one has the power to end the game.

"I remember what I saw."

"He was unhappy boy. Very unhappy. You remember this?"

"That's your story?" My father shakes his head, disappointed that his nemesis would attempt such an obvious move.

Jungmann stands to his full height, removes the pipe, slams the flat of his hand on the table like a petulant child. "He was Kacalek trash. He was no one. Did you know that he loved me? Leoš confessed this to me."

"We were boys playing games."

"For you it was game."

He presses a hidden button. "I am very sorry Rosalye has not come today. Without her we cannot make deal. But, I do not wish that you will feel your journey has been wasted. You would wish to speak with Anezka, yes?" He shouts an order. The door opens. The same five guards usher her in.

Anezka's wrists are manacled in front of her with plastic cuffs. My father is seeing his daughter in the flesh for the first time. Wearing that same fifties-era schoolgirl outfit she had on when she was arrested, the shapeless gray sweater, white smock, plaid skirt, white knee-high stockings. This time her shoulders are slumped, her steely hair is unwashed, matted, and her eyes are sunk into bruised, swollen sockets. Denied the use of her cane, she throws her hip jerkily as she makes her way to the table. The guards remove the cuffs and then leave the room and wait outside. She stands near Jungmann.

I wait for some flicker in her expression to give away what she's been through, but she seems to be afraid of Jungmann and looks away.

"Anezka." Frank is staring at her. "Are you okay?"

There is some superficial resemblance. Both have a round head with a back sloping forehead. What I notice this time is that she has that same faraway look, as though something vital had been misplaced.

That feminine mouth of Jungmann's purses. The sight of Anezka's dishevelment seems distasteful to him. His pipe has gone cold. The tar oozing from the crack in the stem has left a black smear on his finger that looks like feces. I'm careful not let on that I've seen this besmirching smear.

Jungmann takes his time relighting his pipe. "One day of course Anezka will be free. But I think you do not have so much time. Yes?"

It's not really her. It's a shell of her.

"Anezka, I went back to the orphanage." I ignore my father's remonstrance to keep quiet. "To look for your ... your child."

"How is she?" Even though her eyes are glazed with that patina of fear, desire blossoms out of them. Anezka presses her hands together. "How is my little golden bug? She has missed me? You told to her that her mother will come home soon?"

"Enough," says Jungmann.

I can't, I can't tell her, I just can't do it. Has she lost track of how long she's been in here? But, I can't tell her a lie, either. I can't be complicit.

"Guards!" Jungmann shouts. The younger guards hurry in and re-manacle Anezka. The older one waits by the door, back stiff, shoulders straight, no sign of his earlier swagger.

"Anezka." But to say nothing is to send her back with false hope, and that isn't right, either. "She curled up. She died peacefully in her sleep. We gave her a nice burial." Even as my father is translating, the guards are leading her away. Just before the door she stops and looks back. With her eyes in shadow I can't see her expression and it's this that haunts me, the not knowing what she wants to say, what she wants me to do.

Then she's gone. My father says angrily to Jungmann, "This is unnecessary."

"I absolutely agree. It is not my intention to harm Anezka."

"Then for god's sake let her go. Let her go."

"Such an unpleasant habit," he says, considering the smear of tar he'd wiped from his hand onto the table. "You have come to make deal. Okay. Here is my proposition. Rosalye must agree to my proposal for marriage. You will both sign papers giving paternity of Anezka to me. I will change will. Anezka will inherit everything."

"She gets the orphanage now," I say.

He seems amused that I would have the temerity to imagine I am in a position to demand anything. "Very well. If you care so much."

"You are a bastard," my father says.

"You ran away like scared rabbit. I took care to her."

"Taking care of her includes torture?" I say.

"You think to insult me by this? You know where to find us. It is you I think who will hurry. I will expect to hear from you."

He exits. The older guard steps in and beckons for us to follow him into the corridor. I slip on my shoes loosely and take my father's supporting arm. The guard unlocks and opens three barred gates and then we are back in the main corridor and follow him through three more. Along the main corridor we pass guards moving prisoners. With their bad hygiene and tattoos and bad teeth and crude language, the guards can be distinguished from the inmates only by their blue uniforms. From the toothless granny at the front we retrieve our possessions. The cash envelope is missing from my daypack. Pointless to say anything.

Outside the last gate and the peeling taupe wall, the spotlight strobes over our heads and casts macabre reflections among the rusted monsters in the concrete factory yard. Never have I been so glad in my life to take a gulp of fresh air, but the moment I attempt to relax, a sensation like a cutting torch sears through my back and takes my breath utterly away and leaves me doubled over. My father guides me to the bus stop bench across the boulevard by a streetlamp painted cinnabar red, the red of a sunset viewed through smog. I curl up on the metal bench. I tell my father to go to the town square and find a taxi. He won't leave my side. We wait for a bus.

Nothing matters now. Without Rosalye's cooperation, there is no way to meet Jungmann's demands. In the moment I am too sick to care about anything but finding my way back to the hotel and into bed.

Chapter Twenty-Eight

That Night after the Prison Visit:
Last Week of October, 1994

THE MADONNA IN the Landa painting looks especially reproachful. Convinced I had it right when I curled up in my map room, that I never should have allowed my father to tempt me back here, the last thing I want to hear is Milada telling me I need to get up and try to walk. I have blood in my urine. The swelling won't go down. All I want is to sleep.

The only thing worse than no news is good news that is absolutely useless. Milada spoke by phone with Dr. Saudek in Prague. The results from the blood tests were not great, but four of seven blood leukocytes did not cause antibodies to form so they've agreed to do the transplant.

My father is pacing the room, massacring toothpicks. Milada and Josef hover by my bed. What would it take to convince Rosalye to agree to Jungmann's terms? It's up to my father now. I'm done.

Milada has to drive back to Prague. She has a shift to cover tomorrow morning. She suggests that I ride back with her so she can have my back X-rayed in Prague. I'm tempted. But my ordinarily over-protective father gives me the strangest look, or rather, a look I'm not used to in him. He wants one more shot at this. He's convinced he can still win over Rosalye. It's the venue that's the problem. The prison is Jungmann's turf. Despite what she says, she'll never go there. Nor, I let him know, will I, not again, not willingly. Neutral turf is what this calls for. What if we suggested a ceremony at the orphanage? He looks at me.

Milada leaves. She has to. Mainly because I want sleep more than anything else, I decide to stay the night, but I don't agree to more than that. Following Milada's advice, my father gets me off the bed and walks me around the room and brings me water and makes sure I drink plenty even though that will mean other unpleasant consequences.

There's a folkloric dance concert tonight at the Žamberk Municipal Library that Josef wants to attend. I urge him to go, by all means, he's done enough already. If my father wants to talk to Rosalye, if he still thinks that will help Anezka, that's his business. Go, I tell them both. Let me sleep. My father won't hear of it. He won't leave me this way. Josef, likewise, wonders if he should try again with Rosalye.

"For god's sake." The two of them are fussing like my two candle shaving aunts in Cedar Rapids. The pain in my back at least goes numb when I'm up and moving around. How far is it to this concert? Josef points past the balcony. Just off the square by the mayoral house. "Let's all go," I say. "It's better than this hand rubbing."

~⋅∖ ⁄⋅~

FOR TWO EXCRUCIATING hours the wide stage ebbs and flows with a tide of folk dancers washed our way from the Economic University of Bratislava. Pride glows in their sweaty faces. My back is squeezing like a clamp. I suddenly announce I can't sit through another minute. My father is enjoying this so much he doesn't want to leave. "Don't you see it?" I ask my father. "It's like watching old Leni Riefenstahl films glorifying the Olympics and Hitler's alleged master race. Only this isn't in black and white."

"The dances are nationalistic," admits Josef. "Nationalist is patriot with inferiority complex." He demonstrates that he can't raise his left arm to the level of his shoulder. The prison doctor—an older generation nationalist—refused to notice the broken clavicle he suffered during a beating in jail, so it was never set and his fractured bones knit together "like people in village. Each one shove to get on top and no one go anywhere."

"The show's almost over," my father says. "How's your back holding up?"

The long finale commences. At last there is drama. A string band, accompanied by an oboe and a piccolo flute, fills the hall with a haunting atonal sound, by turns bright and then melancholic. Those youthful faces display their joyful aspirations like spring flowers. Soon enough they'll see how grim adults adjudicate their revenge on such eagerness.

My father tips forward on his folding chair. *There's something going on here, he sees something that has him entranced.* Young women, wearing ankle-length pleated skirts with bloomers and rainbow colored aprons and bodices rimmed by hand-embroidered seams, ululate a cappella. My spine shivers. Wearing black ankle boots and knee-length pants with stockings and collarless peasant shirts, the young men yodel and strut like peacocks. *This isn't for show, they're really into it. My father stares as though watching himself.*

The finale finishes with a couples' dance. Boys from one village bounce the bottoms of girls on bent thighs, then swing them over shoulders and taunt their rivals with catcalls. There's a fierceness in the rivalry that isn't funny. My father has picked one of the couples as his favorite. All I see are pink faces pinched with parochial pride and piggy eyes. I realize I'm seeing my father in those faces, the side of him that would abandon his own daughter and his father as well. It's too sad, too sad. I don't know this man. I do see why he didn't want to come back. What happened to Anezka cannot be blamed anymore on his father or on Rosalye, not entirely.

I leave the theater without explaining. Let them follow if they want. At the hotel he catches up with me. I pack my bag hurriedly, worrying that I'll miss the last bus to Letohrad where I can catch the late train to Prague via Brno. I leave things in the room, including that amber vase that had been intended as a gift. The room is paid for the night. As long as adrenaline or whatever it is masks the pain, I'll keep moving. You owe Anezka, I tell him. Stay here. Don't blow it this time.

─ ᾽ι᾽ ─

THE TRAIN FROM Letohrad to Prague via Brno stops at Lansperk. The brakes screech at an excruciating pitch and the car jerks to a halt and we're left in a deafening silence. The interior lights dim, abandoning us, my father and I, the car's only passengers, to murky shadow. The outdoor platform is lit at sporadic intervals by gooseneck lamps. In the inverted conical light given off by those lamps a night fog promises that the air will be chilly and damp.

We wait. The train shudders again. From a distance we hear a garbled voice over a loudspeaker. The ticket office at the station is dark. No passengers are waiting on the platform. Again there is a screech, but no sensation of motion. Finally, my father steps off onto the platform. The forward section of train has moved onto a connecting track. Our section has been left behind.

The waiting room is not locked at night, I know this from Anezka, but I also remember her reporting that a guard strolls by once an hour to prod anyone who has fallen asleep with his nightstick. Vagrants are not allowed to overnight in station waiting rooms. Ticketed passengers are permitted, provided they don't use the room to sleep.

It promises to be a long, miserable night. It's near the end of October and night temps fall below freezing. The waiting room is heated along the fringes by radiators, but the center of the hall is cold enough that we see our breath in clouds when we walk around and our feet under the benches get very cold. The middle of the hall is filled with parallel rows of slatted-wood benches that are hard on backs. The clock mounted above the dark ticket window torments us.

After we're settled more or less, I take a booster shot and eat two wedges of tasteless pasteurized cheese individually wrapped in foil—kitsch cream, I call these pallid wedges—and munch a low-sodium cracker. I offer kitsch cream and crackers to my father. Knowing my more urgent need, he declines.

Our reflections wall off the view to the night outside. It's quiet except for the clock's metronomic tapping on our frayed patience. Once, in the wee hours, a mail cart on metal wheels will roll along a platform on the opposite side, for a moment, in my drowsiness, giving me false hope that salvation has arrived. In the meantime, my throbbing ankles heat up like ovens. My back stiffens from the cold and too much sitting. Every nitrogen-poisoned cell in my muscles screams for relief. Nothing seems more precious than sleep.

My father didn't feel right allowing me to leave alone. Now he is overly solicitous. Can he bring me water? There must be at least a faucet in the washroom. Would I be more comfortable lying down on the bench? He'll drape his coat over me as a blanket and then stand by the heater, and run interference with the guard if need be. He saw me looking at him in the theater. This is about pride. He will not make the same mistake twice.

"This is really torture," he says to make conversation. Then it dawns on him what he just said and he looks sheepish.

"You want to hear about torture?" Recalling Josef's rendition, I paint for my father the image of what must be happening to poor Anezka. "For two or three days, they put you in a room even colder than this. No windows. The walls are not soundproof. You hear screams and praying. Sometimes the sounds are coming from you. They flood the floor of your cell with cold water and take away your clothes, all but your underwear, and they give you a little scrap of a blanket and let you shiver under bright lights. The slop bucket is never more than a meter or two from your nose. There is no way to escape the smell or the light or the cold. To eat they make you crawl to the metal slot that's set at about knee level in the door. The bread has mold and the dishwater soup gives you diarrhea, but you eat it, what else are you going to do?"

"I'm sure it's awful," my father says. His face looks blue and even more drawn and gaunt in the cold light.

"Not always. Then they act like your best friend. Like you're on the same team but you just needed a little wake up. You get better food. You get to sleep in warm dry clothes. In the dark. But in a way, that is worse. They never tell you if it's something you said or didn't say when they throw you back into that cell with the cold water."

"They want a confession."

"They want to break your will. When I first met Anezka, she told us a story from her days as a kid in the orphanage that really stuck with me. I asked her if Rosalye ever came to visit. What would you guess she said?"

"I'm guessing probably not."

"Right you'd be. But Anezka was glad for that."

"Do we have to talk about this?"

"Yes, we do have to talk about this. Know why Anezka was glad? Your daughter was glad she never got visits because the ones who did got their hearts broken again and again and again."

"Okay. Okay, I'm sorry." He paces the rows of benches, breath billowing, his supply of toothpicks exhausted, hands jammed deep into coat pockets. "In 1946, there were ships going back to Europe. The SS America was making a return run. Maybe I could have booked passage. I don't know. Mostly it was wealthy people, movie stars, politicians ..."

"Did you even try?"

"I still blamed your grandfather and Rosalye. I could not forgive them. Anyway, I don't know where I would have gotten the money. In Bohemie town there was talk. New York seemed so far away ..." He breaks off. What does it matter what his intentions were? "Look, I'm here now. Maybe you believe this is a lost cause, but I have to try. Will you help me? I can tell Rosalye likes you. Maybe you could persuade her."

"To what? Marry Jungmann? Sign paternity papers declaring that Anezka is his? You prepared to sign such a document?"

He clicks his tongue. "Just persuade her to agree to meet."

"No. I'm going home."

"What if I can persuade Jungmann to bring Anezka to the orphanage?" he says. "You could talk to her. We have the results of the blood test. It's worth a try."

I frown. "How are you going to persuade him?"

"Well, if he wants to marry Rosalye—"

"Milada believes he'll go before the human rights court," I say. "I'm certain none of the judges or prosecutors got where they're at without getting their hands dirty. It's in their best interest to keep this quiet. You think Jungmann's not working it?"

"No, I don't think so," he says. "I don't think he is."

"You've been away too long."

"I know him."

"What do you mean, you know him?"

"I saw him kill Leoš." My father's jaw, desperate for its customary toothpick, clenches and unclenches.

"What did you see? You saw him actually do it? What weapon did he use?"

"I didn't actually see it happen. Actually happen."

"What exactly did you see?" I persist. It's the lawyer in me, I can't help it. His vagueness at a time like this drives me crazy.

"It was dark in the stalls. But I could still see what Jungmann was letting Leoš do to him. They ran down to the river. I waited. I didn't want to embarrass them. When I got to the river I saw Jungmann pushing down on something. It was dark, like I said, I couldn't see what he was pushing. The next day the best swimmer in the village is found in the river."

"You never reported this?"

"I was so angry with Rosalye I didn't know what to do."

"Forgive my saying so but this thing with Leoš seems to really bother you. I never heard you say anything about him, and finally you come back home to Czecholand and it's Leoš Leoš Leoš." After some time passes without him saying anything, I add, "What is he to you?"

"My father ... I just don't know. There is a good chance ..."

"What? A good chance what?"

"Like I said, I don't know. But Leoš might have been ... my father's ..."

"I can see how this would be a sensitive subject, but what does this have to do with Jungmann? Why does this keep coming up?"

"You saw. He's in denial. He's told himself some other story."

"In his heart he knows what you know? Can we use this somehow?"

"I think it's best we let it drop."

"You think Rosalye needs to hear more about this?"

"I said we should let it drop." He stands in shadow by the wall heater, shivering, rubbing his arms. "I think Jungmann in his twisted mind really thought he was protecting him from the Nazis. People were frightened. That was in the days right after Munich. Beneš was in London. No one knew who to trust."

"That must have been right before you left."

"Yes."

It seems comical to me now, all those years as a kid thinking of my father as a brave hero who would have joined the partisans and lived in the forests in Poland. What it all comes down to is everyone saving themselves and then telling a good story later. Am I any different? Apparently not. I'm still leaving.

―※―

NEITHER OF US talks again for a long time. At some point I'm aware of lying on the bench, his coat over me. The next thing I know a blunt poke against my shoulder has jolted me awake. The hand that's holding the nightstick is purple from lousy circulation, I recognize the symptom from my own ankles. The guard's blue uniform reeks of damp wool and cold. It's his job to harass us, of course. Now I'm awake. Where is my father? I sit up. The guard continues his rounds. There he is, standing by the wall radiator, his arms wrapped over his chest, ear flaps down over his ears, looking gaunt and cold and withdrawn into his loneliness, but then he sees me sit up and he smiles wonderingly, am I okay? I see the apology in his look. He tried to keep the guard away. Before falling asleep I had been remembering how heroic I thought he was, and now he just seems so lonely and so lost, a man no longer of his time, a man who lost his home and who certainly never believed he had real choices, not as I see it, and only now does it occur to him, because I rub it in his face, that he did have choices. But I don't have to abandon him to that shame and loneliness, do I? So I might not make it home. Aside from staying alive, what exactly did I have to do that was so pressing?

─ᐟ↙─

WHEN THE KIOSKS open, with our baggy eyes and lumpy faces we buy fruit and coffee and hang out at the station. While waiting for the train back to Žamberk, I tell my father I'll stay, but this is our last chance. I'm having some difficulty with urination and I'm feeling nauseous and headachy and hypersensitive. Might be sleep deprivation as much as my kidneys. That's why it's an effective torture. You feel everything acutely. You're open to suggestion. You start to believe anything they plant in your psyche, including the notion that abandonment, even torture, can be a sign of love.

Chapter Twenty-Nine

Monday Night Waiting in Žamberk: Two Days Left before the Scheduled Surgery

THE DARK SHADES of gray and ochre splashed against that cold chalky sky in the Landa painting capture pretty realistically the feel of early winter hanging over Žamberk's square. A biting wind blew snow flurries through the park in the late afternoon, dusting limbs with skeletal leaves hanging on, dusting the mausoleum, throwing a veil over the Madonna. The season's first snow caught my father returning from the courthouse. He pulled the flaps on his yellow cap down over his ears. Is it also snowing in Prague? If snow accumulates on the old plum in Yveta's garden, I worry it won't survive, it'll split. We need to get word to her. She must get her boys out there to shake off the snow. My father can't dissuade me from this obsession. He dutifully heads back down to reception to use Dana's phone.

A wedding ceremony has been arranged. Josef talked to Rosalye. My father wisely elected to stay out of it, at least, long enough to give Josef a chance. Meanwhile he met with Anezka's legal counsel and delivered an envelope thick with U.S. dollars, an envelope that officially does not exist, which the counsel, with prodding from Mr. Anton Zamečnik, distributed to the correct judges, after which authorization for medical transfer to IKEM in Prague was filed at the prison. Copies of the authorization were also filed at the records office with the judges' signatures. Still, Jungmann could easily have found a bureaucratic way to delay the procedure, if nothing else by transferring her to a different ward, where other paperwork, other bribes, would be required. But in this one respect, my father's intuition regarding Jungmann proved correct. Call it hubris. Call it delusion. Call it psychosis. All excuses for not calling it what it really is. Jungmann believes Rosalye has always loved him, and will now prove that by marrying him, and Jungmann wants everyone there to witness this grand apotheosis. Does that make him a megalomaniac? He believed in his cause. He believed in the revolution as the path to ultimate harmony. He believed that it was his duty to reeducate the revolution's enemies. But he also believed the Soviets were colonizing thugs. Were it not for his *protecke*, my father's farm would have ceased to exist. But for his beneficence, Anezka's orphanage would long ago have been taken over as barracks for the Soviet cooperative. There would have been neither meat nor uniforms nor a home for her children.

If negotiations go smoothly, the evening will culminate with a modest ceremony held at the orphanage. Tomorrow, regardless of what happens tonight, I will be in Prague, either checked into IKEM's transplant clinic or into emergency care. Today has been a rough day. The headache and nausea have made napping difficult. Because of the beating it's hard to find a comfortable position. Each of my ankles looks like the trunk of a cherry tree. For ten months I've known it was a race against time. The beating handed out gratis by Jungmann's guards merely took the uncertainty out of it.

⸻

MY FATHER PADDLES out of the bathroom wearing an inquiring look on his face. I'm blowing "Clementine" on my harmonica to help him calm down. He's wearing his socks half on and half off—an old habit that means he's worrying, a habit that used to drive both me and Mom crazy.

"Did you know that's my favorite song?"

"Yes," I say. "I know. Your socks …"

He gives me that hang-dog look. "Tonight is not going to be easy."

"Mom's been gone almost three years. You could start thinking about …"

"No, no." Standing before the French doors, my pensive father looks out across the balcony at the snow, which is at least abating. "We have to get you to Prague. You and Anezka. That's all that matters."

My father paces in his half-stockinged feet. I don't have the heart to ask him to stop. His worrying at least leads to some resolve. Grabbing one of his dog-eared Zane Grey paperbacks, he joins me on the bed. A bookstore in Prague sells Karl May westerns translated into Czech from German. He has a stack of those waiting at the flat. He's preparing to be here for an indeterminate duration.

He drops the paperback onto his lap. "I'll do whatever has to be done."

"Including sign the paternity release?"

"If that's what has to be."

"What about Anezka?" Trying to picture her, I keep seeing me. A boy of four or five, in the basement, my hands on a stack of quarters, reveling in the glint of silvery light, the tinkle of what to me was pirate treasure, when he caught me and in a curt voice that frightened me, said, *put those back and don't ever touch them again.* "Remember that amber bowl, you used it as an ashtray? You kept it on your desk down in the basement?" He doesn't recall the bowl particularly. "You'd go down there to smoke your Friday night cigar?"

"Your mother hated cigars."

"When I was young I was convinced you preferred hanging out down in the basement to being upstairs with us. I figured you had secrets down there."

He brushes his paperback aside. Pushes up from the bed, his arthritic knees creaking. He looks out through the French doors into the snowy night.

"There was a time when I really believed I wanted to be a resistance fighter. I wanted to impress my uncle." Still looking out toward the night, he says, "Remember that time you visited your grandfather?"

"You know, to be honest, it was more than just that once."

"I figured."

"Just for the record, he never told me anything. I really had no idea I had a Czech sister until this past January. When I found those letters."

"It's hard for me to tell you this, but when I found out you were seeing him …" He clicks his tongue. His hand reaches for a phantom toothpick. "Well I'll just say it. I felt betrayed. There was no way you could have understood."

"I was trying to understand. But you kept that life separate from us. It was your private basement life. I see now why you maybe didn't want to share it."

"There was no going back. I tried to forget about it."

"But, you had a child." I sink back against the rolled pillow. "In my heart I want to forgive you for that. I try."

"I know. I don't expect you to. But remember, for a long time I believed …"

"You're going to tell me you believed that story about your father and Rosalye. You have to admit, it is a little convenient." But we're running out of time. "What do you think is going to happen tonight? You think Rosalye will go through with it?"

"That's what Josef says. She said she'd do it."

"When you two are in the same room … Anyway." This is his dilemma. On the eve of asking his daughter for her forgiveness, he will be asked to sign a disclaimer waiving paternity rights so that Jungmann can name her as his daughter in his will. Of course, she could simply be named beneficiary of his estate. The issue of paternity especially seems to matter to Jungmann. And all this while watching his old flame marry his old rival.

"I don't want you to do this just for me. I'll go on dialysis."

"Son. I won't let you down."

"Do what's right for Anezka."

"We'll see how it goes."

"Fix your socks. Please?"

It's time. He pulls up his socks. We bundle up. Josef has pulled up out front in an old Volga wagon of indeterminate color—it has so many replaced panels. The rusty, shockless Volga belongs to the mayor's son, who has agreed to chauffeur us. Jungmann, we're told, has been busy today with my cousin Frantiska's husband making hasty modifications in the orphanage. It's an odd place for an odd wedding. The building is condemned for good reason. There is no heat source but that wood-burning stove that's missing its cast-iron doors. With its worm-eaten wooden beams and log walls only scantily clad in plaster, the building is unquestionably a fire hazard. But the building belongs to Jungmann. Very unlikely anyone would cross him but Zamečnik and he's promised to let us have this night without any interference from the human rights court. The wedding will be a ceremony only. Paperwork to be filed later.

─∿─

It's COLD OUTSIDE and the temperature is dropping. No miscreants lounging on the mausoleum with their boom boxes. The square is empty of people. The wind has mercifully died. The roads are still passable and the searing cold and the still air may hold off any further snow. Outside of Žamberk, a thin raiment of crystallized snow glistens on bare limbs that catch in our headlights. Through the woodlands, an icy ground fog rises from the river. The Volga's bald tires give poor traction at best on the frozen asphalt. Our seats, thinly cushioned metal benches bolted to the chassis, send us bouncing and sliding—of course there are no seatbelts—and the jarring is especially hard on my back. I'm wondering how I'll manage the long drive to Prague later tonight in this steel can.

Limbs snapped off in the earlier storm crack under the Volga's wheels like gunshot. More than once Josef, worried that Jungmann's minions will be out here to give everyone an unasked for escort, asks the mayor's son to stop and turn off our headlights and wait. It's a paranoia that never entirely goes away, evidently.

Around the bend at Hnátnice, the orphanage is suddenly there. Hulking, sagging, an immoveable presence. The cracked gargoyles that used to seem charming leer at us tonight as though we should know better than to tempt fate. The heavy shutters have been closed over the windows, yet a thin glow escapes around the edges. What could have been arranged for lighting? Surely not open flames. At least a fire would provide the place a death with dignity. My father thinks it should be torn down to the foundation and rebuilt from the ground up. I want the relic saved. When I walk around in there I feel the spirit of the children. This was Anezka's home. That's what I want to save for Anezka. Home.

Chapter Thirty

Monday Night at the Orphanage:
Preparing for a Wedding

Frantiska ushers us into the caretaker's flat, her brow pinched behind her bulky glasses. Her thick torso is wrapped in a burgundy silk robe that looks too svelte for her, like she borrowed it from Rosalye. She has prepared a bath for herself. She will not be joining us for the ceremony. There are a few messages.

Anezka was released from prison into Jungmann's custody. According to a call from her legal counsel, Jungmann has her release authorization, her passport with the visa, her birth certificate. When she walked out of the prison, he watched her stop to scratch her initials into the peeling stucco on the outer wall before two guards escorted her into the back of the waiting police van. She will be delivered under guard. Jungmann will be along later, after he has changed for tonight's ceremony.

Dana? Did you hear from Dana? What I wanted from her was to find a way to convince him to drop the paternity requirement. "She say, tell Chico, she danced for Jungmann last night private, Salome." I nod, my heart sick for her. "She say tell Chico everything is fine, he has agreed." No way are we trusting this intelligence, but at least the opening salvo in the negotiations has been fired.

Rosalye went missing. Frantiska found her. Where, I ask, shuddering at that possibility.

"*V místě, kde by jste to nejvíce čekali.* We found her in most obvious place."

My father guesses. "The farm. In the blue room." Lest we misjudge her, he adds, "She can seem … haughty, like she's too good for everyone. But I remember how my mother treated her."

The bride-to-be is upstairs preparing herself. We are not allowed to see her. When she's ready, she'll call for Josef to escort her. Until then, we should wait for her in the orphanage.

I take my pulse. Do I need a snack or a booster shot? Usually I can tell. Tonight I can't. My father notices that my eyes are dilated and decides I'm having a reaction. He hands me a six-ounce can of orange juice from my daypack. Would I like to nap until all are assembled? You go ahead, I tell him. Come get me when Anezka is here.

Wielding a borrowed flashlight, he leads Josef across the frozen field, a slight erect proud lonely figure etched out of the dark by a cold slab of moonlight. Winds high up are shifting away the cloud cover. At the tumbled monument to the dead flyer, he kicks snow from the bison and takes his time looking it over. I watch them cross the frozen yard, watch until they open the door upon a reddish pulsing glow and enter what looks to my inflamed imagination like the maw of a furnace.

Chapter Thirty-One

The Orphanage: They Begin to Arrive for the Ceremony

THE SMELL OF kerosene overpowers even the funk of rodent. Near the stove Frantiska's husband has erected an arbor on a raised platform. The assemblage bears an unfortunate resemblance to a gallows. From the arbor a wide bench-swing hangs on ropes. The ceremony will include a courtship scene on the swing. Of course there are no flowers; it's too cold for that. My father and Josef have been feeding wood scraps into the open-bellied stove to beat back the chill before the others arrive. The smoke vents out a flue that is far from air-tight. If there's a high-pressure inversion that smoke will stay in the loft and we'll be in trouble. There is no power to the building. Lighting is provided by several kerosene lanterns with open flames in glass covers, hung from nails pounded into rafters. The lanterns carve an intimate space around the platform. The pulsing glow from the belly of the stove paints an amber stain on Josef and my father and casts harsh shadows that feel like creatures reaching out of the dark.

"I'm feeling better," I tell my concerned father. I nod to Josef. "I can't imagine what you must have said to her."

"You must ask to her." None of us heard her come in. That faux London Fog covers her wedding outfit. She's gone to a lot of trouble to braid her hip-length white hair. Two pinned ram's horn braids elegantly frame her angular face. Tucked from horn to horn is a daisy chain of tiny white flowers. The ruby lipstick has been applied so thickly I worry she's been hitting the Slivovice. Her cold hands fumble with a cigarette.

"You're willing to go through with this?" I hope I don't sound too incredulous.

"We will see if he keeps his word." My father clicks his tongue.

"Just the same," I say, willing to offend him if that's what it takes. "What if he insists on the paternity issue?" Halbrstat, the town historian, will perform the civil ceremony. It was out of the question to approach Zameçnik, the mayor, for this task.

"It is my wedding day. Nothing will spoil it, not even your gloomy looks."

"I'm happy if you're happy," I say. My father's silence speaks too loudly. I cover it with idiotic questions until Rosalye stops me.

"We will begin with courtship swing. He will place flowers in my hair." Unmistakably she has brought the required flowers. There's a sobriety in her tone that stops me from joking about it. "I must not be here when he arrives." Our instructions are given. She wants Josef to lead her in when everyone's here. First will be the swing ceremony, followed by a round of stories, everyone's chance to share a memory of either bride or groom. Objections will be heard at that time. Until then we should just go with the ceremony. She emphasizes this last point, brows lifted. "Understand? You must trust me. I know what I am doing." With that odd request, she slips out to finish her preparations.

My silent father jiggers pensively foot to foot *and looks like Isis doing it* to stay warm. At least I talked him out of wearing that yellow golf cap with the ear flaps.

-~\'/~-

I HAVE TO KEEP moving or my back will seize. Josef walks with me through the hall. The fire lurches at our backs. Shining my light down the row of stout posts and along the outer walls—wide swaths of missing plaster expose thick square logs coated with black tar, the gaps filled with mud and straw chinking— it seems to me that we are in the belly of not a furnace but an ark. An ark built for lost children. An ark built to endure any storm. An ark ultimately cast athwart the one storm it could not ride out: the storm of abandonment. Where did Anezka's children go when Jungmann closed this place four years ago? Josef doesn't know. Why leave it neglected if he had plans for it? Could it still be salvaged, or have worms bored too devastatingly into its structure? Josef won't profess to having an opinion. What if ... I tug his arm, filled with a sudden inspiration. What if we were to start a foundation? Fix up the place, turn it into a shelter for battered women and children? Anezka could be the director.

But Josef is looking dubious. He wants to discuss the ceremony. Rosalye has a punishment in mind for Jungmann and we mustn't question her. "It's your father I worry," he says, whispering. "If he wants fight with Jungmann, it will not go well for Anezka."

"I think he has Anezka's interest at heart." What troubles Josef, I'm guessing, is that my father's latent feelings for Rosalye could be aroused. What troubles me, but I keep this to myself, is that he might decide it's time to talk about what happened to the boy who was found in the river.

"You ready for this?" We're back with my father by the stove.

His mouth opens and he looks at me and his eyes are bleeding with concern. He looks at me and he puts a hand on my shoulder like a girl asking me to dance and he says, "Charles ... Son, I ... Son, I'm sorry. I've given this a lot of thought, and I really want everything to work out ..."

"But? I hear a loud 'but' in this."

"Before Rosalye marries him she has to know. I know we talked about this—"

"Just do me a favor. Let's wait and see how it goes. This can't be just about your need to confess."

"She has to know. I owe that to her."

"She's spent most of her life under the same roof with that guy. You think she doesn't know him by now?"

"It's not just him."

He stops talking and instead busies himself adjusting lantern flames, feeding the stove, testing the ropes on the swing, which has been slammed together out of rough-cut birch still damp from the woods. All those Saturday afternoons when little Anezka waited indoors so that if her mother came for her she wouldn't miss her ... It was just as much my father she waited for, even if she didn't know it. He knew. His sisters corresponded with the family.

We hear the crunch of tires on snow. A car door slams. The reckoning my father has dreaded the past five decades is about to arrive.

Chapter Thirty-Two

A Family Talk at the Orphanage: the Wedding Begins

A MONTH OF INTERROGATION and torture in a cold tiny cell has left Anezka thin, her skin sallow, her eyes swollen and bruised, her hair as toneless as her cat's fur when we found it hanging. She leans heavily on her cane. What we can see of the uniform under her coat, the knee-high stockings, plaid skirt and the rest looks rumpled like it's been slept in. Prison has aged my sister. She looks closer to my father's generation.

Two guards escort her in. My father convinces them that the ceremony is not going to include food and drink so they might as well wait outside in their van and keep it running and stay warm. One of the guards, the same phlegmatic older one who beat me in the prison, is carrying a black flashlight that resembles his nightstick. He taps it desultorily into his palm. His indifference reminds me that I was nothing more to him than a reason to have been late for supper with his miserable family. If he remembers me at all it is because it isn't often you get to beat an American. My skin crawls with loathing, with the desire to attack him. This unprovoked assault, of course, would only prove that more reeducation is needed.

The guards leave. Our party is ruddy in the flickering glow. Uncertain shadows dance around Anezka, who hovers near the fire. I look at my father. He feeds the stove. Soon the others will arrive and he might not have another opportunity, but he can't find it in himself to speak to her. I think he is afraid of his daughter.

"Jungmann has said to me you will sign some paper to say that he is my father."

He clicks his tongue repeatedly.

"I've been wondering," I say to give him time to reflect. "Any idea where that bison came from? The one out there—"

"No, no, I don't know. It was not from me."

While I might not understand his reasons, I do know that he would have said something nebulous rather than pointedly lie. "What about you, Anezka?"

"Where is my child? You will show to me please? *Ano*?"

"Sure, but now is not the best time. Jungmann will be here soon. You guys need a chance to talk."

That only offers my father a way to avoid this touchy moment. "No, you two need to talk. Anezka, we have news from the lab in Prague. The blood tests?"

"Frank. Dad. Not now. Come on."

Anezka lays a hand on my arm. "They took blood, but I know is not for tuberculosis. Nurse say they will not steal my kidney. I must give consent. I ask why? Why they want my kidney?" She looks at my father. "I know more than you think I know."

"The tests were not great," I say. "But there is enough compatibility."

"I will help you. *Samozrejme*. Of course."

"Thank you." I enfold her in a mawkish hug. Such relief. I had no idea how much in denial I had been.

"Before you knock me to ground, come. Show to me where is my child."

Filled suddenly with a bravado I haven't felt since the beating, I guide her out into the snowy yard. Her escorts are in their warm van playing *Mariáš*. I wave to them. At the bison she says a few words in her own language. She stares at the bison as though trying to see through it down to her beloved child. I assure her Dana loves her and would do anything for her. I gush with praise for how well she must have loved her children. Okay, the child I knew was a cat. But you would have to be more obtuse even than I not to see that cat as a surrogate for her orphans. I hug her again, even more mawkishly than before.

—⁂—

THE VANILLA AROMA of Jungmann's pipe announces him. When he pushes through the door, he is not alone. Halbrstat, shorter, thicker, coarser, limps in behind him. The prosthesis squeaks mightily in the cold. Jungmann touches his manicured goatee, the only twitch, the only chink in his façade to suggest he might be feeling something other than naked hubris. Has Dana had a hand in this? His tall lanky frame is buried under a sheepskin coat. Fair enough, it's cold for real. But there's more … a wide-brimmed black Stetson, the top pressed flat and brim rolled as though it'd been tucked into a dusty saddlebag.

And the way it's punched low over his brow. And a yellow bandana at the neck. And leather chaps over worn denims. Tooled cowboy boots with tall heels meant for stirrups. It's John Wayne from central casting.

"Evening." He flicks the brim of the hat without cracking a smile.

My father looks flat out disgusted. "You think she'll be impressed?"

"I am impressed." Escorted by Josef, the bride has entered quietly to avoid the usual fuss. Rosalye's nose is purple from the cold and I wonder again if she has been hitting the brandy hard. Whatever she's wearing is hidden under that faux London Fog.

Rosalye takes stock of her daughter. If there is pity in her, she hides it well. "You have enjoyed your stay at Hotel Jungmann? You've lost weight, I see."

She turns to my father. "You have said your apologies?" He says nothing, eyes her evenly. Josef tends the fire in the stove.

Halbrstat, who is after all her cousin, she ignores as though he were a post. It's Jungmann's turn to fall under her scrutiny. Far from seeming surprised, she gives every sign of approving. "But, you look more Mephistopheles than sheriff. You promised you will shave goatee."

Too late for that now. At her behest, we gather in the lantern circle around the swing. She mounts the platform. Jungmann follows her up and digs his pipe out of a pocket and frenetically scrapes and reloads. Anezka stiffens her spine. I stay close to her to lend moral support. It's fortunate that Milada is not here; the mere presence of Halbrstat would spark a conflagration. My father seems to be listening for a distant sound only he can hear. Even with what's left of my cloudy vision it's easy to see he's waiting for some sign from Rosalye that this is a charade.

"Quiet, everyone," Rosalye says in a stern *I'm-not-playing* voice. She cues Jungmann to deliver a speech. Stroking his cheek, knowing he will be sensitive about this, she removes the pipe from his mouth.

"Her youth is marked by young shock workers ..." In translation it sounds like Party sloganeering. "She has reasoning of million heads ... strength of million of human hands." It goes on, praise for the State that is midwife to ultimate harmony.

"Okay, enough." Rosalye hands him the tiny crown of white flowers. He takes care not to dislodge a single petal. The flowers won't last long in this cold, but he handles them with a feminine tenderness. Rosalye climbs into the wide swing. She invites Jungmann to sit beside her. She pushes off. What a sight. Rosalye with her silver hair in elegant braids, that knock-off coat hiding her dress, her ruby lipstick wonky, her look sharp with purpose. Beside her, Jungmann—with his refinements looking awkward in that John Wayne get-up—obeys her commands. Push off. Slow down. Steady the swing. Now kiss me, shyly, as though it were our first kiss. Their breath billows in the cold air.

This is the adumbrated courtship ceremony. I could even find it touching if not for that cruel set to her mouth, his toadyish fawning. It's as though we were watching a set piece from their club days.

Poor Anezka squints at her mother as though trying to find the missing piece to the puzzle that will solve her fractured life. We have washed up together on the shores of Prague, she and I. But are we nothing more than flotsam in the wake of our parents' history? Milada doesn't think so. That's why she's joined Zamečnik in pushing the case against Jungmann to the European Court of Human Rights. What about Anezka? How can I help her do more than just survive?

The bride to be, satisfied with the courtship kiss, sheds her knock-off London Fog. Her outfit is not a wedding gown. If my guess is correct, the gray smock with the scalloped white collar buttoned at the throat, partly covered by a white apron with a bodice and shoulder straps, is a kitchen maid's outfit. My father stares at her as if he'd seen a ghost.

"Flowers, please." She directs Jungmann to place them just so. He regards her dubiously. Her outfit is not what he was expecting, nor is he pleased with the surprise. The swing creaks. The ropes strain. Delete the jowls and drinker's nose, blacken that long white hair, and you'd have the calculating beauty who played siren to the boys in my father's village.

"Now is time for stories." Our breath forms stratocumulus clouds that are smoggy with poorly ventilated smoke. Rosalye tells her story first. It was an early summer afternoon, long ago, in a meadow resplendent with red poppies "beating like thousand breaking hearts." She turns to Jungmann and adds, "I ask you to undress me. You run through meadow collecting poppies and you cover my naked beauty with poppies as proof of love ..."

"No, stop. That's our story," my father shouts in Czech, interrupting. "You can't do this, not this."

Hearing all that distance disappear from his voice, as though he'd traveled a lifetime in a heartbeat, I decide this travesty can't continue. "Go ahead," I say to him. "Go ahead and tell her."

"We have to talk about Leoš," my father says achingly.

"Truth!" shouts Jungmann. "*Ano*, we love truth, *ano*, feed us truth. 'In midst of blooming May, into faraway confines, above our old castle, flag swaying, we have words. Truth shall prevail! Glory! Glory! Glory!' " He laughs, but then he says, "I am tired from this game. Let us be married and no more nonsense." He calls out to Halbrstat. "Come up here. Let us begin."

"Do not worry for Leoš," she says soberly. "If he has not drowned Nazis would have made hell for him."

"That's an excuse?" I say. "You realize you're marrying your brother's murderer?"

"Murder?" Jungmann says indignantly. "What has your father been saying?"

"We were drinking vodka," my father admits. "It was my first time. I'd never been drunk before."

"You want clean story?" says Jungmann. "Airbrush some bruises you do not wish that your son will see? Okay, I give you clean story and we will both wash our hands. We fought. Leoš fell in and hit head. I could not save. You saw. You were there." Jungmann pauses, looks at my father. "You want to say something more?"

My father, listening to this story, hunched under his coat, jiggering foot to foot like Isis, looks so lonely I want to put a comforting arm around his shoulders but he senses this and gives me a look that says not now.

"Leoš was tender boy," says Rosalye. "I couldn't protect him."

My father has been avoiding her, staring at the fire in the stove, but something clicks. He purses his lips as though sucking on a toothpick.

"You wanted to stop him from talking." My father faces Jungmann now. "I watched you do it, I didn't even try to help him. That's the part I've had a hard time living with. I just let you do it."

"He was your father's bastard," Jungmann says with an amused twist to that feminine mouth. "You hated him. Admit it. But you were coward. You would never make your own hands dirty. No, not you. Like everyone. Leave dirty work to Jungmann. He is not afraid. He alone is not afraid of truth. Truth shall prevail!"

"I felt sorry for him. My father pretended he didn't exist. It was my father I hated."

The irony of what he has just said, with his daughter standing behind him, warming herself by the fire, is not lost on him. He turns to Anezka and says, "I can never expect you to understand …" Then he catches himself and says simply, "I'm sorry."

Anezka says "*Ano.*" Her tone is perfunctory. She looks to her mother. It's not his pity she wants, nor for that matter, mine. If it's an apology she's after, it will have to come from her mother.

The air is growing acrid with poorly ventilated smoke. We won't be able to stay in here much longer. The flickering glow from the fire creases one side of Anezka's face like a burn, like a scar, while the other side is in darkness. Anezka does not move. The little orphan girl is still in her, still waiting for her mother's acknowledgment.

"What happen to Leoš," says Rosalye, "happen to each of us. Our heads were push under. But we found our way here. No more looking back. Let us proceed."

The barrel-chested gnome with the greasy mane of hair tucked behind his ears, the keeper of records, the artist cum security enforcer, hobbles up onto the platform. In Halbrstat's arms is a sheaf of documents.

Among the paternity release forms, the falsified birth certificate, the marriage certificate, and the title to this property, there should be, if Anezka's legal counsel did his job, two additional documents: a form allowing Anezka to recant her confession, and a form releasing her from the court's custody. Anezka's future, my future, rides on this deal going through.

"It is cold," says Jungmann. "Let us put history behind and say vows. I invite all of you to be my guest at Žamberk pub."

"*Dost!*" says Rosalye, rising from the swing. She waits until all eyes are on her. "Nothing will be signed yet. Not until there has been test."

Chapter Thirty-Three

An Orphan Runs Back: What the Fire Consumes

W HAT HAPPENS NEXT is not in the script. Rosalye asks my father to join them on the makeshift altar. Bearing his sheaf of documents, Halbrstat obediently awaits his next command. Rosalye stands with her back to those of us who are waiting by the stove. Jungmann is to her left. My father to her right. Wearing clothes borrowed from Bedřich, the brown corduroy jacket under a heavy WWII vintage P-coat, hands jammed stiffly into pockets, my father looks provincial, like he was carved out of this place.

"One question?" I say. "Who did give that bison to little Anezka?"

"Mother, you said it was gift from my father."

"*Dost*," says Rosalye. "It was gift from man who wanted to be your father. No more questions. Is time for test." Addressing Jungmann, she says, "Show to them. Open your coat."

He is shockingly compliant. A coiled length of lariat is hooked to his belt.

"Place wrists together in front," she commands.

He hesitates, not a good move, apparently, or maybe this is part of an act, I really can't tell. She insults him, calls him a libidinous pervert, a molester of the innocent, a bully, a coward. With the crackling and snapping of the wood in the belly of the stove I only catch part of Josef's translation, but it's enough. She loops the lariat over his wrists, pulls it snug. For her age she's efficient. He complains that it's too tight.

"I will tie you there," she points to a lamp hook nailed to a beam, "if you do not shut up."

My father has the temerity to question her tactics.

" 'You are so beautiful,' you liked to say, 'You are so beautiful.' " She's mocking my father now. "We will see what you remember."

"We were so young. It was a long time ago."

"Stop sniveling. Hold this." She hands my father a glass-beaded rosary with a large wooden crucifix. "Your mother's. Recognize?" He nods. It's the rosary that hung in the farmhouse chapel. That explains why she was there today. "Hold like this." She presses his hands together, crucifix foremost. "Very pious. Nice."

The yin and yang in her life. Neither dares to oppose her outright.

"Mother. Is this necessary?"

"*Ano*, if you want to hear truth."

Our breath emerges in smoggy puffs. The air is thick enough to inspire coughing. Outside in the freezing night there is the sound of large approaching vehicles, the grinding downshift of gears, the screech of brakes. There is no time to wonder about that now.

Squirming causes the rope to cinch even tighter. Jungmann knows better but squirms anyway. At least that truth, the *pain* truth, will prevail. My father, with his gaunt cheeks and pinched brow, looks both resigned and determined to see this through.

"Now we find out which of you truly loved me. Maybe it is neither, *ano*?"

Jungmann, blinking, desperately wishing for his pipe in his mouth, you can tell, wants this over with and no more games.

"Here is my question. I have mole. It is brown and round and small like little bug. I have had since birth. Where is it?" She points to Jungmann. "You first."

"Who cares about mole? We are here to be married." Wrists lashed together, he combs at his goatee like a peasant raking hay. Everyone is watching. His eyes dart to his old friend Halbrstat, but he finds no help there, then that unctuous smile returns and he says with confidence, "It is in place I should not say of course. It would be undignified."

"Stop eating my liver. Where is it?"

"Very well," he says, swollen with faux certitude. "Between your legs, just beside labia majora." Despite the cold his brow has reddened.

"Is your final answer?" She is imitating her favorite TV game show host.

Receiving no help from the audience, he affirms that it is.

My father's turn. His thoughts take him back to that poppy strewn meadow, that anxious virgin boy, that ambitious beautiful girl with breasts like wild colts. He will tell me about this later. That wistful resignation softens into a smile of gratitude.

"Your right arm." He points. "Inside your upper right arm, kind of hidden. You can only see it when you're giving a hug."

"That is *your* final answer?" she says.

He nods. When he's feeling pensive you can see the craving for a toothpick working in his jaw but there is none of that now.

Rosalye reaches behind her and unties and sheds the apron and loosens the back of her maid's smock. The smock hangs from her shoulders. She unwinds the braids. A cascade of white hair shakes free like a waterfall. The smock falls in a heap at her feet. She is wearing nothing under it. Her slack skin is blue from the cold. I would like very much to see the expression on my father's face when he sees the tattoo, but her falling hair hides it.

Jungmann's delicate mouth twitches. The fire snaps. The smoky air burns in the eyes. There is a moment like dreaming, when dreaming becomes waking. My father sets down the rosary. He pulls a handkerchief out of his pocket. He is of the generation of men who still carry handkerchiefs. He daubs at the smudges of lipstick over-bordering her lips. Something comes over him. He rubs at the lipstick as if he intended to erase from his memory the red silk sheets his father once put on her bed.

She opens her arms to my father and gives him the shy kiss she had wanted earlier. Unused to an audience, he returns her kiss stiffly. "I want to ask for our daughter's forgiveness. Anezka?" She stays by the fire, not making it any easier. "I'm sorry I wasn't able to be a father to you."

"Try harder," I say. "Help us understand."

"He is coward," Jungmann scoffs. "That is truth. He run away." He turns a cold eye on Rosalye. "I risk freezing to death in gulag so you will have harmonious home for your children. This is how you give to me thanks? So be it. Sign papers. She will be my daughter. We will say vows and that will be end of it."

"Is it true what my mother has told to me?" Anezka says to František. "You never send for me?" When he offers nothing in his defense, she adds, "Please sign papers. Let us be done."

"I am old now," Rosalye says. "When I was young and beautiful, I was every man's desire. This is also truth. I had no home."

"Glory!" shouts Jungmann. "Truth prevails! Now untie me and we will finish."

Ignoring him, she says to Anezka, "You hear me? I had no home."

Anezka's eyes are dark and hollow. "You believe I will have sympathy for you?"

Rosalye asks my father to hand her the nearest lantern. The lantern's light flickers over the papers. Rosalye hurriedly signs where Halbrstat indicates she should sign and then she instructs my father to sign. I expect him to hesitate, to at least give me a look that says it pains him to do this, but no. He signs. She instructs Halbrstat to cut short the ceremony and skip straight to the vows. In a matter of minutes the deed is done.

"Now you can be happy," she says to Jungmann. "I am your wife."

"One thing you have forgotten," he says. "Untie me."

"I like you better this way."

He grabs the lantern from her hand. With a sweep of his lashed arms he knocks the papers out of Halbrstat's grasp. The papers scatter on the altar. He throws the lantern. The glass shatters. Kerosene spills. Very quickly the papers are burning.

"Go. Have him. But you will have nothing from me."

He looks to Anezka. "I have signed release with court." Like the rest of us she is frozen by the suddenness of the flames. "You are free to go. Get out of here."

"I loved you," Rosalye says to my father. "I loved you so much. I could not understand why you would leave." Flames flick up the posts holding the swing.

"*Jestli chceš umřít, tak si klidně umři, ale já u toho nebudu.* Listen to me!" Anezka is screaming. "If you want to die, mother, you can peacefully die, but I'm not going to be by it!"

There is nothing heroic, nothing elevating in raw pain. Jungmann's eyes open wide, black lips part. He says to Rosalye, "Go. Get out of here."

My father lets himself down from the burning platform. "Come on," he says.

Rosalye laughs. "Don't worry, it is only game we like to play. Isn't it my love? Our little fire game."

The hall is filling with smoke and running low on oxygen. The urge to suck cool air into the lungs is as instinctual as the urge to save yourself when drowning.

⋙⋘

OUTSIDE, THE FROZEN hayfield and snowy yard are lit up like a sports arena. Men wearing heavy black coats and silver helmets, on their arms official looking royal blue patches with yellow trim, rush toward the entrance bearing axes and sledgehammers. Hurry along, we are told. My father shouts at them that there are still people inside. We continue until we are a safe distance away in the snowy cornfield.

Chapter Thirty-Four

On the Wedding Night the Orphanage Burns

THE WWII VINTAGE red and white TATRA fire truck, hood rounded like a roadster's, doesn't inspire confidence. Its lone water cannon, mounted atop the cab, won't do much to stop the fire. Our footfalls crossing the frozen field are muted by the snow. At a safe distance, we stop among corn sheaves to catch our breath. We look back. Men in black coats have battered down the door. No one is going in. Nor is anyone approaching us for questioning about the fire. It's obvious that someone phoned ahead to the fire service.

You smell it as much as see it, an oily smell of creosote. You hear a whipping sound like curtains snapping. You imagine the heat before you feel it. The night air is thickening with a column of black smoke. The hole in the roof draws the flames up like a chimney flue. The outer walls resist the burn. The ark is enduring even this storm. There is still time to go in.

Anezka cannot tear her eyes away from the spectacle of her home burning. "Who called 1-5-0? They are pathetic volunteers. They will only watch."

"My bet is Jungmann." That outburst we just witnessed? He never intended to turn the orphanage over to Anezka. What he hadn't counted on was Rosalye refusing to leave. Is this her final test? That last look he gave her, that was pure desperation. Did he want her to leave with my father? Was this his way of freeing her?

My father rubs his arthritic knees. "Anyone see them come out?"

Anezka is without her cane. She seems to have lost it. Silhouetted against the flames licking along the canted roof, she stands with her back to me. I can't see her expression, but I can guess by the way she leans into the heat that she's planning something. A van with a strobing blue light pulls up. Two men jump out and begin donning gear.

In the melee, the smoke, the men in black, the barricades, the strobing lights, the uncertain radiation of flames playing hide and seek, now here, now gone, it is impossible to know whether those two have got out.

"She did not untie his arms," Anezka muses. "Some clients like hanging torture. You hang from hook with rope tied around wrists. Your lungs weaken. When you drop you feel intense pleasure of relief."

"Keep this to yourself if we're questioned. You are not there. We don't know what's going on in there."

"She will make him pay for burning my home. She will say she do it for me."

"There's nothing we can do. The firemen will get them out."

"She always want to be martyr. She say she sacrifice her life for me. I cannot allow her to believe this lie." She takes off running across the frozen field. Without her cane, her hips lurch and her shoulders dip and rise like a pump. She pushes through the maw of warbling sirens and strobing blue lights. I shout at her to stop. The fire sizzles like a waterfall. It's unlikely she hears. I start after her. The frozen furrows are unforgiving and my feet are wooden blocks. I trip before I've covered more than a few yards. It's all I can do to hoist myself up. I couldn't save my own child if I had to. My father helps me stand upright, holds me.

"*Ty si skutečně myslím, že budu sedět s rukama v klíně a dívat se jak umírás?* You really think I will sit calmly on my hands and watch you die?" He is so agitated his English has slipped. He is furious. Tears are in his eyes. He might have made this mistake once but he's not going to make it again. That is his daughter but I am the son he knows. He has made his choice. He holds me. He won't let me run after her. I don't have the strength to resist.

Men in black coats shout at her, but she has already run past them. The newest arrivals continue their ritual of suiting up in yellow flame-retardant gear and slinging on air tanks and blowing out tubes and adjusting mask straps. Their prep has probably taken no more than a minute or so, but they arrived on the scene late and that delay may mean the difference between life and death.

I see her cane in the snow. I pick it up. It feels like cherry wood and has a bend, probably from a limb taken out of the orchard behind the orphanage. An insignia is carved into the wood. It looks like a bison, though in this uncertain light it's hard to be sure. "Anezka, wait." I have entirely misunderstood her intentions. That man in there, for all his cruelty, is the only father who never abandoned her. "You will need this."

Using her cane this time, I manage to hobble across the field toward the burning building, without going down. Heat rolls over me in waves. Cold sears my back. The loft has captured an angry beast of yellow flame. Smoke eddies, little puffs of vengeful breath, dance along the roofline.

A stern voice broadcast from a megaphone orders me to back away. The crackling is intensely loud. The last gargoyle tumbles. The Tatra's water cannon ejaculates a pathetic stream that splashes over the stone foundation. The choice seems to have been made to let the flames consume the orphanage.

Men in black coats block my progress. "Let me through." I shove. My pulse hammers in my ears. They shove back. "She needs her cane. You don't understand."

But then I see I'm too late.

The two men in yellow fire-retardant suits come back out carrying between them a supine form. No mistaking those white knee-high stockings. A stretcher appears. At the back of the waiting aid wagon, an oxygen mask is lowered over Anezka's face. Her torso shudders and her arms fall outward. She looks to have been hung on a cross. Be sure to give this to her, I say. They tell me to stay out of the way.

"I am her brother." I place her cane on the stretcher beside her. My eyes are watering from the smoke. "See you in Prague," I say. Her expression is unreadable under that mask. Her eyes are closed. I imagine she is calmly sleeping. At last, warm, deep, comforting sleep. "Stay with me, Anezka. I'll wait for you in Prague."

No one notices the cane. It goes into the back of the wagon with her. The doors are closed, the siren turned on. "Have a good sleep," I whisper. "I'll be there when you wake up." The aid wagon screams away. I glance back at the orphanage. That tongue of fire is still lolling along the roof edge as though making up its mind whether to consume this feast or not. The walls are still intact. "It could still be saved," I say to my father, who has come up beside me. The amber of the flames is beautiful. The world has just hardened into the destructive beauty of this semi-precious gem of amber.

Chapter Thirty-Five

Prague: Early Tuesday Morning, End of October, 1994

IN THE FRIGID hour before dawn a crack like fracturing bones wakes me from sleep. I climb out of bed and go to the window. Several inches of fresh snow have collected during the night. The gnarled plum tree leaning over the bench where my father liked to sit has just shattered under the load. Its splintered trunk juts grotesquely skyward. The crash woke my father as well. He enters my room, sits in the moonlight on the edge of my bed. It disturbs me to think of that amputated trunk abandoned in the snow and I tell him so. He promises that when he's home from the hospital, he'll saw it into splits. Yveta's house no longer has wood-burning stoves so he'll have the splits hauled out to the farm.

"We still have an hour," he says. "Better get some rest."

"Sing 'Clementine' for me," I say. "All the verses you know." I reclaim my bed and close my eyes but my thoughts keep churning over what happened.

—◦—

No ONE, WITH the possible exception of Anezka, was with Rosalye and Jungmann in their last moments. What happened is a matter of speculation. Maybe, like Anezka said, her mother had a martyr complex. When Anezka ran back into the building, it was him she intended to save. I'm convinced of this and I told my father as much. In a fire of this size, an odorless gas layer hovers above waist level, replacing breathable oxygen with toxins. Disoriented by the smoke and gas, she couldn't remember where she'd entered. Asphyxiation by gas is said to affect its victims like severe dehydration. Your capacity to reason deserts you. You can't think how to save yourself.

Anezka died in the ambulance en route to Prague. The same ambulance delivered her to IKEM. Her kidneys and pancreas were harvested. We have twenty-four hours from the time of death to transplant the organs. Milada is the on-call anesthesiologist.

After arriving late in Prague—we were driven in that rattling Volga and somehow I managed to sleep through most of it—we got the call from IKEM. I asked my father to follow me into my room to talk. His eyes had a hollow, scoured look and his mouth hung open in a bewildered oval. Even when Mom died I saw nothing like this. "Why?" he said. "Why did it have to end this way?" Every time I tried to push my thoughts toward the hard truth that my sister was dead, they short-circuited to the shock of guilt: I should have somehow stopped her from running back in there. I could have stopped her. If that's what I had really intended I could have found a way. I was at a crux point. No different than Isis at the lip of his cage. Like my father watching Jungmann with Leoš, I watched her go, and I did nothing. To console me, my father sang, low so he wouldn't disturb Josef in the next room, "In a cavern, in a canyon, excavating for a mine, was a miner forty-niner and his daughter ..." It was too irretrievable. I burst into tears.

~\'~

THEN WE SLEPT. The storm dumped snow, the old plum shattered, the storm passed. Moonlight now illuminates a silvery patch on my desk below the window. My Steno—I'd tried earlier to jot notes about what happened but didn't get far—is laid open in that patch of silver.

He puts a hand on my shoulder. "Why did you try to run back in? What were you thinking? You could have died."

"I kept thinking she needed her cane. It had a bison on it. I realized it must have been a gift from Jungmann. I knew she'd want it."

There's a tap at my door. When Milada got the call at the hospital earlier she'd called here. She wanted to talk to me before the surgery. She must have let herself in downstairs with her own key.

Under her coat she's already dressed in her green scrubs. My father leaves the room so the two of us can talk. She sits on my hard box bed.

"Chico." When Milada starts this way I can be sure I won't like what follows. "I am wondering what is right thing to do. You should rest for surgery. Is better for recovery." Her cold hand strokes my overheated brow and I welcome it. "But it seemed wrong that you will expect something that cannot happen."

"Come on, Milada. I was never expecting miracles."

"*Dost*, Chico. You are naïve." She bends. I smell snow on her and she kisses my forehead. "You still have American belief that everything can be fixed."

"You love me anyway, don't you?"

"*Ano*, Chico. *Ano ano ano.* Too much I still love you. If I did not love you this would be easier."

"What would be easier?"

"Listen to me. Please. No more of your million questions. Okay?" She squeezes my cheeks. I attempt to nod. "Okay?" I nod more or less. "Maybe I am naïve like you. All my life I dreamed of escape to America. Last night when I came home, I realized I would be too sad to live away from my sons. My youngest, Martin. Seattle? Grunge? He would be happy. But, my oldest, he is music editor. His passion is Czech folk songs. My second son is studying journalism. He want to write about politics. Both are infected with nationalism like their father. I have thought, okay, they are grown, they don't need mother. But last night we have dinner together. We act like family again."

She presses her cold hand to my cheek. "What is to become of us? You will be expected to stay here for one year after surgery for care. It will be impossible that we will not see each other. What will we do?"

"For one year more you will be mine."

"Chico, no, it is too hard. No."

"I have to do something for Anezka."

"She wished for you to have kidney."

"I let her die. I let her run in there. I could have stopped her."

"She choose this. If what you have say to me is true."

"What is truth? You should have seen my father's face when we heard Anezka didn't make it. It really shook him. Finally he had his chance to try and make it up to her. Then just like that. Snatched away."

"Peel away American skin and you will find deep deep loyalty to family."

"What does this do to your human rights case?"

She laughs. "Do not worry, there are many torturers." She touches my lips to shush me. She kisses my forehead again. I want to hold her. She senses that and leaves me looking after her. Her slippered feet pad cautiously down the spiral staircase. Must be entertaining doubts. Not enough evidently to turn her around.

—☆—

INSTEAD OF CLOSING my eyes, I go to my desk at the window. In the moonlit garden, snow robes the statue of the boy holding his penis. The corpse of the old plum reminds me of the pheasant my father shot down. Crack, boom. I write in my Steno:

> Anezka ran across the field without her cane. Her arms swung crazily as if she were in the race of her life. Well, I guess she was, you would have to say. Why did I hesitate?

From below I hear the first stirring in Yveta's household. Not sleeping well because of the chemo, she is prone to be up well before her boys, puttering in her kitchen. Even the smell of food, she's admitted, makes her want to throw up.

> Really, all I could think was, she needs her cane. In that moment it was everything. She needs her cane. That's what I remember thinking while I stood in that field and watched her run toward the fire. But, am I being honest with myself? Wasn't there a part of me that wanted to save her for purely selfish reasons? I can't stop replaying that image, her hips swinging, her arms pumping. In a weird way, it was a beautiful moment. For the only time in my life I saw someone commit their very existence to something they desired. I admired her for that. I envied her. All that desire. And she was so close, so close.

⌇

IN A FEW minutes we leave for the hospital. Not wanting to rely on a taxi, Milada has returned. I've packed a travel bag and included my insulin kit and spare testing strips. It will take a week or so before Anezka's pancreas will kick in. Rifling through the armoire, looking for something personal to put in my bag, though I told him it would probably be taken away at the hospital, my father pulls out the amber vase. Before driving back to Prague, we'd stopped by the hotel to clear out my things.

"It's really beautiful." He hoists the nearly solid blown glass vase and examines it. The light cannot pass through. The darkened amber turns the tea-color of swamp water teeming with subsurface life.

"It has flaws, but I thought that would make you like it all the more."

"You might want something in your room to hold flowers." He sits beside me on the bed and asks if he can hold my hand. He takes my hand without waiting for a reply. His hand is shaky, rough with calluses, but warm and reassuringly strong.

Milada sends Josef down to wait with the car and keep it running so the windows won't ice over. She sits on my bed beside my father. He offers to rub my ankles but I decline. Ever since the beating at the prison, the swelling has not gone down. The lightest touch is painful. I can't even wear socks unless they're loose.

"Son," he pats my leg, desists when he sees me wince. "I've been thinking I want Anezka to have a nice funeral service."

I nod. "Absolutely. I want to be there."

"Next week we can claim her body. If you don't mind, I'd like to bury her in the cemetery by our church with the Dostals and Lenochs. We can have a proper ceremony when they let you travel."

"What about Rosalye?"

Milada consults her watch. Her look says what she is too polite to say; we need to allow extra time, given the snow.

"Up at St. Vitus, in the bell tower?" My father still feels like he has to explain himself. "You asked me why I didn't come back. Actually, in the 1950s, before the crackdown in 1957, some people were coming back. There was a lot of talk about this in Bohemie Town."

Now that he's opened the tap, I ask Milada to indulge us, just for a few more minutes.

"But I had to ask myself, is this really my country anymore? It sure didn't look familiar in the photos. The Czechoslovakia I left was prosperous. Now there wasn't much to eat. Many of those lucky enough to be alive suffered from diseases they picked up in prison. Most of the young men were dead. Most of the young women were accused of collaborating."

"But you had a daughter here. The only one in her life who tried to help was Jungmann. Think about that."

"I had a family in Iowa. That's what I had to think about." He sighs. In the dark this sigh seems to heave up from some partisan bunker. "In some ways I'm just glad my poor mother was dead. At least she didn't have to go through this. I hate to say it," he apologizes to Milada, "I would have gone back to the farm if Mother was alive, but my country was becoming a sad gray place."

"Is why I had to escape," Milada says. She shakes her head. "Poor *tata.*"

"He's the real hero," I say.

"They tortured him because I escape."

"It was the farm," says my father. No doubt he's given this some thought; my father is not impulsive. When he adds, "I want to help him fix the place up, modernize it," I know that in his mind it's already decided. He looks at me. Would I care to join him in this enterprise?

"You guys go ahead," I say. "Fix what needs to be fixed."

"We could use your help." But it's a token offer. He doesn't really need my help. He just knows I like to keep busy.

"While I was watching Anezka run for her life, I kept wondering what she desired so much that she would take that kind of risk? I still don't know. But I have a theory." Nobody stops me so I continue. "I'm guessing she wanted to tell Jungmann that she forgave him." It's too grave a subject just now so I attempt to lighten the mood with a joke. "Torkey? Remember her? She really is an old fussbudget, isn't she?" Milada laughs. I explain the whiny red-tailed hawk to my father, that she's deathly afraid of the dark, that they have to put her inside at night. "She loves the attention. God, look at me."

"I will miss our cabin," Milada says. My mention of the raptors has her thinking about the Skagit. "That was for me beautiful dream."

"Would you miss it in February?" This is our inside joke.

"Especially in February," says Milada.

"That was our month," I explain to my father. I describe the scene, our first trip to the river. "The sky was white with overcast. The river was at flood stage. Milada and I decided to go for a walk on the other side of the river."

"I enjoyed the river," says my father.

"In February the river floods. Snags break off and pile against the bridge. You think any moment civilization will be wiped out and nature will reclaim everything. I found it pretty scary. Not her."

"It was fascinating," Milada says. "It woke up something in my soul." My father leans toward her hungry for what she has to say. "We stood by river until it was after dark. It was cold and very much wind. Wind move away clouds. Suddenly it was very cold. We look up and we see stars, million and million of stars. I feel river like desire, like desire I have not felt since I was child, like we have gone back to beginning of time for humans on earth."

"You'd go crazy out there."

"Of course. But that desire fed my soul. That was when I knew I had to decide. Run away to America, or fight for justice."

My father's expression pinches with concern. "My generation worried about helping family keep body and soul together."

The two of them button their coats. Mine is hanging down by the front entrance. I follow them down the spiral stairs, wishing I had Anezka's cane. At the entryway they exchange slippers for shoes. Lack of adequate horizontal sleep has left my feet so swollen I can't fit into even my loose shoes. I go out in wool lined slippers. My father pulls on that yellow cap and lets down the ear flaps. Outside, the car is warming. Josef is shoveling the walk.

A plow has left a slush berm. The streetlights are spread too far apart and the berm is dark and the road is crunchy with ice. Crossing to the car, I flail my arms to steady myself. I am Anezka pumping across the frozen field. I will never really know what desire sent her running into that firestorm. I look back through the neighborhood. The snow has knocked down what remained of the leaves. For the first time, through the bare branches of the chestnuts, the upper stories of Milada's *panelak* are visible from here. Which window is hers? The one with the light on? The distance from here to there is surprisingly not very far.

Anezka spent her life burning with what she wanted to say. Then it was too late. "Dad." I pump my arms. I thrust my hips the way she did and manage to cross to him without falling. "Dad, I forgive you." My shouting will disturb the neighbors.

He takes my arm to steady me. "We'll talk later."

When you get around to fixing up the farm, you gotta replace that stove. It heats unevenly. There's no excuse for it anymore.

Chapter Thirty-Six

Epilogue: a Few Months Later in Prague

TONIGHT'S OPERA IS not at the national theater. *Our* opera is second string, but Milada's youngest son is in the orchestra pit. The old opera house is thankfully only a short walk from the Museum metro stop at the top of Wenceslas Square. I'm getting out more these days, but am easily exhausted. The theater's Rococo interior—fluted, gold painted stucco, urchins and angels leaping from every surface—is too busy for my taste, but my father, sporting a salt and pepper wool jacket with a white shirt and a three-button vest, looking ever more European and professorial, ogles the lobby like a boy digging up treasure. The period interior is giving him such obvious pleasure—*a slice of beloved history*—I swallow my critique.

Anda-Louise Bogza, a popular soprano from Bucharest, is singing the lead role. This explains the unusual crowd. Aunt Magda, my father's favorite little sister, is on her way but running late. We've arranged for seats in the front row where the aisle is wide enough to accommodate her portable oxygen tank. Milada waves to her neon-spiked son. Shortly before the house lights go dim, Aunt Magda rolls in with an usher's help. There's a hugging, shoulder squeezing, crying scene right in front of the orchestra pit. *Frank, look at you, crying for purely sentimental reasons. And so solicitous. Can I bring you something, a glass of champagne? Are you comfortable? Please tell us if this is tiring and we'll leave.* In Iowa, he'd spent his life modulating his accent, steeled against a phantom that never materialized. Here he talks, he laughs, he hugs. Here, where they don't even pretend to hide the cruelty, he's alive.

Like the rest of the crowd, he cheers wildly at the soprano's curtain call. It wasn't all a smashing success. At times the orchestra drowned out the singers, and the trumpet flatulated notes that even the strings' perfume couldn't hide.

When the conductor comes out, an Italian man sitting next to my father leaps to his feet, cups his hands to his mouth like a megaphone, and boos with enough gusto to suggest he felt as double-crossed as Tosca herself. "You butcher! You killed Puccini!" he yells.

"Try Janáček," yells a German. "Maybe you will do *From House of the Dead*."

The smile thins on the conductor's face. The audience, mostly tourists, laughs. Mercifully, the house lights come on. The conductor bows and hurries off.

"Do not waste pity on him," Milada says of the conductor. She's wearing a short-skirted black dress with three strands of garnets wrapped at her throat, her hair piled extravagantly. She looks gorgeous. "He has health. He is young and talented. So tonight were mistakes. He has future."

My father disagrees. "I'm the lucky man. I am with my family in my birth land and free of the hungers that will eat him alive."

It's suggested that we continue this conversation over dessert. We catch one of the taxis lined up outside the emptying theater. Despite worrying that it will be late for me, my father asks to stop by the Vltava to show his sister the swans drifting through reflections of the castle lights. He's full of history tonight. Memories banked now can't replace the history they lost, but they don't seem to obsess over that. They enjoy talking about what they do remember. Using her *protekcé* at Café Slavia, Milada snags a standing-only table, tough for me, but Aunt Magda can lean on her walker and just seems thrilled to at last spend time with her older brother.

A famous hangout for literati the likes of Hašek and Škvorecký, the café is in a gray last-century building so nondescript you'd walk right past. The interior, on the other hand, all original art deco—glass sconces, mirrors, sleek curved metal, all lines streamlined—drips with the period chic that connoisseurs love and that has my ordinarily taciturn father raving. We stand at a stylish pedestal table. Milada orders a round of the café's famous dessert, warm strudel with crème. I take a bracing regimen of immunosuppressant pills three times a day and have to be very careful in crowds to avoid sneezing and handshaking—I wash my hands constantly and do not use handrails—but wonder of wonders I can eat this food. Saudek warned me not to expect to recover eyesight. At least the retinal bleeding has stopped. Aunt Magda gasps for air through her hose but she looks up at us, beaming.

"František," says Aunt Magda, returning to the debate interrupted at the theater. "You speak as though your life were over. Now you are home."

He kisses her on the forehead. "It's good to be home."

We enjoy our strudel. The crowd, obvious Americans in jeans, Czechs in local drab, Germans and French in sophisticated theater clothes, are oblivious to our joyful reunion. My concern slings back to my father's remark about the conductor.

"I think it's time." *Deep down, the shame festers. You feel complicit, if only because you are alive and idle.*

"I think it's too soon. Dr. Saudek is saying it takes at least a year before you get your strength back and your organs are stable."

It's true. I've already had one scary near-rejection episode that landed me back in the clinic hooked up to drains and an insulin drip. "No, it's time. I've got to put it out there and see what happens." With help from the mayor's *protekcé*, we got title to the orphanage property. Thanks to the fire, it will have to be rebuilt from the ground up. My father claims the fire did us a service. But that is my father's specialty. We're applying for non-profit status so we can accept donations. In this economy, I'm afraid that means catering to Germans and Americans anxious to do business here, but until the local economy is back on its feet it's a compromise we have to make. Once we're up and running, we'll staff the shelter strictly with locals. Josef will be our manager. This is what I want Anezka to have wanted.

"He is right," Aunt Magda says to my father. "Desire like his must to be honored. You cannot expect he will keep tongue behind his teeth."

He looks sadly at his sweet little sister. So quietly I have to strain to hear, he says, "I am sorry I was not here."

"Now you are here and you have your son."

Milada looks at me with that hard glint she gets when she talks about escape. *Don't let anything stop you. And don't look back.*

Photo by Jonathan Pierce

SCOTT DRISCOLL, AN award-winning instructor (the University of Washington, Educational Outreach award for Excellence in Teaching in the Arts and Humanities 2006), holds an MFA from the University of Washington and has been teaching creative writing for the University of Washington Extension for seventeen years.

Driscoll makes his living as a writer and teacher. While finishing *Better You Go Home*—a novel that has been several years in the making and which grew out of the exploration of the Czech side of his family in the 1990s after Eastern Europe became liberated—Driscoll kept busy freelancing stories to a variety of magazines, both commercial and literary. He most often writes feature stories on subjects ranging from health to philanthropy to education to general reporting for *Alaska* and *Horizon Airlines Magazines*, but he also does profiles and book reviews, including an October 2010 profile for *Ferrari Magazine 11*, and a July/August '08 profile in *Poets and Writers Magazine*.

Driscoll's short stories and narrative essays have been published extensively in literary journals and anthologies, including *Image Magazine*, *Far From Home* (a Seal Press anthology), *Ex-Files: New Stories About Old Flames* (a Context Books fiction anthology featuring high-profile writers such as David Foster Wallace, Jennifer Egan, and Junot Diaz), *The Seattle Review*, *Crosscurrents*, *Cimarron Review*, *The South Dakota Review*, *Gulfstream*, *American Fiction '88* and others.

Driscoll has been awarded seven Society of Professional Journalists awards, most recently in 2009 for social issues reporting, and including best education reporting and general reporting 2004. His narrative essay about his daughter's coming of age was cited in the *Best American Essays*, 1998, and while in the MFA program, he won the University of Washington's Milliman Award for Fiction (1989).

You can find Driscoll on the Web at www.scott-driscoll.com.

Made in the USA
Charleston, SC
20 July 2013